I0690660

SEA OF GHOSTS

THE WARRIORS OF TIR NAN OG

BY ALISON SCOTT

The sail come from the south, catching the light as the ship crossed the wind. "Ciarnan!" Gil pointed to the mast.

The Irishman scrambled up, slung one leg over the yard and peered into the glare.

"Warship?" Gil shouted.

"Knarr."

"Alone?" Arnkel called.

"I see no other."

Gil called the Irishman down.

"How does she ride?" Arnkel asked as Ciarnan's feet touched the deck.

"Low in the water."

"Ah," Arnkel shook his head. "Well laden. That is dangerous. The wind might rise. And then? Laden ships founder. We must relieve him of his burdens."

"He'll make quieter waters before any storm," said Gil.

Watching the knarr escape, Arnkel said, "You do not sail this ship alone, my friend. And some here would have this prize."

All down the coast of Alba, Gil set a cautious course, sailing far out to sea, beaching each night far from habitation. Crossing another firth, his restless crew again watched laden knars slip out of reach. They camped that night on a windswept strand in Northumbria. The mood was sombre, everyone weary of wind and sea.

Overnight, the weather turned. Rain and sleet spatted tent cloth. Leaving the strand under oar, he took his course from landmarks and memory, raised sail and set off into the keening wind.

At midday, the clouds broke. Between squalls of snow, sun lit yellow beaches and fresh ploughed fields. A church bell chimed.

Rachel and Danni ran to the rail. "Look! Lindisfarne!" The muinntir shone white with fresh fallen snow. He was closer in then he ever intended. His eager crew gathered at the rail.

Gil sensed movement behind him and was turning when the blow struck. Brushing the side of his head, it slammed into his shoulder, breaking his grip on the tiller and hurling him to the deck.

A sword blade glistened in front of his face and Arnkel Fish-Tail was at the helm.

Pro Christo Domino

A wedding dance of blood,
A wedding night of fire.
Old men's wrath, young men's pride
Call Hrolf's Isle to war.
> *Amid the swallows of my roof beams,*
> *I read my course.*

A debt I cannot pay,
A fight I must not win;
On Helgi's strand, I duel with Hakon's bride.
> *Amid the swallows of my roof beams,*
> *I read my course.*

Bright Fire-Hair, sweet Valkyrie,
Summons Odin's will: I lay
The keel of peace on Northern sands.
My pennant at his masthead,
Broadaxe takes the dragon way.
> *Amid the swallows of my roof beams,*
> *I read my course.*

Fair Caledon! My lady flies on sunlit wings.
Ermine-cloaked, I dance the dance of Alba's kings.
> *Amid the swallows of my roof beams,*
> *I read my course.*

from *The Saga of Floki Magnusson*
circa 900 (?) AD

The glory of young men is their strength,
> But the beauty of old men is their grey hair.

All streams run to the sea.

Kethuvim

CHAPTER ONE

L ionheart balked, head down, feet planted firm. *It's the other way.*

Gil shook the looped lead rope serving as reins. *Not today.*

We always go the other way. Gil looked out at the white flecked sea, misty in the August dusk. What was it about hill ponies that everything always had to be the same? He gave Lionheart's flank a solid thump with his heel.

I take you to Norway. I take you to Francia. I take you to Rome, even; and now we're home. And you still want to stand under the same tree until your hooves fall off. Who said travel broadens the mind?

What's a mind?

Gil dropped the reins, raised both hands to his head and mouthed a silent scream. Then, with a weary shrug, he guided the reluctant pony between two low stone buildings at the rear of Floki Magnusson's longhouse. Hidden from view by the sweeping new turf roof of the hall, he slid down from his improvised sheepskin saddle and drew the looped lead rope over Lionheart's head.

Lionheart rolled his eyes in a sudden panic. *I smell cows.*

Gil grabbed his forelock and pulled his shaggy head down to eye level. *You smell cows because we're behind the dairy. And you are NOT afraid of cows. Camels, maybe. Cows, no.* He un-looped the lead rope and tied it to a gnarled little birch tree grown up against the wall. Lionheart shook his head, rubbing his halter against the tree. *Don't do that!*

It's too tight. I can't move my ears. Gil sighed and loosened the already loose strap behind the pony's flattened ears. *And my mane is caught.* Gil patiently re-arranged strands of mane. Then he lifted the sheepskin padding off Lionheart's withers and gave the dark stripe that crossed his back and shoulders a quick rub with a handful of dry grass. "The Lord's holy mark upon him," Aidan called it. Gil grimaced. Not having much effect.

He left the pony tugging experimentally at his tether and slipped cautiously around the corner of the building and through the open door. In the cool dimness of the cow byre, he gathered an armful of hay, brought it back out, and laid it down in front of Lionheart.

Lionheart gave it a wild-eyed look and whickered frantically. *You're leaving me here! Why are you leaving me here?*

Gil closed both hands around his nose. *Because I don't want anyone to see you. OR hear you.*

Lionheart stood twitching his fur while Gil plotted a route past the longhouse that would take him unobserved to the strand. Just the thought of the little skiff waiting safely above the tideline brought a warm glow to his heart.

He glanced at the sky. Still only two stars beside the day-lit moon. Time enough to cross to the island, see Janetta, and get back before the last stragglers came down from the farms.

JANETTA likes to see me. Lionheart shook his mane sulkily. *SHE says I'm pretty.*

Look, I like to see you, too. Only, not now.

I want the pony pen.

I'll come back and put you in it. Soon. Eat your hay. And be quiet.

Janetta gives me oats.

Oh, Janetta would give you the moon, if you asked.

Lionheart flicked one ear and rolled one eye to the sky. *Can I eat it?*

Sure, Gil nodded wearily. *You reach it; you can eat it.* He left the pony stretching his pretty neck moon-ward and sprinted for the strand.

Drying fishing nets gave cover from the longhouse to the low dunes. Lying flat on the landward slope, he peered through windblown beach grass, surveying the sand and shingle shore. Floki's splendid warship, *Silver Dragon*, took pride of place in the noust nearest the longhouse. Her mast was down and shrouded by her awnings; her painted figurehead faded from her long journey under southern suns. Gil's friends Ragi and Ciarnan were at work scraping barnacles from her hull.

Keeping his head low, Gil scanned the strand beyond. Four more longships rested above the tide, black awnings sheltering their decks. He knew them all by their figureheads; *Sea-Stag*, *Wave-Loper*, *Foam-Steed*, *Tide-Trampler*. Floki's chieftains were gathering for the wedding of Grimhildr Thorolfsdottir and Ulf Kolsson, on whose farm Gil had worked all summer.

And from whose farm he had departed in secret and ridden in haste, to keep his tryst with Janetta on the Holy Isle.

Half hidden by spray, its shore already grown dim, it beckoned him from across the strait. The tide was full, the crossing treacherous. But it was not the low roar of the white frothed rousts that brought his head up in dismay, but the unexpected sight of a rapidly approaching sail.

Who? At this hour? The ship turned across the wind, her striped sail shifting and all her graceful length revealed. His heart leapt. *Sea-Raven!* Hakon Ragnaldsson's *Sea-Raven*, come home to the strand on which she was born.

For an instant, he was back in that weary summer, laboring at Master Shipbuilder Eyolf Grimsson's side. His calloused hands knew every strake, every thwart, every hard-won inch of the ship he helped build, from her swaying masthead to her keel. "She's fast," he murmured proudly, as she bore down on the shore. His eyes swept the set of her sail, the slice of her prow through the surf. "And if I helmed her," he whispered, "she'd be faster." And, though the man on the steering board was renowned throughout the North for his seamanship, it was true.

"Come *on*, Hakon," Gil muttered. "Get her beached and get out of there." But Hakon Sea-Friend, cousin and foster-brother of the earl, was also renowned for his caution. The sail slipped down the mast, oars flashed, and *Sea-Raven*, humbled, approached Hrolf's Isle at the stalwart pace of a merchant's knarr.

Gil groaned. As fond as he was of the dour, kindly Shetlander, Hakon Ragnvaldsson was, just now, the last person he wanted to see. He glanced with frustrated longing at the skiff in her nest of sea-grass, looked back at the strand, and groaned louder. *Correction. There* was the last person he wanted to see.

A party of men and women had emerged from the longhouse, streaming down the gentle slope to the strand. At their head strode a tall, lean man with an assured gait and an unmistakable mane of bright yellow hair; Earl Floki Magnusson welcoming his cousin to his shores. Gil dropped his head on his forearm and pounded the damp sand with a frustrated fist.

Of course. No ship approached Floki's longhouse without alerting the guards on the hill. Not this summer. Plenty of time to prepare a welcome. He looked up wearily. At the earl's side, the pleated linen sleeves of her dress fluttering ghost-like in the dusk, was Danni, Gil's childhood friend. Her dark hair flowed loose, yet, unadorned by a woman's headdress, but she carried herself with adult dignity, as befitted the earl's betrothed.

Her brother, Percy, round and sturdy in his britches and bright blue tunic, walked just behind, solemnly conscious of his role as earl's cupbearer. *And what's missing from this picture?* Gil winced. *The earl's helmsman, duty-bound to be at his side.* He glanced again at the darkening sky. A scattering of stars now hung over the sea. Only the most hard-working farmers would yet be out in the fields. And he doubted Floki ever regarded him as hard-working, either on land *or* at sea.

Sea-Raven's rowers raised their oars and the ship glided silently to the shore. Ropes were thrown and Floki's warriors rushed to catch them. Gil caught sight of Ismail among them and ducked guiltily behind his screen of beach grass. Lying to the earl was one thing. Lying to his best friend, another. But at least it saved Ismail from lying on his behalf.

The gathering fell silent then, as the gangplank was lowered and Hakon and his lame, grey-bearded father, Ragnvald, descended to the strand. Floki greeted the old man with filial respect, and then, laughing, wrapped Hakon in his powerful embrace and swung him off his feet.

Raised as brothers, they had sailed together and fought together all their lives, and, as often, fought with each other. But none doubted the bond between them, even now, when other bonds were fraying like sea-weathered rope.

Floki released his cousin and turned smiling to the assembled company. A cheer went up and others rushed forward. First, Ulf, the short, stocky bridegroom, and Grimhildr, his formidable bride, as tall as the earl and never without her throwing axes, worn, with her womanly scissors and comb, at her waist.

The earl's parents, Magnus and Shony, followed; then Aidan, his priest, with his Noble Cat trotting at his heels and the crow, Feannag, wheeling and cawing overhead. One by one, the whole gathering greeted the guests, and when, at last, they drifted up to the longhouse, dusk had deepened into darkness.

Lady Day in Harvest was past; the endless daylight of high summer, past, too. Night had returned to the Northlands, vanguard of the winter darkness to come. The wind rose, flattening the beach grass. Moonlight shone on the white water of the roust, and ragged clouds chased each other across the stars. Even with his earl's blessing, it was no time to put to sea.

Gil got slowly to his feet. The longhouse fire beckoned: companionship, warmth, safety. He raised his eyes to the sea and the island. He would see her tomorrow. He had seen her yesterday. But it wasn't enough. He had to see her tonight. With a quick glance down the empty strand, he sprinted for the skiff.

Dragging the little vessel to the water's edge, he raised her light mast, waded with her into the shallows, and fastened the steering oar. Then, jumping aboard, he freed the sail and, as he caught up the sheets, thought suddenly that the one person who would understand was the earl, who had sailed to Rome and back for the sake of love. Not that understanding would make him any more forgiving.

Away from the lee of the shore, the skiff heeled hard. Gil tightened the sheets further, and the bow wave foamed over the rail, splashing his already soaked britches. He grinned happily; the longhouse and his duties forgotten. Nothing to think of but wind and tide. Keeping the roar of the half-seen roust off his right shoulder, he set course for a small, pale crescent of sand; the only place on all the Holy Isle where any ship, however small, could make landfall.

Helming the skiff, after helming *Silver Dragon*, was like playing with a kitten after wrestling with a tiger. *Or a Noble Cat,* he thought wryly. The little craft skidded across the wave tops, like a skipping stone, her slender mast bending before the wind. But she was, for all that, a true miniature of the Northmen's great warships, fleet and seaworthy in the right hands.

And, thanks to the earl he was flagrantly disobeying, his were the right hands. *This is where he first taught me.* He smiled. It seemed a lifetime ago. His mind flitted from sea to sea: all the places where Floki had shown him the helmsman's trade. The cold Northern waters of Shetland and Norway. The storm-tossed winter sailing home from Rome. The wild coast of Francia. The tide-race of Yula's Isle. His ignominious landing on Kernow, where he sheared *Silver Dragon's* steering oar in pride and stupidity.

He forgave me that. What's being late to a feast compared with that? Comforted, he ran the skiff up onto the island strand, and dragged her safely above the tide. Then he drew the sword, which, like every man on Hrolf's Isle this summer, he kept always at his side, and with its point, marked a circle in the moonlit sand.

Casting a last guilty glance across the strait, he stepped neatly inside, chanting as he did:

Bless to me my sister,
Bless to me my brother.
Bless to me, O Changeless One,
My Change-Thing, my Other.

As always, sound struck him first, even as his feline ears unfurled: the tinkling of pebbles in the surf, the rustling of grasses, the splash of tiny fish. And there! His head flicked around: that pleasing clatter. Swishing his tail, he leapt from the circle into a landscape grown huge and bright.

The sound came again. His whiskers trembled as, one paw raised, he sniffed the air. Then, striped back low and tail horizontal, he trotted toward the sea. Somewhere, far at the back of his feline mind, his human self pleaded: *Other way!* But Cat had found the source of the sound, and ears pricked forward with delight, pounced.

It didn't go well. The clattering thing tasted of salt, his teeth skidded unpleasantly on its surface, and when it slipped from his grasp, something nipped meanly at his nose. And his paws were wet. Cat sat down and washed.

Gil's human self pounded imaginary fists on the sand. *It's a crab, idiot.*

Cat washed another paw.

Crabs don't work.

Cat washed a third paw.

You've tried crabs before. They never work.

Cat finished the last paw, swished his tail, and pounced on the crab.

After the fourth attempt, he lost interest and remembered why he was there. Shaking the last bit of water from his toes, he loped inland.

Nose twitching, he followed the scent of peat smoke up a little hill, and paused at the top, with one paw raised. Twin curls of pale blue rose from the low turf roof of the island's only dwelling. Cat chirruped happily and bounded over the rough ground to the building's door.

Crouching there, tail flicking, he listened to the sounds within. Nearest and loudest was a rhythmic rumbling, like the growl of a giant beast. He briefly flattened his ears, but his nose told him the beast was human: Grimhildr's brother, Bjorn Break-Neck. Gil's shipmate and friend, he was Floki's fiercest, most loyal, and least imaginative warrior. Sworn to slay any man who set foot on the island, he would mournfully slice Gil to pieces.

Untroubled by that, Cat crouched, yet listening. Between the rumbling growls which his human mind determined were snores, two other sounds passed through double walls of stone; a sweet, far singing, and the whisper and tap of a spindle on the floor. Cat began to purr.

Trotting on light, sure paws, he circled the house. Twice as long as it was wide, it was, in truth, two separate buildings; a second dwelling added to the first, now neatly enclosing its only door. There was, however, one small window, in the furthest wall, shuttered tightly against the night. Beneath it, Cat sat down and gave a plaintive meow.

A happy cry sounded within and a quick scuffling of feet. The shutters unlatched and flew open and Janetta's face appeared, pale in the moonlight and veiled by her long, black hair. With another cry of delight, she held out her arms.

Cat leapt to pass through the waiting circle, but was, instead, enveloped in her warm embrace. Snuggling him against her chest, she swiftly re-latched the shutters and waltzed with him around the floor. Cat hissed protest, but she ignored him, singing softly and stroking his striped head until the hiss died away, replaced by a purr.

Wait a moment. I didn't sail all this way just for you to get your ears rubbed. Make an effort!

Reluctantly, Cat wriggled free and bounded into the round, wicker creel holding Janetta's unspun fleece. Emerging, with wool tangled in his hair and the creel jammed on his feet, Gil sat awkwardly on the floor to extricate himself. Janetta knelt waiting beside him. "You came! Even today!"

Freed at last, Gil jumped up, lifted her to her feet and into his arms, and tumbled with her onto her low straw bed. "I had to see you." He pulled her close and kissed her shyly. "The farm was empty without you." She sat up, as shyly, and pulled away.

"Look. See what I make." Rising, she ran lightly to a small wooden kist, and carefully retrieved a folded cloth. In the dim firelight, she spread out, at the edge of the mattress, a tiny bed covering, sewn from white linen, embroidered and trimmed with braid. "For Grimhildr," she said. "I had to stay to finish it."

"For Grimhildr?" his voice rose in amazement and she pressed her fingers against his lips. "But it wouldn't cover ...."

"For her *baby*," she shook her head, despairing of him.

"Baby? Grimhildr?" A vision arose of Grimhildr's throwing axes disarming the earl and Hakon Sea-Friend on the shore of Mont Tombe. "Do you really think ...?"

"But of course there will be babies. What is marriage for?" She returned her handiwork to the kist, came back smiling, and lay down beside him again. "What of the chieftains?"

"It's early," Gil said uneasily. "I'll be back in plenty of time."

"It is not early," she said. "It is late." But she slid into his embrace and they lay kissing and caressing while stars wheeled past the smoke-hole in the roof. "At least we do not have Grimhildr between us, now," Janetta murmured.

"Or Bjorn," said Gil grimly.

She laughed aloud and quickly buried her face against him. "Does he wake?" she whispered worriedly.

Gil shook his head. "Snoring like Lionheart."

She giggled again. "He probably sleeps on his feet, too. Like a pony."

"Right up against that door."

She relaxed and whispered, "Do you remember her headdress? The way she slept in it? And sat up when I struck it."

"And threw me out."

"But she let Cat in."

"Not for long." His Cat-self ruffled its fur at the memory of flying through the air, launched by Grimhildr's big hand.

Janetta sighed. "Imagine. She is really to marry tomorrow, at last!"

"If she takes time off from shearing sheep."

"But the shearing is finished," Janetta said innocently.

"I know." Gil sniffed his hands wearily, "A hundred sheep-worth, I know."

"You are very good. Ulf is proud of you."

"Glad I'm good at something."

"But you're good at everything! The plough. And the sickle. Even milking. Though that, of course, is women's work," she added primly.

"Didn't stop the earl making me learn."

She smiled. "He is proud of you."

"Some chance!" He snorted loudly and she slapped her fingers over his face.

"Hush. Bjorn stirs."

"Shifting hooves," said Gil.

She listened and then lay close again. "I remember," she said dreamily, "I spoke of *our* wedding. And you said I must not, because dreams spoken of do not come to truth. But see, now, soon it will! This Lentron, your first year is done. The farm is yours, and we are betrothed. And the next, we are wed!"

"And the next ...." he reached shy fingers and fumbled at

the clasp of her tunic. Just two clasps and it would fall free and then, just the frail linen dress beneath ….

Smiling, she removed his hand. "You must go." She sat up, and the clasp, successfully loosened, tumbled to the floor, striking a hearth stone with a resounding clang. In the room beyond, two booted feet thudded on packed earth.

"What man?" roared Bjorn, unbarring the outer door.

Janetta's face went white in the firelight. "Quickly!" she shoved Gil toward the creel. "He does not harm a cat!"

In the moments it took Gil to cram his feet back into the wicker circle and mutter the blessing, she had unlatched the shutters and was waiting with hands outstretched to lift Cat through the window. Preserving his dignity, Cat leapt past her and soared out into the night.

He landed amid a row of turnips, a yard from the huge sheepskin boots of Bjorn. Enormous sword in one hand and a throwing axe in the other, the big Northman turned in a circle, scanning the moonlit landscape. Fortunately, he hadn't the eyes of a cat. And Cat, who did, streaked for the shelter of the nearest clump of gorse.

"Who goes?" roared Bjorn, sensing, if not seeing, movement. Cat growled and ran for the shore, with a steady thud of boots shaking the ground behind.

He does not harm a cat.

Fine. But a cat can't sail.

Meowing in frustration, Cat crossed the sand to the waiting skiff in three long bounds.

Gil was in and out of his circle and dragging the skiff into the water when Bjorn reached the strand. Spotting a man and a boat and a flapping white sail did not require the eyes of a cat. Bjorn thundered to the sea's edge as, with a desperate shove, Gil launched the skiff and leaped on board.

Bjorn's axe flashed over his shoulder and slammed into the mast, showering him with splinters. Then, with half fastened oar and half gathered sheets, the little vessel took off racing into the night. The tide, fierce and unforgiving, was for once his friend. In moments, he was safely at sea, a widening gap of dark water separating him from Janetta's outraged guardian.

The big Northman dwindled to a dark lump on the pale strand, and his angry shouts faded before wind and tide. Gil returned his attention to the sea, peering into the murk for a glimpse of the watch fires. The longhouse, with its new turf roof, was no longer the vivid landmark it had been when roofed with sails. Spotting a ruddy flicker, he steered toward it and relaxed: the tide-race, once so terrifying, now was simply exhilarating.

The wind had got up and he thought of reefing the sail, but he was enjoying the ride too much to bother. Dark water splashed over the rail and he grinned with delight. As always when he sailed alone, he heard Floki's laughter over one shoulder. And, over the other, Hakon Sea-Friend's dire warnings of doom.

At sea, timid is part of fine. Right, Hakon. Gil held the sheets tightly beneath the sole of his boot and re-adjusted the tacking spar. The prow lifted clear of the water and the skiff flew.

In his element once more, he thought wistfully, and not for the first time, why did his Change-Thing have to be a cat? Why couldn't he have been a selkie, like Floki, and swim to the island in the sleek, grey fur of a seal? Somewhere deep within, his Cat-self ruffled its own fur in disgust.

At least, he thought gratefully, Bjorn had not recognized him. No more able to lie than Percy, Bjorn would faithfully report both the intruder and his failure to slay him, to the earl. Then, Gil realized grimly it made no difference. There were just two men in the North Isles who could make that landing in the dark: Earl Floki Magnusson, and Gil Lake of Tir nan Og. He might as well have left footprints on the waves.

All he could hope was that amid the excitement of his sister's wedding, Bjorn would forget.

Gil set a course that kept him well offshore until past the watch fires and the unseen guards, then came about, dropped the sail, and slipped into his hidden landing under oar. Confident that he'd not been noticed, he lowered the mast, yanked Bjorn's axe free, and inspected the damage before furling the sail and hiding the axe within its folds.

Then, adjusting his sword belt and combing the sea tangles from his hair with his fingers, he traversed the strand at the tideline as far as *Silver Dragon's* noust, and came up beneath her dragon prow, into the open.

The guards hailed him, at once, moving quickly from the shadow to bar his way. Then, recognizing him, they stepped back with apologetic nods to the earl's helmsman, rightfully checking his ship, and letting him pass. Gil strode by them, working hard to look the part.

Song and laughter greeted him long before he reached the longhouse doors. He passed between the two watch fires, and quickened his pace, eager to enter at a moment of maximum distraction.

Two shapes bulked at either side of the entrance: Floki's personal bodyguards, not men to argue with. Gil gave the well-armed pair a cheerful smile and held up empty hands. They beckoned him closer, studying him carefully though they knew him well enough. Then, with grudging shrugs, they moved to unbar the doors; the nearer man pausing in the shadows of the roof to shove something large and un-budging aside. Gil stopped in his tracks. The large thing shook its shaggy head and whickered happily.

Gil stared. *Lionheart?* The pony shook his head again and his lead rein slapped against the roof post to which it was tied. *What are you doing here?*

Lionheart lowered his nose to the ground and his ears flicked disconsolately. *My halter was loose.*

YOU made me loosen it.

And I was lonely.

For what? Gil couldn't take his eyes off the neat seaman's knot securing the lead rope. *You hate every other pony on the face of the earth. Who tied you here?*

I heard wolves.

There are no wolves on Hrolf's Isle. WHO tied you …?

Lionheart twitched his ears and, without difficulty, emptied his mind. With a growing sense of doom, Gil pushed past him, and, as the guards swung open the doors, slipped swiftly in, and as swiftly behind the backs of a row of standing, cheering Northmen.

Behind his screen of swaying, stamping bodies, Gil quickly

scanned the crowded, fire-lit hall. The two long tables had already been cleared, the feasting done. Astrid and Jorunn, serving girls of the home farm, were cheerfully filling ale horns.

On low stools beside the long hearth sat Niall, the Irish *file's* son, and Eoin, the earl's poet, with Eoin's lean grey dog sleeping at their feet. Each held a harp on his knees; the poet's a splendid instrument of polished cherry wood inlaid with silver; the boy's harp, plain and battered and small, gave no hint of the powers it could summon.

Together they sang and laughed, sharing jests in their own Irish tongue as they played a lively wedding song. The farmers and seamen at the tables sang along, raising their ale horns and pounding the boards, while Ulf, the bridegroom, adorned in a woman's tunic and linen headdress, stamped up and down the hearthside in a raucous dance. Ragi of the High Island and Arnkel Fish-Tail paraded either side, planting kisses on Ulf's hairy cheeks.

Gathered on the broad sleeping benches under the eaves, the women of the islands clustered around Grimhildr and ignored them, admiring instead the array of gifts for hearth and farm. Soapstone bowls from Shetland rested on a fur bed covering from Norway. A fine new axe and a sturdy foot plough lay beside scissors and combs, horn spoons, and a cooking pot. A single oar stood in for a new skiff brought over from the Horse Island.

Irish linen was pored over by grandmothers, and Gil spotted Danni and Rachel giggling together over two vast linen night shirts for bride and groom. Girl children wrapped themselves shyly in the woolen bridal shawl, while two small boys took turns rocking each other in a carved and painted cradle.

Cheeses, hams, and casks of ale surrounded a splendid ram tied to a roof post. In an open space between rolls of silk carried back from Rome, lay the earl's own gift: a large, ornate metal key that would hang from a girdle around Grimhildr's waist, signifying ownership of her fine new farm.

Cautiously, Gil stretched up to glimpse the High Table at the head of the longhouse. A row of grey-bearded men sat deep in conversation, their solemnity at odds with the mood of the hall and their own lavish dress.

Bright-colored tunics, fur-trimmed cloaks, the fire-lit glow of silver arm-rings; all spoke of warriors of substance, gathered for celebration. But their faces told a different story and their silver wine goblets rested on the table before them, little touched. Though Magnus Redbeard, sitting with his sister's husband, Ragnvald and his nephew, Hakon, swigged defiantly from an old ale horn and cast a sour glance at his son.

Surrounded by his five chieftains, with his grey-robed priest a sparrow among peacocks at his side, Floki took no notice. Yellow hair intricately braided, arms and throat adorned with gold, a blood-red tunic over the snowy linen shirt Danni had sewn, he rested against the tall back of the High Seat, listening thoughtfully to the nearest of his companions.

Percy, his cupbearer's duties done, sat on the edge of the earl's chair, wrapped in his ermine cloak and leaning sleepily against his shoulder. With an arm around the boy, Floki watched the carousing in the hall with a gentle, remote smile. As if, Gil thought, he was already far away in Norway, in bondage to the old sea-king whose son he had lost.

The chieftain beside Floki leaned closer, over the empty chair at the earl's right. The helmsman's seat. Gil looked around uncomfortably for some humble place on the long benches where he might slip in among his friends, un-noticed.

Ulf, Ragi and Arnkel danced nearer, right to the foot of the hall. Whirling around, the two young men swung their ungainly bride off his feet and the wall of men shielding Gil parted before Ulf's flailing boots. Granted an unwanted clear view of all the longhouse, Gil saw Danni's eyes open wide and Aidan briefly shake his head. But it was too late.

With a slight nod toward his companion, Floki rose to his feet. Still with his gentle smile, he swept his gaze down the long tables lining the hearth and then raised a commanding arm. "Please. I beg you. Rise. My helmsman honors us with his presence." He bowed slightly toward Gil.

Faces turned, surprised and puzzled. After a moment's awkward pause, the men on the long benches got to their feet. The music stopped and Ragi and Ulf staggered to a halt. Arnkel glared. Ciarnan stood up with a look of total astonishment.

Beside him, Ismail quietly rose, his dark eyes bright with amusement, and gave Gil his own small bow.

The chieftains at the High Table were less amused. Turning affronted faces toward Floki, they stayed solidly in their seats. He smiled again, as gently, and said without compromise, "Up."

One by one, they got to their feet. Hakon's face was baffled; Ragnvald's bleak. Aidan stood quickly, his troubled gaze shifting from Gil to the earl and back to Gil. Only Magnus Redbeard stayed seated. Floki turned toward him and made again the same firm gesture.

The hall fell so silent that Gil could hear the flutter of flames in the hearth and the rustle of mice in the eaves. With a fierce shake of his wild red hair, Magnus lumbered to his feet. Floki smiled. He looked down the hall and beckoned Gil. "Come."

Gil's feet felt frozen to the floor. He stepped forward and tripped over his own boots. Regaining his footing, he walked hesitantly into the hall. Every eye in the room was on him; the men at the tables, the women among the wedding gifts, Danni and Rachel equally appalled; all watched his clumsy progress. The children clung uncertainly to their mothers. Even the ram stared, its glittering yellow eyes baleful.

Passing between the two rows of men, Gil made his way up the hall beside the glowing hearth fire. A memory came, unsought, of his long ago arrival at Hrolf's Isle, as a prisoner, and his terrifying ride up the ward hill, certain he faced execution at the hilltop monolith, Odin's Stone.

He stumbled again and caught the side of one table, and went on, past the two silenced harpers, the blind poet Eoin turning his head to listen to his footsteps. Niall, the *file's* young son, watched, sad and frightened. Gil's friends, Ciarnan and Ragi, seemed caught between concern and suppressed hilarity, but Ismail's dark eyes grew troubled at Gil's discomfort.

The last few steps were the hardest. Gil slowed and Floki smiled again and beckoned him closer. With no sound but the scrape of his boots on the packed earth floor, Gil crossed the open space at the end of the hearth and stood in front of the earl.

Floki's smile broadened. When he spoke, his voice was soft, but not so quiet that the others at the table would not hear. "I bow to you, Helmsman. At your age, I would not dare to insult a single chieftain. You have insulted every chieftain in the North."

"Floki, I'm sorry, I ...." Gil's words fell over themselves.

"I do not ask you to speak."

"But ...."

"And I warn you this: an untruth in acts is as much an untruth as an untruth in words. It is a lie, like any other lie, and I do not wish to be lied to. Let us say only this: I am aware what hour you came down from the farm. Had I not been aware, I would have half the island searching for you. Times are trying, and you, for reasons that escape me at present, are valuable to me. Fortunately, beasts are honest, even when men are not."

He paused and said, raising his voice so those in the hall could also hear, "However, it pleases me that you are here. I have work for you."

"Tonight?" Gil said, surprised.

"I do not ask you to speak," Floki reminded him. He looked around the hall and back to Gil. "Tomorrow, as you perhaps forget, there is a wedding. Ulf Kolsson and Grimhildr Thorolfsdottir must pledge themselves, hand-fasted through Odin's Stone."

"I know ...." Gil murmured.

"*Helmsman*," Floki's eyes flashed, though his voice remained mild. "Is it not *possible* for you to keep silence?"

Gil sensed movement at the earl's side, and turning his head, caught a brief look of warning from Aidan and nodded warily.

"Now," Floki continued, "Considering this is the case, it would be a great sorrow if Odin's Stone were not there. If, perhaps, it was stolen away in the night." He cast a mournful look around the hall and returned his gaze to Gil. "Therefore, I ask you to go and mount guard on Odin's Stone. I trust you to keep it safe."

A brief guffaw came from among the men on the benches. Floki looked up. "This is no matter for jests."

Silence fell again in the longhouse and in it, Gil heard his own perplexed voice saying, "But it weighs a couple of tonnes."

Floki laid a hand on the High Table, vaulted the board, and landed a foot from his helmsman. He caught Gil's long hair in a powerful fist and jerked his head back hard. "Guard Odin's Stone," he whispered so only Gil could hear.

He strode off down the hall and men at the feasting boards shrank back, clearing a space as he vaulted another table, snatched a fur up from a sleeping bench and flung it at Gil. "That is your bedmate," he called. "You need seek no other."

Ciarnan and Ragi covered their faces, smothering laughter. "What?" Floki called. "You are jealous?" He snatched up two more furs and flung them at the two boys. "Bed-mates for you also. Go with him." Their smiles faded and they held their ground. "*Now,*" Floki said, his voice smooth as silk. Muttering both boys clutched their furs and followed Gil to the doors.

"Helmsman," Floki called pleasantly, "There is a pony just beyond. You may use it, should you choose to ride."

CHAPTER TWO

L ionheart balked, head down, feet planted firm. *It's night.*

Good guess! Gil looked grimly at the sky, now black and rich with stars. The moon was down but the Milky Way cast all the light they needed. Lionheart stumbled.

I can't see!

Yes, you can.

Lionheart made slow, hoof-scraping steps.

Well, at this rate, it won't be night when we get there. Gil looked over his shoulder. Ragi and Ciarnan had managed to extract ponies from the pen, bridle them, and ride out in the time it took Gil and Lionheart to shuffle to the foot of the hill track. The boys' mounts pushed eager heads past Lionheart's rump, excited by the night smells.

"Does he not *move*?" Ragi called irritably.

"He's warming up," Gil called back.

I'm cold.

You're not cold and ….

My feet don't work when I'm cold. Lionheart manufactured another stumble. *And I can't see.* He sidled sideways, blocking the path. Ragi's pony shied and kicked out. Ciarnan's reared. Ragi cursed under his breath.

With a sigh, Gil swung his leg over Lionheart's neck and jumped down. He caught the pony's bridle and strode ahead, pulling him up the path.

"You are walking?" Ragi cried.

"It's faster," Gil called over his shoulder.

Ragi groaned.

Ciarnan called quizzically, "Why are you keeping that beast?"

Gil turned and grinned. "I'm not. Floki says I can salt him down for winter. You're looking at the Christ's Mass feast."

Lionheart's head came up, and the white of his eyes shone in the starlight. *Salt me?*

Last chance.

Gil jumped back on board and Lionheart trotted, dainty feet finding a sure footing, up the ward hill track.

By the time they reached the summit, Gil was enjoying himself. The night held the first chill of Northern autumn. The starlit view of sea and islands would lift the darkest mood. And, best of all, he was far from the longhouse and its earl.

Behind him, he heard the boys laughing, making jests at his expense. He turned and grinned good naturedly, glad of their company, even if they were less than pleased to be here. He drew Lionheart to a halt and jumped down from his back. Dragging the looped rein over the pony's shaggy head, he walked the last few feet and stood gazing up at the great monolith the Northmen called Odin's Stone.

Taller than Bjorn, and sunk deep into the earth, it loomed black against the sky, its hollowed out center forming a star-filled window into the night. Laying his hand on the stone's cold surface, Gil smiled ruefully, remembering his first terrified sight of it, convinced he faced a bloody execution at its foot.

It seemed now a benign presence; like Cille Aidan's Great Circle, it was far older than the Northmen's tenure of the islands, its true meaning and purpose lost in vanished minds. But the Northmen had found their own uses for it: landmark, beacon site, and tomorrow, symbol of binding trust.

Gil stretched up and rested his fingers on the smooth surface of the circular aperture and smiled again. Grimhildr and Ulf would join hands through it easily enough. But when his turn came, someone would need to lift Janetta up to reach. *We'll ride,* he thought. *Pledge ourselves from the backs of our ponies.*

What ponies? Lionheart's ears flicked back suspiciously. *And who's talking to you?*

From below in the darkness, a voice called his name. Ragi appeared, silhouetted against stars and sea, as his horse mounted the last rise before the stone. "Gil, friend. You are fortunate!" He waved cheerfully, "It is yet here."

"Surprise, surprise." Gil squinted sourly at the huge monument. It would take an army to move the thing. He tugged Lionheart's head up. *Come on, you. I've got somewhere nicer.*

Reluctantly, the pony ceased cropping grass and ambled behind as Gil led him past the sailcloth covered wood stack laid ready for the ward fire that would summon Floki's chieftains to Council. Or war. No need of that tonight. Gil shrugged uneasily. They were all here. As he was painfully aware.

He went on, and in a sheltered grassy hollow beneath the summit, he tied Lionheart's lead to a sturdy heather root and undid the girth securing his sheepskin excuse for a saddle. He pulled it free; the fur from the longhouse that he'd draped behind it tumbling to the ground.

"Ho!" Ragi called down to him. "Do not forget your bedmate!"

With a wry grin, Gil collected the fur and climbed back up to the summit with it wrapped around his shoulders. Stopping a few feet from his waiting companions, he turned in a slow circle. All around, glowing softly in the starlight, lay a glorious expanse of land and sea. Dark islands, their shores rimmed with surf. Bays and straits and inlets stretching, white-flecked, to the dim horizon.

He bent his head back, taking in a sky more white than black, so vast the number of its stars. The Milky Way flowed across the heavens, a creamy river mirroring the tide-races below.

He looked down the way they had come. The two watch fires were a faint red flicker on the shore; the longhouse itself wrapped in darkness. Beyond lay the dark strait, its white-frothed rousts shining in the starlight. Their low roar rose easily to his ears, but the Holy Isle, itself, was shrouded in night, the little house where Janetta slept lost in inky black. But he knew it was there, just as in the darkest night he would always know *she* was there, safe in the guarded depths of his heart.

"He looks for his sweetheart!" Ciarnan laughed.

"But his sweetheart is here!" Ragi held up his own fur, peering lovingly at it in the dim light. "Oh! Janetta," he warbled. "You are so beautiful!" He swung the fur around as if dancing a reel, and then clasped it against his chest. "Your lips are so warm." He caressed it lovingly. "And your eyes are so ... hairy."

"That's enough." Gil strode forward, snatched the fur, and flung it to the ground. Silence fell, broken only by the roar of the distant rousts and the sighing of the wind through the hollow of Odin's Stone.

"It is a jest," Ciarnan said uneasily.

"I know." The words came out harsher than Gil intended. Facing Ragi, he shrugged slightly, to soften them. But the feelings he had for Janetta, the way they were wrapped up in his feelings for the land and the sea and everything beautiful in his life, left no room for jests.

"He means no harm," Ciarnan said. Ragi said nothing. His hand rested on his sword belt. Then, slowly, it slipped from it and hung listlessly at his side.

"I take back the jest," he said quietly.

Gil nodded. "That's okay." As always, it surprised him when they deferred to him. But something had shifted between them since he returned from Rome, a boy no longer, but a man with blood on his hands.

He smiled then and sat down at the foot of the monolith. "We could play King's Table," he said cheerfully.

They scratched out a board in a patch of bare earth and made playing pieces from stones and twigs. But in the dim light, they kept mixing them up and eventually they abandoned the game and just leaned back against the stone, huddled in their furs and talking quietly.

Ciarnan shivered and peered at the eastern sky. "Come, dawn," he pleaded. "I freeze here."

Gil smiled. "You shouldn't have laughed."

"Oh, friend," Ragi grinned in the starlight. "If you had seen your face!"

"'Mount guard on Odin's Stone!'" Ciarnan mimicked the earl's menacing voice.

"'But it weighs ....'" Ragi fell back laughing. "I do not believe how you argue with him."

Gil covered his face. "It's my mouth. It just keeps talking

away, whatever my brain says." He grimaced. "I thought he was going to kill me."

"You? Never."

Gil shook his head. "Me. You. Anybody." He paused. "If he thought he had to, to keep his chieftains loyal." They argued then, but he knew he was right. "It's a game," he said at last. "It's all a game of King's Table. And this," he flicked an unmarked stone into the heather, "Could have been me. I humiliated him. He let me off lightly. It's more than I deserve."

Ragi leaned forward suddenly and took up the charred twig they had used as King. "If that was you, then this is the earl!" He waved the twig in Gil's face. "It is not your fault his chieftains rebel. It is his own. They know he sails to Norway, on Saint Matthew's Eve." He snapped the twig in half and flung it aside. "Who follows a dead man?"

"He will return," Gil said.

"In seven years, were he to live. But he will not live. They seek another to lead them. You should do the same."

"Never," Gil said, surprised at his own vehemence. Calming himself, he said then, "Hakon Sea-Friend will be earl."

Ragi laughed and Ciarnan joined him. "Reef the sail! Reef the sail!" they chanted in unison.

Then Ragi said softly, "It is no trouble to me. Young men prosper under a weak earl." He looked up at the stars. "My uncle on the High Island is old. He never marries and has no children. Soon, he dies, and his farm comes to me. Then, I ask for Rachel."

"You?" Ciarnan laughed gleefully. "The earl prizes her as a daughter. Chieftains beg for her in vain. And he gives her to a skinny farmer from the High Island?" He swung a rough hand to slap Ragi's head.

Ragi ducked and said coolly, "But it is not Floki Magnusson I ask."

No. Gil leaned quietly back against the monolith, feeling the cold of the ancient stone seeping through tunic and cloak. *Of course not.* Floki Magnusson would not be here to decide Rachel's future or that of anyone else. And he, of all people, should know that.

He had been with the earl when, grieving as if the child were his own, he buried their young hostage on that bitter Roman strand. He was beside him on the harsh winter voyage home, when he vowed to bind himself in slavery in reparation for the boy's death. And, at Candida Casa, it was Gil he charged with holding him to that bold, insane vow, should his own resolve fail.

Small chance of that. Gil looked up at the fading stars and thought of his first crossing to Norway, a sailing that led to this moment as surely as the stars followed their own high courses.

There, too, he had been beside the earl in his failed attempt to rescue his cousin and his lady. He had seen his fury at the sea-king's treachery and witnessed his terrible vengeance: the old man, bereft of all regal stature, weeping and reaching out trembling hands as Floki's warriors bore his child away. And yet, even then, Gil had not believed the treacherous old chieftain would keep his promises.

But, one by one, he did. The hostages of Hakon's lost ship were returned. Recompense was paid for the wounded, and for two who had died, and for the ship, *Storm Serpent*, herself. At last, all the terms of the boy's ransom were met, and against all protest, Floki Magnusson prepared to pay his debt.

All summer he sailed the islands with Hakon Sea-Friend, shoring up alliances with his uneasy chieftains, and instructing his cousin and his helmsman in the affairs of the earldom. The harvest was brought in. His tithe to the Church and the wages of his poet were paid. *Silver Dragon* was made ready. And on Saint Matthew's Eve, Gil would take the helm for his second crossing to Norway, bearing his earl to his self-imposed fate. Seven years in bondage to the old Norse king. Or, as all but Floki seemed certain, a swift, brutal death. Either way, Gil would sail back alone.

For the first time, keeping watch in the long grey dawn, he forced himself to imagine Hrolf's Isle without its tempestuous, wise young earl.

Ragi might well have a farm to offer Rachel, but Ismail, he knew, held her heart. Would staid, practical Hakon Ragnvaldsson care? What would become of Danni, betrothed to a slave in a far land, or a widow before even a wife? And what of himself, a boy just reaching manhood, half-schooled in the arts of war?

Since the day he had come to Cille Aidan, he had lived, restlessly and resentfully, under the menacing protection of Floki Magnusson's sword. Now, with the earldom teetering and the forces of the Golden Knight closing in, Floki was leaving them on their own. "*Damn him,*" Gil whispered impotently to the night. Beside him, Ciarnan stirred from his sleep.

"Gil?"

"I'm here."

"You wake?"

"I'm awake."

Ciarnan wrapped his fur closer and said, "What think you of Jorunn?"

Surprised at the sudden shyness in the boy's voice, Gil thought of the young serving maid. Fifteen, probably; grown suddenly tall. Slim and graceful, with fine dark brows arching quizzically over clear, blue-green eyes. A ready smile and a quick, light step at her work. "Nice," he said. "She's really nice."

"She has accepted me."

"Accepted ...?" Gil said dumbly.

"We are betrothed. And," Ciarnan paused, and less shyly, added, "I have tasted a little of the pleasures to come."

"*You,*" Gil said, "But aren't you ...?"

"I am not a monk, my friend. I leave my vows when I take up my sword to follow Floki Magnusson."

"But you're meant to go back to your father! You promised the earl you'd sail with Hakon on his Dublin trip."

Ciarnan stretched his arms languidly over his head. "What earl?" he said. With a cheerful laugh, he curled again under his fur and went back to sleep.

Then, with dawn greying the sky and paling the stars, Gil slept, at last.

Just before waking, he dreamed of Danni. Not as she was now, tall and womanly, at the side of the earl. But the child Danni he had known at Greene Mountain Falls, standing on the Lookout Rocks, calling his name, and holding up sun-browned arms that, even as he watched, grew feathered and became wings.

Lionheart woke him, snorting and pawing impatiently at the turf. He sat up, hearing her call him still. Far above, a grey-winged bird circled in the sea-lit dawn. Ciarnan and Ragi were quietly watching, both with faint discomfort. Few Self-Bound Men were ever truly at home with a Change-Thing.

"The earl's lady," Ragi said boldly. "I think he sends her for us." Gil laughed and shook his head. Floki, fine falconer that he was, might send Rachel's sparrow-hawk. But Danni's wild-goose Change-Thing obeyed no man, not even the earl.

"She flies only to fly," Gil said simply, watching, as always a little enviously, as her broad wings took her far away over sea and islands, the whole of the North Isles her own.

When she returned, soaring back over the ward hill, Ciarnan and Ragi were collecting their ponies for the ride back to the longhouse. "Come with us," Ragi called over his shoulder, "I think it is safe now." He shrugged toward the grey bulk of the monument. "The trolls do not carry it away in daylight."

Gil smiled, still watching the circling bird. "You go. I'll follow you." The sun caught her wings as she turned, and with outstretched neck, swept down over the startled ponies' heads and through the center of Odin's Stone.

Instinctively, he reached his arms out, but her momentum, as she transformed from hollow-boned bird to strong, young woman, took him off his feet, and they tumbled together to the grass. For a moment, they lay giggling, as the children they had once been. Then both drew back, and they scrambled to their feet.

Ragi grinned at Gil. "One moment more, and I tell the earl. And this is you." He drew a finger across his throat.

Gil laughed lightly, but Danni's dark eyes grew somber. She turned quickly away. Then her gaze fell on Ciarnan, and her face lit with a teasing smile. "All the serving girls are getting ready for the wedding," she said. "Jorunn looks very pretty in her new shawl." Her smile broadened. "But very lonely, too."

Ciarnan quickly gathered the reins of his pony. "She is not lonely long," he laughed, and mounting, kicked the placid beast into a gallop. Ragi watched as they careered madly down the hill. Then he mounted his own horse.

"And Rachel?" he said, searching Danni's face. "She is pretty also?"

Danni's smile faded. "Rachel is always pretty."

"And?"

She shook her head. "She is not lonely, Ragi," she said with a gentle smile.

Gil stood beside her as she watched the two boys descending the hill, one exuberant; the other, determined. His own gaze strayed from the riders below to the girl at his side.

Her cheeks were brown from the harvest sun, the tails of her glossy dark plaits bleached golden from swimming in the sea. Bracelets adorned her arms, strings of bright beads circled her throat, silver brooches fastened her braid trimmed tunic; all gifts from her sea-faring beloved that told every man she was spoken for. Gil felt boyish and shy around her now. "You're very pretty, too," he grinned. "But maybe I'm not supposed to say that." He drew a mocking finger across his own throat.

She was quiet. "You should have challenged him," she said.

"Ragi?" Gil stepped back. "What? Fight him for your honor?" He shook his head angrily, "It was a *joke*, Danni."

"Not my honor," she said solemnly. "Yours. They must respect you or you will lose all authority."

"*What* authority?" he laughed sourly.

"You are earl's helmsman. Whether Floki Magnusson is earl, or Hakon Sea-Friend is earl. Why does he sail with you to every longhouse in the islands? Why does he seat you at his right in his own? *When* you can be bothered to get there."

Gil groaned, slumped down again on the grass at the foot of Odin's Stone and put his head into his hands. "I was sure I'd get back in time."

She sighed and sat down on the ground beside him. Drawing her skirts down over her bare feet, she rested her head back against the mossy surface. He raised his own and they looked deep into each other's eyes. "When are you going to grow up, Gil?"

"Probably sooner than I'd like?"

"Yes." She looked out over the sea. "I saw Cille Aidan."

"What, now? This morning?"

She nodded. "There were men there," she said.

"Who?"

She shrugged. "Strangers. Vikings. They've made a mess of it."

He jumped to his feet. "Tell the earl!"

"Why?"

"*Why*?" Because they've been raiding Hrolf's Isle all summer. And now we know where they are."

She stood, also, and shook her head. "They're small fish, Gil. He has bigger things on his mind."

"Yeah," he said. He wrapped his arms around himself. "Suicide."

"It's not that, Gil."

"It sure looks like that to me."

"I know. But not to him. Floki loves life. He's fearless. But he loves to live. And he expects to live. If the Norse king has any sense, Floki will be leading his warriors for those seven years."

"And if he doesn't have sense?"

"It's a debt he has to pay." She paused. "All the more so because he is earl and there is no one to make him pay it."

"He asked me to," Gil said dully. "He asked me to hold him to it."

"Then you must."

He whirled around and slapped the old stone so hard his whole hand stung. "It's so pointless! It won't bring Eirik back. It won't make peace with the old king. Hakon will never be able to marry his daughter."

She looked down toward the longhouse where another, happier wedding party was already gathering. "He will. If the debt is paid."

"With his cousin murdered or a slave in her father's house?"

"It's not about feelings, Gil. It's about keeping the rules."

Turning, she gestured in a broad arc to the landscape below them: stubble fields and pastureland, heather hill, moor, and loch, all ringed by the restless sea. "It may look wild and lawless," she said. "But it's not. There are rules about everything. Rules about farmland. Rules about beasts. Tools. Ships. How the harvest is shared. The fishing. The plunder. Floki broke the rules."

"I know that, Danni. I hated him when he took the poor kid hostage."

"Eirik was a fair hostage," she said.

"Bullshit. He was ten years old."

She nodded. "I was there, Gil. I remember Eirik. The way he teased Gudrun about Hakon. The way he followed his brother Kari around, copying him. He worshipped Kari. And when Kari died that summer, Eirik put on his sword and took his place." She paused. "He had to. He was the last brother left. Without a son, the old king is fair prey to anyone and his kingdom is a battlefield. *That* is the rule Floki broke; he took the man's last son. He took the heir."

Gil nodded slowly. "And now Floki is taking his place."

"Yes."

"And Hrolf's Isle will be the battlefield."

She turned abruptly away. "We have to go." With her back to him she said, "The wedding party will be here by None. We shouldn't be here before them."

"Another rule."

She looked back and bleakly met his eyes. "Yes. Another rule."

She rode behind him on Lionheart, her feet swinging lightly as if she were yet a carefree girl. The pony snorted happily, picking his sure-footed way down the hill. "It's fun riding him again," she said. "It feels like old times. Rachel and I were out on Frosti and Freya, two days ago, but we had to go gently. Freya's in foal."

Gil laughed. "We're all growing up." He ruffled Lionheart's mane, behind his ears. "Even you." Lionheart shook his head and snapped companionably at Gil's leg with his big white teeth.

"Do you miss home?" Gil said suddenly.

After a long while, she leaned against his shoulder and said, "I miss my foster-father."

"Your ... at *Finlaggan*?" he cried, picturing the wolfish chieftain on his magnificent ship.

"He was so kind," she said simply.

"Sure." Gil twisted around on the pony's back and stared at her. "But that wasn't *home*, Danni. What about *our* home." He paused and said angrily, "Your real father."

"It's so long ago," she shook her head sadly. "Let me down," she said then.

"It's okay," he muttered.

But she said quickly, "I know. But they mustn't see us like this." She touched his shoulder and pointed down the hill.

They had reached the last low ridge above the home farm. The longhouse roof, its turf bright with late summer flowers, lay below; the sea sparkling beyond. Figures, small in the distance, milled around farmyard and byres. The neighs of excited ponies rose to their ears. "The wedding party," Gil said, halting Lionheart.

She slipped down, and Gil jumped down too. "Can I walk beside you?" he said uncertainly.

She grinned and pushed him slightly. "Of course. But like ships. Clear water between."

They walked then, side by side, leading the pony, who ambled contentedly, free of his burden. Behind a clump of scrub willow, Danni stopped and sat down on a sun-dried rock, examining her skirts and sleeves and picking off twigs and bits of grass.

"There isn't time to go back to the Nunnery," she said, loosening the ribbons that bound her plaits. "I have to do my hair."

Gil laughed, looking down to the steep roof of Aidan's little church and cell, and the small house beside it, which did indeed resemble a monastic dwelling. Floki had built it for Rachel when he first brought her to Hrolf's Isle. Now, Danni, too, slept there, secluded from the longhouse by the sanctuary of the church.

"Having a little trouble thinking of you two as nuns."

Danni smiled. "So is Ismail," she said.

"And Floki?"

"The earl is very respectful," she answered in a quiet, stranger's voice.

She drew a small, braid-trimmed pocket from beneath her tunic and took from it a silver comb and a small polished-metal mirror that Floki had bought from a merchant Dane. Laying down the mirror on her spread skirt, she combed out her sleek, brown hair, until it flowed, sun-burnished, down her back. Then she bound the ribbons around her forehead, checking the effect in the mirror resting on her knees.

She looked up, saw him watching and smiled shyly. "All right?"

He nodded. "You should be the bride," he said solemnly.

"What?" she cried, her eyes sparkling, "Marry Ulf?"

"You know what I mean."

She stood up, the treasured mirror and comb held carefully before her. "I will be."

He turned away. The wedding party had begun to flow toward the hill, festive garments making a colorful river. Children ran shouting. Dogs barked. "Who is going to look after these people?" he said.

"Hakon Ragnvaldsson. And you."

"No, Danni. I am not." He paused. "Okay. I'm a good steersman. Fine. I'm okay with a sword. Pretty ordinary with a bow. I ride well enough."

With my help, Lionheart put in.

"With a little help from my *friends*," Gil said wearily. "But I don't belong here. I'm always making mistakes. I don't *understand* the rules. I sound about twelve when I talk in Norse. And Floki says I can't even add up right, so he's sending me to *school* with Aidan."

"He goes himself," Danni smiled.

"Right, fine." Gil was still bemused by the earl sitting beside him in Aidan's cell, practicing Latin letters with a quill and ink. "So, we're both school kids. But that doesn't make me Floki Magnusson. I'm *really* a kid, Danni. I'm sixteen years old."

She nodded. Then she flipped the mirror around and held its polished surface in front of Gil's eyes. He stepped back and stared. The gleaming metal showed him a young man with tanned forehead and newly lean cheeks. Blue eyes, habitually narrowed against sea glare, gazed calmly back. Beneath one, running almost to his jaw, a white scar cut through the brown fur of a youthful beard. He murmured, "I haven't seen my face since …."

"Since home," she said.

And, other than in the deceptive waters of some tidal pool, it was true. Wonderingly, he raised his fingers and traced the fierce white line, his legacy from the fire-raising at the Deer Isle.

"Suits you, Helmsman," she said.

Shaking his head uncertainly, he turned the mirror over and placed it back in her hands.

At the foot of the hill, they met the bridegroom's party. Sturdy Ulf Kolsson, with face still dark from southern seas, hair and beard trimmed and combed, and even his farmyard boots brushed clean, held the be-ribboned bridle of a fine black gelding. Flanked by his brothers and cousins, and surrounded by his farm workers and serving maids, he had the proud bearing of a man who had seen the world.

Beyond, at the doors of the longhouse, the bride's party gathered around Grimhildr. Seated already on a tall white mare, with the earl holding the reins, she looked startlingly pretty with her red hair freed from its headdress and crowned instead with a circlet of flowers. A treasure chest of jewelry from Ulf's Roman journey brightened her blue tunic. Her snowy linen sleeves fluttered in feminine pleats.

"Check for the throwing axes," Gil muttered.

"Still there," Danni whispered back. Her eyes strayed as she spoke, and Gil followed her gaze.

A group of young girls came running with baskets of flowers plucked from the longhouse roof, and crowded around the white mare, weaving blossoms into her mane and tail. Then, giggling wildly, they turned upon the earl, who knelt obediently on the beaten earth as they plaited flowers into his long yellow hair.

Around him, his warriors laughed and shouted, but he remained patiently kneeling until the children were done.

Gil watched in silence. "Danni," he said cautiously. "He doesn't listen to me, or Hakon, or Ragnvald. Or anyone. But he'd listen to you."

She was silent, still watching the laughing children and their playful earl.

"Danni ...."

"That's why I say nothing," she said.

"Danni ...." he protested.

"He lets me fly, Gil." She turned to him, her face tear streaked. "I let him fly, too."

CHAPTER THREE

From the corner of his eye, Gil saw the sail. Just off the headland, a fleeting shape, pale as a gull's wing in the summer mist. He looked to the earl. But Floki, like the others gathered at the summit of the ward hill, had his back to the sea, facing the bride and groom.

Gil turned again to the water. The sail was gone. *Or never there.* He rubbed his eyes, dry and itchy from lack of sleep, and shrugged. Probably a merchant, if it was ever a ship at all. He'd get no trade today.

"Gil," Janetta tugged his hand, drawing his attention back to Ulf and Grimhildr standing solemnly on either side of Odin's Stone. Leaning forward, they reached together into the stone's cool shadows, their big, work-weathered hands clasping in an iron grip. Exchanging a brief nod, they released their hold, turned to the assembled company, and stood side by side.

Grimhildr gave her stocky farmer a brief glance and announced to all, "I am Ulf's woman." She brushed her hands together, as if finished with cheese-making, or shearing a sheep.

Half a head shorter than his six-foot bride, but solid as a weathered oak, Ulf thrust his thumbs into his belt and rumbled, "I am Grimhildr's man." Then he crouched, wrapped his arms around Grimhildr's legs, and hoisted her over his shoulder. Grimhildr squealed with girlish delight, and he strode off down the hill, only relinquishing his rosy-cheeked wife, when the earl came running with her mare.

Ulf's brothers brought his black gelding; bride and groom were set aboard their mounts to ride to their wedding feast.

Ciarnan and Jorunn threw a straw baby, and the gathering broke up with shouts and laughter. Small boys struggled to lift small girls. Percy hand-fasted a serving maid through Odin's Stone. On foot and on ponies, the younger men raced each other down the track, while, at the rear, the earl walked with his cousin and his sober chieftains, his lady by his side.

Janetta sighed sweetly, watching the bride and groom. "They are so happy." Gil looked down on her dark head. In his heart, the words echoed secretly, *I am Gil's woman. I am Janetta's man.* He felt dreamy and dazed with love for her. His concerns about the sail slipped effortlessly from his mind.

When they mounted Lionheart, again, together, the pony gave a rib-shuddering sigh and lowered his nose to the ground. "He is tired!" Janetta reached around Gil to pat his neck.

"He is lazy," Gil said, grinding his heels into Lionheart's flanks. *Down the hill. Now.*

Down the hill. Clip. Clop. *Up the hill.* Clip. Clop. *Down the hill.* Clip. Sigh. Clop. *Up the ....*

"Oh, forget it." Gil swung his leg over Lionheart's neck, jumped down, and reached his arms up for Janetta.

She can stay. She feels nice.

And I don't feel nice.

Your feet are too long. They tickle.

Fine. I'll cut them off.

Cut them off! Lionheart's ears pricked forward. *Cut them off!* Clip. Clop.

Outside the little church, Aidan was waiting, with the earl's mother, Shony, at his side. Grimhildr and Ulf dismounted and knelt while Aidan sprinkled them with holy water and spoke a Latin blessing over their heads. The chieftains watched with impassive faces. The earl's father folded his arms.

"May the good Christ grant you a hundred children!" Shony cried, laughing.

Magnus thrust a fist in the air. "And may Odin make them all sons!"

The men and the boys cheered heartily. Floki extended his hands to bride and groom and raised them to their feet. "Ah, let them have daughters, too," he smiled. "Life would be sad with no women." He bowed gently to the girls and farm wives who cast triumphant glances at their men.

Magnus glowered. "And do we feast, now, like in the days of the old gods? Or do we only pray?"

Floki smiled again, a little sadly. "We feast, Father. Come," he said gently. "Come with me."

Magnus shrugged, turned, and walked alone to the hall. The chieftains shuffled, uncertain who to follow, until Floki beckoned them forward. Hakon and Ragnvald walked apart, seeking their own middle ground. Gil watched uneasily; then turned with relief to the necessity of tending his pony.

At the mossy water trough, Lionheart snuffled up huge, noisy gulps, raised a muzzle dripping with slime, and rubbed it against Gil's chest. *Oh, thanks so much.* Gil grimaced and wiped his hands down his tunic. Lionheart snorted suddenly and shied, as Arnkel and Ragi barged in beside him, filling a wooden bucket to the brim.

Grinning, they backed behind the pony until the bride and groom appeared, on foot, their mounts ambling behind. "Here, Ulf!" Ragi called. "I bless you, too!"

Gil turned as he bolted forward, bucket raised high. "Oh, don't …." he protested.

But in an instant the earl was there, catching Ragi around the middle, lifting him off his feet and hurling him, head first, into the trough. The bucket clattered to the ground, splashing Gil's boots. Lionheart reared in alarm. Gasping and spluttering, Ragi floundered upright, with his face covered in horse slime, mouth twisted in outrage.

"You do not mock my priest," Floki said quietly and turned back to the bride and groom.

Ragi scrambled to his feet, standing dripping in the trough, and shouted after him, "Who guards your priest Saint Matthew's Morn?"

Floki whirled, a cold fire in his eyes that Gil knew well. Aidan ran from the couple's side, and raising both hands, barred the earl's way. But Ragi remained, standing in the water trough, frozen with terror.

Silent as a wraith, Shony had mounted the trough's wooden frame and stood now behind the dripping youth, her sword at his throat. "From whom should the good father need a guard?" she said silkily, "Tell me. I will deal with him."

She pressed the blade closer until Ragi croaked, "No one. No guard. He needs no guard."

Around them, even the battle-scarred chieftains stepped carefully back. Shony jumped down and Ragi, shivering, carefully climbed to the ground. Then Grimhildr strode forward, wrapping her bridal shawl close, one hand drifting to an axe head, "And why should he ever need a guard? He who helps all and harms none?"

The women and girls all nodded, and whispering among themselves, left their men and clustered defiantly around Shony and the bride. Men and women faced each other across the yard, the new bridegroom scratching his head uncertainly. Then, a handsome, dark-haired young farmer looked toward Aidan and said, "Without his medicines, my Thorhalla dies in child bed." He walked away from the men and went to the side of his wife and child.

Muttering passed through the ranks of farmers and warriors. Sea-weathered Svein Snaggle-Tooth announced, "He heals the arm I break when the skiff founders on the Spear Isle." Gruffly, he, too, joined the women. Another shook his head plaintively, "He listens to my frail-witted father and makes him smile." With a shrug, he crossed the yard as well.

Gil saw Arnkel fade carefully out of sight in the crowd, leaving Ragi alone, facing accusing eyes. The earl suddenly laughed and threw his arm around the youth's drenched shoulders. "Enough solemn talk! It is a wedding, not a burial. Come, I give you clothing. You do not dance dripping like a stranded fish." With his arm still around Ragi, Floki led the way to the hall.

Gil was already at his place among the chieftains, when Ragi re-appeared. Dressed in the earl's fine clothes and looking like a chieftain's son, himself, he strode the hall with a bold swagger and claimed a seat beside Rachel. Across the breadth of the longhouse, Ismail rose quietly from among the young men and moved to her other side. Twisting a lock of her long red hair, Rachel stared resolutely ahead.

Gil's gaze drifted longingly to Janetta, sitting far away, with the young women, but he stayed resignedly where he was, until Floki came from his bedchamber behind the High Table. Flinging his ermine cloak over his shoulder, he took his place beside Gil and turned to Aidan at his left. "My helmsman graces me with his presence," he said cheerfully. "But now my cupbearer vanishes." He raised helpless hands. "I am like the prophet, Good Father, without honor ...."

Aidan laughed softly. With a wary glance at the earl, Gil pointed to the hearthside. "He's there."

In a heap of straw, beside the blind poet and the *file's* son, Percy sat humming loudly to their harp music and patting his two baby goats. True to his promise in Rome, Floki had sailed away one summer's morning in a small fishing skiff and returned a few days later with the pair tethered in the bow.

Some said he had sailed to Caledon for them, others, all the way to Norway. A few muttered that they were stolen from the selkies in their land beneath the sea and would bring ill-fortune. But they seemed to Gil pretty ordinary goats, black and shaggy with glittering yellow eyes, grazing all day on the longhouse roof.

When Floki beckoned, and Percy jumped to his feet and ran to him, they came clattering after, nosing about the legs of the surprised chieftains and then standing up with small front hooves resting on the board. Floki regarded them with an indulgent smile while Percy poured wine into the chieftains' silver goblets. Then he, himself, took the wooden cup that hung from a cord around the boy's neck, and filled it with water and a small splash of wine.

Percy sat down on his little stool behind the table and sipped it solemnly as he ate. Then, as always, he climbed up onto the edge of Floki's seat and sat leaning against him as the chieftains ate and drank. Wriggling around, he proudly held out the cup to Gil.

"It's beautiful," Gil said, taking it in his hands.

"Floki made it," Percy said. "From a tree," he added.

Gil smiled. "Except for that bit." He pointed to the band holding the miniature staves of wood together, like the hoops of a cask. "It's silver."

Percy nodded seriously. "That piece is from a silver tree," he said.

"Now, there's a tree men would seek to fell." Ragnvald chuckled and leaned past Gil "May I see the cup?"

Percy thrust it into his hands, rotating it so the decorative figure on the silver band faced toward him. "It has my wolf on it. Like this." He turned his shoulder, showing his golden arm band.

"Ah, Fenrir," Ragnvald smiled. His long, lined face softened and a playful light briefly touched his somber eyes. "A wolf not to be trifled with." He brushed his hand over Percy's head and placed the cup back in his hands.

"He's my friend," Percy said happily. He offered the cup to be admired by Aidan and then each of the chieftains in turn.

"The gods meet their ends, but children still play," Ragnvald smiled again at Gil, and shifted his lame leg with a grimace of pain. He looked older and leaner and sadder than Gil remembered him last, when they parted at sea, off the coast of Alba.

Small wonder: in the time between, he, whose son was in chains in a foreign land, lost, too, his cheerful ruddy-cheeked wife, Gunnhild. Magnus Redbeard's sister, and as unlike him in nature as alike in face and build; she had been the one source of light in Ragnvald's gloomy hall.

But a ship had come in, that spring, with sickness aboard, and it had swept their islands like a summer squall. Ragnvald, crippled and battle-scarred, it had left unscathed, while she whose youthful charm and motherly care had won Gil's heart, fell ill within days. And, as they yet sailed the Irish Sea on their long journey home, she had died, without ever seeing again the son they had freed.

That, Gil knew now, was what life was like here; always precarious, neither just nor fair; death taking the young and vigorous as readily as the frail and old. He looked down at the goat kids sleeping in small black balls and thought of Hakon's lapdog lying mournfully at Gunnhild's feet. It, at least, had seen Hakon home once more.

"Foster-son," Ragnvald turned then to Floki, "Have you not verses for the wedded pair, as you had so often for me?"

Floki bowed to his foster-father, rose, and joined Eoin and Niall by the fire, and while they stroked their harps, he recited a playful poem in honor of the bride who had sailed a longship to Rome and disarmed an earl on a Frankish shore; and of the stalwart groom, who had won a troll-maiden for a wife.

Ending his recitation, he took an ale horn from a passing serving girl and raised it to the bride and groom. While all in the hall took up their own and drank with shouts and cheers, he returned to his seat beside Gil.

"Fine words," Ragnvald said happily. "I thank you, Fosterling." The chieftains nodded and solemnly raised their silver goblets.

"Oh, fine words," Magnus Redbeard echoed suddenly. "My son is never short of words. Or music." He glowered at the Irish harpers and lurched to his feet, empty ale horn in hand. Floki at once signaled to Jorunn who came running to fill it. Magnus swigged it down and looked blearily over the longhouse tables. "He lies alone in his bed making verse, like a poet. He chants his psalter like a monk. And sings sweetly as a dairy maid." He swung his big, aggrieved head side to side and cried plaintively, "Are there any men left in this hall?"

Laughter and cheering died, and a shocked silence filled the longhouse. The wedding guests all turned from Magnus to the earl. Floki acknowledged his father's words with a small whimsical smile, sat quietly for a long moment, and then leapt to his feet and drew his sword.

Gasps of alarm swept the hall. The chieftains rose, murmuring protest. But the earl only smiled cheerfully, and still holding up the sword, turned to his foster-brother. "Hakon, cousin, I need two."

Relief flooded Hakon's face and with a nod of understanding, he drew his own sword and handed it to the earl. "I thank you,"

Floki smiled again, shrugged off his ermine cloak, and with a blade in each hand, leapt over the table and strode down to the flickering hearth.

Hearing his footsteps, the blind harper inclined his head, nodded to a soft-spoken command, and began to play a sweet lithesome tune. Niall listened briefly, and touched his own strings, and the perfect notes of the High-King's harp rose to counter Eoin's melody.

Floki turned to the High Table and raised both swords. "For you, Father." Looking up, he threw the blades high into the air; one, and then the other; a flashing, deadly dance of steel soaring above his head and then tumbling down.

Cries of alarm again echoed in the hall, and then gasps of relief as the hilts of each slipped safely into his hands. Then, bowing to Magnus, he fell to his knees and laid both swords down on the beaten earth floor; Hakon's first, and then his own over it, forming a razor-edged cross.

Looking up, he beckoned Jorunn and bid her bind her handkerchief around his eyes. When she was done, he remained a few moments, kneeling quietly, head yet bowed. Then he rose to his feet and the music rose with him, clear and strong, the sightless musician eerily aware of his every move.

Floki raised his linen-bound face to the unseen rafters of his longhouse, lifted his arms above his head, and gave a joyous shout. Then he leapt over the blades, his feet as sure in the darkness as the harper's fingers on the strings. Back straight as a ship's mast, he began to dance, stepping in and out of the crossed blades with graceful solemnity. The music quickened and he circled, turning fleet-footed across one sword and then the other, never once touching blade or hilt as the musicians played faster and faster.

Both harps joined in the melody, the harpers' fingers flying, and the music grew louder and faster still. Floki whirled and spun, jumped with both feet curled behind him, and landed facing opposite. He jumped again, turning to the clapping chieftains. Swift feet weaving a dizzying pattern, he danced on in flagrant darkness until the music came crashing to an end.

Whirling, he yanked the blindfold off, swept one arm down,

caught up one blade, whirled again, claimed the second, and holding both up in triumph, faced his father. Laughing and sweat-soaked, he gave another joyful shout and flung himself full length on the floor, the deadly blades crossed again in filial submission.

Gil felt the table shake with the pounding of feet on the beaten earth and the thumping of ale horns on the feasting boards. "Again! Again!" Erling Maiden-Face shouted, and others took up the chant.

Floki raised himself to his knees and shook his head. "Again, and I am dead," he panted. Still breathing hard, he climbed to his feet, sheathed his sword, and handed the other across the table to Hakon. Hakon took it and clasped his cousin's hand in a hearty grip. Danni half rose from her seat to greet him, eyes shining. Still clutching the earl's fur cloak, Percy giggled with excitement, clapping his pudgy hands.

Floki took his seat again, enfolding the boy in a gentle embrace. "We would have wine, now, Cupbearer," he whispered. Percy jumped up and resumed his dutiful solemnity, pouring wine for Floki and then each of the chieftains. Magnus waved him away and lurched to his feet, clutching his ale horn, and as the chieftains raised their silver goblets to his son, he held it up, too.

"Very pretty," he growled. "And while you dance so prettily, other men find better uses for their swords." He gulped the last of his ale and walked away.

A leaden silence fell over the High Table. Gil heard Ragnvald's weary sigh, as he set his goblet down, untouched. He saw Aidan rest a gentle hand on Floki's wrist. But the earl himself only nodded, as Magnus lumbered down the hall, dipped his drinking horn into the ale cask and held it to his lips.

"You danced that at Einar's Holm," Gil said angrily. "And Magnus loved it. I remember him cheering."

Floki took the wine jug from Percy and drew the boy close. Wrapping the cloak around him again, he smiled wryly. "It is a long season since I win my father's praise. Look! Even my ale displeases him!"

Magnus had gulped down the horn's contents and stood

wiping his lips and grimacing before he dipped deep into the ale cask again. "Well, he drinks enough of it," Gil muttered.

Floki laughed. "Each mouthful drowns the taste of the last." He looked up, to the rafters of his hall where the swallows were settling for the night. "The dance is from Alba. A chieftain's son in Caledon showed me the steps." He smiled suddenly. "The Saracen was with me."

"Palamedes!" Gil said.

Floki nodded slowly. "Would he were here. Or we, there. Riding again through Caledon. Those were good times." He lowered his gaze and watched Magnus weaving slightly on his return to his place. "But he is far now from Alba, and I, soon, farther still." He straightened suddenly, setting down his wine goblet. "You must return there. You are not done."

"*Alone?*"

Floki smiled, his eyes still on his father. "Do I waste my breath all summer? You make alliances, Warrior. Here. In Francia. And then in Caledon. All men will rise against a tyrant, in time. But they must be well led. The time has come. You will lead them."

Gil stared at the earl; wordless, terrified, and insanely proud. Then Magnus re-appeared, swaying and drunk, in front of him, and for once Gil was glad to see him. He staggered, missed his footing, and lurched heavily into the high back of Floki's chair.

Immediately, Floki stood, offering his steadying arm. Magnus brushed it aside and settled with a thud on his own seat. Then, as Floki, too, took his place again, Ragnvald rose deliberately to his feet.

He raised his silver goblet, swept the hall with his gaze, and then turned and cast his sworn-kinsman, Magnus, a look of slow-burning fury. "Fosterling," he said, and though he addressed Floki, his gaze remained on Magnus. "Again, I thank you. Fine words and then a fine dance. A very fine dance. So fine," his voice broke into a throaty growl and the anger in his eyes flared dangerously, "That I would have you dance it at my own son's wedding, when that day comes."

He drank heartily from the goblet and Gil leaped to his feet and raised his own. One by one, the chieftains stood, also, and drank, until only Magnus and the earl remained sitting; Magnus glowering with resentment, and too drunk as well to rise, and Floki gazing quietly again at the rafters.

"I will bless Hakon's wedding," he said.

"Bless it?" Hakon cried. "What, cousin? With a bucket of water, like Ragi? Then we turn you on your head in the trough as well!"

The table exploded in laughter, half amusement, and half relief. But Floki yet sat in silence, staring curiously at the darkness beneath the eaves as if he saw something there among the swallows that no other man could see.

Shaking his head, suddenly, he looked around as if freshly awakened and then jumped to his feet. "The wedding dance!" he cried gaily. "Come, now, bride and groom, lead us!"

The tables were cleared and shoved back against the sleeping benches, the cooking pots hurried away, and the pot chains hooked up above their heads. Men, women, and children; bairns in arms and old people on staves all flowed into the center of the hall. Hastily choosing partners, they formed a column of couples that soon became a ring, encircling the whole long hearth.

Gil ran to partner Janetta before anyone else could claim her. Ciarnan captured Jorunn. Ismail and Ragi collided with each other in their haste to win Rachel, both losing her to a handsome young Shetlander from Hakon's crew. The two harpers touched their strings, and Grimhildr and Ulf, hands joined, proudly began the dance.

Like Floki's witchery with the swords, it started with slow steps and solemn dignity, a formal procession, twice circling the hall. Then the music quickened and with it, the dancers' pace. While Gil struggled to keep up, the couples turned and spun and swung each other in circles. Moving from hand to hand and partner to partner in bewildering sequence, they formed sets of four and then of six, made arches with their arms and as all passed beneath, changed partners yet again.

Stumbling a few paces behind, Gil felt himself guided, re-directed, and shoved firmly into place by warriors who had trusted his steersman's skills from Hrolf's Isle to Rome. Men better accustomed to oar and sword amazed him with their grace, dancing proudly with their silver laden women.

Thundering past like the bear he was named for, Bjorn yet turned his partners as lightly as if they were glass. Arnkel, less restrained, swung each off her feet. Craggy Svein Snaggle-Tooth tripped by, hand in hand with his impossibly beautiful half-Irish wife.

Even Ragnvald joined in, thumping awkwardly on his stiffened leg. Three of the chieftains followed, but two remained sitting morosely with Magnus, while Hakon stood off to one side, leaning against a roof post and watching with troubled eyes.

Away at last from his embattled High Table, the earl danced with his people. Yellow plaits flying, face free of care, looking scarcely older than Ragi; who, in his borrowed clothes, could be a brother; he held the eyes of every woman in the hall.

Freed also from his duties, Gil swung happily from Jorunn to Danni, to ancient Asa who refused to release him without a kiss, and on to Bergljot of the thick golden braids, and Hrodny and Asgerd and Grimhildr, surprisingly light-footed, and alarmingly, to Bjorn.

"How'd that happen?" he cried helplessly to Ismail, who was suddenly in front of him.

"You on wrong side." Ismail patiently re-aligned him in the dance.

"How are *you* so good at it?"

"African," Ismail grinned. "We have rhythm, remember?" Then he was gone and Janetta was there again and nothing else mattered.

Ragi swung by, lost his footing and skidded to the edge of the fire. He staggered upright, found his partner, and went on, eyes always searching the hall for Rachel. On the next round, he grabbed an ale horn from a table as he passed, dipped it into the cask and downed it while he danced. *Like Magnus*, Gil thought, troubled. But then the dance took him and he forgot everyone's troubles, even his own.

Another change of partners, another wild swing, and he faced Rachel, pink-cheeked and glowing, arm-in-arm with

Ismail. He reached for her hand, but Ragi barged into the circle, clasped Rachel's wrist, and pulled her roughly to his side. Men shouted and old women scolded. Ragi ignored them, dragging Rachel out of the dance.

"No!" Ismail lunged forward. "She is not a sack of meal to be thrown about by you." His hand closed on Ragi's shoulder. "Let her go."

Ragi shoved Ismail's arm aside and reached for his sword. Before the blade cleared the scabbard, Ismail's was in his hand. Around them, the dancers scattered like chaff in the wind. The harpers' fingers stilled on their strings. Children cried and ran for their mothers. Then suddenly the earl was there, a powerful hand around each youth's wrist. Smiling amiably, he tightened his grip until both swords clattered to the floor.

"No man sheds blood at a wedding," he said. "It brings ill-fortune." Still smiling, he let them go, watching carefully as each retrieved and sheathed his fallen weapon. "That is better." He looked up. "And what wedding is this with no music?"

The harpers began at once to play, and the dancers sought their partners again. Rachel ran to Ismail, embracing him fiercely. Ragi stood quietly watching, and then turned and walked alone out the great longhouse doors.

They slammed closed behind him and the dancing resumed, but couples had circled the hall only once when a shout from outside cut through the music and with a thud and clatter the doors fell open again. Hands reached for swords and then relaxed as Ragi staggered back in.

Gil's first thought was that the night air, which sobered most men, had somehow made Ragi drunker. He took two steps, halted and swayed; another two, and he reached out with a hand that flapped oddly. And then suddenly he fell and men rushed to his aid.

Held up by their arms, he sagged to his knees. His body twisted and Gil saw the sodden red stain spreading sickeningly across his back. Aidan and Floki were beside him, then, lowering him gently to the floor. Ragi looked up at the earl. His eyes were wide and puzzled. "The guards?" he said, choking on blood. "The guards?"

Floki jumped to his feet and with a quick wave of his hand sent a dozen warriors racing through the doors. Then he knelt again beside the blood-soaked youth. Women came running, tearing their underskirts for bandages. But neither the earl nor Aidan showed any haste. Both had seen Death often enough to know his face.

Ragi's dimming gaze searched the room and fell at last on Rachel, standing weeping in Danni's arms. Floki beckoned her closer as Ragi reached out a shaking hand. "Fire-Hair," he whispered. Rachel closed her eyes.

Still not looking, she fell to her knees and let the earl draw her nearer until Ragi's blood-stained fingers closed on a lock of her long red hair. She sobbed, face buried in her hands. "It is well," Ragi said. "It is best." A happy light brightened his eyes. "Now I never lose you." He clutched the hair closer to his chest as the light faded and Aidan murmured his Latin prayer.

Floki got slowly, wearily to his feet and then spun around as running feet sounded outside. Erling burst through the doors, windswept and wild-eyed. "To the strand!" he shouted. "They burn the ships!"

CHAPTER FOUR

The rain came, blessedly, at dawn. Gil raised his head, savoring the soft touch of it on his soot-smeared face, the hiss of its fall on still smoldering wood. He rested the axe-head against a charred strake and dared to look around.

The strand was dismal in grey mist. Between each of the beached ships, heaps of charred timbers smoldered, hacked free to save the rest. Axes yet sounded. Gil flinched at each blow.

The wind rose, as always at first light, cutting through his soaked clothing. All night he had trudged in and out of the sea, filling endless buckets of water. Driven by desperation, he had not felt the cold. Now, he shivered and wrapped his arms around himself. Then he raised the axe and splintered more wood from the ship he had helped to build.

Eyolf Grimsson stopped beside him and rested his hands on the axe. "Enough," he said, nudging the charred strake with his boot. That grows cold." He cast his gaze down the damaged ship, white beard bristling, vivid blue eyes intent; the same look he'd cast over Gil's apprentice work.

"*Eldivdr*," Gil said suddenly. "Firewood." He pretended to toss something over his shoulder.

The old shipwright glowered uncertainly and then suddenly laughed, a big, booming laugh Gil had never heard before. "Tree-Nail!" he shouted. "So bad, always, you make! *Eldivdr*!" He held up forefinger and thumb as if they grasped a small piece of wood and flung it happily over his own shoulder. He seemed remarkably untroubled by the destruction of his work.

Gil shook his head. "How can you laugh?" he said, weariness freeing his tongue.

Eyolf's thick eyebrows lowered. "What else? Do I weep like a woman?" He shrugged his broad shoulders. Then he said, almost kindly, "What I build, I build again." He touched his forehead. "The ship is here."

Gil watched him walk away and join the earl beside *Silver Dragon*. They stood side by side, looking down the strand, talking quietly, Eyolf stroking his beard. *Like a couple of farmers,* Gil thought suddenly, *surveying their fields. A good day's work.*

How could they be so calm? Warily, he raised his eyes to the ship behind them. Surprised and relieved, he saw little damage. Scorch marks where a fire had been lit below the bow; the dragon figurehead splintered and blackened with smoke. And nothing else. Surely, they would have targeted the earl's ship first?

Then, with sinking heart, he understood. The real damage lay all around; his chieftains' ships, hacked and torched on the violated safety of his shore. *They left it on purpose,* Gil thought. *To make it worse.*

Floki slapped Eyolf's shoulder and spoke a few more words and left the shipbuilder with a cheerful smile. Gil had never admired him more, nor felt more willing to do anything he asked. He stood waiting as the earl approached.

Halfway to where Gil rested against *Sea-Raven's* lowered mast, Floki stopped beside Ulf and Grimhildr, struggling together to salvage her slashed and charred sail, bound yet to its half-burnt spar.

Both yet in their stained and sodden wedding finery—Grimhildr with her beautiful, embroidered skirt tucked up into her belt—they had worked uncomplainingly through their wedding night, as had every able man and woman in the longhouse.

Without his loyal people, the earl's humiliation might have been insurmountable. With no ships, they were as helpless as snared rabbits, awaiting the inevitable conclusion of the fire-raising: an army on their shores.

But Gil could see, even now, that every hull was secure, the harm to decks and upper strakes repairable. Old sails could serve while the damaged were also repaired. If it had to be, they could be at sea again in a day. *Ragi saved us,* he thought painfully.

He glanced unwillingly to the turf-roofed church, where his friend's body lay growing cold, its own fires forever doused.

Suddenly exhausted, Gil slumped against the mast and closed his eyes. The axe handle yet clutched in his hands, he felt himself drifting into sleep.

"Helmsman!"

He jerked awake, forgetting for a moment where he was. The reek of smoke and the ringing of axes brought him instantly back. Floki beckoned him from where he stood with Ulf and Grimhildr on the ember-strewn sand.

Gil shouldered the axe and stumbled down the gangplank to the earl's side. Floki nodded a welcome and then turned the bridegroom inland. "Ulf, my friend, you have work yet to do this night."

"What night?" Ulf grumbled, a cheerful light in his eyes.

"It is work a man can do, as well, in the day. Grimhildr will show you. She is very knowledgeable."

Grimhildr loosened her skirt hem from her belt with one hand, and with the other, gave the earl a sharp slap across his jaw. "As if you would know." Sliding her arm through Ulf's like a proper matron, she strode vigorously up the strand beside her husband.

"Ah, Warrior," Floki laughed. "To be young!"

"But they aren't young," Gil blurted.

"This morn," Floki smiled after them, "they are." He looked down at Gil. "You are weary, Helmsman?"

"A little." Gil struggled to grin. Floki took the axe and slung it over his own shoulder. He studied Gil quietly.

"I must meet with my chieftains, now," he said. "I would have you beside me." He paused and Gil sensed a new uncertainty.

Please, he begged in his heart. *Don't ask me. Tell me.*

"If you will," Floki said.

"Gladly," Gil answered at once.

Floki laughed and put his free arm around Gil's shoulders as they walked to the longhouse. "You will be less glad when you see their faces."

The haze of smoke drifting over the island reminded Gil bitterly of their triumph over the Golden Knight on the Deer

Isle. "I guess this is his revenge," he said.

"Our friend?" Floki laughed grimly. "Only the beginning." Gil cast him a quick, desperate glance, and then looked away. "You are not alone," Floki reminded him. "You have companions."

"One less tonight," Gil said painfully.

"All men lose friends, Warrior. This is the world. But others live. The young Saracen; a fine fighter. The monk of Hy. Fish-Tail, though he is not to be trusted. Erling; trust him above all." He paused. "Hakon will stand by you."

"Against your father?"

Floki slowed and stood still on the smoke-shrouded strand. "Yes. But do not ask that of him. Find another way. And you make new friends," he said. "These," he swept his arm out, encompassing the assaulted ships, "Win you allies. It is their captains' battle, now, too."

Gil looked from the ships to the earl. "You think so?" he said warily.

"I know so, Warrior." Floki raised both arms and shrugged. "Yes. Yes. They blame me and are angry with me. I know this, too. But it is not Floki Magnusson who fires their ships. They are Northmen, Warrior. These are their dearest possessions. Better for him if he ravished their wives."

"Are you serious?" Gil gasped.

Floki slapped his head. "I am never serious, Warrior. Do you not know me yet?" He returned his companionable arm to Gil's shoulders. "Respect Hakon. Do not push him too far, and he will hold Hrolf's Isle for you. You have other work. Ragnvald gives you a ship. Thirty warriors, Shetlanders. Grim as a grey day at dawn, but good seamen, good fighters."

Gil shook his head hopelessly. "Why would he do that for me?"

"Because I ask him and he keeps his word. For *Silver Dragon*, you raise your own crew."

"By myself?" Gil cried.

Floki gave him a grim look. "If you cannot find thirty willing men on all Hrolf's Isle, you are not worth the time I spend on you."

"Okay," Gil muttered.

"*Good.*" Floki said. "You learn. Now, with them, you sail to Francia. Palamedes is a gracious man. He wearies, no doubt, of the forest. And Lance'lot, also."

"My father," Gil whispered.

"And your lady's father, the Earl de Troye; he too would lie in his own bed in Caledon. All men seek their homes. And what of your friends of the tournament field?"

"The Men of the Forest!" Gil said. "Morians would join me. And ...."

"Yes!" Floki applauded. "You see? It will be easy!"

"What? With, like, two ships and maybe a hundred men and ...."

Floki grimaced. "Don't be Hakon, Warrior. One Hakon is enough."

He paused again, then, where the path divided; the main track leading up to the longhouse, and the lesser one bearing left along the shore, to the church.

It was the moment Gil had dreaded, but he followed the earl past the girls' Nunnery, and Aidan's cell, with its stone cross and the bell hanging from its wooden trestle, to the church door. Ducking after him beneath the stone lintel, he stepped warily within.

Grey light crept through the narrow windows, barely penetrating the darkness. The single flame of the sanctuary lamp drew his gaze to the altar, and as his eyes adjusted to the dimness, two more lights emerged: twin candles set on the floor. Between them, wrapped in white linen and stiller than in any sleep, lay his friend who had played King's Table on the ward hill and bragged of his High Island farm.

The Noble Cat emerged from the darkness and brushed gently against Gil's leg. Feannag rustled feathers on the window ledge. Below, Aidan sat on a low bench, his psalter held up to the candlelight. Rachel curled like a little girl beside him, her head on his knees. At his other side, Danni and Janetta huddled in each other's arms. Steeling himself, Gil stepped forward and knelt by the shrouded body.

Face washed clean of blood and grime, hair and half-grown

beard combed, Ragi looked too boyish now to be the swaggering warrior who had danced at the wedding in the earl's fine clothes. Danced, and drank ale, and laughed. And argued .... Half-closing his eyes, Gil let his fingers fall on skin cold as stone, and whispered goodbye.

Janetta looked up and her tear-stained face brightened and he wanted more than life itself to run into her arms. But he stood, instead, and turned back to the earl.

Floki knelt, also, then, and touched Ragi's forehead, brushing back his hair with a gentle hand. "Ah, Man of the High Island," he said, "A long road you travel for love." He crossed himself and rose to his feet. "But what better cause?" he smiled sadly, "What better cause?" Nodding to Aidan, he turned Gil toward the door.

Outside, in the harsh, grey light, the earl's face was calm and peaceful. Gil thought suddenly of how often he had done this; here, where death came so readily from battle, or drowning, accident or illness. And for this, too, he knew, there were rules.

As soon as a ship could be made ready, Ragi would return to his own people. Warriors would accompany him. Silver; an amount ruled appropriate by the chieftains; would be paid to his kin. The earl's poet would record his achievements in verse. And Ragi of the High Island would join his fathers, a wraith and a memory in tales around the hearth. And Gil hated it all.

"I don't want Ragi to be a story!" he cried aloud.

Floki turned and gave him a wry, puzzled smile. "Warrior?"

"I want him to be Ragi, still. Just a real person." He looked away and muttered, "Alive."

"All men die, Warrior." Floki casually blocked the treasonous punch Gil threw at him, caught Gil's nape in his lion's paw grip, and gave him a rough shake. "All men do die."

He lifted the axe he had rested against the church wall, slung it again over his shoulder, and started back to the longhouse track. But as they reached it, he turned suddenly, his eyes on two riders approaching from the hill. "Wait, Warrior. We will learn their news."

Shading his eyes, Gil studied the riders, too. Four pairs of men had been sent out to find the household guards, missing since the firing of the ships. Two had returned in the night;

their search fruitless. This pair, also, rode unaccompanied. As they drew closer, he recognized Ismail, slim and graceful on his brown pony, Chocolate, and Arnkel Fish-Tail, riding—as he did everything—belligerently, big shoulders hunched, as if in argument with the horse.

Floki waited until the tired animals slowed to a walk. "Do you find them?" he called.

Both Ismail and Arnkel shook their heads as they dismounted. Ismail, who could track a mouse through a barley field, said clearly, "No sign. No horses pass that way. No men."

Arnkel shrugged. "I say they are never on the hill," he announced, "But killed on the strand and thrown in the sea. The tide will bring them back."

"Or they will swim," Floki said drily.

"Dead men ...?" Arnkel blinked, baffled.

Floki laughed. "Yes. Unlikely." He nodded toward the hall. "Tend your beasts, Fish-Tail, and take your rest. I thank you." He turned to Ismail. "Young Saracen," he said gently, "your lady keeps vigil with Ragi in the church. Go comfort her. And ask the good father to join me in the hall."

Ismail looked down at his hands. "I cannot," he said.

"What say you?"

Gil jerked his chin toward the church, and mouthed, "Go."

"I cannot," Ismail repeated. "He dies because she chooses me," he said simply. "How can I go to her now?"

The earl was quiet. He looked back to the longhouse. "I do not see her drive him out into the night. Nor do I see you do that. Men make their own fates, Saracen." He smiled slightly and his voice softened. "Now do my will."

Gil held his breath, but Ismail ducked his head, turned, and trotted obediently to the church. Floki watched. "He is too honorable to be a Northman, Warrior. We send him to Palamedes." He smiled and then pointed down the strand. Two more riders were descending the steep path from the headland. "Perhaps Svein and Erling have better fortune."

But Svein and Erling were also shaking their heads as their weary mounts plodded to a halt before the longhouse. "Not on the hill," Svein said.

"Nor on the strand," Erling agreed. "But," he added, "A ship has been in beyond the headland. The keel drag is fresh yet. Perhaps they take the bodies away."

Floki raised an eyebrow. "What, Erling?" he said. "Carrying them over the headland? Those two frail striplings I choose as guards? And for what purpose? A noble burial? I had not imagined our visitors so thoughtful."

Gil heard the words dully, as from a distance. *A keel drag. A ship has been in beyond the headland. A ship ....*

"Then where are they?" Svein said querulously.

"Far from here," Floki said. "Taking their ease."

"Ah," Erling sighed wearily "I see."

"I pay them well, Maiden-Face, but not, it seems, well enough." Floki shrugged and held out both arms fondly. "I thank you both for your efforts. There is food in the hall. Break your fast and take your rest."

"The guards!" Gil cried, suddenly understanding. "The guards betrayed us!"

"*Yes?*" Floki seemed less angry than exasperated, and that, more with Gil's incomprehension than with the thing he was trying to comprehend.

"The *guards* killed Ragi?"

"Did he, himself, not say so?" Floki smiled wearily and shrugged. "As the High One says: 'When passing a door post, watch.'" He set the axe down outside his unguarded hall and laid a hand on Gil's shoulder. "Helmsman, it has been a long night."

Very carefully, Gil said then, "Floki, there's something I didn't tell you."

"What? That you are an idiot? It is well, Helmsman. I know this."

Gil shook his head, too weary for teasing. "I saw their ship. From the ward hill. I saw a sail by the headland. Everyone was watching the hand-fasting. I turned and saw it."

"And?"

"I didn't tell you!" Gil cried, anguished. "The wedding ... Janetta ... I forgot."

Floki nodded solemnly. After a long silence, he said,

"Warrior, we should not allow you near women. In the morning, I pledge you, a holy monk, to Aidan. But that is a small matter." He paused. "Think, now, Helmsman. Think carefully. If you *do* tell me, what do I do?" Gil shrugged. "I cannot launch ships for every sail that passes. So, I do this: *I warn the guards.*" He punched Gil's shoulder cheerfully, his eyes sparkling with amusement. "Come, Helmsman. We have work to do. And there will be little to laugh at in here."

Floki pulled open the heavy doors and the early sun slanted through them, casting bars of brightness through air yet thick with smoke. Last night's fires, revived by weary kitchen maids, heated cauldrons of broth and girdles of sweet-smelling barley bread.

At either side, men and women sprawled asleep on the broad benches, still in their grimy wedding finery. Weapons and tools lay abandoned amid shawls and ribbons and head cloths, all discarded in the haste to save the ships.

Jorunn and Hrodny hurried forward with bowls of broth, but Floki gently turned them aside, his eyes on the far end of the hall. Barely visible in the murk, the chieftains waited, seated at the High Table in a long grim row, as if they had not moved since last night.

But their soot-grimed, sea-sodden clothing told another story. And at the first sight of their faces, Gil instantly doubted the earl's blithe confidence in their forgiveness. It was clear enough to him who they blamed for the burning, regardless of who had laid the fires. And the looks they cast his own way were no kinder. If these were to be his allies, his enemies were only half his troubles.

Red Kol, and his son, Ragnar, seated at the far left, side by side, greeted them with identical expressions of dismay. Kol, his once auburn hair now snowy white, was, after Ragnvald, the oldest man at the table. But he so matched his red-headed son in youthful vigor that they were taken, by strangers, for brothers. Big, genial men, they farmed Hrolf's Isle's north coast and were frequent visitors to Floki's hall. Today, they were less than genial.

Beside them, Hrafn Bare-Chin stroked his wispy beard and

sighed. His lands, like those of Egil Thorsson, called Split-Helm, lay across the strait on the Horse Isle. Both men looked like they wanted nothing but to be back aboard their ships, sailing home. *Who could blame them?* Gil thought. He remembered how willingly they had followed Floki to Norway and knew they deserved better than what had befallen them last night.

Gauk Njalsson, whose own island lay beyond the Spear Isle, looked up at the earl's approach, stony-faced. Ragnvald, even older and more tired this morning, shook his head by way of greeting, his conflicting loyalties written on his features. His own son, Hakon, seemed stunned, as if unable to imagine his audacious cousin experiencing such defeat.

Only Magnus Redbeard, perched by himself on an upturned ale cask, looked cheerful. "Ah," he said, "Here is the man who so treasures his guests that he fires their ships to keep them close!"

Ragnvald looked up at the roof-beams. "Enough, brother," he murmured, "Enough."

But Floki only laughed. "And there," he waved his hand to his father, "Is the man who drinks the cask dry, only to have a seat!" Gil struggled not to laugh. But no one else even smiled.

Floki took his place, then, on the High Seat, beckoned Gil to his side, and called to the serving girls, "Come now. We will break our fast."

The chieftains all shook weary heads and waved the girls away. Hrafn Bare-Chin said quietly, "We want no more of your hospitality, Floki Magnusson. I would only that I were across the strait on my own shore. And, indeed, I would be there already, had I a ship worthy of the sea."

"And you shall have," Floki said gently, "Soon. Listen." He smiled slightly as they reluctantly bent ears toward the longhouse walls. Beyond, hammer blows sounded above the perpetual sighing of wind and sea. "My shipwrights and carpenters, the best in the North, are already at work." He paused. "Eyolf Grimsson surveys the damage and it pleases me to tell you, it is far less than first thought."

"That is small comfort," Gauk Njalsson growled, but he shrugged slightly as he spoke.

"Come, now," Floki smiled again, and as if coaxing small children said, "Eat. Hungry men make poor judgements."

To Gil's surprise, one and then another acquiesced. Bowls of broth were served and huge mounds of warm bannocks laid before each man. Gil clutched his own bowl and drank the warm liquid gratefully, and, as gratefully, accepted a second. Bannocks and cheese followed and the more he ate, the hungrier he felt. Around him, the chieftains sipped morosely, and then more eagerly, and their conversation lifted from its monotone of exhaustion, to ordinary, if subdued, speech.

The longhouse doors creaked open and discussion ceased, mid-sentence, as hands reached for swords. But it was only Aidan, obedient to the earl's summons. He drew the doors closed again behind him and made his way quietly between the benches of sleeping men and women, to take his place at Floki's side. Relaxing, the chieftains greeted him with restrained courtesy and returned to their breakfast.

Ragnvald brushed crumbs from his iron-grey beard and said solemnly, "Fosterling, it is bad enough that your own guards betray us and slaughter one of your warriors. But surely you understand," he raised both bushy eyebrows, "the knife was meant for you! Dressed in your garments, the boy is your double! They take their chance."

"I know this, Ragnvald," Floki said calmly. "And when he escapes, they panic and flee."

"His ending, and our good fortune," Gauk Njalsson said.

"I know this, too."

Ragnvald stared at his foster son, his eyes filled with a mix of puzzlement and outrage. "Your *own guards*, Floki! The men chosen to protect ... does this not trouble you?"

"That the boy dies in my stead troubles me, Ragnvald. As it would trouble any man."

A low chuckle came from the end of the table. Magnus Redbeard rocked back on his ale cask seat. "Do not be so sure," he said. "I have known chieftains who kept two and even three doubles, to draw aside unseemly blows. A wise practice," he nodded knowingly to his son. "Each died in old age on linen sheets."

Ragnvald raised his hand in protest. Red Kol and Ragnar shook their heads. But Floki only sat quietly, looking across his hall in the dim light. Then he said, slowly and regretfully, "No, Father. This is too far. This must end." There was a nodding of agreement, a muttering of support, but in the instant of the chieftains' reaction, Floki was on his feet, and none of them moved fast enough to stop him.

One savage kick took the ale cask from under Magnus, and he sprawled on his back on the floor. Gil saw the cold battle light in Floki's eyes and knew Magnus Redbeard was a dead man, even as Floki reached for his sword.

"No!" Ragnvald shouted, and the sleepers on the benches started and stirred as the chieftains rose as one to restrain their earl. But it was Aidan who, faster than any fighting man, caught him and with arms around his waist pinned the deadly sword arm to his side.

"Mortal sin, my friend," he murmured softly, tightening his powerful grip. "Mortal sin." Gil stared in open-mouthed relief as the earl straightened from his fighting stance and slowly lowered his hand from his sword hilt. Aidan stayed yet, holding him firm and as the anger faded from Floki's eyes, Gil remembered the night the gentle, scholarly priest had flung his own drunken young self bodily onto a pony's back.

Floki suddenly smiled. "It is well, Good Father. I harm no one." He turned and his smile broadened, lighting his tired features. He slapped Aidan's shoulder. "And when the old gods return and the wolf, Fenrir wreaks his wrath, I would have this warrior at my side!"

He turned then to face his father, lying stunned on the floor. Fear yet haunting his eyes, Magnus got slowly to his feet, and still unsteady from the night's drinking, staggered a few steps from the table. "Redbeard!" Ragnvald called imploringly. "Stay with us, I beg you." Magnus hunched his shoulders, shaking his big head grimly.

But then Floki said, "I beg you, also." And, freed by Aidan, he walked slowly to his father and knelt on the floor before him. Magnus again shook his head. But then he suddenly reached out and touched Floki's yellow hair, as if he was yet the child he had once been.

"On your feet," he said gruffly, and turned back to the waiting council.

Floki obediently stood, but instead of returning to the table, beckoned them to the door in the back wall of the longhouse, which led to his bedchamber. Nodding toward the weary sleepers on the benches, he said, "I think we disturb their rest enough. And," he added as the chieftains crowded into the room behind him, "perhaps not all we would say should be shared by so many."

The earl's one private space in all of Hrolf's Isle always surprised Gil in its simplicity. A narrow bed and a kist for clothing on one side of the hearth, and on the other, a second, smaller bed and a desk with hanging oil lamp. It was scarcely larger than Aidan's cell and with the earl's psalter resting open on the desk, could be mistaken for that of another monk, but for the battle-axe and shield hanging on the wall above.

A mound of furs on the smaller bed erupted suddenly in a tousled brown head as Percy sat up, blinking sleep-blurred eyes. Two small, woolly black heads rose beside him and he reached quickly for his pets.

"Floki Magnusson," Red Kol groaned behind Gil, "Are we to meet now in a byre?"

"And why should we not?" Floki crouched quietly beside the boy's bed. "A byre is an honorable place. The good father will tell you."

"I have enough of your jests," Kol groaned, wrinkling his nose.

Floki shrugged, lifting one and then the other baby goat from the bed and setting their small black hooves gently on the floor. "No jest. A byre *is* an honorable place. And, I think they smell no worse than you." He gently shook Percy awake. "Cupbearer, it is morning. Go now to Jorunn for breakfast and come then back to me."

Percy looked from Floki to the circle of bemused chieftains. "Is Ragi dead?"

"Ragi is dead."

"Is someone else dead?"

"No one else is dead."

Percy nodded in his solemn, wise way, got up and padded from the room. Floki caught the goat kids before they could follow. "Your breakfast is on the roof." He opened the latched shutters of the small window in the outer wall, dropped them out, and shuttered the window again.

Gil remembered when the opening was just a straw-filled gap in a turf wall. But its purpose was unchanged: a secret exit for the boy and his protector in an attack. And now, he thought, suddenly chilled, those who would claim Percy and his fabled treasure had been within a hundred feet of this room.

He took his place on the floor and sat cross-legged while Floki put fresh peats on the fire. Aidan knelt, youthfully supple, beside him. Around them, the chieftains hunched on beds under the slope of the roof, as if besieged there, as they were, in truth, beyond the walls.

Ragnvald stroked his long grey beard with gloomy impatience. "Fosterling," he growled, "When you are done with kitchen maids' work, I would speak with you." Floki's lips quirked in a smile, but he continued stoking the fire.

"Speak, Foster-Father. Even kitchen maids can hear."

"You have failed us," Ragnvald said.

"I have." Floki laid a last peat on the fire and looked up. "I fail you thrice over. You come for celebration and meet strife. You come assured of safety and meet destruction." His words were echoed by wounded mutterings of agreement. "I fail you as a friend and I fail you as a chieftain. And you, Ragnvald, I fail as a son."

Another round of muttering circled the room. Floki waited for it to subside and then said, "Have others more to say? Is there some other grief I have caused?" They looked from one to another uneasily, until Gauk Njalsson shrugged and with a glance at his compatriots, said, "I think that is enough."

Floki smiled slightly. "I would say more than enough." Gil watched him, puzzled by his calm. The earl stood suddenly and raised his arms to the hanging battle-axe and lifted it from the wall. It was a formidable weapon and looked at home in his powerful hands. He passed it to Gauk. "Feel the weight of it."

Gauk took it, bracing his arms to hold it steady.

"Forged in Norway," Floki said. "It is not mine. I borrow it from a man in Eire who had no more use of it, being dead."

Magnus chuckled at the back of the room.

Floki continued, "I do not use it often. Too heavy. Fine in open ground, but a burden to carry. Like all weapons, it has its place. And its time. But this," he took the axe from Gauk and returned it to the wall, "Is neither."

He turned, eyes suddenly alight. "We are attacked in the night by a handful of Vikings. Who, but for a small treachery, never reach our strand. I will deal with them. Myself, my helmsman," he nodded to Gil, "Perhaps one other. At most." He shrugged, and then swept them all with his cold grey gaze. "This is not warfare, but raiding. And you, my friends, who have done both, should know the difference." He smiled again.

Gauk ducked his head sheepishly, but Egil Split-Helm said, "When I was a boy out a'viking, I would be proud indeed to strand five chieftains and their earl with them."

The mutterings rose again. Floki held up three fingers of one hand and said, "Three days my friends—two, if Eyolf is, as often, over cautious - and you are at sea. Until then, I give you my house and my table. My barns are full. There are beasts in plenty on my fields. Wine from Rome and the best ale-wives' ale. You will rest, and eat, and drink at your pleasure. My harpers will play for you, my poet, sing for you. And you will sail in the end with gifts worthy of your fine names.

"I ask only this: that the blame for what happens here falls on no man, but me. Not my bold cousin," he nodded towards Hakon. "Not my helmsman. Not my brave father. These men are without fault."

He turned to his foster-father. "Ragnvald, you are eldest and furthest from home; for you I leave this room and sleep on the benches, without."

"Where I always sleep," Magnus said sourly.

Floki cast his father a weary glance. "That I build a fine house above the hall for my mother and yourself, is my pleasure and my duty. That you take snoring drunks instead for bed mates, is your choice." He let his gaze drift across each of the chieftain's faces. "Is the matter settled now?" he said.

For a moment, Gil thought it was. But then Hrafn Bare-Chin rose to his feet. Stroking his frail beard, he spoke in slow, thoughtful tones. "When a squall comes across the strait, it blows hail and rain over the fields, but as quickly it is gone and the sun returns. A small thing. But it only reaches our strand because powerful winds blow it from the sea.

"When *those* winds come, crops are flattened, ships founder. It is the wind that blows these Vikings our way that I fear, Floki Magnusson. And for that, we have none to blame, indeed, but you."

A sudden murmur of affirmation and complaint arose as the chieftains fell upon his words like dogs on a bone. In the midst, the door latch clicked and all heads turned in alarm. Percy froze in the doorway, still clutching a half-eaten bannock.

"Be at peace," Floki said wryly. "My cupbearer slays few." He smiled and held out his arms, and Percy ran fearfully into them. Then, remembering his responsibilities, he found his wooden cup amid the rumpled furs of his bed and solemnly hung it, as a badge of office, around his neck.

"Indeed," Ragnvald said softly. "He slays few. But many are slain in his cause." Eyes dark with regret, he said, "Our troubles begin the day this child comes to your father's house."

"He comes to the priest," Magnus interrupted, and with an angry glance at Aidan, said, "I say our troubles begin the day *he* comes." He laughed roughly, but the anger glinted yet in his eyes.

Floki shrugged and smiled. "A priest and a simple boy. Ah, much to fear there, no doubt."

"Do not laugh at us, Floki Magnusson," Egil Split-Helm leaned forward, beard bristling. "The boy has powerful enemies. You draw them upon us all by sheltering him."

Floki met his eyes, a cold challenge in his own. "Would you have me cast out a stranger?"

Ragnvald raised pacifying hands. "No, Foster-Son," he said wearily. "We would not. None can fault your hospitality and that is as it should be. But it is not just the boy ...."

"What then? Would you have me abandon his sister, who

comes to us a girl of tender years? Or my helmsman, who guides my ship to Rome? Or perhaps the Saracen who fights nobly at my side? With which of these shall I break trust?"

Ragnvald shook his head. "You do not make this easy, Fosterling." He looked up at Gil and when he spoke next, a black fear gripped Gil's heart. "You bring from Camelot a girl already pledged."

"Yes. Pledged to my helmsman."

"Now," Ragnvald said. He raised his hands again, this time in frustration. "Oh, Floki, be reasonable. Stolen brides have peopled these islands. But not brides pledged to kings."

"I have taken her into my household, Ragnvald. Speak no more about her."

Red Kol jumped to his feet. "And you speak no more of your household, Floki Magnusson. It is ourselves who will care for them in years to come. While you pursue this madness in Norway. They are not yours, but ours!"

Floki stood in silence, facing the older man. "Take your seat, Kol," he said gently. "You are weary." His hand drifted almost casually to his sword hilt. Kol angrily tossed back his thick white hair but sat again on the bed.

Floki smiled approvingly and said, "That I leave you for a while is true. But I leave you well led, and well-guarded, by my heir."

All eyes turned to Hakon, sitting quietly on the edge of the clothes kist. But Magnus balled a hand into a fist and shook it at his son. "Your heir is my fosterling. He does not answer to you, but to his father and to me."

"Hakon Sea-Friend is not my heir," Floki said. He stepped lightly behind Gil and suddenly rested his hand on Gil's head. "My heir is here."

Gil jerked back with a jolt, as if the earl had actually struck him. Cries of disbelief filled the room and again all eyes turned to Hakon. But the dark man's face was impassive. And where other men might look angry, he looked simply relieved.

"That boy!" Magnus thundered.

"He is sixteen," Floki said, adding, "I raid Eire at sixteen. Not that you notice."

"But Fosterling," Ragnvald's always reasonable voice shook with protest. "He is not you. He is but a stranger from a strange land, who struggles even to speak our tongue."

"His sword hand will translate when necessary." Floki laughed. His own hand rested yet on Gil's head. "And it is well he is not me, since it is I who failed you."

He stepped back then to his place near the window and his laughter stilled. "He has sailed further than any man among you; rescued hostages, brought back plunder, and learned more of the ways of the world than you, for all your years, will know.

"Which of you has seen the towers of Camelot? Which of you has sailed the Roman Sea? Who has done battle in the streets of Rome? You, Red Kol; have you seen a horse with toes?" He nodded to Gil. "He has. And you, Gauk, have you hidden amid the bones of saints? He has. Egil, could you ride with Frankish knights in tournament? Hrafn, have you climbed the citadel of Mont Tombe?"

He paused and they all studied Gil with wary new assessment. "Yes, he is young," Floki said. "But his knowledge outstrips his years. And Hakon Sea-Friend, who was born on the day I was born, will hold this house, while he sails out to war." The chieftains nodded thoughtfully. Floki said, "And always, there will be my father, whose head, Red Kol, though not as white as yours, is not empty." Magnus grunted querulous agreement. Kol stroked his beard.

But Hrafn sat up straight, laid his hands stubbornly flat on his knees and said, "But there would *be* no war, were it not for these strangers and their cause." And like flotsam floating on the sea, the chieftains turned with the tide.

"A king's jealous ire may be bought off," Ragnvald said. "Brides are easy for kings to find. But," he shrugged uneasily, "there are stories. Since you first return from Caledon, and we hear them still. Stories of treasure."

Excited murmuring passed around the room. "They say it is worth more than all the silver in the North!" Kol's son Ragnar declared.

"They say," Gauk Njalsson leaned forward and whispered, "the boy, your cup-bearer, is himself a great king's son, sent away to the priest because of his infirmity. The treasure is his inheritance."

Egil Split-Helm joined in, "Some say, the son, indeed, of the Golden Knight who now rules Camelot. Spirited away by the brothers of Hy!"

"Some even say," Red Kol's voice grew strangely solemn, "the treasure is Arthur's and the boy, Arthur's son. And you keep both in waiting for his return."

"No doubt you will be first in his household," Hrafn protested, "but what of us?" He looked around his fellows as if gathering strength and then said, "We ask only this: keep the boy. Keep your helmsman's stolen bride. But only return this treasure. What use is it to you in your slavery? What use to us, if it brings murder and burnings and drains away the strength of our households with endless fighting?"

Floki smiled. "Tell me the name of one man who has seen this fabled treasure. One!"

Red Kol shifted his feet and glanced uneasily at Gil. "They say," he began, "Your helmsman tricked you, and stole this thing. And yet won your forgiveness."

Floki nodded. "I am a forgiving man."

"I say," Kol's voice hardened, "your forgiveness comes lightly. This is a story. The treasure is here, and always was."

Floki sighed. He wrapped his arms around himself, leaned wearily against the wall and said at last, "How can I argue with one so shrewd?" He gave them a small, defeated smile, and turned to Percy, who sat cross-legged, beside Gil. "Cupbearer?" he pointed to the wooden vessel, hanging on its braided cord, around the boy's neck.

Percy got up and slipped the cord carefully over his shaggy brown head, and with innocent trust, handed his cup to the earl. Floki studied it solemnly, and then held it out to Red Kol. "Here, then," he said. "The treasure you seek."

Kol's jaw dropped. Floki stepped closer, holding out the cup, and he shook his head, thrusting it away with both hands. Floki shrugged. "Hrafn?" he held it out again and Hrafn, too, brushed it aside. Ragnvald groaned.

"Fosterling," he whispered, "We come to your house in

peace. A man dies in front of us. We suffer grievous harm. We work throughout the night. And now, we are so weary that eyes close even as we speak. Will you mock us even now?"

"I mock no one, Foster-Father. I offer a treasure." And he repeated the offer to each of his outraged chieftains, who each re-coiled in baffled fury.

Then, leaning against the wall and still holding the cup, he said quietly, "I have offered you what you request. You have refused. Therefore, I judge, you accept my terms as they stood. The strangers stay. My helmsman inherits the earldom. The service you owe to me, you owe to him, Saint Martin's Eve. That is agreed?"

They stared at him, and each other, in a confusion so complete that no one spoke. "It is agreed," Floki said for them. "And now," he set the wooden cup on his desk and stretched tiredly. "I ask for a few moments peace, while I set things in order for my Foster-Father, in this room."

Aidan rose, and with his own, quiet authority, shepherded the chieftains from the bedchamber. Gil got up to follow, but the earl's hand on his shoulder held him back. When the door latch clicked closed behind them all, Floki fell back on his bed, dragging the fur over his face to smother the laughter that shook his lean frame.

After a long while, he sat up, shaking his head, still, and smiling at Percy and Gil. "Cupbearer," he said. "There is water, there, in the jug. I would drink." He directed the boy to an earthenware vessel on the floor. Percy lifted it, carried it laboriously to the desk, and set it beside his cup. He looked up enquiringly at Floki, who nodded encouragement.

But when he took up the cup, he made no attempt to fill it, but instead fumbled determinedly at the silver band enclosing the staves. "There," Floki said gently, "that is right. By the jaws of the wolf." Percy pressed firmly on the fine-drawn teeth, and Gil saw something move. The boy looked up again to Floki for help and the earl reached his arms around him, and with his own fingers, drew out a tiny silver pin. The band fell free, exposing a jigsaw of wooden pieces, below.

"This one?" Percy's eyes went again to Floki, who nodded.

Percy pressed a wooden square and it, too, moved.

"Very good."

Gil stared, fascinated, as, eyes half shut with concentration, the boy lifted a polished oblong free. "It's a puzzle!" he cried, forgetting entirely the purpose of the vessel, in seeing it dismantled. A third piece slid. A forth turned as if on a pivot. A fifth lifted free. And then suddenly a crack appeared.

Percy's face lit up with happy excitement, and Gil became aware of a silvery light filling the room. He whirled, but saw nothing. He looked back, and was aware of it again: there, in the dark corner. There, touching the earl's fine cloak. And yet, when he raised his eyes to focus on it, there was no light at all, or rather, a light that existed just to the edge of what eyes could see.

He looked back to the cup. It lay in pieces on the earl's reading desk, with the psalter and the earthenware jug. Percy was sitting again on his bed, his hands reverently holding nothingness.

"Cupbearer?" Floki beckoned and the boy got up, set the thing that was not there carefully down, lifted the jug, and poured. Head swirling, Gil watched the water gush from the clay vessel and stop mid-air, filling emptiness with the shape of a simple goblet.

The last drops splashed. Percy lowered the jug, and with both hands offered the water-cup to the earl. Floki closed his long, calloused fingers around the impossible thing, lifted it, and drank. Gil grabbed the edge of the desk.

The earl lowered the diminished water-shape and offered it to Percy, who sipped from it proudly and with a beaming smile, offered it then to Gil. "Drink, Helmsman," Floki said. "It is only water."

Slowly, Gil reached out a shaking hand until it touched what he could not see. And then terror engulfed him, as in the Chapel of Pentecost when the unicorn showed him the core of the earth, and blackness swept in, like the sea over a drowning man.

CHAPTER FIVE

G il rested his hands on the lowered mast of the skiff and looked across it to the earl. "What if they had *agreed*?" he said suddenly. "What would you have done?"

Floki continued unfurling the sail from the yard. Without looking up, he said, "I give it to them." He raised his gaze then to Gil's shocked face and laughed. "It does not happen, Warrior. I know men. They weigh every man's treasure in the scales of their own hearts. You say so yourself when you take the reliquary in Caledon. Men follow what they see. Here, they see only a boy's wooden toy."

Gil nodded. He looked out to the white-flecked waters of the strait, and the Holy Isle, a black silhouette in the grey dawn. "I thought," he said awkwardly, "It was out there." He hunched a shoulder toward the roust roaring with the incoming tide. "With your brethren."

Floki stood lightly on a rowing bench, and together they lifted the mast into the keelson. "It was," he said. "But a day comes and you have need of it. I think I do not send you to them. They are strange. And besides, you do not swim that well."

Gil grimaced, his mind flitting unwillingly to the depths of the tide-race. He turned from it to the curving white strand. The shore was empty now of ships, but for a scattering of fishing skiffs above the tideline, and the earl's *Silver Dragon*, in her noust. Little sign remained of the fires that had burned there three nights before. Eyolf's shipwrights had finished their work. Charred and broken timbers were cleared away and the tide had washed the sand clean. Gulls drifted peacefully above the longhouse where most of the household were yet asleep.

He looked down again at the skiff. Though he had loaded her himself with provisions and bedrolls, and a surprising amount of weaponry, he had no idea where they were going and knew better than to ask. He watched, startled, as Floki added an iron clad spear to the bows and quivers, battle shields and throwing axes, already aboard. Floki looked up suddenly, saw him, and laughed. "We pay a visit to old friends, Warrior," he said. "It is poor manners to arrive empty-handed."

"Old friends … the guards!" Gil said. "You know where they are!"

"I know where others are, and they may well be among them."

"They're with the Vikings at Cille Aidan!" Gil stopped short. "I mean, that would be a good place."

"Warrior, when we say too much, saying more is never wise." Floki raised an eyebrow and smiled. "I know you meet her on the hill. It is well for you I am not a jealous man." His smile remained, untroubled. Gil nodded. Not for the first time, he wished he knew when the earl was joking. "Still," Floki added mildly, "That is not how I know they are there."

He looked up. A man had appeared outside the distant longhouse, a bladed weapon glinting on his shoulder. Hoisting a heavy burden under his arm, he sauntered casually down the strand. "Good." Floki nodded and turned back to the skiff. "We take her out now. Our company is complete." He slipped the strap of a leather book satchel from his own shoulder and laid the satchel carefully on top of his battle shield. "Aidan would test my learning upon our return. So, you will sail, and I will study."

Gil squinted at the approaching figure. "Magnus," he said. "*Magnus* is coming with us?"

Floki slid a weathered log beneath the skiff's graceful stern and placed his hands on the low rail. "I say one other. Myself, my helmsman …."

"But *Magnus*? After …."

"My family disputes are not your affair, Helmsman."

"Okay," Gil muttered. He gripped the opposite rail and gave the hull so sharp a shove that he lost his footing in the sand.

Floki suppressed a grin as he scrambled erect. Together, they rolled the skiff over the log and as Gil placed a second beneath the stern, the earl said, "He is a fine warrior. You will be glad of that."

Gil said nothing. Magnus reached them as the skiff slid into the sea, timing his arrival neatly with the completion of the work. Wading into the water, he dumped a small ale cask aboard.

"You bring your own bench, Father," Floki smiled.

Gil looked with alarm from the cask to the double-bladed weapon over Magnus' shoulder. Magnus swung it down and added its hefty weight to the small armory in the boat. "I take this back to Ireland. It does not suit my son to be a thief." He grinned, prodding the leather book satchel. "Not now that he grows so holy."

Floki smiled again and jumped into the skiff. Reaching a hand to Magnus, he said, "A father, indeed, must guide the morals of a son."

Magnus growled something, ignored the courteous hand, and clambered heavily aboard. Gil shoved the craft into deep water with an inward groan. *Oh, great. Magnus, a cask of ale, and an Irish battle-axe. Happy sailing, everybody.*

But, as soon as they were underway, Magnus yawned lazily, stretched out on a fur on a bench, and propped his feet on the rail to resume his interrupted sleep. Even before they were through the wild waters of the roust, he was snoring; a compliment to Gil's seamanship. Or maybe just to last night's ale.

As the longhouse slipped behind them, and Gil set his course for the open sea, a new concern abruptly entered his mind. "If Magnus is with us, and Hakon is sailing to Shetland...."

"Ragnar Kolsson watches my household."

"*Ragnar?*"

"And six of his father's best warriors. They stay on when Kol sails. Perhaps you do not see from the Holy Isle."

"I was just taking her home!" Gil protested. "I didn't even set foot on the strand. Ask Bjorn!"

"So, I guess right." Floki smiled to himself, his eyes yet on his psalter.

Gil gave the steering oar a savage shove and yanked the sheet in hard. The skiff heeled abruptly. Magnus' snoring head lolled. Floki turned a page. "She sails better with a light hand."

With a sigh, Gil loosened the sheet. "Okay. Just tell me this. How did you persuade Ragnar to stay? The last I saw of him, he was madder even than his father."

"Ah, yes. But you do not pay attention. True, they are not pleased with me. And that first night they would gladly turn their back on my shore forever. But they cannot. And so, with much ill-humor they accept my hospitality." He paused and carefully closed the book resting on his knees.

"Red Kol is a widower," he said then. "He so loved his wife, that he wants no other. And Ragnar has had no wife at all. Men without women …." he shrugged. "Kol's hall is a dismal place. An old grandmother stirs the soup pot. The fire burns low. There is neither light, nor song, nor story. All is gloom. They work late, rise early. What else is there to do? They forget when it is bath night. Everything smells of oxen and sheep."

Gil grinned, but Floki continued, quite serious. "Beneath my roof they find a table always bountiful. My poet is rich in verse. The music of the harp enchants. Soon, they enjoy themselves, behind their frowns. And then, even the frowns are gone.

"Meanwhile, I speak with Ragnar. Many times, I praise his skill in battle. This is no lie; he, too, is a fine warrior. But he lives in the shadow of his father. So, when I ask if he would guard my hall, he is willing, and proud. Also," Floki added cheerfully, "I promise him a wife."

"You what?"

"I promise that the earl will provide a wife. As I provide a husband for Grimhildr, Warrior. By Lentron, next, if not sooner."

Gil sat up straight on the steering bench. "By Lentron—but you won't …."

"Not *myself*, Warrior," Floki said patiently, "The *earl* keeps this promise." He shook his head, "Oh, come now. This is not difficult. Ragnar is handsome. His farm, well-stocked. You provide a good dowry."

"But …."

Floki narrowed his eyes. "Are there no women in your

hall who would have husband and children? Surely you can persuade just *one*?"

Gil's mind flitted wildly from one pretty young face to another, each more outraged than the last. "Surely," he muttered.

"Good!" Floki gave him a sunny smile and returned to his book.

It was a peaceful sailing, the skies fair, the wind steady from the west. Even tacking across it, the skiff made fine speed. By Saxt, they were rounding the precipitous western headland of the Horse Isle. Gil nudged Floki from his studies to re-set the tacking spar, as he turned, and with the wind over his shoulder and the prow lifting above the chop, he sailed on, retracing the journey that first brought him to Hrolf's Isle, a year and more past.

Then, it had been Floki's henchmen, Wolfskin and Sheep, at the helm and himself a prisoner bound in a fishing net, his face in the bilge. He dropped his gaze from the sea ahead to the studious earl and his sleeping father, both calmly relying on his hand on the oar. He, too, had come a long journey.

Floki put his book away and took the helm, while Gil dozed in the sun. Then Magnus woke and he also took his turn. His mood had brightened and he and Floki talked amiably of the harvest and the livestock, like the farmers they were. The armory in the bow seemed oddly out of place.

The long day drew on pleasantly, with board games and storytelling, and meals of ale and dried fish, until, with the late summer dusk falling, Gil rounded a familiar headland and saw before him a low sand island shielding a narrow strand and the ruins of a longhouse he knew well. "Einar's Holm," he murmured.

But both the earl and his father had seen something more. "Head up," Floki said, and as Gil turned the craft into the wind and the sail fell slack, he too saw the wisp of blue smoke rising above the blackened shell of Magnus Redbeard's hall. Suddenly, the armory seemed very important indeed.

Still, there was no warship resting on the strand, only a fishing skiff, smaller than their own, with a net stretched to dry over upraised oars. The only other sign of life was a four-horned sheep in front of the ruined longhouse and two black goats cropping grass on the new turf roof of the byre. Around them drifted the smoke of a hearth-fire below.

"There's someone *living* here!" Gil cried.

Then a figure appeared from behind a broken wall, a woman, slender and ghost-like in the dusk, her skirts and white headdress fluttering in the wind as she strode down to the shore. "Derla," said Magnus, tugging uneasily at his thick beard. Floki nodded.

"Take us in, Helmsman." Ducking beneath the sail, he made his way forward and as Gil turned downwind, toward the strand, he lifted a coiled rope and stood waiting in the bow.

A few yards out, Gil loosened the oar and the little craft glided gently through the shallow surf. Floki threw the bow line to the woman who caught it and drew them in, so neatly that they could step out without wetting their feet.

Close up, Gil saw that despite the slim grace of her body, she was not young. Her skin was lined and weathered, and the hair beneath her linen headdress was grey. Her eyes were grey, too, and oddly familiar, as was the sudden white smile that lit up her features as she greeted the earl.

"Ah, fishing again." She took both his hands and leaned forward to kiss his cheek.

"It is that season," Floki replied. Then he switched suddenly into another language, the Pictish tongue he spoke with Shony, his mother.

The woman answered, a few terse sentences, and then, looking down into their boat said, again in Norse, "I see you bring good nets."

"And good hands to hold them," Floki said, and beckoned Gil forward. "My helmsman, Gil Lake of Tir nan Og."

The woman looked Gil up and down, reached out, and squeezed his upper arm. "Young," she said.

"But strong. And brighter than he looks," Floki offered helpfully. The woman laughed and again Gil felt something familiar about her. Floki stepped back, suppressing laughter himself. "My father greets you also," he said pointedly.

Magnus shuffled forward, and with head bowed, mumbled

a few Pictish words. "Redbeard, you grow more charming with each passing year," she said. Dismissing him, she turned again to the earl. "You may eat with me, but you will wash first," she said. "All of you."

Floki nodded like a small boy. "Yes, Derla."

"I bring water and towels." She strode off, the wind flicking her headdress jauntily, and disappeared within the re-roofed byre. Magnus watched her go.

"How long is she here?" he asked.

"Since she comes down from the shielings. She will be away again, come spring. You know her ways."

Magnus grunted and turned back to the skiff. Together they hauled the craft above high tide, securing her bowline to a solid driftwood log, and lowering her mast to its cradle. Before they had finished unloading the weapons and provisions, Derla returned with a water jug and an armful of linen towels.

She stood, arms folded, her back to them, while they stripped naked on the shore and washed. To Gil's happy surprise, the water was warm and there was even a bar of soap, carefully wrapped in sweet-smelling grass. "You may turn, Derla," Floki called when they were dry and dressed again. "Our modesty is preserved."

"Then you preserve something that never exists," Derla said, giving him her quick, white smile. She stepped closer to the heap of weapons, lifted the Irish battle-axe, and held it up, appraising it. Then gripping it in both hands, she swung it in a powerful arc, burying the blade in the driftwood log. "A fine piece," she said. With a nod of satisfaction, she walked away. Then, turning over her shoulder, she called, "Bring the sail, Redbeard. There are walls for you," she added, with an imperious wave toward the burnt-out longhouse, "But no roof."

Gil stared as Magnus humbly loosened the sail from its yard, bunched it in his powerful arms, and lumbered off to the ruins of his own great hall. "Doesn't he *mind*?" he whispered.

Floki laughed. "What? Derla? She speaks thus to all."

"But it's his own house."

Floki smiled quietly, slinging his shield over his back and collecting the bows and quivers, the spear, and his psalter. "He is afraid of her," he said. "All the Northmen are. She belongs to the old peoples of the islands, who held them before they came." He nudged Gil toward the three throwing axes. "Take those. Also," he continued, "They think she has powers."

Gil looked up, startled. "This is not so," Floki said mildly. He studied the byre, where Derla had again disappeared. "Words come to her, at times, unsought. As they come to me. This is not a power, but a weakness. It is a part of myself that I cannot control. The same, with Derla."

"It's a gift," said Gil

"Call it that, if you choose. Either way, it is not a thing to fear, though those who do not have it, may think it so." He shrugged.

"Are you sorry you have it?" Gil said warily.

"Am I sorry there is a sky or a sea? It *is*, Warrior. That is all." Shouldering his burden of weaponry, he started up the path to the longhouse. Gil followed, his own shield over his back, the axes in his arms.

They passed two weathered wooden stakes, which he suddenly recognized as the frame for the target on which he and his friends had practiced archery. At once, all of lost Einar's Holm fell into place in his mind: the longhouse with its row of shuttered windows, its fine dragon finials, and sweeping turf roof. The dairy and outbuildings. The pony pen. As they passed Magnus rooting about amid the fallen timbers, and approached the byre, Gil said boldly, "Are you afraid of her?"

Floki turned and laughed gaily, shaking his head. "No more than any other man is of his grandmother," he said.

"His what?"

"His grandmother. She is my grandmother, Warrior." He grinned at Gil's wide-eyed astonishment. "All men do have them. Indeed, they have two. She is my mother's mother."

"Oh." Gil nodded, astonishment giving way to another flood of recognition. *Of course. The familiar smile. The sharp replies.* Though it was not Shony that Derla brought to mind, but the earl, himself.

"So why …?" he began stupidly.

"Why is she here? Because she so chooses. She is a wanderer, as her people were. A woman of the shielings."

Gil stopped outside the byre. He glanced over his shoulder at the sea, the unguarded strand. "Is she safe here?" he said uncertainly.

"As safe as she wishes to be." Floki's eyes suddenly narrowed. "Do you think, Warrior, I do not offer her a place in my household?" He shrugged. "It is there for her. Perhaps she comes, one day. But I think not. She has her own places, here, and on other shores. In summer, she is on high ground. In winter, by the sea. She troubles no one." He shrugged again. "Besides," he added softly, "It is from Derla my mother learns swordplay. Few would take either on."

A sudden scuffling brought Gil's head up in alarm. Floki laughed again as two long-horned shaggy beasts appeared, glaring down from the roof. "And there are these! Who would take *them* on?"

"This is where you got Percy's goats!" Gil cried.

"Of course not," Floki said evenly. "I steal them from the selkies under the sea. Do you never pay attention?"

Gil grinned and shook his head. But then he said suddenly, "Is Derla ... has she a Change-Thing?"

Floki smiled up at the black, shaggy creatures. "That may be so," he said. "That may be so."

Inside, the byre was remarkably tidy and clean. Kists were arranged as benches either side of a fire that burned brightly on a new stone hearth. Fish dried in the greenwood rafters. Cheeses were stacked in the shadows beside jars of meal. Nearer the hearth, sheep and goat skins carpeted the swept stone floor.

A straw and bracken mattress was spread by one wall. Against another stood a loom and an ancient harp. Both were smaller than usual, as were the wooden kists. Nothing in the room, Gil realized, could not be loaded on a pony's back, or into the hull of the skiff on the shore. Like the Northmen with their black tents and awnings aboard their ships, Derla could recreate her home wherever she chose to rest her keel. He felt a small stab of envy for anyone who could be at once so secure and so free.

They took places around the hearth and when Magnus joined them, shared a fine meal of fish seasoned with herbs, bannocks fresh from the hearthstones, cheese and butter, berries, honey, and cream. Afterward, Gil dozed by the fire while Magnus played the little harp and Floki and Derla talked quietly in their shared Pictish tongue.

Derla looked up suddenly, and switching to Norse said, as if Gil, too, had been included in the conversation, "So, then, let me see your sword work." She stood, stepped into the open space between the bench and the wall, and tossed him his shield. Smiling, and looking alarmingly like her grandson, she drew her sword.

Gil cast Floki an uncertain glance. The earl rose, as did Magnus, and both retreated prudently to the opposite wall. "Warrior," Floki murmured as he passed, "do not hold back. She will not."

Gil nodded. He drew his own sword and raised his shield. Derla lifted hers and smiled at him over its rim. Then she moved so fast that Gil found himself staring at the empty place where she had been. Simultaneously, his shield flew from his arm, propelled by a lightning fast kick and a ringing upward blow swept his sword effortlessly aside.

He stumbled, caught his balance, and regained his hold on the hilt. But Derla's arm was around his neck and her blade in front of his face. "Too slow." She lowered the sword and stepped back. "Try again."

He tried ten times. The closest he got to her was a modest tear in her apron. She was as light on her feet as a fawn and as quick in her movements as a fish. He felt he was fighting a wraith, with no human form at all. When at last she called a halt, having disarmed him again and again in ever more inventive ways, Gil slumped against the wall, too exhausted to care.

"Very good," said Derla.

"*What?*" he whispered.

She smiled, a kind, even motherly smile and turned to Floki. "The boy is capable," she said.

Gil shook his head. Cautiously, he raised his eyes to the earl. To his surprise, Floki looked faintly proud.

Magnus grunted. "That is well, Derla," he said. "Since my son names him his heir."

Derla studied Gil and nodded thoughtfully. Then she turned again to her grandson, saying only, "You are young to choose an heir."

"All men die," Floki gave her a slight smile.

"And some die sooner than others," Magnus growled. "Does he not tell you he sails to Norway, in three days' time? Into a den of wolves, to be slaughtered, as a point of honor." He gave a weary shrug that undid the sourness of his words, and a startling look of pleading came into his eyes, as if Derla might dissuade, where he had failed.

But Derla only nodded again, untroubled. "My grandson dies at no man's hand," she said. Then she smiled and beckoned Gil.

Hesitantly, he stepped forward until he was standing before her. The pale grey eyes that had challenged him ruthlessly over her battle shield, now shone with a dreamy soft light. And though she never took her gaze from his face, he felt she was looking through him and past him to some other faraway place. Her voice was gentle when she spoke. "You will have happiness," she said. "Though a day comes when you think all happiness is ended. You will yet have happiness."

They slept that night with their sail for a tent in the ruins of Einar's Holm and rose again before dawn. Eating hastily in the darkness, they set out in silence from their shelter. But Derla was already up, milking her goats in the first grey light. "I wish you good fishing," she called as they passed. Magnus raised the big battle-axe in cheerful reply. With swords at their sides, shields on their backs, bows and quivers over their shoulders, they mounted the hill.

Even so laden, they moved fast, climbing the slope that once Gil had ridden in terror, clinging to Lionheart's mane. Then, with rainy light brightening in the east, they were on the heather moorland. Long-legged and tall, now, Gil kept up, stride for stride, with the earl and his father, loping easily over the rough ground, leaping burns and skirting bogs, his memories of the landscape still vivid from the past. How long the distance had seemed then! And how quickly they covered it now. Already the Great Stones were in sight.

Floki halted when they reached the nearest of the monoliths, scanning the dim, brooding circle in the strengthening light. "The pool, Warrior," he said quietly. "Do you see it?"

Gil searched their surroundings for a glimpse of silken water but saw nothing. Magnus shook his head. "It'll be by the church," Gil said. "If it isn't here."

"Good," Floki said. "A better place." Gil threw him a questioning glance, and he said, "More cover." He led on, up to the Wood of White Trees, and in the narrow path through them, he slowed to a walk. Stopping suddenly, he turned to face Gil. "Do you trust me, Warrior?" he said.

"Trust you? Of course."

"No, Warrior. Do you *truly* trust me?"

"I said so."

"Without thinking. Now think. You know me years now, but do you truly know me? Do you trust me?"

Gil thought carefully and said, "As much as I trust anyone."

Floki laughed softly. "A very good answer. We will see now what it means." He walked on, and with Gil at his side said, "I would do, now, with you, what my father claims I do with Ragi. But," he added cheerfully, "I think you survive."

"Use me as your double?"

"As decoy." He rested a hand lightly on Gil's shoulder. "Derla tells me there are five men at Cille Aidan. There were three. Then two joined them. My two," he added drily. "She sees all, from the hill and from the sea; she will be right. It is, of course, you they come for."

"*Me?*"

"Warrior, we are three days from Saint Matthew's Feast. Do you forget your purpose?"

Gil shook his head. "The Crossing will be open, I know. But I'll be halfway to Norway."

"You will. And so, too, the boy and the treasure they seek. But our friends do not know this. And so, they wait here for you. And," he paused, "I give them, now, what they wait for."

They had reached the end of the wood path and stood looking down on the grey quiet sea and the familiar outlines of Cille Aidan. Stripped of their thatches and blackened by fire, the small round cells stood open to the sky. The church, too, was roofless, its stone cross fallen and the bell and bell frame gone. Where the frame had stood, just outside the doorway, a small perfect circle of water glistened silvery with reflected light.

"The Wandering Pool," Gil whispered. Floki nodded, but stayed still within the shelter of the trees, silently studying the jumble of stone buildings below. All around them lay the messy evidence of a casual encampment: scorch marks from impromptu hearths, animal and fish bones, grey undergarments spread out on stones to dry. From the smell drifting over all, it was obvious they were not bothering to walk to the cliff top latrine.

"There," Magnus muttered. He pointed to Aidan's scriptorium. Gil saw it had been roughly roofed with sailcloth. A cough sounded from within, echoed by a loud snort. "They sleep without a guard."

"Perhaps." Floki's eyes swept the remaining cells and the shore with its upturned skiff and heaped fishing net. At last, he turned to Gil. "Go, now, to the pool. Stand, look within. Do not turn. Do not move. Whatever happens, do not move."

"Okay," Gil said uneasily.

Floki took both his shoulders in his big hands and turned him so they faced each other. "Do you trust me?"

"I said …."

"Yes. But I must know." He looked deep into Gil's eyes, and then released him. "Do not move. Trust me."

Gil nodded again and stepped warily from the cover of the trees, half-expecting to be instantly felled by an arrow or an axe. Spared, he walked on, making his cautious way down the familiar track to his long ago home.

Just outside the low stone *vallum* that marked the boundary of holy ground, he glanced back. The earl and his father had vanished. Birds flitted innocently at the edge of the wood. *Okay.* Setting his face forward again, he went deliberately on, past Danni's cell, and his own, past the scriptorium with its snoring occupants, to the forlorn remnant of Aidan's church.

He wanted suddenly to enter it, for Aidan's sake. But, obeying Floki's orders, he stopped just short of the empty doorway, at the edge of the circle of wind-rippled water that had chosen to place itself there.

It looked smaller than he remembered, but then, maybe it changed its size as it moved from place to place. Surely it changed its depth; a mere six inches today, to the murky sand bottom. And a thousand years deep, a day from tomorrow.

Stand. Look within. Conscious of the scriptorium behind his unguarded back, Gil took a deep breath. *Okay. I'm doing it.*

Something clattered behind him, a stone hitting stone. *Do not turn.* Then another stone soared over his head and cracked into the hull of the upturned boat on the strand. *Do not move.*

Shouts sounded, muffled by thick stone walls. Awake now, in moments they would be on him. He stared at the water. Then a new threat grew from beyond; footsteps running up from the strand. Desperately he fought the urge to reach for his sword. To turn. To simply run.

Wild thoughts surged through his head. What if it was all a trick? Like the trick Floki played on the chieftains? All the talk about being Floki's heir, just a flattery to beguile him, like he beguiled Ragnar Kolsson? What if he, himself, was a sacrifice; a peace offering to Magnus? Heart pounding, he stared at the opaque water that reflected everything and told him nothing. Like Floki. Floki the storyteller. Floki the game-player. Ever the Change-Thing ... gentle and honorable one moment, a murderous Viking the next ....

Trust me.

But who are you?

The water stirred. Heavy booted footfalls shook the springy ground. A shadow crossed the pool's surface. *Run.*

Do not move. He heard the words as if the earl was at his side and froze. Something swished across his shoulder, soft as the wind and silent as death, catching at strands of his hair. An awful meaty thud was followed by an even more awful scream. Unable to stop himself, he looked up.

A man was standing just across the Wandering Pool,

skewered through by Floki's iron-tipped spear; still standing, still agonizingly alive. Another scream came from his open mouth and was drowned in a torrent of blood. The body collapsed to its knees and fell forward, staining the water red, the spear twisting it sideways until—twitching and kicking—it died before his eyes. Gil's hands flew to his mouth.

Do not move. Fingers pressed to his lips, he stood rigid. Something whistled past his ear and he heard another scream, to his left. Another quick swish and another scream to his right. *Three of them,* the last rational piece of his mind told him. *Two left. Do not move.*

Cries of outrage rose behind him and then suddenly stopped just feet from his unprotected back. *Where were they?* Again, he fought desperately to hold his place. And then, suddenly, the earl was there, stepping from behind Gil's own ruined cell, standing tall and quiet, his hands empty.

"Yes," he spoke clearly, looking past Gil to whoever was beyond, "I am dead. A mere wraith, returned from Valholl to pay your unpaid wages. Goodbye, my friends."

A berserker howl split the morning air and Magnus Redbeard burst from behind the cell wall, the Irish battle-axe raised over his head. Turning the double blade, he swung it sideways and charged. *Do not move.* Gil closed his eyes as flashing steel swept by his face, but the sound alone would remain with him forever; the rending of bone and flesh, the dying screams, and Magnus' full-throated laughter, over all.

They threw the bodies from the cliff by the latrine. "Let the maas pluck their eyes," said Magnus, wiping blood from his hands.

"They will not care," Floki answered quietly. "But let the sea take them, all the same." He sounded weary and walked in silence back to the blood-spattered church.

He spoke little on the journey home to Hrolf's Isle, but sat alone in the bow, studying his Latin psalter, while Magnus sprawled comfortably with his feet again on the rail. But, with dusk falling, Floki summoned his father to the helm and went forward again and sat with Gil beside him. "You do well," he said, with a brisk nod.

Gil shook his head. "I didn't do anything. I just stood there."

"It is far, far harder to stand before a sword than to wield one. You do well. My father thinks so, too, though you will not hear it."

Gil grinned weakly. "No."

Floki looked up, then, at the sail, straining above them, and said, "The Crossing lies unguarded now." Gil nodded uncertainly. "The boy and his cup await on Hrolf's Isle." He returned his gaze to Gil's face. "Clear water and a fair wind, Helmsman. What is your course?"

"My course?" Gil stared back at him, astonished. "But you …. Saint Matthew's Eve …."

"I think Erling can find Norway."

"But Hrolf's Isle!"

Floki leaned back against the rail. "Hakon is a good man. My father, less good, but more powerful. If they fail, there will be others." He smiled wryly,

"No ship another cannot helm.
No horse another cannot ride.
No lass another cannot love.

Sigrid, my other grandmother, tells me this when I think too well of myself." He smiled again. "I offer you a gift, Warrior. Not a burden. You are free to choose." He paused and said softly, "All men seek their homes."

Home. Gil stared back at the skiff's stern: Magnus hunched over the tiller and a wake stretching behind them, all the way to Cille Aidan. But his mind raced ahead, over the bow, to the Holy Isle, and Janetta. Leave? Leave Janetta? *I'll take her home with me.* Was it even possible?

Floki laid a hand on his shoulder. "There is one thing more I would show you, Warrior, before you make your choice. But go, now and take the helm from my father. I would have your hand on the tiller, through the roust."

With a cheerful grin, Magnus relinquished the skiff to Gil, stretched lazily and took up his favored position with his back on a bench and his feet on the rail. "So," he said, with a sly glance at his son, "the old plough-horse sees the young go to the fields, raises his head and shakes his mane—he would follow. So, you take him, harness him to the plough awhile. He does well, and when he tires, is content again in his field." He yawned placidly and closed his eyes.

Floki turned a page of his psalter. "At least he is not in the stew pot."

"Or salted down for the Christ's Mass feast," Gil muttered, struggling to hold the oar in the tide race. Dusk lay over the water. Ahead were the twin watch-fires of Hrolf's Isle. When the prow struck the fierce cross-chop of the meeting tides, Magnus was already asleep.

Gil himself slept that night in his blood-stained clothes, sprawled on a bench in the longhouse, oblivious of the preparations for the journey going on all around him. But the earl shook him awake before dawn even arrived. He was on Lionheart's back, cantering up the hill, between Floki and Ragnar Kolsson, as the sun rose.

It seemed a simple courtesy to escort the younger chieftain back to his father's lands. But when they parted with Ragnar, within sight of his north coast hall, Floki turned off the track over the hill and rode toward the morning sun.

Lionheart trotted after, ears pricked forward, perversely in a good mood because Gil wasn't. *Stop joggling,* Gil muttered, his teeth clattering on a rock hard bannock. *I'm eating my breakfast.*

I can't. This is how my feet work.

Well, walk.

He'll leave me behind! Floki's pony had broken into a canter.

Good. Then we'll sneak off home and back to bed. Then, thinking better of it, Gil stuffed the whole bannock into his mouth and with a muffled, "Move it!" kicked Lionheart into a canter, too.

They rode on, until the steepening ground forced them back to a walk. And then, on a heathery cliff top, looking down on the sea, Floki drew his mount to a halt. Gil glimpsed the Church Isle, over a dip in the land. Another low island lay far to the North, a dim blue shadow on the horizon.

Floki dismounted and, beckoning Gil to follow, walked

carefully toward the edge of the cliff. Then, with Gil behind him, he stopped suddenly and held up a warning hand. Gil stopped and looked down. A foot from where the earl was standing, the heather parted and a strange light shone up from below. He opened his mouth to speak but Floki instantly clapped a hand across his lips.

Then, with Gil's silence assured, he knelt in the heather, stretched forward, and lowered himself carefully to the ground. Beside him, Gil did the same and with fingertips gripping wiry roots, pulled himself nearer until they lay side by side. He looked down and stifled an involuntary gasp.

Before him, a great chasm cleaved seventy feet of rock, revealing a glimpse of distant sand and sunlit sea and the swaying masthead of a ship, rocking gently in sheltered waters directly below where they lay.

Suppressing, again, a cry of astonishment, he stared down the mast to the ship's deck. Men moved about it, coiling ropes and mending a damaged sail. More seamen were ashore amid tents and casks of provisions. *A camp. A Viking camp. But as different from that at Cille Aidan as night from day.*

Gil wriggled nearer the edge and peered out toward the sea. The chasm was huge, a sea cave, part of its roof fallen prey now to the very surf that had formed it eons past, long before Northmen or Picts or any men at all.

The cleft grew wider as it neared the sea and sand beaches extended both sides of the trapped tide. On one shore, another longship lay beached, her mast lowered. Men gathered there, too. *No*, he thought. Not Vikings. Warriors. No raiding party but a disciplined force of fighting men.

Breathing deeply, he wormed back from the edge. He had seen what the earl had crossed Hrolf's Isle to show him. He need not see any more.

They returned in silence to their grazing ponies, mounted, and rode back the way they had come. When they reached the track across the hill, Floki beckoned Gil forward and they rode side by side toward home. "One of these," he said then, "is the ship you saw. From here, the fire-raisers sail."

Gil looked back. "How did you know they were there?"

"I do not. But it is where I hide a ship, if I so need. And I know this: he does not leave this task to five men, two of them traitors who may be bought again. Cille Aidan was a trap. Even old ale-sodden Vikings are more secretive in their camp. They let themselves be seen. He uses them as decoys, as I use you." He shrugged. "They would kill the guards later, anyhow. Traitors cannot be trusted."

"And their own three?"

Floki looked out across the hill. "At the end of winter, if fodder grows short, we cull the cattle. We keep only the best."

Gil shivered. "A trap within a trap," he said. "Like Rome."

"Men have little imagination. What they do once, they do again. Even clever men, like our friend."

Gil reined Lionheart in on the last little ridge and looked down at the longhouse. "So, what are we going to do now?"

Floki shrugged again. "Nothing."

"*Nothing?*"

"They will not stay, Warrior. As I say, it is you they come for. When Saint Matthew's Feast passes, and you have not come, they will withdraw."

"Until Christ's Mass," Gil said. "And then they'll be back." He paused and said angrily, "Again and again. Until they win."

"Or you win," Floki said quietly.

"Then should I fight them? After Norway? Should I come here?"

Floki studied the longhouse roof thoughtfully, and then turned to face Gil again. "And if you win, what then? A man who commands so many ships can spare another two." He slipped down from his pony, looped its reins over his arm, and walked on through the fields.

Gil followed, leading Lionheart, and stood watching curiously as the earl leaned down, grasped the stalk of a grey-green nettle with his left hand, and yanked it free. He opened his fist, showing Gil the welts raised by its sting. "It pains me, so I cut it down," he said. He drew his sword and sliced the plant off clean, low to the ground. "What then?"

"It grows back," Gil said with a shrug.

"Because I do not take the root." Floki leaned down again,

dug his fingers into the ground and hauled up a tangled root ball. Shaking the earth free from it, he tossed it aside. Then he opened the fingers of his left hand again and held out to Gil the stinging leaves. "It is well," he said as Gil gingerly took them. "I crush it. It gives no more pain."

Gil closed his own hand around the cool damp tangle, harmless now as grass. "So I go to Caledon," he said, "Right?"

Floki smiled. "You are earl, Saint Matthew's Eve, Warrior. Not I."

CHAPTER SIX

"Warrior, where is North?"

Without taking his eyes from his landmark on the Norwegian coast, Gil lifted one hand from the tiller and pointed over his shoulder.

"You are certain?" Floki's smile was a faint glimmer in the starlight. He had risen from his place by Danni and come silently to Gil's side.

"Yes." The wind, from the North all day, had veered easterly, bringing scents of land. Sea birds flocked homeward as dusk fell. Frigga's Spindle was rising in the East.

All the long way from Ragnvald's Shetland hall, they rode calm seas, under skies so clear that the snows of Norway were his guide for half the crossing. But light winds meant a slow journey and dusk found them still far out to sea.

Gil didn't mind. The sky filled up with stars, as familiar now as the scars crisscrossing his own hands. The sights and sounds and smells of the sea told him where he was. And he was in no hurry for this strange, peaceful journey to end.

They had sailed at dawn, leaving behind Floki's foster-father, a lean, lost figure clutching the whimpering lapdog left by Hakon in his care. "The saddest chieftain in the North," Floki said quietly as green water opened between him and his uncle's strand, and Gil, too, could imagine no lonelier earl than Ragnvald. His wife beneath the turf, his son far now on Hrolf's Isle, and his beloved fosterling a dead man in the eyes of all.

But then Floki smiled suddenly and said with rock certain cheer, "Yet, ten summers hence, he has more grandchildren than his creaking old knees can bear."

"How?" Gil mouthed, shaking his head.

"How? The usual way, Helmsman. How else?" He had laughed and tugged Gil's long ponytail of hair. "You are too serious, my friend. Do the cares of the earldom weigh on your heart?"

Gil shrugged. Whatever, no cares weighed upon the man who had relinquished that earldom. Surrounded by friends and family, as light-hearted as if sailing to his own wedding, he played board games with Rachel and Percy, traded verses with his poet, or lay with his head in Danni's lap, sharing kisses and caresses in the autumn sun.

As if time stood still, Gil thought, watching. But it did not. And though the deck was laden with gifts of ale and meal and the men and women aboard were dressed in their finest clothes, *Silver Dragon* sailed to no marriage feast. And the priest who accompanied them carried not water for a wedding blessing, but oil for the anointing of the dead.

"And where is your mooring?"

Gil pointed instantly to the hidden bay where they had first rested their keel when last he was here. "They haven't seen us. That's the hill of the ward fire."

Floki looked up at the dark height. "It is well. They will see us tomorrow. We will make certain. And where is North, helmsman?"

"Same place I left it," Gil said with a smile, his eyes and his mind on the approaching shore. Floki laughed quietly and held out his hand, palm up raised. Something small and shining glittered in the starlight.

"Your Falling Star agrees."

"Grandpa's compass!"

"Warrior ...."

Gil shook his head, fiercely, before Floki could finish speaking. "It's my gift to you. I'm not taking it back."

"I think, now, you need it more than I."

"Why?" Gil said angrily. "Was I wrong? Was I wrong even once?"

"No."

"And still you think I'm not good enough."

Floki shook his head. "You are very good. But against the sea, in the end, none of us are good enough."

"Now *you're* Hakon."

"Hakon is right, Warrior. Tedious, but right." He paused, turning the compass in his hand. "I like this thing," he said suddenly. "Sometimes, I hold it in my hand at night and watch its small wing fly ever North … how does it know, Warrior? How does it know?"

Gil shook his head. "It's magnetic. It's pulled by …." he stopped, furious with himself for never listening at school, never learning, so now he could not tell this curious, innocent man something so simple. "It works," he muttered lamely.

Floki leaned back on the steersman's bench, watching the sail blotting out stars. "I would see Tir nan Og, if I could," he said. "Where men make such things." Then he laughed. "I think, Warrior, that though I leave you now and send you, alone, on this great journey, I still try to stay with you? So, I try to give you the Falling Star … to keep you safe. This is a foolishness, I know."

Gil turned sharply to face him. "You want to keep people safe? How about turning this ship around for a start."

"That is not possible." Gil shook his head in frustration. Floki remained silent. After a long while, with the surf on the approaching shore already sounding, he said, "I make this vow on the strand at Rome. And you, at Candida Casa, pledge to hold me to it."

"Okay," Gil sighed. "So, I take you there." He raised his head and signaled to Ismail to stand ready to loosen the steering oar. "And if by some insane chance, he accepts your offer and doesn't just kill you, tomorrow, what's to stop me sailing back here with an army?" Floki said nothing. "We took this hall with a handful of men," Gil whispered hoarsely. "We could take it again. And settle this," he shrugged a shoulder toward the sea-king's strand, "Like Northmen."

"Call for oars," Floki said.

Gil's head whipped around to face him. "*I* am helmsman. And I am earl. Remember?"

"You still need oars," Floki smiled. "The wind is falling and you're in the lee."

"Oarsmen!" Gil shouted. He glared at Floki's teasing grin.

When the sail was down and the oarsmen bending their backs, Floki said, "I can make of you a warrior. I can make of you a seaman." He paused, "I can make of you an earl. But the man, Warrior, the man here," he lightly touched his chest, "The man under all those things, that, only you can make."

His eyes on the dark strand, Gil said, "So, it's all about honor in the end." He glanced quickly sideways and gave a hopeless shrug.

"Perhaps," Floki said, unruffled. "But, if not honor, then prudence."

"What?"

"Should you come there, as you say and he has been wise rather than vengeful, it is myself you will meet at the head of his forces."

"You'd fight me?" Floki nodded. "Erling? *Hakon*?"

"I must, Warrior. I pledge him my sword." He smiled reasonably. "Now, if you are not certain you can defeat me, then be a true Northman." He tapped the scabbarded sword at Gil's waist. "Use that, now, when I am without arms." He smiled again at Gil's shocked face. "No? Good. That will save Ragnvald, Hakon, and my father the trouble of flaying you alive." He laughed cheerfully and then leaned forward, threw his long arms around Gil, and held him in a brief, fierce embrace. "Godspeed, Warrior."

Then he rose and strolled lightly up the deck between the ranks of straining oarsmen, as *Silver Dragon* rode the surf ashore, catching his balance perfectly when the keel thudded into sand.

Gil woke at dawn to the staccato of sleet against the black tent cloth and the low rumble of a pounding surf. Slipping from Janetta's side, he ducked out from beneath the shipboard shelter and stood on the snow-rimed deck, squinting into an onshore gale. The wind had backed westward and risen ferociously. Winter had arrived, overnight.

Sea grasses lay beaten flat. Blown salt froth tumbled across the strand and trembled in patches on their deck. Beyond, the tumbling waterfalls of the ward hill headland reversed their courses and blew upward in fountains of spray.

Gil's eyes swept the surf, layer on layer of crashing waves, piling one on the other in their haste for the shore. *I'll never get her off this strand,* he thought wildly, even as he plotted a course out through the breakers that would leave their hull intact.

He turned inland and scanned the crescent bay. The waves-pounded strand and the grassland above were empty, but for wind-driven gulls. The sea beyond was empty, too, a day for the hearth fire.

But then, out of the mist of blown spray, two figures appeared, cloak-wrapped, walking close together at the surf's edge. Gil's eyes flew to the ward hill. No fire; but the two kept walking purposefully toward him. His heart lurched. Trapped by a falling tide and the onshore gale, lightly crewed and even more lightly armed, his ship was a sitting duck. And sheltering here, from whence they once had launched an attack, mocked any claim of peaceful intentions.

He turned quickly to raise the alarm and then stopped and looked back, puzzled. The two walkers had halted, and then one knelt down on the sand, beneath the other's outstretched hand, yellow hair bared to the sleet. *Floki. Kneeling for absolution from his priest.* Gil's last hope that somehow this day would not happen vanished like so much blown foam.

It took four attempts and every man and woman on the oars to get *Silver Dragon* afloat. Twice her proud dragon prow was beaten back onto the shore. A third time, she broached to the wind and tilted dangerously, drenching her oarsmen and exposing her hull to the pounding surf. "Get her around!" Erling howled to the rope men. "Get her around before she goes over!" And before Gil knew, the sea broke her keel and reduced her whole glorious length to firewood.

And then, at last there was clear water between him and the strand, and with her rudder down and the power of twenty long oars, she was under his control. Swinging her into the wind, he headed to sea, with Ciarnan and Arnkel Fish-Tail swimming, hauled along by their ropes until Floki plucked one, and Grimhildr the other, from the surf. Immediately they took up two more oars.

Gil allowed himself an instant to search the benches for Janetta and found her, across from Danni, her cloak whipped loose by the wind, her black hair torn free of its braid. As light as sea froth herself, she bent her back with uncanny strength. Rachel, drenched and determined, balanced Ismail, mid-ship. Ulf rowed across from his bride and despite her girlish glow, her strokes were as powerful as his.

Only Percy, of all their company, was spared the rough wood of an oar. Tucked in beside Bjorn and lashed securely to him by a stout line, he huddled with eyes squeezed shut and fingers pressed to his face, crying hysterically for Floki.

Gil heard Floki's shouts of re-assurance from his own bench, near the stern, but no one could stop a moment, even to comfort a child, so close was the balance of power between oarsmen and onrushing seas.

Ahead lay the first tidal bar, a long, low wall of foaming surf. The tide, turning as they launched, was now falling with alarming speed. In the distance, thin lines of spray-drenched sand broke through at left and right. Gil steered a course through them, where dark water showed the greatest depth, uncertain of clearance, even for the longship's shallow draft. But they surged through and with a shudder of relief, he set a course for the next channel.

A narrow riptide, so fast flowing between its banks of sand that it spun whirlpools on either side; it, too released them unscathed. Gil raised his eyes and fixed them on the final bar, seeking vainly for deep water. An unbroken line of foaming breakers lay in his way. If there was a channel, he could not find it. He looked once over his shoulder. There was no way back, even if he could turn without foundering; the lines of breakers had closed.

Fighting panic, he glanced desperately at Floki and received in return a cheerful grin. Torn between admiration and fury, he tightened sweaty hands on the tiller. Then, alone at the helm, he chose his course, a narrow gap where the backs of the wind-sheared waves were greenest, and swung his oar with a small smile of his own. *Why not? What better way to die?*

They hit the breaking surf so hard that for a moment Gil thought he had grounded her. But the keel cut through, the hull bending and twisting like a living thing. Seas smashed over both rails, green water surging amid the feet of the oarsmen.

And then, to left and right, the sea vanished, and in the troughs between the enormous crests, yellow sand appeared. Gasping in sheer horror, Gil braced his shuddering oar with his whole body and steered for open sea. Again, the waters parted and he glimpsed the sea floor.

Shouts of alarm sounded thin as children's cries against the awful roar of wind and surf. Gil's gaze, sweeping his crew as he prayed they were all still aboard, stopped suddenly, arrested by a thing he never thought to see: terror in the eyes of Erling Maiden-Face.

Then he heard a shout from below, at his right. "He is Moses!" Aidan called across to Floki, "He takes us through the sea on dry land!" Floki's laughter brought another smile to Gil's lips, as priest and penitent earl exchanged a salute, then bent their backs to their oars, one as powerful and fearless as the other.

And then they were through, surging suddenly across the final line of breakers and out into blessed open sea. When Gil turned to look back, there was no water left where they had crossed.

Again, he swept his eyes over his crew; all here, drenched, terrified, and exhilarated. His gaze returned to Floki and as they shared a nod of satisfaction, Gil permitted himself a sudden sweet moment of pride: in the worst seas he had ever seen, the best seaman he would ever know had not relieved him of the helm.

Clear of all hazards, they raised the mast. The great wing of the sail tumbled down, and Floki's golden pennant whipped free. Arnkel and Svein hauled in the sheets. Ismail set the tacking spar. Oars were shipped, and *Silver Dragon* fairly flew, south-southwest, on a fine broad reach.

Gil took her far, far out to sea. Glad to be away from that shore, and reluctant to return to it, he was more than happy to beat westward all the way home. But when both the mist-shrouded ward hills were in view, Floki bade him turn landward again, toward the sea-king's strand.

As he headed up into the wind, Sleet battered his face, dripped from his hair, and clung to his growing beard. A more different day than when last he saw this harboring, he could not imagine, nor an approach more different than that grand arrival, with seven ships abreast, shield racks ablaze with color, and warriors lining their rails.

Now, the racks were bare of adornment, the passengers were few, and but for Floki's bright pennant, the wind-battered ship might have been a lone, lost knarr, seeking shelter from the storm.

Then, as she came about and for a moment lost way, the pennant fluttered, fell, and wrapped around the mast. The sail bellied out and the boys released the spar as *Silver Dragon* lunged downwind. But the pennant stayed, caught in its own snow laden folds, still as a shroud.

Gil heard a low groan and saw Bjorn staring up at the mast with the eyes of a frightened child. "Odin leaves us," he sighed.

"Bjorn." Floki laid a gentle hand on the big man's arm. "It is but a flag. A piece of cloth. It does not speak of Odin. Or of anything."

Bjorn shook his head. "It is an omen. A bad omen."

Floki smiled and then suddenly laughed. Brushing the snow from his beard he said fondly, "Bjorn Break-Neck, my friend, once before we part, I would hear of a *good* omen. Surely, they come in both kinds."

He laughed again, but no one laughed with him. In mournful agreement with Bjorn, Erling, and Ulf, Arnkel and Svein all shook their heads. Floki squinted up at the snow-filled skies. "Gods of my fathers? Has no one any sense?"

He whirled around and pointed from the luffing sail to the squall-flattened waves. "It is the wind! It turns and it eddies. You have never seen such before? Do sails not at times blow backward and water-devils play in the surf?"

But they all kept their eyes fixed on the masthead and Gil found his own drawn to the trapped pennant, willing it to break free.

Then, suddenly, Ciarnan jumped up from his bench, ran forward, kicked off his boots and mounted the swaying mast. Barefoot and agile, he scrambled up, amid the thrumming shrouds, into the full force of the wind.

Floki shouted his name and then turned to face Gil at the helm. "Call him down." Ciarnan slipped, slid several feet down the snow plastered pine, and scrambled up again. "This is not worth a life, Warrior. Call him down!"

"Ciarnan thinks it is," Gil muttered. And as the Irishman reached the yard, he kept stubborn silence. A gust slammed into the sail, showering them all with chunks of ice. Ciarnan lost a handhold, snatched at the trembling rakke, steadied himself, and mounted the yard. Then, balanced precariously thirty feet above the sea, he reached up and yanked the pennant free. It spun out in a streak of gold, bright as sunlight against the wintry sky.

Legs wrapped around the yard, Ciarnan sat watching it for a moment of triumph, then swung down onto the mast and half slid, half fell its icy length, leaping the last ten feet to the deck. Surrounded by cheering shipmates, he calmly wiped his bloodied hands on his shirt and returned to his bench.

Floki saluted him with a nod and a small smile and then turned to Gil. "And had he fallen?" he said quietly.

"He didn't." For an instant, Gil took his eyes from the distant strand. "Men follow what they see," he pointed up to the fluttering flag, "And now they see Floki Magnusson."

Grimly pleased, he turned his eyes again to his goal. Ahead lay a far better harboring than that they had left. A broad, deep water cove ran inland to a long white strand with nousts for many ships. Even at low tide there was easy clearance for far heavier vessels than their own.

Above the strand, the sea-king's fine hall stood stormbound, its turf roof white. Beyond, the steep rock-walled valley was lost in spindrift, its scattered farmhouses blurred smudges in the snow.

The burnt-out barn that Gil remembered had been re-built, but half the harvest was yet in the fields. Stacks of sheaves bearing snow headdresses stood forlorn like abandoned wives. Half-laden wagons were covered in white while the harvesters sheltered from the storm.

"We are not the only unwelcome guest," Floki said. "Winter comes early and brings its own griefs. Take her there, Warrior," he gestured to an empty noust, a modest landing at the edge of the strand. "Where merchants and poor cousins rest their keels."

Gil adjusted his course, aware that everything they were seen to do had meaning, messages without words written on sea and sand.

"They see us!" Erling pointed to the ward hills. The glow of fire, pale through the driven snow, flared over one hill and then the other.

"That is well," Floki said, and to Gil, "Reef the sail."

"*Reef*?" Gil shook his head. Why? She's sailing like a dream."

"Dreams can be frightening, Warrior. Give them time to awaken."

Reluctantly, Gil signaled the boys to clip his dragon's wings. When they were done and the ship settled sedately into her wash, he surveyed her progress sourly. "Happy now?"

"Ah, now I have a Northman!" Floki laughed "I am happy." He stood beside Gil at the helm until they were close enough in to see figures emerging from the longhouse and spreading out along the strand. Steel glinted in the pale light.

"I think they're awake," Gil muttered.

Floki calmly studied the gathering forces on the shore. Then he said, "If this does not go well, Warrior, I would rest on the Holy Isle."

"*What*?" Gil stared.

"Aidan knows." Floki nodded and smiled and then walked forward to meet his fate.

Gil called for oars and as the sail came down, leaving only the bright pennant at the masthead, Danni rose and went to stand beside Floki at the rail. Released by Bjorn, Percy ran to join her, and stood between them, an arm around each.

The wind had lessened slightly but the snow was falling more heavily than ever, fat wet flakes that etched everything in white. Percy huddled close to his sister, shivering, even in his fine cloak, and Floki took off his own, wrapped it around the boy and stood, then, the snow caking his red tunic and bare head.

It hardly mattered. They were all soaked through from the sea and the storm and, with the struggle to hold his course eased, Gil was shaking with cold, himself. On the strand below, the waiting ranks of cloak-wrapped warriors looked as miserable as themselves.

Steering oar raised, he brought his ship smoothly into the noust. Ismail and Ciarnan threw the bow ropes down and, welcome or not, they were drawn up onto the Norwegian strand. Though as they let down the gangplank, swords were quietly unsheathed below.

Floki's own sword rested in its fine silver-trimmed scabbard in Gil's hands as, together with Aidan, they descended the gangplank; Aidan and Gil slightly behind, Floki, unarmed in the lead.

At the foot, he walked forward alone and was instantly surrounded by a ring of steel. He held up empty hands as they circled him, and when they moved to confront Gil as well, he called, "He is my helmsman. The sword he holds is my own." He nodded to Gil, "Give it to them."

Carefully, Gil handed the sheathed weapon to the nearest of two snow-plastered Norwegians. With an uncertain shrug, it was accepted. Floki smiled encouragingly. He turned and looked up at the ship and said quietly, "My family would join me."

Shielding their eyes against the driven snow, the men on the shore squinted up at *Silver Dragon*. Danni, Rachel, Janetta, Percy, and Bjorn clustered together around the gangplank, waiting in silence. Percy peered tearfully out of the enveloping cloak and waved at Floki, who smiled, raised his arm to wave back and was blocked at once by two men with swords.

But then another stepped forward, an older man with a magnificent sweep of greying blond beard and flowing moustache blowing like horse tails in the wind. "Enough," he said. "He would comfort his child. Where is the harm in that?"

The two swordsmen lowered their weapons warily and stepped back. The older man smiled a cheerful smile, belying the hostility all around. "Bring them down," he said. He signaled to the surrounding warriors to move back, as Janetta, Danni, and Rachel came to stand beside Aidan. Grimhildr and Ulf lifted Percy over the rivulets of out-running tide and set him down on the strand. The ermine cloak trailing in the snow, he ran, arms-outstretched, to Floki. But Floki turned him gently back and, sniffling, he clung to Grimhildr instead.

Stroking his snow covered moustache, the Norwegian studied the bedraggled gathering on the shore and then glanced up at the regal pennant snapping in the wind. He turned puzzled eyes again to Floki. "Who are you, lad? What brings you to our shore?"

Floki smiled slightly. "You know me. I came once in anger. I return now in peace to pay the debt I owe."

Again, the moustache was tugged and then recognition, and with it, dismay, swept across the weathered face. "Floki Magnusson," the man whispered, "I would not have known you. You have changed. So much has changed!" He sighed and then leaned suddenly closer. "Lad, give the boy to me, and go. Take your family and your ship to sea, now, before any other hears what I have heard."

Floki smiled and shook his head. "I beg you, summon your chieftain," he said.

With a sad, hopeless shrug that set the ends of his moustache trembling, the Norwegian turned and relayed Floki's request, and a lean young warrior set off at a bounding run toward the storm-shrouded hall. Then they all stood together, waiting; not quite prisoners and not quite captors, shivering and battered by the uncaring wind, until a shout announced the runner's return. All eyes were raised again toward the unseen longhouse.

Five figures came, like ghosts, out of the blowing snow, walking abreast, cloaks closely wrapped, garments wind-plucked. A semi-circle of guards fanned out behind them. Gil strained to pick out the big-shouldered belligerent form of the sea-king. He should be centermost, flanked by his most trusted chieftains. But the figure in the center was slim and a head shorter than those surrounding. Puzzled, he turned to Floki. "Which is he?"

But, eyes on the approaching Norwegians, Floki only shook his head. "Now, as I told you," he said. Laying a hand briefly on Gil's shoulder, he stepped away.

Gil moved back to stand between Janetta and Danni. Each had their place: Grimhildr and Ulf kept Percy between them, Grimhildr with her cloak ready to cover his eyes. Rachel stood beside her, her eyes on Floki and Gil knew she would remain, watching unflinching whatever fate befell him.

He glanced quickly at Danni. She kept her place, but her whole body bent forward, like a wind-battered reed, reaching out to her beloved. Her face was white, calm, and still, only her eyes fiercely alive.

Aidan, alone, remained at Floki's side, guardian not of body, but of soul. As the five reached them, Floki gently laid a hand on his shoulder and thrust him back, out of harm's way.

Then, at the last moment, a vicious gust of wind from the sea threw a white curtain of hail and sleet over all. Gil strained forward, seeking the old chieftain among the shadows. The wind dropped and the flakes thinned. A slight movement drew his eyes to the central figure: a gloved hand slipping from within an encompassing cloak to draw aside its fur-trimmed hood. Wind-whipped strands of white-blond hair veiled a face so beautiful, so impassive and with eyes so cold that it might have been carved from ice.

"Gudrun!" Danni gasped. But the sea-king's daughter seemed aware of no one but Floki.

"My lady." His strong voice sounded thin in the storm. "I would speak with your father."

"You will speak with me, Floki Magnusson."

"My lady …."

"You have come too late. My father is dead. I am chieftain of this hall."

Floki stood utterly still, the wind and snow battering him unnoticed, as if not comprehending what had been said. Gil saw, stunned, that he who had planned this so carefully, had prepared for every possible circumstance, had not prepared for this.

Gudrun watched and after a long silence said bitterly, "He died in the hungry time, old and ill and suffering, with the name of his last, lost son on his lips. Because of you."

"Oh, my good lady." Floki lifted an instinctive hand to offer comfort and it was brutally slapped aside by a guard.

Gudrun turned and her gaze wandered, distracted, over the group on the strand and the others yet aboard the ship, seeking one face. "Where is my brother?" She sounded puzzled and shielded her eyes against the snow to seek him again.

"He is not here," Floki said.

"Not here?" She stared, astonished, and then outraged. "You break your word!"

Floki shook his head. "My lady," he said slowly, "He is with his father."

"What say you?" Confusion and then more anger crossed her face. "Where is he?"

Gil heard a groan behind him and turned and saw the gentle older man who had met them bury his bearded face in his hands.

Floki spoke clearly, measuring the words as if to a child. "He died of a fever on the Roman strand. I buried him there with honor." He paused. "I wept over him, as if he were mine."

"*You! You* wept for my brother?" Her eyes flashed. "Guards!"

Two men stepped forward with unsheathed swords. "Gudrun, child ...." the man behind Gil implored. Gudrun looked up to the speaker.

"I am your chieftain, Olaf, not your child." She flicked a hand, gesturing from the swordsmen to Floki. "Kill him."

CHAPTER SEVEN

The guards came from either side, and calmly and gracefully, Floki strode forward to meet them. Grimhildr swept her cloak around Percy and Gil struggled not to close his eyes. Beside him, Danni gave a low, anguished animal cry. And then, like a dark whirlwind, she darted from her place and swept past him.

Gil lunged to restrain her, but with furious strength she shoved him aside, running out between the swordsmen, running to her love. She reached Floki and flung her arms around his neck, entwining her slender body with his. Twisting around, she faced Gudrun. "If he dies, I die with him. Kill us both."

With shouts of dismay, the chieftains closed in, as one, to stay the swordsmen's hands. But the swords were already lowered, the uncertain eyes of the executioners on the face of their fierce young earl.

Anger and anguish warred in her pale, cold eyes. "My sister … Danni," she whispered, and then with hardening voice, "step back. I will not have you harmed."

"Go," Floki gently lifted her arms from his neck, "It is time." He looked up to Aidan, "Good Father …." Aidan stepped forward to take her but Danni only tightened her grip.

"Gudrun." A craggy, scarred old warrior swept snow from his hair with a three-fingered hand. "Let this young chieftain speak in his defense. A moment," he said wearily, "before you end a life." An eager muttering arose among Gudrun's uneasy council.

Her eyes still on Danni, Gudrun slowly nodded.

The old warrior turned at once to Floki. "Why have you come here?" he said.

"To pay a debt."

"To die."

"If that is the price."

The warrior shook his head hopelessly. But another, then, stepped forward, a swarthy dark-haired man who reminded Gil of Hakon Sea-Friend. "Have you a better offer?" he said.

Floki smiled slightly and Gil had a sudden startling remembrance of him bargaining with a jewelry merchant on Hrafn's Ayre. He turned to Gudrun, meeting her gaze with good-natured calm. "Lady, I offer you myself, living, not dead. I offer you my sword and my loyalty. For seven years, I will serve you and fight your cause against foe, friend, or kin, at your bidding."

Two of the chieftains nodded vigorously. "Gudrun, this is a good offer."

But Gudrun cried angrily, "Seven years? Seven years from your thrice seven and more? My brother had only ten." She nodded brusquely to the guards, who, with eyes darting uneasily from face to face, stepped forward again.

The old warrior flung an arm out, blocking them. His eyes narrowed against the sleet, he said clearly, "His cousin, Hakon Ragnvaldsson is powerful, and his father and uncle as well. They will avenge this."

For a moment, Gudrun hesitated, her resolve faltering at the mention of Hakon's name. Then she shook her head vigorously, casting a cascade of snow from her hood. "Let them," she said.

"You bring war to our shores, Lady," said a big, fair man.

Her eyes flashed scornfully. "Are you not fighting men?"

But then Floki said, "There will be no fighting. My heir stands before me," he held a hand out towards Gil, "He will carry out my wishes, and my wish is that my death is not avenged."

The eyes of the council turned to Gil, assessing him. The old warrior snorted. "You set a cub against a wolf pack. Your father's name is known throughout the North. Will he agree?"

"And who would trust him if he did?" Gudrun cut in. "Sea-scum island Viking that he is?" Her fine features hardened.

"No. I cannot face my father's wraith and let you live."

As if to applaud her, the wind gusted violently, swirling a funnel of snow along the storm-swept beach, caking hair and beards with sleet and lashing bare skin with slivers of ice. Percy shrieked and cried. Men cursed. Even Gudrun turned her face aside.

Then, suddenly, Olaf burst forward from behind Gil. "Enough!" he shouted, his voice and his moustache shaking with outrage. "Enough, Gudrun. Your father would not leave *anyone*, not even sea-scum Vikings, to stand on his shore in this weather! By all the gods, give these people the shelter of your hall!"

Gudrun stared, in silence. With widening eyes, like one suddenly awakened, she surveyed the gale-wracked strand, the half-beached ship, battered yet by the surf, and her drenched and freezing crew. "I forget my duties," she murmured; strangely, to Floki himself.

Then she stepped back and addressed her warily watching chieftains. "Do as my uncle says. Food, drink, shelter for all. When all are cared for, we meet again in the hall." She turned back to Floki and to Danni and suddenly held out her arms. "My sister, come with me. I care for you myself."

Danni hesitated, but with Floki's gentle urging, she went uncertainly to Gudrun's side and allowed herself to be led from the strand. The chieftains stamped after, shaking snow from their cloaks. Olaf watched, and then took off his own cloak, wrapped it around Floki's shoulders, and with his young prisoner beside him, followed his earl to her hall.

Gil ran hurriedly to join them, but Floki smiled and shook his head. "Secure your ship, Warrior. I will not be harmed. There are rules."

Gil stepped back, watching uneasily, and then turned to his waiting crew. With the vigorous help of their erstwhile adversaries, they dragged *Silver Dragon* fully ashore, lowered her mast, and shrouded her against the weather. Remembering the gifts Floki had brought for the sea-king, he had the casks of ale and meal off-loaded and borne up to the hall. Then, with his ship safe and his crew in the now welcoming hands of the

Norwegians, he made his own way, half guest and half prisoner, up the strand.

A skinny cheerful lad, hardly younger than himself, but shyly awed by his rank, guided him first to the wash house in a stand of firs beside a burn. The sweet scent of burning pine brought him instantly back to Mona and Gudlief Egilsson's hall, where the warmth of the wash house belied the cold plotting of Floki's untrustworthy kinsman.

But, on entering, the blast of hot steamy air on his frozen skin was so welcome and the scene before him so jarringly unreal that he just stood in his heavy wet clothing, dumbfounded.

Surrounded by a dozen naked, towel-wrapped captors, Floki sat on a bench between Olaf and the scarred old warrior in animated conversation with his likely executioners. "Warrior!" he called cheerfully, amid much laughter, "This fine woman will attend to your needs."

He turned back to his companions, as a stout blonde figure, swathed in aprons and red-faced beneath a linen headdress, bore down on Gil, pulling at his clothing. "Off!" Before he could move, she was stripping him naked, much as she might pluck a chicken. Wise enough, after Mona, not to argue, he gave in to her vigorous scrubbing until, pummeled and soap-stung, he collapsed in relief on a bench.

Floki and the Norwegians returned to their talk of overlords and taxes, harvests and weather, and snows of old, far earlier and far worse than this, while Gil sat bemusedly watching and soaking up the blessed warmth.

Peering through the steam for his crew, he spotted Ismail and Ciarnan, sitting with eyes closed and legs stretched out to the fire. Across the hearth, Bjorn, hairy as a vast black bear, rocked happily in the heat. Aidan, lean and muscular as a warrior, sat beside the poet, Eoin, who bent toward the fire, his head tilted, weaving his surroundings from threads of sound.

One by one, the occupants of the wash house moved back from the fire and dressed themselves in the clean, dry clothing provided by their hosts. But Floki and Olaf remained, deep in the inevitable tracing of bloodlines and when they came upon a common ancestor, Gil was hardly surprised, so much did

Gudrun, with her pale hair and icy eyes, resemble Floki. But his own mind was not on the past, but the immediate future, and the reckoning that awaited them in the hall.

When, clad in wondrously dry and clean breeches and a beautiful deep green tunic, he himself moved to the door, he was the last to leave. Olaf had gone out with Floki, just ahead, but when Gil joined them, the Norwegian hastened off to speak with a servant, leaving them, for a moment, alone.

Gil watched his curious moustache blowing in the wind and then turned in bewilderment to Floki. "How can you be so calm?" he burst out. "They're going to kill you! What does it matter what your grandfathers did?"

Floki smiled, and with his gaze still following Olaf, laid a hand lightly on Gil's shoulder. "It is hard to kill a man once you meet with his family. Once you share laughter and talk of your fathers' days. Besides," he nodded toward the wash house, "Men without their clothing are never so fierce. Nor so angry."

Gil grimaced. "Maybe you should take *her* in there."

Floki laughed, his eyes sparkling, and covered his face with one hand. "Warrior! I lay down sinful thoughts before Aidan. Do not send me back to him again!"

Olaf returned, moustache bouncing, a broad smile on his weathered face, as the serving man trotted toward the jumble of outbuildings behind the hall. "I take it upon myself to secure a good ale for the feast," he said. "Lest we become too serious." He laughed, and resting his arm around Floki's shoulders, escorted him to the longhouse as if they were the oldest of friends.

Gil hesitated, and then followed, a reluctant few paces behind. The sea-king's hall loomed before them and he knew too well that, no matter how gracious the welcome, once within, they may as well be in a prison.

His eyes settled on Olaf's broad back. Cheerful and hospitable, so quick to intervene on their behalf, he was yet Gudrun's uncle. And, however distant, another of Floki's often treacherous kin. Gil's mind flew again to Mona, and Gudlief Egilsson, as bountiful in his welcome as Olaf, even as he plotted to betray them. And, had it not been for Floki's quick-witted cynicism, he would have succeeded.

But here, Floki seemed as irrationally trusting as a child, and Gil, as irrationally perhaps, felt determined to defend him. He looked up to the sloping, snow-covered roof. No warriors lurked above the eaves, though his own memories conjured Bjorn and Grimhildr, mounting to the rooftree and smashing through the turf with their axes. And the oak doors that they themselves had barred, trapping the old king inside as they stole his son, now swung wide, beckoning them in to warmth and shelter.

Olaf and Floki had gone within; the guards waited politely. With heavy heart, Gil followed and heard the great doors thud shut, the bar scraping closed, behind him. Instinctively, he looked left and right, over each shoulder. No swordsmen stood ready to spring out; only a pair of giggling servant girls, admiring Olaf's handsome companion.

Trust Floki to enchant the women, even here, Gil thought wryly. Then he looked up and saw ahead the one woman in the hall immune to any charms. Slim and slight in her father's seat, she sat in regal silence, her chieftains on either side. Two places had been left empty at the High Table; that on her right, for her uncle, and on her other side, the seat of the honored guest, for Floki.

The long tables flanking the hearth were lined with men and women of her household, with Gil's crew and Floki's family scattered among them. Few in number, and weapon-less, they presented little threat, and yet Gil was well aware that armed men held places beside each. And when Percy jumped up from his bench and ran joyfully to Floki, his wooden cup bouncing on his chest, swordsmen instantly blocked his way.

But a clear, ringing order from their chieftain sent them back to their places, and Gudrun herself rose and ordered a small stool to be brought and set beside the chair reserved for her adversary. She remained standing until Olaf and Floki had taken their places, and then signaled the serving women that feasting might begin.

Gil made his way forward and found an empty seat between two young Norwegians. A girl with ropes of yellow hair poured ale. Numbly, he drank, his gaze sweeping the peaceful hall, his mind conjuring images from the past: the twin lines of Floki's swordsmen holding the floor and the sea-king's warriors backed against the walls. The old chieftain and his dark, angry bride disturbed in alarm at their breakfast. And Floki, splendid as a young king himself, striding into the longhouse with his ironic gift of barley. *A farmer's silver.*

Now, neither farmer nor earl, he sat drinking wine with his fair, dangerous host, in the hall he had once taken at sword-point. Gil wondered what Gudrun's father would have thought. And what of her beautiful, haughty stepmother?

He looked up then, searching the hall for her, but finding her neither at the High Table, nor among the women on the long benches, decided her stepdaughter's hospitality was more than she could bear.

For, if Gudrun's courtesy was forced, none would have known. A fine meal was set before them; musicians with harps and flutes played and sang while they ate. The gifts of meal and ale Floki had brought were displayed and commented upon and, bizarrely, further gifts—cheeses and a live, half-grown ram-lamb—were presented to him in return. These were passed into Gil's care, after the appropriate speech of gratitude, and he could see Percy joyfully eyeing the lamb, a companion for his goat kids on Hrolf's Isle.

Then, quite suddenly, the feast was ended. The tables were cleared. The musicians retreated with the serving women through an inner door. Gudrun rose and announced she would hear petitions. Had any in the hall a grievance against another? Her cool eyes swept the longhouse with calm authority and Gil was again reminded of Floki, holding his own court on Hrolf's Isle.

But here, this day, there were no disputes over livestock, nor complaints of injuries. "Does any man make petition?" Gudrun repeated. There was silence, in reply, and then a sharp intake of breaths and a stir of surprise, as Floki got to his feet. He faced Gudrun, nodded to each of her chieftains in turn, and returned his gaze to his host. "I make petition," he said.

Cries of amazement arose from the benches and a light touch of laughter. But Gudrun remained utterly calm. "Against whom do you hold a grievance?" she said.

Floki smiled lightly. "Against you." A shout of protest echoed in the silent hall. "As chieftain," he continued, "And your father's heir."

More protests came from the benches, querulous and outraged. Gudrun silenced them with a flick of her hand. "Very well." She turned from Floki and looked out to the hall. "My council will hear this petition," she said.

It was a signal, Gil realized, for all others to depart. Men and women rose, as one, and made their way from the longhouse, shepherding the visitors before them. Percy reached out tearfully to Floki, as Danni led him away. Erling looked in alarm to Gil and Bjorn protested, but armed men surrounded them both. Gil leapt to his feet. Two lean swordsmen bore down on him, too, but he dodged them, running forward to the head of the hall.

Five warriors tackled him before the High Table, throwing him to the floor. Jerked back to his feet, arms pinned behind him, he was spun around to face Gudrun, while rough hands searched his clothing. "I'm not armed," he muttered angrily and was punched hard in reply.

"Release him," Gudrun said.

His arms freed, Gil straightened and wiped blood from his mouth. "I do not leave my earl," he said. Her icy eyes met his and he saw a flash of respect. But then one of the searchers gave a shout of triumph and held up something that flashed in the firelight.

"My father's knife!" Gil cried, like a startled child. So accustomed was he to carrying it, sheathed always at his belt, he had forgotten it was there. But that belt now cinched in his borrowed tunic, and he had carried a weapon into the hall. "I forgot ...."

Floki mouthed, "you idiot", as the knife was set before Gudrun. He turned to her patiently. "It is but a small blade he uses for gutting fish. But," he added with an amiable smile, "It is a gift from his father and hence a treasure to the boy and must be returned to him, before he leaves."

Gil watched, astonished at Floki's boldness as he then lifted the knife himself and laid it in Gudrun's uncle's hand. Olaf nodded sagely. "That will be done. All men have small things that matter."

Floki smiled again, "That is so." He reached inside his tunic and instantly two of the chieftains drew swords. Still smiling, he said, "But I have only this. A threat to nothing but the affections." He drew out a small pouch hung by a cord around his neck. Gil remembered the gold and amber necklace he carried always for Danni, but the object that fell from the pouch to the table was smaller than that, and silver.

Gudrun's eyes widened, their expression briefly softened. "Hakon's ring," she murmured. She lifted it and stroked it gently. "He wore it always."

"Indeed, he did," Floki said. "But now he wears yours that you sent as a pledge, with me. And he would have you wear this."

She held it yet, as if reluctant to let it go, but she shook her head. "The gods have decided we are not to be joined. It cannot be." She held the ring out to him.

He smiled. "How wise you are to know, so well, the thoughts of the High Ones. And you so young." Then he reached out and closed both his hands around hers, the ring between them. "Take it. Perhaps they change their minds. Who knows? And if so, better to have it from a living hand, than one dead."

He released her and she stared at him, shocked, then closed her hand in a fist around the ring. Floki turned to Gil, "I thank you for your loyalty," he said, "But there is no need. These people know well the law, and I am kept safe within it."

Gil saw a small flicker of pride pass over the chieftains' faces. They nodded graciously. Then the scarred old warrior held up his maimed hand. "Still, the boy, as his heir, has rights also. And a man should have beside him one to defend his cause."

Nods of solemn agreement passed down the line of chieftains. Olaf looked to Gudrun. Still clutching Hakon's ring, she said, "He may stay." She turned back to Floki. "Speak your grievance, now."

Floki sat in silence beside her, for so long that the chieftains cleared their throats and made small gestures of impatience. He set his gaze far down the hall, in the empty space between the tables, where the hearth fire burned low. So intent were his eyes on that emptiness that those at the High Table instinctively looked there, too.

"He is not there," Floki said, "The man with whom I dispute. And so I charge his wraith: You sold my kin into slavery," he said, speaking to nothingness.

Gil looked instinctively over his shoulder, and then forced his gaze back to the table before him. Floki continued. "You broke your pledge, and hence my trust, and for the sake of those I am sworn to defend, I take your son ..."

"Speak to me," Gudrun said angrily. "Not my father."

"... as the only guarantee of their safety," Floki finished. He returned his gaze to her face. "Very well," he bowed his head graciously. "The charge now lies with you."

She stared at him. "And is there, in this, no fault of your own? None?"

"I was in error," Floki said calmly. The chieftains muttered and he sat again in silence. Then he said, "Your brother would make a fine chieftain. Young enough to listen to his advisors and not over-rule men who had lived and fought before he was born."

Gil saw small smiles cross the faces of three of Gudrun's council. Floki said again, "I was in error. I take your brother. I should instead take you."

Olaf's mouth fell open. The scarred warrior shook his head and smiled in astonishment tinged with admiration. Gudrun stayed icily calm, her fingers still clutching Hakon's ring. She turned to face him. "And would you have wept over me, if you had buried me, also, on a foreign strand?"

"Oh, my lady," he smiled, "I would, had not Hakon Sea-Friend slain me first."

She smiled then, too. "Then I do the same for you. Tomorrow, at dawn." She stood, the business of her council finished.

Gil grabbed the edge of the table and shook his head. *No. Not like this. So light and uncaring. Like the dismissal of a servant.* He opened his mouth to make useless protest. But other voices were clamoring already as Gudrun's council all rose to their feet, as well.

A white-haired man who had not spoken before said quietly, "This is not within the law."

Amid the chorus of agreement, Olaf's voice stood out. "Gudrun! His complaint against your father is just. You thought as much yourself. As did we all. He offers a reparation he barely owes. Accept it!"

"And shelter my brother's murderer beneath my roof?"

Olaf groaned and slumped into his seat, head in hands. The fair man who had spoken on the shore stood, arms folded. With a glance upward, he growled, "This is not your roof, alone, lady. Others raised the beams, others laid the turf. Others defend it with steel. Provoke this man's kin and it is our households, our farms and sheep and cattle, our sons and daughters, who will pay!"

"Gudrun," Olaf said through the half-parted fingers of his hands. "You have enemies enough."

"I will deal ...."

"Your stepmother ...." the maimed warrior began.

"I will deal with her."

"You have not dealt with her yet," he returned. "Nor her dangerous husband."

"Her paramour."

The man shrugged. "She is free to wed him now. But, wed or not, she has a claim through the child."

"It is not my father's child."

Olaf leaned back in his seat, whimsically stroking his long moustache. "Five men might hold that honor." He marked them off thoughtfully on his fingers. "She was as generous as a queen cat in the straw. But your father, indeed, was one of the five."

He straightened, his jovial face suddenly deadly serious. "Your situation is not good. You are your father's heir, but so, too, is your new half-brother. You have my loyalty and that of each man here, but we are few and three of us are old. This man," he gestured toward Floki, "comes to you as a gift. Indeed," he smiled wryly, "A gift from the gods. His swordsmanship is justly famed and his thinking, as justly. He is fearless and men follow him. He brought seven ships from his wild islands and over-powered your noble father."

"By trickery!" she cried.

"Gudrun," Olaf smiled again, his head tilted gently, "How else are battles won?" He paused and said solemnly, "With his help, you may well win your own. For you indeed have enemies enough. But shed this young chieftain's blood as if he were some petty Viking, and you will have many more. Whether or not he accepts this dishonorable death."

Gudrun sat in stony silence and then turned abruptly to Floki. "Then I give him an honorable death. We will duel. Odin grants life to the just."

Floki smiled and shook his head. "Odin grants life to the better swordsman. And though you have indeed become the warrior I saw in your eyes, you will not be my equal."

"Not swords then, but the bow. Or the axe. No warrior is best at all the arts of war."

He smiled again. "Would that were so."

For the first time, Gudrun smiled also. "You are not renowned for your humility."

Floki ran his fingers through his luxuriant hair and looked up winsomely. "Yes, I am vain. Of my good looks and my verse making; my grace at the dance and the way I catch the women's eyes. But of my fighting skills I am only truthful. Good lady, I have done harm enough to your father's seed. I do no more. Let two of your best warriors face me in this duel. That would be fair."

Gudrun shook her head, but there were eager nods from her chieftains.

"Or three," Floki added. "Fairer still."

"No, no, lad," Olaf intervened. "Three is too many. I cannot allow that."

"None," Gudrun said angrily. "My father fought his own battles. I will fight mine." But her council, caught up in this new solution, ignored her, and began citing names of swordsmen and laying down rules of combat.

More wine was called for and goblets re-filled, Olaf ensuring that Gil, still standing awkwardly before the High Table, also be served. Having settled on the chosen warriors, they had moved on to matters of compensation, for injuries and for death, turning at intervals to the white-haired man for details of the law.

"He has no children," one put forward, speaking past Floki as if he were not there.

"Ah, but the helmsman is his heir," another added, "And there is his cousin. And his parents."

"Both yet living?" a third addressed Floki.

"Both yet living."

The white-haired man took note, with brisk nods of his head.

"The cupbearer?" Olaf enquired.

"He is my fosterling."

Olaf looked to the white-haired man.

"There must be compensation to him. And the parents. The cousin. The foster-father. The heir, of course. Is he blood kin?"

"No."

The white-haired man nodded again and Gil realized the price of compensation varied accordingly. He sipped his wine in silent amazement as Floki's skills and accomplishments, his breeding and potentials, were discussed before him as if he were some prize beast at market. Though, Floki himself seemed perfectly at ease with it all.

"The young woman?" Olaf asked politely. "You are pledged?"

"Yes."

"Ah," Olaf stroked his moustache, glanced at the white-haired man, and looked back at Floki. "Is she? Possibly ...?" his broad cheeks reddened as he gestured vaguely to his own ample waistline.

"I have not known her," Floki said.

"Ah." Another nod from the white-haired law-master.

Gudrun, who had sat in silence throughout, her gaze on the high roof beams, suddenly got to her feet, set her wine goblet on a high shelf on the paneled wall behind her, and walked out through the inner door in sheer, astonished frustration, Gil imagined, perhaps equal to his own. But Olaf cleared his throat, blushed again, and said, "Women's needs," and they all nodded sagely and returned to their debate.

"Our own warriors?" the three-fingered man put in, "Is there reparation to their kin, should he slay one. Or both?"

The white-haired man nodded. "Yes. We pay that."

"And should he survive?" The fair man hunched a shoulder toward Floki.

"He is a free man," the law master said simply. "The debt is paid."

Gil relaxed, his fingers loosening their white-knuckled grip on his goblet. He had seen Floki in battle. Two warriors, even the best two warriors in Norway, would cause him little pain.

And then, through a fog of relief, he heard the creak of the door, not the small, inner door through which Gudrun had left them, but the great oak entrance at the foot of the hall. The last light of the dying day swept in, paling the firelight. Gil spun about, reaching for the sword that was not there.

She was standing alone, framed in the doorway, a bent bow in her sure, white hands, the arrow already set to string. Gil whirled and flung himself between her and Floki, even as the arrow flew.

Sprawled across the table, he heard its deadly swish above his head, then a clang like a struck bell and the solid thud of splintered wood. Bright liquid splashed his outstretched hands, red as blood but light and sweet: *wine*. He raised his eyes and stared.

Gudrun's arrow protruded from the split paneling above the heads of the astounded chieftains, its feathered shaft quivering like a dying bird. Below, her wine goblet lay shattered, the stem bent and broken, the silver bowl spinning yet in a wine-splashed arc on the shelf.

Floundering amid the over-turned drinking vessels on the table, Gil pushed himself awkwardly erect, only to be instantly pinioned by two powerful hands. Fingers biting into the flesh of his biceps, Floki shook him so hard his teeth clacked together. "*Why?*" he demanded, pale eyes alight with fury. "*Why? Why? Why?*" Still stunned by what he had done, Gil shrugged uncertainly. "What possible good could come from *you* dying here?"

"I didn't think," Gil mumbled.

"Well, *think*, Warrior!" Floki cried. "Think!" He released Gil roughly and swept a trembling hand across his own face. Then, looking back, he said softly, "I thank you for your loyalty. It is more than I could ever deserve." Gently, he moved Gil aside, as Gudrun's light, sure footsteps sounded in the empty hall.

She came and stood before him, her cheeks yet rosy from the sea wind and her eyes bright with proud, young triumph. He bowed to her graciously, then turned and, placing both hands on the arrow, wrenched it free of the wood, held it up before her, and snapped it in two. An uneasy muttering swept the chieftains, but Floki smiled then and extended one half of the arrow to Gudrun, keeping the other himself. "My lady," he said, "We will duel."

In the darkness before dawn, Gil rose from his place on the sleeping benches. He shook Ismail awake and by the fading glow of the hearth fire, they made their way to the doors. Unsure of the line between courtesy and command, they had accepted the shelter of Gudrun's roof. But Gil had slept little, his mind on his ship, undefended on the strand.

Sliding the heavy bar as quietly as they could, they slipped out into the night. The dozing guards woke and saluted them hesitantly, as uncertain as themselves if they were prisoners or guests. With a quick nod, Gil led the way to the strand before they could change their minds.

Winter and its snow had vanished overnight. A fine gentle wind blew in off the sea. Even before dawn, the air was warm. On the shore below them, *Silver Dragon* rested high above the tide, untouched by storm or treachery. A loud baaing broke the silence. "Look!" Ismail laughed and pointed to the deck. A small woolly shape stared down from the bow, tugging at its tether. "Percy's new friend."

Gil smiled. Gudrun's gift had been delivered overnight. He mounted the gangplank and found the ram-lamb munching a nest of straw. The cheeses were stacked nearby, under a new tarpaulin. All else on the ship was in order, exactly as he had left it.

He felt a twinge of guilt for having mistrusted their fair host, but it was not enough to prevent him walking all around the hull in the dim light, checking for unseen damage. *Trust no man.* The words jolted through him. Floki's words. Now they were his own. "She's fine," he said, a little awkwardly, to Ismail.

"Check the rudder," Ismail smiled.

It too was untouched. They nodded to each other, with satisfaction and turned back to the hall. Day had broken; the valley and its farms emerging from darkness, the high tops of the surrounding mountains touched by the rising sun. Mist yet lay in the hollows, but the day would be fine, the wind already lifting the battered uncut barley.

A cluster of farm lads came down from the fields, whistling as they walked. Gil knew from their jaunty stride alone that they had not heard of the duel. Though the milkmaids, standing in shawl-wrapped huddles, looking down to the strand, surely had.

Ismail nudged him. "They are grieving already."

Gil stood still, watching them. "No need," he said at last. "She will win."

Ismail stared. "She is that good?"

"Maybe." Gil shrugged. "But it doesn't matter. He won't take the chance that she's not." He smiled hopelessly, and continued walking, his mind returning, as it had since Floki accepted Gudrun's challenge, to their own homeward journey and their earl's last sailing to the Holy Isle.

They met on the strand, at Terce. The tide was out and the wide expanse of dune-lined sand offered space for the duelists and an amphitheater for the witnesses, gathered to ensure the outcome was undisputed.

With Ismail at his side, Gil came early to the site. Down the strand, his crew, dressed again in their own garments, were quietly preparing their ship for the sea. The duel over, he would sail at once, swearing in his heart to never see this shore again.

Olaf led the way from the hall, carrying four bows in his arms. A boy followed with a quiver of arrows. Behind them, Floki and Gudrun walked side by side, their windblown hair bright as the ripened barley. At the steep descent to the flat sands, he took her arm, like a young man escorting a girl in a dance.

Gil looked at the quiver of arrows and felt sick. "This is so crazy," he muttered.

Ismail smiled sadly, "But it is not war."

The chieftains took their places in a solemn row. Gudrun's household clustered behind them, her serving girls weeping and the young men in stunned silence. Floki's people stood apart; Erling with his arms folded grimly, Ciarnan and Arnkel Fish-Tail wary and watchful. Ulf and Grimhildr sheltered Percy between them. With Janetta at her side, Danni wept, wrapped in Aidan's arms.

"Where is Rachel?" Gil said suddenly. He searched the shore for her, but she was not among the watchers, nor the last of the crew, coming up from *Silver Dragon*. Ismail shook his head. "It is too much."

A deep sadness settled in Gil's heart, but he could not blame her for her desertion. Had he any chance of turning away, himself, he would have taken it.

He watched as Gudrun was handed her bow by her uncle and Floki offered a choice of the remaining three. He lifted each, quickly and lightly, and chose one without hesitation. Olaf nodded approval. "It is a fine weapon."

"My own is finer made," Gudrun said. She extended it to her opponent. "You must have it."

Floki smiled, "Fine indeed, but too light. This other is better."

There was a murmur of approval from the chieftains that all was being done in the proper way. Arrows were selected; one, only, each. Then Olaf led the young duelists out onto the open strand. They stood back to back as he walked in a solemn circle around them, expounding rules that they already knew, before retreating to the chieftains on the dunes.

The white-haired law-master gave the first command, and,

bow in one hand, single arrow in the other, they walked steadily away until he bade them halt. The watchers drew in sharp breaths. Fifty paces separated the two; far enough to demand skill, but close enough, too, to make likely a clean death. They waited in silence, Gudrun facing to the south, Floki to the north. Gil turned instinctively in the same direction, and seeing *Silver Dragon* with her mast raised, was suddenly glad that Floki was seeing her, too.

Gil was still looking at the ship when he heard the last, sharp command. He spun about, but Floki was faster, faster than Gudrun, too. Already his arrow was set and the bow drawn back, Gudrun drawing hers, seconds after.

The two households stood frozen, the chieftains straining forward. In a blur of movement beside Gil, Grimhildr swept Percy under her cloak. A second blur, over his shoulder, distracted him, and when he looked back he saw what he had dreaded to see: the smile and the quick flick of the wrist. The bowstring hummed and Floki's arrow soared innocently skywards, arcing out over the dunes.

My grandson dies at no man's hand. But a woman. A woman. Gil closed his eyes. And then, in the darkness, he heard Gudrun's sharp cry. A tumult of shouting arose around him. His eyes snapped open again and he stared, uncomprehending.

White and shocked, Gudrun clutched her wrist, staring upward, as her arrow, flying wildly askew, skittered across the wave tops and disappeared into the sea. The chieftains crowded forward, shouting and gesturing. The sleeve of her dress soaked red with blood. Floki lowered his bow and walked calmly toward her.

"But how?" Gil cried. "I saw the arrow...."

"There." Ismail pointed high above the heads of the duelists. Silhouetted against the bright morning, a small, swift shape parted the squawking gulls, swung inland, and vanished beyond the dunes.

"Rachel," Gil whispered.

She was still breathing hard when she suddenly appeared, slipping easily through the excited crowd, unnoticed in the chaos of shouting and amazement. Eyes shining, Ismail leaned close to her and plucked a small white feather from her hair. She studied it and shrugged. "Seagull. Silly things everywhere."

On the strand below, Floki was gently binding Gudrun's talon-raked wrist, with strips of linen torn from his shirt, while all around the chieftains debated the fate of the duel. Three insisted upon a second attempt, but Olaf countered that it was clear now that Floki would not defend himself. "It would be murder," he declared. "Out-with the law."

"Few who are murdered are first given a weapon," the fair quiet man reminded them.

"Then let him fight with men," another protested.

"Let him go," a woman's voice shouted and the serving maids began to shout, too.

"Odin sends the hawk," a man called. "The young chieftain must not die." Others took up the cry, until suddenly the old law-master held up both hands, silencing them all.

He spoke slowly and calmly, "The law does not provide for this, so I must think." He sat down on a grassy bluff and settling his chin on one fist, closed his eyes.

Both households waited. Floki finished bandaging Gudrun's wrist. The boy with the arrows admired Gudrun's bow. Released from Grimhildr's cloak, Percy ran to his sister, who stroked his head distractedly, her attention fixed on the white-haired man. Rachel smoothed her tangled hair back into place, removing another feather. Throats were cleared and boots shuffled restlessly, but no one spoke for all the long while the law-master thought.

At last, the old man raised his head. "It is not the hawk that is Odin's bird," he pronounced, "but the raven." An uncertain muttering greeted his words. "Still," he continued, "A hawk is swifter than a raven." He paused, allowing time for more muttering. "And Odin is All-Father and hence *all* birds are Odin's."

Sighs of relief came from the serving maids. "*But*," the law-master went on, "The hawk might have flown of its own."

Olaf shook his head firmly. "No wild hawk would fly against man or woman."

"A tame hawk may," the quiet, fair man put in. "Indeed,

readily, at the command of the falconer."

The law-master gave a solemn nod. He narrowed his eyes and addressed Floki. "Have you such a hawk?"

Gil held his breath as Floki turned, looked directly at Rachel and smiled innocently. "I have no hawk obedient to my command."

"Ah," said the law-master and again closed his eyes, and sat again in long, thoughtful silence. The wind ruffled the sea. Gil heard the soft thrumming of *Silver Dragon's* shrouds. He jumped when the old man suddenly rose to his feet and began to speak.

"That the bird speaks of Odin, or not, I cannot judge," the law-master announced solemnly. "But all know Odin rewards courage. We have seen courage enough this day." Raising both hands, he said clearly, "I rule the duel over. The debt is paid and the young chieftain goes free."

Gil heard an anguished cry of relief, so strong as to be indistinguishable from grief. Danni ran from Aidan's embrace across the open strand, her arms outstretched to Floki. He caught her and swept her up into his own, laughing and kissing her as if she were already his bride. To cheers from his household and some from their opponents, too, he set her gently onto her feet and looked up to Olaf and the law-master.

"If Odin rewards courage, then your chieftain also deserves reward." He turned to Gudrun. "Good lady, I give you back my freedom. I stay at your side and serve you until your household is secure. Then, and only then, I return to my own."

Smiles broke out on the faces of the chieftains. Gudrun solemnly drew back her wind-swept hair and studied Floki in silence. Then, suddenly, she too smiled, nodded and took his hand. Clasping it in her own, she turned to face her followers and raised their joined hands high. "Let it be understood," she said clearly, "That between Gudrun Helgisdottir and Floki Magnusson, all debts are paid and these two households are at peace."

It was three days before Gil sailed; three days of summer sun in which they joined together in the harvesting of the barley, and two nights of feasting and story and song. By the third morning, both the snow and the duel seemed faraway and unreal.

He was at ease now among his Norwegian companions, as at home on Hrolf's Isle, accepting their mockery of his strange accent and standing up for Arnkel Fish-Tail in his dizzy infatuation with a dairy maid called Jodis. When he left the sleeping benches at dawn, he pretended not to see the couple locked blissfully in each other's arms.

A rising mist and an incoming tide promised good sailing. He crossed the strand, mounted the gangplank of his ship, and walked the deck, methodically checking provisions and oars and rigging. At the tip of the lowered mast, he paused, unwound and released the golden pennant, and rolled it carefully in his hands.

"You are early, my friend." Gil jumped, looking quickly around. "Here, Warrior," Floki called. "I bid my dragon farewell." He stood on the strand, looking up at the gilded figurehead. "And I tell him to obey you."

Gil laughed, not quite sure that he was joking. Floki surveyed the ship with a keen eye. Gil said, "I've checked everything."

"You have a helmsman now to do that, while you lie in your bed."

Thinking what Erling might say to that, Gil grinned weakly. "I think my helmsman has other things to do."

"Ah, yes," Floki laughed. "Erling, too, finds a woman at last. The small fair one with the lips that say no and the eyes that say yes. I wish him well. He has lived like a holy monk these years since my pretty hawk clipped his wings." He smiled. "She is indeed terrifying," he said fondly.

Gil remembered the kiss Erling stole from Rachel, that long ago day at Einar's Holm, and Shony's fierce retribution. "Your mother's sword was more terrifying."

"Only a little." Floki stretched up and touched the strakes

below the figurehead and turned away. "Come, Warrior. You must make your farewells."

"Wait," Gil said. He held out the rolled pennant. "I took this down. It's yours ... but I want to keep it. I want to fly it."

Floki tilted his head quizzically. "You must have your own, Warrior. Blue," he laughed, "to match your eyes, so the women will swoon when you are yet far out to sea." Gil smiled but shook his head. "It is expected, Warrior. You are their earl."

"But you are mine."

Floki stood a moment in silence. Then he pressed the pennant back into Gil's hands. "No. But I make you a good helmsman, when next we meet."

The golden pennant fluttered at the masthead when they put out to sea. Gudrun's household gathered on the strand to watch. Gudrun herself came down from her longhouse with Danni, their arms entwined around each other's waists. When all had boarded; Erling and Arnkel last, clutching treasured love tokens, Danni yet lingered beside Floki on the strand. "Stay with me and be my sister!" Gudrun cried.

Floki waited in silence. Danni hesitated, her eyes on Gil, maneuvering his ship from the noust. Then, sadly, she shook her head. "You've kept your pledge," she said simply, "Now, I must keep mine."

Floki smiled, "Ah, this thing called honor. It undoes us all." Then he caught her up in his arms, carried her through the water and set her lightly aboard. She leaned down to him yet, as the oarsmen turned the ship, and then ran to the stern and mounted the steering board by Gil. The sail rode up the mast. *Silver Dragon* heeled and clear water opened between ship and strand. Danni scrambled up on the rail, clutching the dragon's tail and stood looking back, until nothing could be seen behind them but their wash, white as a bride's veil on the sea.

CHAPTER EIGHT

Lionheart balked, ears back, staring at the thing Gil had flung over the pony pen gate. Gil tugged at the lead rope. Lionheart shifted his weight to his haunches and shivered, rolling his eyes.

It's a saddle. Gil sighed wearily. *Don't act like you've never seen one.*

The saddle is gone.

No. The saddle WAS gone. Because I've been riding around a peat bog of an island for half a year. Now I'm going to Francia and I NEED A SADDLE.

Lionheart lowered his head hopelessly. *The saddle is gone.*

Have it your way. Here comes a figment of my imagination. He hauled the high-cantled jousting saddle off the gate and flung it on the pony's back. Lionheart sagged in the middle and groaned while Gil fastened the girth.

Think that's heavy? Well, here I come on top of it. Gil vaulted grimly aboard. Lionheart sagged again, then arched his back and bucked. Gil slammed his feet into the stirrups, tightened his knees against the unfamiliar leather, and grinned. *Not a chance.*

By the time they met Ismail, coming down from the fields with Chocolate, also saddled, and Ciarnan, bareback on a big grey plough horse, Lionheart had given up and was trotting aggrievedly up the hill track.

Ismail jumped down, hacked a young hazel sapling free from a thicket, and with a few swift blows of his hand-axe, transformed it into a leafy lance. He held it up, "Noble Sir Bannock-Face! I challenge you!"

"You're on, Sir Herring-Head!" Gil swung down from the jousting saddle, enjoying again the novelty of stirrups, and cut his own lance.

Riding further up the hill, they chose as tournament ground a damp stretch of sheep pasture dotted with gorse bushes and sloping steeply into a marsh. Ciarnan dismounted, and relishing the role of herald, shouted grandly, "To the field!"

Gil turned Lionheart and galloped away over ground so rough that only a hill pony could master it. *Fine*, he thought. *Good training*. As he had learned jousting with Lance'lot in blizzard-swept Caledon, the reality of battle was a long way from the mock warfare of the lists. He spun Lionheart around to face Ismail and Chocolate, raised his shield, lowered his hazel sapling, and charged.

On the first pass, they were both disarmed, the springy green wood bending almost double against steel-bossed shields. Ciarnan collected the fallen weapons and they charged again, the ponies jumping bog pools and stumbling over thickets.

Splinters flew and they pulled up, Ismail with half a frayed lance clutched gamely beneath his arm and Gil with less than a third. Two more passes left them holding leafy stumps. Ismail dropped his ruefully. "Next time, I make better lance."

"Next time, we make better knights." Gil grinned, breathing hard. "Out of practice. And I need to fix these stirrups. My knees are up to my chin." He kicked his feet free of them, as they cantered back to Ciarnan.

"You grow," Ismail smiled.

"Yeah. And Lionheart doesn't." Gil looked up at the sky. It was a fine autumn day, but the sun had tilted westward and they were long past the endless daylight of summer. "We'd better move or Red Kol will be in his bed before we get there." He paused, looking to Ciarnan as well. "And I want to show you something along the way."

It was a long ride over the hill, and even though Gil resented Hakon's instance that he have bodyguards as appropriate to an earl, he was glad of their company. Far more than if he had accepted Hakon's own choice of attendants: Thorfinn and Thorgeir, two grim-faced brothers from Gauk's Isle, as famed for their sour natures as for their sword hands. The boys might be no match for them in battle, but they were swift and agile, and, more important, they were friends. Having seen even Floki betrayed by hired men, Gil had decided loyalty was preferable to prowess.

Still, a part of him missed his freedom on the hill, as he missed his trysts with Janetta on the Holy Isle. But an earl had responsibilities a carefree boy had not. Hakon had judged those solitary crossings also too much a risk, and Janetta now slept on Hrolf's Isle, secure beneath Shony's roof.

Even with Hakon away from the island, first in Shetland, and now on his autumn Dublin trip, Gil obeyed his wishes. The wills of a shared earldom must not be seen in conflict. But he chafed restlessly under the Shetlander's exacting caution, yearning for the day when *Silver Dragon* set sail, and he would answer to no man but himself. A day that would not come, however, until he completed her crew.

So far, that had proved easier than he had hoped. Young men, weary of the drudgery of the farm and the confines of the island, dreamed of adventure on the sea. And of silver. Gil knew, now, that whatever he paid his oarsmen from the treasury Floki had left him, they would expect to supplement it with raiding. Somewhere, some merchant setting out, even now, with dreams of his own, would finance *Silver Dragon's* sailing.

It was the way of it. Even Hakon Sea-Friend, trading in the markets of Dublin, would come back from Ireland with more than seeds and tools. For all his grave demeanor, he was as much a Northman as his cousin, and this was their world.

But the old men of the island, who sent *Sea-Raven* off on a tide of knowing jests, were less good-humored when their own households were involved. Riding from hearth to hearth, Gil had learned quickly: the sons were no problem. It was the fathers he had to win.

A farmer with six young men beneath his roof would spare one easily, or even two. A man with only three was concerned with the autumn ploughing, the bringing in of the peats, the laying up of the boats. The hours of winter were short, but there was work enough to fill them.

Gil listened patiently while eager boys' eyes watched his every gesture. Sometimes the offer of more silver was enough. Others wanted assurances of laborers. For some, no argument succeeded. And Red Kol, with one son only to work his windswept fields, was one of those. But Ragnar Kolsson was the best swordsman on the island and Gil was determined to have him aboard.

Drawing up his too-short stirrups, he crossed the leathers over the saddle's pommel, and letting his legs hang loose, set out to cross the island to Red Kol's hall, with Ismail and Ciarnan just behind. His boots brushed the tops of gorse bushes and snagged in brambles. When Lionheart splashed across a burn, he had to pull his feet up to keep dry.

Mid-stream, the pony shied and stumbled, hooves clattering on rocks. Gil grabbed his mane to keep his seat, eyes intent on two figures striding out of the marsh, voices raised in argument. The boys hurried their mounts forward on either side, but Gil held up his hand. "It's just Arnkel," he called back.

Arnkel Fish-Tail, who he himself had sent out this morning to gather withies for Eyolf's boatyard, stood at the marsh's edge, with an armful of the cut willow switches and more filling a leather sack slung over his back. The second figure, a girl with thick blond braids tied back beneath a kerchief, faced him determinedly. "Bergljot," Gil murmured. Bergljot Gunnarsdottir from the hall, whose father farmed beyond Ulf Kolsson's lands.

They leaned toward each other, backs stiff, heads close, Bergljot's kerchief bobbing with vehemence, Arnkel's face red with anger, oblivious of Gil's approach until Lionheart whinnied a greeting to a packhorse tethered beyond. Startled, they both looked up. Then Arnkel suddenly grinned.

"Hey! Sliepnir!" He turned abruptly from Bergljot, and looking glad of the interruption, pointed at Lionheart and Gil's dangling feet. "Sliepnir! Six-legs!"

"Ha, ha." Gil smiled wearily. He glanced at Bergljot. The girl stood with arms folded, watching Arnkel impatiently. Gathering his reins, he nudged Lionheart discreetly to move on.

"It is good!" Arnkel persisted. "You put feet down and help

him up the hill!" He made a many-legged horse shape out of both hands.

Gil smiled again, but Ciarnan said quietly, "He's better than the nag you ride. And," he added, "Sliepnir has eight legs."

"Oh? Has he?" Arnkel turned red, annoyed to be corrected by an Irishman. "So, I give him eight legs!"

He bolted across the open ground between them and gripped the cantle of the jousting saddle to vault aboard.

"Don't ...." Gil warned, but already Lionheart was doing one of his extraordinary four-footed sideways shimmies. Body extended, legs scrabbling, Arnkel held on a moment too long and, losing his grip, sprawled, cursing, in the burn. Bergljot laughed aloud.

"Well, what did you expect?" Gil said evenly. Arnkel climbed, dripping and furious, to his feet. Gathering himself, he closed on Lionheart, raising a fist. Gil shook his head. "Don't even think about it."

"If I want to, I do it," Arnkel glanced at Bergljot and back at Gil and laid a deliberate hand on his sword hilt.

Instantly, Ciarnan and Ismail reached for theirs. Gil watched, unmoving and silent, until Arnkel slowly let his hand fall. Then he smiled and nodded carefully. "Thank you for the withies," he said. "When you pass the hall, you'll find a fleece lying by the door post. Please bring that to Eyolf, too." He smiled again and with a light salute of his hand and a brief nod to Bergljot, he rode on.

Lionheart forgot about the saddle and concentrated on being skittish instead, leaping at non-existent shadows and rearing twice when a seagull flew overhead.

Relax. Gil tightened the reins. *It's over.*

He hit me.

He did not hit you.

He said I had six legs. Lionheart stumbled in indignation.

No. He said WE had six legs. Like Sliepnir. Only Sliepnir has ...."

What's Sliepnir?"

Odin's horse.

What's Odin?

A god. Sliepnir's the god's horse.

Lionheart pricked regal ears. *A god's horse.* He trotted with noble demeanor for a while, then stopped, swishing his tail. *What's a god?*

Oh, let's not even go there. Gil sighed, swinging his dangling legs.

The track skirted the ridge of Odin's Stone and broadened on the leveler ground beyond. The boys came up and rode either side, their ponies jostling companionably. "Arnkel is not pleased with you," Ciarnan said cheerfully.

"He'll get over it."

Ismail smiled. "Bergljot is not pleased with Arnkel."

Gil turned and nodded. "I noticed."

Ismail's smile broadened. "So, maybe, she will be wife for Ragnar?"

Gil shook his head, "Don't think I didn't ask. But, no, Bergljot is one of the four hundred thousand girls on Hrolf's Isle who said 'No.'" He sighed, disconsolately flicking Lionheart's mane with the reins. "You wouldn't believe how many reasons girls can think of to say no. 'He's too old. He isn't old enough. He's too tall. He isn't tall enough. He looks too much like his father. He *doesn't* look like his father ....'"

Ismail laughed softly. "They love somebody else. That is problem. You find one who loves no one at all; she loves Ragnar."

Gil smiled with satisfaction. "I think I have."

In sight of Red Kol's hall, Gil turned Lionheart off the track and led the boys out along the cliff top, following by memory the way Floki had taken weeks before. Finding the narrow cleft in the over-hanging heather was a bigger challenge, with only the undulating hillside, and the alignment of distant islands, for guide.

Ciarnan and Ismail watched curiously as he reined Lionheart in on a small rise and dismounted. Beckoning them to do the same, he led the pony cautiously toward the cliff edge, testing the ground before him with each step.

Lionheart balked and he gave the bridle an irritated tug, keeping his eyes on the ground. *Move.* He tugged again. Lionheart reared, jerking the bridle from his grip, and Gil stumbled backward and felt his left foot slip into nothingness.

The boys laughed and then shouted in alarm as, flailing at air, he teetered on the crumbling ground, wrenched his body forward, and then flung himself blessedly on his face in the heather. Ismail and Ciarnan backed their ponies hastily to safety, staring at the ground. Gil struggled upright, grabbed Lionheart's mane, and cautiously turned.

The cleft lay at his feet. Rain in the night had weighed the fading heather down, covering the gap in the rock completely. He looked up at his pony, twitching his sensitive ears at the faint sound of the sea far below, and patted his mane.

When they had tethered their mounts at a safe distance, Gil led the way back to the cleft, which he had marked now carefully with a cross of broken heather twigs. Stretching out on the ground, he pulled himself to the edge and looked down. On either side, Ciarnan and Ismail did the same. As one, they cried aloud. Gil smiled. This time, there was no need for silence.

No mast swayed beneath the heather; no ship's deck lay far below. As Floki had assured him, the Golden Knight's raiders were gone, leaving nothing but the scorch marks of their fires to show they had ever been here.

"So deep!" Ismail turned his face toward Gil. "If Lionheart does not shy ...." He grinned and made a tumbling figure with his fingers.

"Old Sliepnir has his uses," Gil grinned back. "Come on," he got to his feet and edged cautiously back. "I want to find a way down."

At the cliff edge, the ground fell away precipitously to the sea and a pebble strand. Clinging to heather roots, they felt their way gingerly into a chute between two spines of rock and scrambled down, skidding on their heels and clutching at sea grass, riding an avalanche of sand.

Midway, they came upon an animal track which angled more sensibly down and followed that, coming out on a broad rocky shelf, crusted with seaweed and dotted with tidal pools. Gil jumped down onto the packed sand below, and with an eye to the restless sea, walked quickly to the hidden inlet beyond.

Shielded by a promontory of tide-marked stone, it was invisible to a landward approach and accessible only at low tide.

Even now, with wavelets lapping his boots as he worked his way around the promontory, it was virtually cut off. But on the far side of the rocky wall, the beach broadened into an inviting strip, wide enough to rest a ship, its upper reaches dry even at high tide. The strand below the opposite rock wall was even wider, and between the two, sea water ran deep and clear, to a broad crescent of shaded sand hidden within the hillside.

"So beautiful!" Ismail whispered, looking up at the high, broken ceiling where shafts of light, flickering with crying sea birds, drifted through the narrow cleft.

Gil looked up too, marveling at the play of sea and shadow and sunlight. *Like the church in Rome. Maria Rotunda, where Rachel came as a child.* But no man's hand had built this.

"So fine a harboring!" Ciarnan cried. "It takes a longship."

"Two," said Gil.

Mindful of the incoming tide, he walked quickly along the strip of sand, into the dim interior, until he was standing at the farthest reach of the inlet, where the walls narrowed and the rock ceiling closed in, forming a true cave.

Above the tideline, the keel drag of the Golden Knight's ship still marked the sand. Far back, where any smoke would swirl, unseen, below the rock roof, were the blackened remnants of his raiders' campfires. A litter of fish and animal bones lay charred amid half-burned twigs. And something else; something pale and fragile. Gil crouched and pulled from the ashes a scrap of scorched vellum. In places, the carefully scribed words could yet be seen.

"*Benedictus Dominus Deus Israel ....*"

Gil whirled. Ciarnan was standing behind him, reading the Latin he had learned as a boy-monk at Hy. He, too, crouched then, on the sand, raking the ashes and retrieving more scraps of vellum. "Ah, here," he said then. His hand fell on a rectangle of leather-bound wood, the cover of the ravaged book.

He stood, brushing ash off and revealing fragments of the leather that held yet a patterning of tooled knot work. Three patches of brighter color stood out, even under the coat of dust. "See, here," he said, his voice emotionless, "They take the hinges, the clasps. They are silver. Gold. This," he held up the beautifully worked leather and his handful of vellum, "Is nothing to them." He gave a manly shrug; then brushed a sooty hand across his face and turned away.

Gil said quietly, "We could take it to Aidan. Maybe he ...."

Ciarnan spun back, his jaw set and his eyes cold. "For what purpose?" He dropped the pages and the binding back into the ashes and kicked sand over them with his boot. "See? It is nothing to me as well. I am a Northman, now."

Gil watched him stalk away. Then he knelt and laid his own vellum page down on the sand and weighted it pointlessly with a shell. He looked up at the soaring roof above him, shimmering in its ever-changing light, and thought of Hakon Sea-Friend, even now on Irish shores, playing the Northman's game. And then, of himself, helming *Silver Dragon* on the sea-road to Francia, with thirty young men beneath his sail.

He sat back on his heels and closed his eyes. *Sheep, cattle, merchants' silver, if I must. But not this. Never this.* Rising quickly, he hastened to join Ciarnan and Ismail where the tide was already lapping at the sea-cave's guardian walls.

Eager to be away, Gil led the boys at a canter back along the cliff path, until they again looked down on Red Kol's hall. Sturdy cattle dotted the pastureland. Fields and byres were tidy and well cared for. He nodded, pleased. Having found a girl who was willing, he wanted to do right by her. And by her suspicious father.

"Willing," he considered, as he turned Lionheart's head to the farm track, was perhaps an exaggeration. Asgerd's own words were, to be exact, "Not if he were the last man on the Island." But Janetta and Rachel had both laughed when he morosely confided his latest failure.

"That is good!" Janetta said. "She has noticed him."

And Rachel added, "And she fancies him." To Gil's incredulous look she said loftily, "Well, she's not going to tell *you*, is she?"

Encouraged, he tried again; reciting the prospective husband's virtues at her father's hearth, while her parents listed their daughter's fine qualities in return, and Asgerd spooned milk down the throat of a half-grown lamb and looked bored.

But then, the milk finished, she tugged the lamb's ears fondly, wiped her hands on her apron, and with a weary sigh, agreed to meet Ragnar Kolsson.

"Are girls a different species?" Gil asked Ismail suddenly.

Ismail gave him his wide white smile. "You do not know this? You the earl of Hrolf's Isle?"

The twelve-year-old serving maid who opened Red Kol's door to them, stared wide-eyed at Gil, too awed to speak. Hastily tucking wisps of pale hair beneath her kerchief, she beckoned them into the hall; then scurried out, pointing to the fields beyond, her eyes still on Gil as he passed.

Ciarnan punched his shoulder. "Another conquest! The women of Hrolf's Isle tumble before you!" He raised a hand to his forehead and pretended to swoon.

Gil winced. "She's probably trying to remember who I am." He made his way cautiously into the hall and stood grimly surveying its shadowy depths.

"So dark," Ismail murmured.

Peering into the gloom, Gil made out the wan glow of a hearth fire, burning so low that the smoke made no effort to rise to the roof, but swirled at chest height through the room. Barely visible in the murk, a hunched, shawled figure bent, witch-like, over a cauldron.

"She will stand all day before *that* boils," Ciarnan muttered. He shivered and wrapped his cloak close.

Farm implements littered the straw-strewn floor, left where they were dropped at day's end. The remnants of a meal sat forlorn at one end of a long feasting board, though Gil suspected feasts here were few and far between. The floor was so thick with mud tramped in from the farmyard that he could not tell if stone or bare earth lay beneath. Above, drying fish festooned the rafters, mingling their smoky tang with the byre scents below.

Gil whispered, "I see why Floki thought it needed a woman."

"It needs a fire-raising," said Ciarnan.

Gil smiled wryly and then jumped as something moved in the straw and let out a loud squawk. The old woman at the cauldron never looked up, even when the squawk came again, even louder. Gil's eyes fell on the source: something grey and bright-eyed, creeping toward him on splayed grey feet.

"It is devil!" Ciarnan jumped back.

Ismail laughed. "It is seagull." He crouched and held out his hand. But the creature advanced instead on Gil, as if acknowledging his rank.

"He keeps a *seagull* in here?" he groaned.

"You have goats," Ciarnan reminded him.

"*Percy* has goats. And they're going. Soon."

The goats were a bone of contention. Gil had drawn the line at the ram-lamb they brought back from Norway, shutting it firmly into a pen before any attempt could be made at bringing it in. But Percy drew his own line at the now large and boisterous goat kids. "Floki said I could keep them and it's *Floki's* room."

That Gil did not dispute, and indeed he had tried hard to relinquish the earl's private quarters to Hakon. But Hakon, in his solemn courteous way, was as stubborn as Percy and slept aboard his ship rather than take Gil's entitlement as his cousin's heir.

It was expected. A lot was expected, Gil had come to realize in the weeks since his return from Norway. It was expected that he would sleep apart from his warriors. It was expected that he would take Floki's place at the High Table. It was expected that he would pass judgements on disputes of boundaries and livestock and fish pools, between men old enough to be his grandfather. And, he thought dismally, looking down at the grey speckled back of the seagull, *it was expected* that he find wives for men who didn't know a house from a byre.

The seagull stamped its feet, cocked its head, walked in a circle, and making a shrill peeping whistle that seemed to come from everywhere, looked up at Gil. "What does it want?" he protested.

"Food," Ciarnan said. He pointed to Gil's mouth. "Cough up some fish, like its mother does."

Gil looked up at the herring-laden rafters and down at the

gull. "What are your wings for? Get your own!"

It walked in another circle, peeping disconsolately, and then suddenly raised its wings and ran flapping to the door. The latch clicked open and the little serving maid scurried in, inched her way around the seagull and then stood twisting her hands together and staring again at Gil.

Red Kol followed; a sickle in one hand, a whetting stone in the other; white hair and beard tousled by the wind. The gull retreated from his stamping feet but rushed back as Ragnar stepped quietly into the hall and began circling and whistling before him. Smiling, he crouched down in the muddy straw, drew a piece of dried fish from a pocket, and dropped it into the bird's open beak.

"We have guests," Red Kol said sharply.

Ragnar nodded and smiled again, gave the seagull a second piece of fish, and then gathered the bird up in his arms, where it remained, placid as a housecat with its beak resting on his shoulder, as he stood and crossed the room.

Red Kol lowered his bulk onto a bench and indicated with a nod of his head, that Gil and the boys should do the same. When they were seated, and Ragnar, still holding his seagull, had perched on the end of the feasting board, he took up his whetstone and gave the sickle a rasping scrape. "Early in the day for talk," he said, striking the sickle again. "Work does not end with harvest."

Gil nodded agreement.

Ragnar smiled wearily, "Work never ends."

Kol cast him a sharp glance. "Do beasts cease to eat? Does the land plough itself? Does rust no longer come upon tools because the sun has set early?" Ragnar shook his head and stroked the gull's sleek feathers.

"No, father," he said quietly.

"Then work does not end." Red Kol tossed back a lock of his snowy hair and fixed his dark eyes on Gil. "The answer is 'no,'" he said. "He does not sail with you." Before Gil could reply, he went on, striking the whetstone on the sickle with each sentence. "I have one son." Scrape. "No grandson." Scrape. "Not even a nephew or a fosterling." Double scrape. He lowered the sickle and laid the whetstone on his knee. "My wife dies young." He swept them all with an old man's weary gaze. "Too young." His voice trailed to silence. Gil opened his mouth to offer sympathy, but behind him, Ismail suddenly spoke.

"In my village, when I am child, there is a man, as you, only one son. Then, that son marries. Each year, there is child. Some years, two! Soon, he has so many sons they call him Grandfather of Village!" he laughed lightly, nodding to Kol.

But Kol only shook his head and shrugged one shoulder toward Ragnar. "He does not marry."

"Maybe ...." Gil began, but Kol raised the whetstone and struck the sickle a ringing blow, cutting him off. He worked away at the blade, holding it up and studying the edge, then scraping again. Then he set both tools down and looked out across the smoky room.

"There are men," he said, "Who light up a hall the way the sun lights the sea." He paused. "Men like the earl."

Gil smiled and nodded agreement. Kol wasn't the first man to forget the earldom had changed hands. But then Kol turned and looked straight at him and said, "And men like you."

Gil heard Ciarnan's smothered bark of laughter. Even Ismail was hiding a grin. He shook his head emphatically, but Red Kol persisted. "Surely, this is so! Look," he jerked his white-bearded chin toward the serving maid, "That child does not take her eyes from you." He turned and addressed the girl, "You! Go help your grandmother."

The serving maid ran to the old woman at the hearth, her face red. But no redder, Gil was sure, than his own. "Those are the men women choose," Kol concluded. "Him," he gave Ragnar a dismissive but not unfriendly nod, "They do not notice."

Gil took a deep breath. "One has," he said.

———

Back on his pony and riding away, Gil offered Ismail a gleeful high-five. "Good man!" he grinned. "You got us our meeting."

Ismail shrugged uncertainly. "Do you think he really comes?"

Ciarnan joggled up behind them, bareback on his plough horse, and laughed. "If his father lets him."

"No problem there." Gil twisted around in the jousting saddle, hand on the high cantle. To Ciarnan's doubtful look, he added, "When he started asking about her father's cattle, I knew we'd won."

"And Asgerd?" Ismail said then. "Does *she* come?"

Gil nodded. "I think when Asgerd decides something, it's decided. And nothing stands in her way."

"Except a seagull?" Ciarnan grinned.

"That is *really* no problem."

"You sure?" Ciarnan scratched his head, incredulous.

Gil smiled. "The whole time I was there, she was hand-feeding a lamb that was at least as old as Percy's and might just manage to eat grass."

"A pet?" Ismail asked.

"Well, like the seagull. Something orphaned, needing to be cared for. And she's someone who needs to be caring for something. Like Ragnar."

"Hey, you clever man!" Ismail smiled.

"Not half as smart as you, with that story from your village. How old were you then?"

Ismail shrugged. "I am not yet born. It is old story. Another time. Another village. But all villages the same. And all men the same."

"And women?"

"All different," Ismail grinned.

Gil looked ruefully out over Lionheart's ears at Hrolf's Isle, stretched out before him. "Why didn't he make *you* earl?"

Gil rose before dawn on the morning of the meeting, creeping from his pitch-black bedchamber without disturbing even a goat. But, as every morning, a huddle of people awaited him around the newly stoked hearth fire, with concerns and complaints to be addressed.

Most were small and easily managed; a lame cow which

he sent to Shony, wise in such things; a kitchen maid with a burnt hand who he took, himself, to Aidan. An argument over a fishing net borrowed and not returned was settled by a loan of Gil's own.

Other larger grievances, an accusation of the theft of a lamb, a sudden feud between Arnkel Fish-Tail and Bergljot's brother, must be kept for the gathering of the chieftains upon Hakon Sea-Friend's return. Which could not come soon enough as far as Gil was concerned.

Leaving the longhouse, he searched the horizon hopefully for Hakon's sail. But the sea was empty; the rousts gentle at slack tide and the Holy Isle misty and peaceful in the late autumn sun. He remembered Janetta telling him how Floki would retreat there to tend the little garden alone and laughed softly, understanding.

But at least now he was free for a day on the hill, escorting Asgerd to the shielings for her carefully planned tryst with Ragnar Kolsson.

High and windswept, crowning the island in all its sea-wrapped beauty, the summer shelters were a traditional meeting place of young men and women, where, tending their mingled cattle, they could share laughter and song and quiet moments far from the eyes of their elders. Gil himself had gone there with Janetta throughout the summer, looking after Ulf Kolsson's beasts and lingering into the long, white nights.

Now, with winter coming on, the hill would be loud with young voices calling back and forth as each farmer's cows were gathered from the common herd and driven, with summer calves at heel, to the shelter of lower ground.

Ragnar and Asgerd could meet by apparent chance among them, share a simple meal, and work side by side. Even Red Kol would approve. And, with luck, Gil and Janetta could do the same.

She was waiting patiently on her pony at the foot of the hill track, his inevitable bodyguards waiting, too. Lionheart flicked his ears forward, catching sight of her, and began to trot, his usual miseries over the saddle forgotten.

Why don't I just give you to her.

Lionheart whickered happy agreement.

And then, Gil thought dangerously, *I could get a real horse.*

A real horse?

Well, bigger.

Lionheart's ears flattened and he stepped sideways, working up a buck.

No, no. Bad idea. Joke. Too late. *But the good thing about the jousting saddle,* Gil smiled to himself as his pony bounced, spring-loaded, into the air, *it's about impossible to get bucked out of.* Firmly planted between over-sized pommel and luxuriant cantle, he sat like a rock until with a shuddering wheeze, Lionheart gave up.

Aidan's bell was ringing the third hour when they at last left the home farm and Gil's duties behind. The day was glorious, the sea white-flecked and with the tide turning, the gull-haunted rousts again sounding their distant roar. Janetta brought her pony up so close to Lionheart that they could hold hands as they mounted the hill, while Ismail and Ciarnan had the courtesy to drop far behind.

And, thankfully, the good sense to hurriedly catch up, when they spotted Magnus Redbeard ahead, laboring with a pick at a small rocky spring. When they drew abreast, he straightened his back and surveyed them sourly. Gil smiled and said, "A fine day, Magnus."

"Fine for those with time to play." Magnus hunched a shoulder toward the spring. Ferns and moss grew so thick around it that the water was a dark glimmer in their shadows. "I clear this at seed time. While you and my son are chasing shadows in Rome. No one clears it since."

"I'll send someone," Gil said quickly.

"Pasture without water is no pasture."

"I said ...." Gil stopped. "Fine." He turned Lionheart aside and rode on.

Once beyond hearing, Janetta said, "It is not about the spring."

"Oh, no," Gil murmured, thinking how an earldom could dwindle in a man's mind to one resented heap of stones. Then he laughed, "I know! I'll send Red Kol. Since they're the only two on Hrolf's Isle who work!"

A sturdy brown mare, roughly saddled with a sheepskin, stood untethered and unattended outside Asgerd's house, a pretty buff foal beside it. In the doorway, Asgerd's parents waited side by side, dressed in their best formal clothes. Silver brooches and strings of bright beads adorned her mother's blue tunic. A fine velvet cloak was draped over her father's broad farmer's shoulders.

When Gil dismounted, guiltily conscious of his own shabby work attire, they stepped forward and made small, precise bows; an honor he was sure he did not deserve, though no doubt *it was expected*.

He smiled, looking around cautiously for a sign of their daughter. "She makes herself ready," the woman said. "She would make a good appearance."

Her husband let out a gruff, gleeful laugh, silenced by a look from his wife. But he turned, then, and shouted into the interior, "Daughter! The earl awaits you."

Gil smiled again, awkwardly, and then Asgerd burst from the house, striding past her parents, plaiting hanks of honey-blond hair as she did. Whipping the strands together with swift, rough hands, as if it were the tail of a horse, she finished, knotted a scrap of frayed linen around the end, and nodded cheerfully to Gil.

He thought suddenly of Danni, when they were children, and grinned, glad anyhow to be put back in his proper place. Giving Janetta a friendly smile, Asgerd saluted Gil's bodyguards, ran to the waiting mare, and vaulted aboard, revealing the startling sight of a pair of man's breeches, beneath her skirt.

Catching up a halter-rope rein, she pressed light heels into her mount's flanks. The mare's head came up, ears pricked joyfully, and she leapt forward, and with her foal romping beside her, galloped from the yard. Gil hastily swung into his saddle and sent Lionheart galloping after, with the rest of Asgerd's attendants trailing behind. The mare slowed as the track steepened and Gil brought Lionheart up at her side.

Asgerd turned and grinned. She was a tall, long-limbed girl, broad-shouldered as a man, with a lean, sun-tanned face and a wide happy smile that lit up her grey eyes. "Forgive me," she said, "But if I stay, my mother sends me back for silver beads and brooches, so Ragnar Kolsson knows we are not poor. We are not. But if that matters to Ragnar Kolsson, I do not want him for a husband. Or even a friend."

Gil watched as the foal ran to its mother and nuzzled against Asgerd's leg. She crooned to it and drew a slice of apple from a pocket beneath her tunic. He smiled. "I think I know what matters to Ragnar," he said. "And it isn't silver."

When the others had caught up, Asgerd drew her mare into line with Janetta's pony and the two rode ahead talking and laughing together. Gil dropped back with Ismail and Ciarnan. "I think she needs no escort," Ciarnan said.

Ismail grinned, "Perhaps Ragnar needs escort?"

"He's on his own," said Gil.

The shielings lay in the center of the island, scattered over a hollow of yellowing grassland. There were ten in all, small, windowless stone buildings, with doorways so low that a tall man must bend nearly double to enter. Some were roofed with thatch; most, just tented over with sailcloth. Of those, three had already been stripped of their roofs for winter, their rough wood rafters bare against the sky. Peat smoke rose, sweet-scented, above those yet in use.

Black, brown and buff cattle sprinkled the surrounding hillsides and in the distance, two boys were driving a small, lowing herd down from more distant pastures. Nearer, a group of girls perched on little wooden stools and sang softly together as they milked cows tethered only by love. Nearer still, Ragnar Kolsson teetered on the stone stoop of the first rough shelter, peering anxiously down the track. He waved an arm, as if they could possibly miss him in all that emptiness, then stood, boyish and awkward, hands hanging loose at his sides.

"So much for playing hard to get." Gil grinned and nudged

Lionheart forward. But Asgerd, with another touch of her heels, sent her own horse cantering ahead to the shieling. Gil laughed. "Not playing hard to get either."

She jumped down, roughly smoothing her skirt over her half-hidden breeches and strode forward with a happy smile. Ragnar opened his mouth to speak but then ducked his head like a balking pony and stared fixedly at the ground before his feet.

Look at her, Gil pleaded silently. But Ragnar stayed transfixed by his tuft of grass. And when Lionheart halted before the shieling, Asgerd had found her own piece of turf on which to fix her now unsmiling gaze.

Gil swung down from his saddle and hurried to intervene, but Janetta leaned down from her pony, smiled, and shook her head. "He is a man," she whispered.

"Not acting like one," Gil whispered back.

She smiled again. "Come. Let them have only each other."

They retreated then, leading their ponies over one of the heather-brown ridges that rimmed the hollow, with Ismail and Ciarnan following behind. Once out of sight of the shielings, Gil sent the boys off on the useful pretext of seeking out home farm cattle, freed Lionheart from his despised saddle, and tethered him with Janetta's pony, to graze. Janetta spread a linen cloth on a mossy rock and laid out a small feast of bannocks, blackberries, and cheese, which they hastily devoured before, crumb-sprinkled and berry smeared, they fell happily into each other's arms.

The sky above cleared to a perfect blue, and the wind died away to nothing. Gil stretched out luxuriantly on the warm grass, listening to the lowing of cattle and delighting in the reds and golds that the sun somehow found in Janetta's black hair. *I am in the most beautiful place in the world, with the most beautiful girl in the world. NOW, I am earl of Hrolf's Isle ….*

"Should we not see how they are?"

"Give them time," Gil said dreamily. But, sitting up and gauging the angle of the sun, he realized a whole lot of time had already passed. He got up and tentatively crept back up the little ridge and slowly raised his head, ready to duck in an instant if things had advanced more than he should see. But a quick glance dashed that happy thought.

Their meal finished, the couple sat stiff as two stumps of wood, their faces half turned aside. Their ponies, grazing behind them, looked friendlier by far. Ragnar studied the broad backs of his hands. Asgerd held out a clump of grass to the foal. Neither said a word.

Gil lowered himself out of sight, crept back to Janetta, and flopped down in despair. "He's hopeless. I'm surprised she hasn't just jumped on her pony and ridden home."

"She does not wish to ride home," Janetta said. "She likes him. And he likes her. They do not have words; that is all."

"Well, if they can't speak, they can't get married, can they?"

Janetta smiled, untroubled. "There are other ways of speaking than words." She pulled him closer and kissed him, but that just made it worse.

"If Asgerd did that," Gil groaned, "*Ragnar* would jump on his pony and ride home." He rolled on his back, staring gloomily at the sky, and then sat up again and slapped his forehead. "I should have brought her *there*. If she had seen him with that seagull ... Yes! The seagull! Why didn't I think of that?" He jumped to his feet. "Quick! Your hair ribbons," he said.

Janetta stared, bewildered, but obeyed. While she loosened the bands of braid binding her long loose hair, Gil searched their sheltered coire for a gorse bush and came back with a thorny twig in his hand. Still baffled, Janetta held out the ribbons as Gil broke off the longest thorn, and, wincing, drove it into the soft flesh between two fingers.

"Why do you do that?" she cried. "It will hurt!"

"Sure does." He grinned, took the ribbons, and made a careful circle on the ground.

"You will be the Cat? Here?" she stared still at the thorn impaling his hand. "But why that?"

"Because I haven't got a broken wing." He grinned again, jumped into the circle and whispered the blessing to the wide blue sky.

It hurt even more when he was Cat. Though Cat was sensible enough to sit down and try to gnaw it free. "No! Go," Janetta gave him an undignified shove from behind, and Cat got up and trotted, limping, toward the ridge. At the top, in view of the shieling below, he sat down and licked his paw.

Asgerd saw him first. Slumped disconsolately beside Ragnar, her boots stretched mannishly out before her, she suddenly straightened and stared at the small patch of orange that had appeared amidst the heather. "Look!" she cried, her face brightening. "It is a cat. A little cat!" Ragnar raised his head, his gaze following her pointing finger. Cat looked up at the movement and then returned to gnawing at the thorn. "What does it do here?" Asgerd said, "So far from any farm?"

Ragnar got slowly to his feet. Cat did the same and stood on three legs, the sore paw raised. "It is lost," Ragnar said. Cat lowered his paw and, sniffing the air, limped toward the shieling.

"And look! It is lame," cried Asgerd.

Ragnar nodded his red head solemnly. "It is lost and lame."

Cat limped closer. When they both moved cautiously to meet him, Cat shied away, limping convincingly back up the hill. Asgerd and Ragnar signaled to each other, moved apart, and began a cautious circling stalk.

Cat sat down and nibbled morosely at his paw until Ragnar's hands clamped suddenly around his furry middle. Forgetting his purpose, he let out a yowl of outrage and scraped red claw welts down Ragnar's wrists. Ragnar laughed gently and closed his big friendly fingers on Cat's scruff. "Fierce cat," he said admiringly. "Fine, fierce cat." With his free hand he tickled behind Cat's ears.

Finely and fiercely, Cat hung helpless, forelegs splayed, scruff pinned. His nose wriggled at a new human scent and then Asgerd was there, taking each of his forepaws between gentle fingers, until she found the thorn. "Poor cat," she murmured. "Poor lost little cat. Poor lost little cat with a thorn … ow!" She grinned and giggled, holding up the fresh-plucked gorse-spine with one hand and sucking the bloody fingers of the other.

Then she leaned forward and to Cat's consternation, kissed the top of his head. Her messy, half-undone plait of hair flopped over him, tickling his nose and he batted it away with his newly de-thorned paw. Ragnar laughed and lifted the hair carefully and smoothed it back over her shoulder.

Asgerd looked up and Ragnar's fingers slipped from her plait. Above Cat's head, the couple smiled hesitantly into each other's eyes. *Time we were out of here*, Gil reminded his Other.

But Ragnar had shifted Cat onto his broad forearm and was stroking him under his chin with one calloused finger, while Asgerd tickled each of his ears. Blissfully, Cat began to purr. "He likes you!" Asgerd cried. "You must keep him." Cat purred louder.

Hey, fur-face! Move. Asgerd, maybe; but I'm not making love to Ragnar Kolsson! With a last rumble Cat reluctantly wriggled free, sprang to the ground, and loped, pleasingly four-footed, up the hill. Asgerd crouched down low and called to him. Cat slowed and looked back, holding up one paw.

Ragnar leaned down over the girl, his gentle hand on her shoulder. "He will not stay," he said. "He has gone to the wild, as they sometimes do. We must let him go."

Cat swished his striped tail, stalked to the crest of the ridge and sat down, looking wild. Asgerd sighed. "I so wish to have a cat. But my mother says they steal the cheese. Surely, it is the mice that do that." She scuffed a boot against a tuft of grass.

"I have three fine cats," Ragnar answered her, "who steal no cheese. And one is in kit. I bring a kitten to you, when I return from Francia. It is then young and foolish, yet, and will charm your mother."

Asgerd watched Cat longingly and gave a doubtful shrug. "Perhaps if you cover it with silver."

Ragnar laughed, suddenly the bold, confident swordsman. "I bring that, too," he said.

Yes! Cat jumped up, streaked over the ridge, bounded down the other side and leapt joyfully into Janetta's arms.

CHAPTER NINE

"What's that for, Gil?" Percy squinted his eyes nearly shut and rubbed his nose with the back of a grubby hand. Gil slid a hazel sapling into place, waited while Ismail bound it with a withy, and picked up another. "What's it *for*, Gil?"

"It's a fence." Gil stepped back, surveying his work. A screen of neatly slanted hazel poles, strengthened by a driftwood frame, enclosed three sides of a square, abutting the stone wall of the cow byre. Within, a new turf-roofed lean-to stood ready.

"What for?" Percy repeated.

Gil turned and grinned. "You."

Percy scratched his head. Ismail finished trimming another sapling and handed it to Gil. "We make better fence than lance, I think."

Gil smiled. "Solved that problem." He shrugged a shoulder toward the boatyard on the strand. "Master Shipwright Eyolf Grimsson: two lances, steel-tipped, coming right up."

"Is it for my goats?"

Gil fastened another pole.

"*Gil.*"

"It's for your sheep," Gil said. "Okay?"

"Okay." Percy stared suspiciously at the turf-roofed shelter.

"*And* your goats."

"Gil! You promised!"

"I did not promise."

"But Floki said …."

"Floki," Gil said for what felt like the thousandth time since Norway, "is not here." He looked grimly up at the sky.

A trailing vee of wild geese appeared above the Holy Isle,

winging their way southward. Gil watched, knowing soon he would follow under his own great wing of sail. Another high dark shape angled in from the heights of Hrolf's Isle, drew nearer, and slipped into a place at the edge of the vee. "What are you looking at, Gil?" Percy prodded him unhappily.

"Your sister." He watched her enviously, so free and far from everything.

Percy looked up. "Is she flying away?"

"No."

"She will."

Gil shook his head. *Not now*, he thought. *Not until she's kept her promise ....*

"She will," Percy said again with solemn certainty. "One day."

A shout from beyond the byre caught Gil's attention. A horseman appeared, galloping down from the southerly promontory, waving an arm. Ismail watched his approach. "Karl," he said.

"And here comes Ari," Gil grinned. "Not about to be beaten to it." From the heights to the north, another rider appeared, shouting and gesturing, too. The boys were cousins from the Horse Isle, both fourteen; the youngest who would sail with Gil. He had entrusted them with the watch of the longhouse strand, a vital but not too challenging task, which they embraced with rivalrous enthusiasm.

The two horses veered closer and on the high ground above the longhouse drew side by side and galloped abreast before skidding to a halt beside the cow byre. Karl was quicker from the saddle, but Ari, the faster runner, reached Gil first. "Sail!" he gasped, pointing wildly at the sea.

"Two sails!" his cousin panted stumbling to Gil's side. "Beyond the Spear Isle!"

"It's the Golden Knight!" Ari cried.

Ismail straightened and set aside his bundle of withies. Gil dropped the hazel sapling he held, ran to the rear of the longhouse, and scrambled up a roof pillar onto the over-hanging eaves. With Ismail on his heels, he raced up the long slope of yellowing turf until he stood astride the rooftree, looking far out to sea.

Late autumn dusk was already dimming the horizon. Low cloud, borne on a stiff north-westerly, shrouded the Horse Isle, and the rousts of the tide race were hazed in spray. A blue smudge against the darker blue of dusk marked the distant Spear Isle. Close-hauled against the wind, the two ships rounded its southern tip, struggling to outrace the night.

Gil watched until they came about, revealing the graceful profile of the first. Her white sail was unadorned, her masthead bore no pennant, but he would always know her anywhere.

"Do we fight?" Karl shouted eagerly from below. Ari waved his sword.

"Yes," Gil called down with a grin. "But not today. It is Hakon Sea-Friend home from Ireland."

"*Sea-Raven*," Ismail smiled. "But whose ship is that, then?" He pointed to the second sail, checked red and white, the colors barely visible in the murk.

Gil's grin broadened. "Yours," he said.

Ismail spun around so quickly that he staggered on the sloping roof. "What?"

"Ragnvald's kept his word," Gil said. "A ship and her crew. Thirty oarsmen. And we have thirty. Sixty fighting men. More, if we wanted." The news that Ragnar Kolsson had joined him had swept the island like a brushfire. Now, everyone wanted to sail. "She's yours, Ismail."

Ismail watched the approaching ship and shook his head. "No way."

"You'll be fine."

"I am land man," Ismail pleaded.

"You," Gil laughed softly, "are anything you decide to be. Horseman. Swordsman," he paused. "helmsman. Nobody learns things faster and nobody learns them better. You're brilliant with the skiff."

"When I'm not ...." Ismail tilted his hand back and forth, miming a choppy sea and looked convincingly sick.

"Even then." Gil glanced back at the ships. "You'll helm her and leave me and *Silver Dragon* standing. Then *I* make you earl."

Night had fallen when the weary crews guided their ships to land, hulls black in the flickering light of the watch fires, loosened sails, fluttering ghosts. *Sea-Raven's* dark-winged figurehead loomed menacingly over the strand. From the Shetlanders' prow, a white swan with curving neck and fierce black eyes glared down above the name, *Star-Seeker.*

Gil called an order and his rope men surged into the sea, shouting for lines. Shadowy figures moved on the decks above and ropes snaked out into their hands. Working together with the oarsmen aboard, they hauled both vessels up onto the strand, while Gil waited, cloak-wrapped in the icy wind, to welcome his brother earl home.

It was a quiet return; tired men seeking only food and sleep. But tomorrow, the ward fire would flare at Odin's Stone, summoning the chieftains to greet one earl and bid another farewell. Then, amid feasting and song, the tales of adventure would be told, and the bounty of trading and of raiding displayed for all to admire.

For now, the only treasure to be unloaded was a fine Irish bull, purchased for the home farm in Dublin and bellowing already to his prospective brides ashore. Hakon himself led the beast down the gangplank, his crew stumbling down after. Hair and beards wind tangled, cloaks crusted with salt, they walked with the unsteady lurch of men long at sea.

The Shetlanders followed shyly, young and wide-eyed at their first adventure, and not half as dour as Floki had promised. Indeed, their helmsman, a sturdy older man called Svein Sveinsson, beamed cheerful good humor as they strode up the fire lit pathway to the hall.

———

Three days later, *Star-Seeker* sailed the tide-race of the Holy Isle, a crew of Shetland and Hrolf's Isle men on the oars, and Ismail at the helm. Aboard his own beached ship's deck, Gil stood up on the rails of the half-built pony pen and craned his neck to watch.

Her checked sail reefed and taut, the longship heeled beautifully, riding the crests of the breaking waves. The African boy's slim body was braced against the steering oar; Svein

Sveinsson stood rock steady at his side. "Thank you, Ragnvald," Gil murmured. A better ship and a better crew, he could not have asked.

A flood of gratitude filled him for the grey-bearded Shetlander showing him such unearned loyalty and then for the loyalty of so many others. The men on the shore provisioning his ship. The carpenters and shipwrights repairing damaged strakes. The women of the weaving sheds painstakingly mending her sail. The women of the kitchens packing fish and meal into casks. The blacksmith sharpening old tools and forging new ones. The farm boys bringing down bedding and fodder for the ponies.

He smiled as Ari and Karl raced each other to the gangplank with new lengths of timber for the pen, scuffling to be first up onto the deck. Young men's eagerness and young men's courage made a longship crew. But the hard work of an island sent her to sea.

The boys arrived at his side, panting and throwing punches. Gil re-directed their energies to their hammers and mauls. "Make it sound," he warned gruffly. "Loose ponies sink ships." Awed, they went to work with new solemnity. Gil turned his face aside to hide his grin, and looked out across the strand, adorned now with the warships of his chieftains. Their presence spoke louder than any words of the trust placed in him; a trust he must not fail. His eyes flicked instinctively to the guarded heights overlooking the shore.

"What are you watching?" Ari said uneasily.

"Birds. Get back to work." Gil jumped down from the rail with a sudden memory of Danni perching there on their first voyage from Einar's Holm. So long ago: Lionheart bemoaning his sea-bound fate; Ismail sea-sick and lost; himself, half terrified, half exalted by the glorious expanse of northern waters. And Floki Magnusson swaggering at the helm; so fierce, and yet, Gil thought back, so young as well; a boy himself, in love with a girl from a faraway land.

He looked up to the longhouse where curls of wood smoke proclaimed preparations for the night's feast underway, directed by that same girl. His chieftains would be already gathering around the long hearth. Giving the boys their final instructions, he descended the gangplank to take up his duties as earl. As always, there would be serious matters to discuss, and after the feasting and gift-giving, and before the recitations and song, the usual petitions would be heard. But, thankfully, now Hakon Sea-Friend would be at his side.

An earl for the longhouse, Floki had called him, and Gil had no doubt that Ragnvald's somber thoughtful son would address old men's disputes and young men's feuds far better than he could himself. Then, at last, all would be done. Buoyed by his poet's praises and his chieftain's farewells, he could turn his eyes to the sea. As he strode up the busy strand, stopping half a dozen times to answer queries or settle disagreements, his heart felt light and his mind free, as if *Silver Dragon's* prow was already questing south.

In the open space before the hall, Ciarnan was schooling the two ponies Gil had bought on the Horse Isle for Janetta and Rachel. Riding one and leading the other, he cantered in a wide ring, turned and cantered the opposite way. Gil watched, admiring the Irish boy's easy grace; bareback, legs hanging loose, head slightly cocked, listening to the sound of their hoof beats by which alone he seemed able to judge their fitness.

Hrafn, the black mare Gil had chosen for Janetta, was slim-limbed and glossy, with a delicate head and a mane and tail sweeping the ground. Hoping he had not been deluded by appearances, he called, "How is she?"

Ciarnan slowed both ponies, turned them, and trotted to Gil. "Very fine," he reached and patted the mare's sweaty neck. "Both very fine. Grani is stronger," he ruffled the mane of the dapple grey beside him, "But Hrafn the swifter. She will do well for Janetta who is so small. And Grani will give Rachel a challenge so she forgets Freya, left behind, and loves this one. Also, she will not be a Sliepnir." Ciarnan grinned, pointing at Gil's long legs.

"Good," Gil said. "One Sliepnir is plenty." He felt shyly proud. No one knew horses like Ciarnan, and Ciarnan's praise was not easily won.

He went on toward the open doors of the hall, but suddenly

stopped, staring at his newly built goat pen by the cow byre. A bright splash of color showed, low down, through the slatted fencing. "Percy?" he called suspiciously.

Making a swift detour, he trotted up to the fence and leaned over the top rail. The two black goats playfully head-butted, trying out their new-sprung horns. The Norwegian ram vigorously tugged tufts of grass. Wrapped in his bright red cloak, Percy sat cross-legged at the foot of the byre's stone wall. "Get up off the ground," Gil said. "It's too cold."

Percy stayed stubbornly sitting. "*They're* on it."

"They have fur. And hooves."

"I have ...."

"Get up, Percy."

The boy's lip came out in a pout, but seeing Gil's face, he quickly stood. He wrapped his arms around one of his evicted pets. "They're cold."

Gil leaned over the fence and patted the other. "Under all that?" He buried his hand in the goat's shaggy fur.

"They're cold *inside*," Percy said firmly, "and I'm going to sleep in here with them."

Gil looked down at the longhouse where five chieftains awaited their earl. *Why goats, Floki? Why not kittens? Or maybe a puppy?* He nodded solemnly to Percy. "Fine. But if Vikings come to steal you in the night, shout *really loud*, okay?"

"Vikings?" Percy rubbed a pudgy hand against his nose.

"Like *really* loud."

Halfway back to the hall, Gil slowed, hearing the footsteps behind him. "I'm coming now," Percy said. "But only for tonight."

Gil smiled, leaned over, and wrapped the red cloak closer. "Now that's a really good idea. Because there's a feast tonight. And I need my cupbearer to pour the chieftains' wine."

After the grey, cold light of the fading autumn day, the hall was a haven of warmth and color, rich with the scents of baking bread and roasting meat. The golden glow of the hearth fire and the flickering flames of torches burnished the beautiful stolen wall paneling that Gil guiltily loved. Men and women in tunics and cloaks of red and green, violet and blue, crowded the long room. Their voices mingled cheerfully with the gay notes of the harps, as Eoin and Niall, back to back before the High Table, playfully traded melodies.

And then, as Gil stepped past the watchful bulk of Bjorn Break-Neck at the door, the speakers fell silent, the harpers stilled their fingers, and even the children, clustered around the blind poet's dog, ceased their play. Expectant faces turned toward Gil, and two old men, toasting their outstretched legs by the fire, respectfully got to their feet.

"No," Gil whispered, feeling a strange mix of embarrassment and disbelief; an eerie parody of his all too recent walk of shame before Floki's mocking gaze. Only, the pillared high seat was empty now, and there was no mockery in any of the eyes fixed on him. Even Hakon Sea-Friend, standing modestly before an array of tools, cloth, weapons, and silver ware—fruit of his Dublin voyage—bowed his head slightly as Gil passed.

But, as the gathering parted around him, Gil was aware of one voice that spoke boldly yet, one man who had not turned to greet him. A bearskin flung over his shoulders, arms and neck adorned with silver, an ale horn in his hand, Magus Redbeard commanded the hall that had been his son's as once he commanded Einar's Holm.

And, as at Einar's Holm, his gaze passed over Gil as if he were no more than a roof post. Neither raising nor lowering his voice, he continued regaling Hrafn Bare-Chin of some battle tale, even as Hrafn's eyes strayed uncomfortably to the face of his young earl.

Nodding to the old chieftain, Gil walked calmly to his own private quarters at the head of the hall. Percy trotted after, watching Gil, and then Magnus, and then Gil, with puzzled eyes. Gil shepherded him through the door in the paneled wall behind the High Table, with a smile. But when he closed it behind them, his hand was shaking on the latch.

In the seclusion of the small bedchamber, he stripped off his shirt, poured water into a basin, and washed, cooling his temper as he did. Then he poured fresh water for Percy and while the boy took his turn, he chose clean shirts from a kist for them both.

"Magnus is your friend," Percy said amiably as he dried his face. As happened sometimes, his conviction was all the stronger for lack of evidence.

"You think so?" Gil smiled again, pulling the clean shirt over the boy's head.

"He just *pretends* to be mad at you," Percy added. "*Inside* he's your friend."

"Like the goats are cold inside?" Gil fastened the silver clasps of the fur-trimmed cloak Floki had given the boy and adjusted his gold arm ring to reveal the etching of the wolf, Fenrir.

Percy shook his head. "You're joking; but the goats *are* cold inside."

Gil grinned, slipping into the shirt that Janetta had sewed from linen of her own weaving. "Right. And Magnus is my friend. Inside."

Cheerful shouts sounded beyond the door. Gil quickly drew his best tunic over the white shirt, self-consciously added the silver collar that Hakon insisted he wear, and buckled his sword belt around his waist. Then, with Percy beside him, proudly bearing his cupbearer's wooden goblet, he returned to the hall.

A burst of noise and color met them as they stepped through the door. The harpers by the fire plucked a lively rowing song and all of the company sang along. Between the two long feasting boards, the crew of Star-Seeker, garments yet damp from the sea wind, paraded around the hearth.

Paired as on rowing benches, they swung mock oars, with Ismail mounted on the shoulders of the last pair, helmsman of a living ship. Svein Sveinsson ran forward with an ale horn and, raising it high, splashed golden liquid over the African boy's head. From behind the High Table, Gil applauded, laughing and shouting with the rest. But then, seeing him there, Erling Maiden-Face slapped a heavy hand on the board before him and called for silence. At once, the music stopped, the laughter stilled, and again all eyes turned to Gil

"No." He grinned and waved. "Don't stop ...." But it was

already too late; the mock ship lay becalmed. *Star-Seeker's* young crew hurriedly lowered Ismail to the floor and then retreated with him to stand in the shadows of the eaves, their faces turned respectfully toward their earl.

For a wistful moment, Gil watched as Ciarnan joined them, pummeling Ismail in rowdy congratulation. Then, squaring his shoulders, he laid a hand on the pillared back of the earl's high seat and called his chieftains to the feast.

When all were seated in carefully determined order, he stepped back, ceding to Hakon Sea-Friend his cousin's central place. But Hakon only smiled, ducked his head, and took a lower chair. Gil stood for a stunned moment, and then quickly beckoning Aidan to his side, he mounted the pillared high seat, earl of the longhouse by default.

But one chair still remained empty, as Gil had known, all too well, it would. Looking out over the hall, he took a deep breath and called clearly, "Earl's Father! Honor me at my table."

Confused looks crossed faces below and a surprised muttering passed down the High Table. But Magnus Redbeard cocked his head slightly and studied Gil, one eyebrow quirked in assessment. Then, with a shrug, he rose and strode up the hall.

"Well done," Aidan said softly.

Gil watched until Magnus had lowered himself onto the chair between Hakon and Hrafn Bare-Chin. Then, with a wry smile, he murmured, "It's a start." He turned to the women waiting at the hearthside below and signaled for the feasting to begin.

Cheers greeted the tousled, sweating kitchen maids, hurrying from the fire with their platters of venison and game. Louder cheers welcomed their sisters with the ale jugs. The girls turned proud faces aside as the younger men flirted and flattered for larger portions, second fillings of ale. Skinny and boyish among them, Ari and Karl grasped fruitlessly at ale horns passing over their heads, then glowered up at the High Table. Gil caught Danni's eye and they both smothered laughter.

He watched her fondly as she moved about her future husband's hall, bright as a southern bird in an emerald green tunic clasped with silver. Linen sleeves fluttering like snowy feathers, she bent to this guest, turned back to that, listening to old men's grave reminiscences and young men's boasts with equal graciousness. *How far you've flown, my childhood friend.* He raised his eyes then, shyly seeking Janetta, and found her crouched among the children at the poet's feet, ensuring each had their rightful portion.

At his own table, servings were lavish and fine wine flowed freely. His chieftains ate and drank, tense postures easing. Nervous glances to the doors lessened. Restless hands steadied on wine goblets. A comfortable silence fell over all.

Still, Gil was well aware that part of every man's mind was out on the strand with his ship. And, indeed, the larger number of each crew had been left cautiously aboard. But Floki had done the same at his kinsman's hall on Mona. And if Floki, himself, had failed them here, why should they trust his untried heir?

Second servings were finished; third, offered and declined. Percy re-filled the wine goblets and the harpers gentle music drifted up from the floor. Gauk Njalsson grew nostalgic, reminiscing over days past when he, too, was young, sailing adventurous seas. Egil Split-Helm shared battle lore. "Surprise," he growled to Gil, thumping his silver goblet on the board. "A small force. Fast-moving. And surprise."

Gil nodded. His would, indeed, be a small force, and even he knew that without surprise on his side, their adventure would be short.

Hrafn Bare-Chin drew maps in spilled wine, depicting coastlines from Orkney to Dofras, with the best, most secret harborings. Magnus suddenly laughed, pointing to a bulge of land on Hrafn's wine-map. "There. The finest harboring of all the eastern coast," he paused, "For those with skill to make it. And *there*," he drew a rough cross, "Lies Lindisfarne. The finest prize." He grinned a wolfish grin. "Is that not so, good father?"

"A prize indeed, Magnus," Aidan smiled. "I would not deny."

"Then that is our loss," Gil said clearly. "Winter is coming. We must sail quickly past." With his eyes locked on Magnus' own, he beckoned Janetta to bring more ale.

She came at once with a brimming jug, setting it down beside Magnus, and, as if he were Gil's only guest, asked if all was to his satisfaction? Would he like more to eat? A different tune from the harpers? Should the poet recite?

Gruffly, Magnus shook his head, but she won from him a faint bemused smile. Gil watched her achingly as she retreated down the hall, wanting nothing more than to be alone with her again, on the island across the wild sea.

He let his mind drift to a fanciful future: Janetta his bride, their own children among those around the hearth ... they would need more space ... he'd raise the roof, build a sleeping loft. And a wash house, so his guests might warm sea-weary bones ....

"You will choose an heir?"

"What?" Gil turned. Red Kol was leaning past Aidan, his eyes, under their bushy white brows, intent on Gil's. "An heir," he repeated. "Who will be your heir?"

"*My* heir?" Gil blinked in confusion.

"No man sails out certain of his return," Gauk Njalsson nodded solemnly from his place.

"But Floki will return," Gil blurted. "Whatever happens to me." A small silence fell. "And Hakon ...." he stopped because Hakon was shaking his head.

"I was not my cousin's choice," he said simply.

Hrafn Bare-Chin carefully sipped his wine. Then, leaning back, he said, "We would indeed welcome Floki Magnusson's return. But once a man puts out to sea, winds blow many ways."

"And," Egil Split-Helm put in, "Even Floki Magnusson, fine warrior that he is, chose an heir."

"It is the custom," Ragnar Kolsson gave Gil an encouraging smile, and all nodded agreement.

Gil sat stunned. Floki had indeed chosen an heir, but Floki was preparing to die. Did they think the same of him? Raising his eyes and looking out over the hall, he spoke softly to the man at his right. "Do I do this?"

"It is the custom," Aidan murmured.

"But who?" Gil whispered desperately, his gaze yet on the men at the feasting boards below.

"Honor the man who seeks no honor," Aidan said. "Whose will is to do your own."

Who seeks no honor ... Ismail! Ismail who never sought anything for himself. His eyes went instantly to the slim dark boy sitting happily among their friends, with Rachel, as always, at his side. Ismail who had braved the sea he feared for him. Who would do anything for him ... and for that reason alone, Gil knew he could not ask.

His gaze slipped regretfully away and then came abruptly to rest on Ciarnan, the Irish prince who left his father's kingdom to be a Northman ... *Who better can I trust than the man who would not be earl?* Straightening his back, Gil looked from left to right, and addressing his gathered chieftains said, "Ciarnan of Hy is my heir."

"The *Irishman*?" Red Kol's wild brows rose.

"Another boy," Gauk Njalsson sighed.

"He is older than me," Gil said stubbornly. "And he too has sailed to Rome."

"He is capable," Ragnar agreed. "With a sword. With a horse. With a ship."

"He is a churchman!" Magnus groaned.

"He is a king's son," Gil returned.

Magnus shrugged and drank a swig of ale and wiped his mouth. "Why not choose the good father?" He nodded toward Aidan, and then put prayerful hands together and smiled at the roof beams. "And make all of Hrolf's Isle a holy *muinntir*?

Gil laughed. "Oh, I would, if he would let me." Then he looked hard at Magnus and said, "And if you'd seen him aboard *Silver Dragon*, laughing with your son while every other man was terrified, you would choose him, too. But, since I cannot have Aidan," he turned gently to Percy, "Cupbearer, please bring Ciarnan to my table." He sat back, carefully ignoring the mutterings of his chieftains, as the boy walked solemnly down the hall and tugged at Ciarnan's sleeve.

When the two stood across the table from him, Gil nodded a brief, private greeting, and then spoke aloud for all the hall, "Ciarnan of Hy, when you left your brothers of the *muinntir* and your father in Ireland to follow Floki Magnusson, you made a vow. What was it?"

Ciarnan rocked back on his heels, eyes half-closed. Then, looking warily back at Gil, he said, "That I would return to them when my cousin Donal's death was avenged. But it is not yet!" he protested. "I am not done!"

Gil silenced him with a sharp flick of his hand. "I am earl, now, and I relieve you of this vow." Ciarnan's face broke into a smile, but Gil spoke over his mumble of gratitude, "For this reason only: my chieftains request that I choose an heir before I sail. And *with their agreement*," he said evenly, "I choose you. Will you defend Hrolf's Isle in my place?"

"Gladly." Ciarnan's eyes shone with a fierce happy light. "I defend Hrolf's Isle for you, for Earl Floki, and for every man here." A cheer arose from the benches in the hall, drowning the confused protests at the High Table.

Aidan laughed softly. "Well done, Gil Lake of Tir nan Og. I close my eyes, and another sits beside me."

Gil smiled to himself, wondering if that other would be pleased or infuriated by the comparison. Then he turned to his left and with a broader smile said, "Earl Hakon! Show us the treasures of Ireland!" Sitting back, then, he cautiously sipped at his single serving of wine, while the attention of the longhouse shifted to Hakon and *Sea-Raven's* proud young crew.

Sturdy sea-kists were carried from beneath the eaves and set out in the center of the hall. Lids prised free, they revealed stores of linen and kitchen ware, tools for farm and shipboard, coils of rope, fishing nets, sacks of seed for the spring sowing, a new plough to break winter ground.

Gil admired and praised as was expected, complimenting Hakon on fine bargains struck, and passing a Saxon throwing axe around the table for each man to weigh. Hakon stood the while, smiling within his dark beard, and then called for one final kist to be opened in view of all. Within lay rolls of iridescent silk, glass beads, silver brooches and arm rings, pearls and velvets and lace: the cargo of some hapless merchant knarr whose fate Gil did not wish to know.

Amid jests and knowing laughter, gifts were distributed, first to Shony and Magnus and then to the chieftains. Lastly,

Hakon stood before Gil and laid down on the table a warrior's hauberk, its supple chain gleaming in the firelight. "You grow!" he smiled, and, arms stiff at his side, mimicked a man bound too tightly by his armor. "Soon you do not breathe!"

Gil lifted the mail shirt and thanked Hakon gravely, but Hakon only laughed, "Wait. There is more. My cousin sits like a king in his furs; why should not you?"

Gil, who could think of a million reasons why not, shook his head. But Hakon lifted from the kist a cloak of deep blue felted wool, lined with silvery fur. By the proud glow in the Shetlander's eyes, Gil knew this, too, was no mundane purchase, but a prize won in the old way, in some raid on Irish shores.

Hakon held the cloak out. Gil accepted with the graciousness such a gift deserved. He slipped it over his shoulders, shutting from his mind whose blood had been its price. Warm and silky within, as Cat's own fur, it fitted him like a glove.

CHAPTER TEN

When the gift giving was finished and Hakon had taken his place once more at the High Table, Gil stood, the cloak yet about his shoulders, and with a quick glance at his fellow earl announced, "We will hear petitions, now. Has any here a grievance against another?"

He swept the longhouse with his eyes, expecting old warriors with quarrelsome grudges, young men with feuds. Instead, three women emerged from a cluster of farm wives and advanced on the head of the hall. None were young, but the one in the middle so ancient, tottering on unsteady legs, that Gil signaled to Ismail to help her. But the two on either side waved him away, gripped the old woman by her elbows, and propelled her briskly forward, until all three stood before Gil.

"What can we do for you?" he asked the oldest gently.

"Tell him," said the woman on her right.

"Not what *she* tells you," the woman on the left cast the other a malevolent look over the ancient one's linen-draped head. The old woman raised vague blue eyes at Gil. Her face was brown and wrinkled from a lifetime of wind and sun, her smile toothless.

"Who are you lad?" she said.

"He is the *earl*, Asa," the first woman cried angrily. "He is to give judgement on the linen."

"The linen?"

"Our mother's linen, Asa. Your sister's linen that she willed should be mine."

"Listen to her!" The second woman spun around and faced the long benches. "Have you ever heard such lying?"

The old woman stared at Gil. "Where is the earl?" she said.

"I am earl, now," he answered gently. "With Hakon Ragnvaldsson. See, he is here." He signaled to Hakon, but the Shetlander, deep in conversation with Gauk Njalsson, only nodded vaguely.

Asa gave Hakon a brief glance, champed her soft lips, and turned back to Gil. "Earl Floki is dead?" she said sadly.

"No! Earl Floki is in Norway." *But he'll be dead soon enough if I ever get my hands on him.* "How can *we* help you?" he said loudly, facing Hakon. Hakon saluted him with his wine goblet without turning. *And the earl of the longhouse with him, in a moment.*

"I have no need of help," she smiled contentedly, and then added, "These are the daughters of my sister Thordis, who we buried at seedtime. Helga," she shook a gnarled finger at the first woman, "speak properly to the earl, now. You also, Hildigunn. They never had any grace," she confided to Gil. "Born on a waxing moon, both of them."

Hildigunn stepped forward and leaned over the table with such boldness that two of the council rose to their feet. "I am here to claim my inheritance. Our mother left her linen kist to me. She chose as witness her sister, who, for all her babbling, knows this perfectly well."

"She knows nothing!" Helga protested. "Not even her own name."

Gil cast a last, futile glance at Hakon, and then nodded slowly. "Could you maybe *divide* the linen? Half to you, Helga, and the other half ...."

"Why should she have half my linen?"

Gil sat back and closed his eyes, recalling suddenly his first sight of this longhouse, himself a terrified boy, and Floki Magnusson in this seat, ruling with a mix of wisdom and the sword. Then, without opening his eyes, he slowly smiled. He sat like that for a deliberately long while, listening to the uneasy shuffling of the women's feet. Then he looked up and with a gruffness he did not remotely feel announced, "You will divide the linen. Shony, Earl's Mother, will oversee this. One more argument —"

"Why —?"

"*One* more argument and I find the poorest widow on Hrolf's Isle and give it all to her. Agreed?"

They stared, furious and frightened in equal measure. Then both nodded and with a new timidity turned to retreat. Asa smiled sweetly and patted Gil's arm. "You are a good lad," she said. "Where is the earl?"

Where indeed? He smiled back and closed his eyes again as Ulf and Erling escorted the next petitioners to his table. At his right, he heard Aidan's soft laughter, and then a loud bleating. His eyes snapped open, seeking Percy and an illicit goat, but fell instead on a half-grown brown ewe-lamb held protectively in the arms of one of the farmers standing before him. He smiled, thinking of Asgerd. "That is a fine lamb," he said, nodding to the man.

"It is mine," said the other. "He steals it."

The first farmer sighed, then suddenly set the lamb down on the earl's High Table, turned, and with another sigh, punched his accuser in the jaw.

"No!" Gil rose to his feet. But Ulf and Erling were there already, hauling the two apart.

"I steal nothing. He lies."

"You were seen, Glum! Skinning your own dead lamb and tying the skin on this one's back to fool the ewe."

"So? I find it motherless. I leave it, orphaned, to starve? That is better?"

"You *return it to me*. I have ewes also."

Glum leaned suddenly over the lamb that was nibbling breadcrumbs from the board. "So? You do not tell me, 'I am Bruni's. He who lies in his bed until the sun has set, while I stray.' Why do you not say this?" He turned to a chortling audience on the benches and shrugged dramatically. Then he faced Gil. "I nurse it. I raise it. It drinks my ewe's milk and eats my grass. How is it his?"

"*He* has a sheep," Percy said in a small peeved voice, plucking at Gil's cloak from his cupbearer's stool.

"*Yes*," Gil said. "I've noticed. Hakon?" he pleaded.

"A fine lamb," said Hakon Ragnvaldsson.

Pushing the lamb out of the way, Gil bent his head close to

Aidan's. "They both have a fair claim. What do I do?"

"Like the linen. Divide it. A lamb each."

"But there's only one! How do I make two lambs out of one?"

"Ask the ram."

Gil shook his head and then sat back suddenly and grinned. Wrapping his fine cloak closer, he stood solemnly to make his judgement. "Glum keeps the lamb. When the time comes, he runs her with his ram. Her first ewe lamb goes to Bruni. All others, he keeps. And all from *his* lamb, Bruni keeps. Agreed?"

Bruni shrugged ill-naturedly but nodded. Glum thought a long while. "And if there are twins?"

"Then *I* get one for my patience!" Gil picked up the lamb and shoved it into Glum's arms. "Go. And take this with you." Still glaring at each other, the two returned to their places. The council sipped wine and nodded approval.

"Ah, Solomon," said Aidan.

Gil smiled weakly, watching Erling and Ulf as they walked down the benches, seeking further petitions. At the foot of the hall, they turned to Gil and shook their heads. Relieved, he took his seat again and called to his waiting harpers for music. But before their fingers could touch the strings, shouts sounded outside the longhouse. Bjorn spun about, sword in hand. The doors burst open and instantly every fighting man in the hall was on his feet. But through the door came only a fair-haired girl, cheeks rosy from the cold air and eyes alight with fury.

"Bergljot?" Gil whispered.

Two men stumbled in immediately behind her, each with his arms pinned behind him by one of the young Shetlanders Hakon had posted outside. The first was a scarred old warrior with grey hair streaming wildly around his red face, and the second, a younger version, hair still blond, features yet unmarked: Gunnar Osvifsson, and his son, Sigurd; Bergljot's father and brother.

"I make petition!" Gunnar roared.

Bergljot spun about. "You do not!" she shouted. "There is no need."

"No!" her brother shouted back. He looked up at Gil at the

High Table. "Make them release me," he demanded, struggling against his captors to reach his sword. "I deal with him the way he deserves!"

Gil shook his head. "Who, Sigurd?" he asked uncertainly.

"Him!" Gunnar pointed at one among a group of young men watching with suppressed laughter from the benches. "Arnkel Thorleiksson. The man who shames my daughter."

"Fish-Tail?" Gil glanced warily at the tall man who sat, seemingly untroubled, amidst his friends.

"No one shames me!" Bergljot turned angrily to her father.

"Because you are shameless," Sigurd cried. "But if he dies, our family, at least, has no shame!"

"If he dies," Bergljot cast a fierce glance at Arnkel, "I am a widow." Arnkel met her gaze with a slow smile and a languorous shrug. "I *am*," she cried indignantly. And looking up to Gil, she said, "He is my husband. We handfasted through Odin's Stone. Make him acknowledge me." She paused and brushing her hair back said boldly, "*And* my child."

"Child?" Gil shook his head, "But you don't have ...."

"What are you, a child yourself?" she cried furiously. "I am *pregnant*. And *he* is the father!"

"Oh!" Gil heard his own stupidity as he spoke. He turned awkwardly to Arnkel. "Are you?"

Arnkel shrugged again. "I may be." He looked around at his smiling friends. "But I have heard of others who also may be."

"That is a lie!" Bergljot shrieked. "There were none. And you lie again to deny me! We are married!"

"When?" Gil said. "When *was* this wedding?"

Composing herself, the girl faced the High Table again. "Before he sailed with you to Norway." She looked sadly back to Arnkel and said, "And you were happy with me then ...." Her voice trailed off and then, with renewed anger, she again addressed Gil, "But then he returns and he is happy with me no more."

Gil's mind flashed to the Norwegian girl asleep in Arnkel's arms. He closed his eyes. "Right."

"But it is *too late!*" Bergljot shouted at Arnkel. "The child is coming and you are its father. And my husband."

Gil addressed Arnkel quietly, "Did you handfast with Bergljot?"

Arnkel grinned. "Your cupbearer handfasted with Hrodny on the day of Ulf Kolsson's wedding. Are they wed?"

"That was a jest for all to see," Bergljot cried.

"And ours was a jest for none to see." Arnkel smiled. The young men on the benches laughed and thumped their ale horns on the board.

"Silence!" Erling called. But they ignored him, laughing louder.

Aidan laid his hand on Gil's sleeve. "Ask for the witnesses. If there are no witnesses, there is no marriage."

Gil rose to his feet. The laughter died, and the young men ducked their heads. "Bergljot," he said gently, "please name the witnesses of the handfasting."

For the first time, she was silent.

"Daughter!" Gunnar shouted. "Answer the earl."

Gil faced Arnkel. "Who witnessed the handfasting at Odin's Stone?"

Arnkel gave another of his lazy shrugs, and, looking around his supporters, said, "Odin?"

In the laughter that followed, Gil turned hopelessly back to the girl. "Weren't there *any* witnesses?" he said. "None of your friends …."

"It was the middle of the night," she answered, in a small girl's voice.

"You handfasted in the middle of the night?" Gil shook his head, remembering his own dark exile at Odin's Stone. "*Why?*" he cried incredulously. "Why couldn't you wait until morning?"

A gleeful shout went up from Arnkel's friends, and Arnkel, grinning broadly, stood to address Gil. "If you do not know, my friend, I cannot tell you. Not here, in front of the women."

The entire longhouse erupted in laughter, even the older men chortling and shaking their heads. Magnus thumped his ale horn on the High Table and slapped Red Kol's back. Bergljot stood frozen, alone in the midst of the hall, until her father strode forward, clasped her arm, and dragged her, no longer protesting, to the door. Sigurd, his arms yet pinned, was hastened after by the guards. At the foot of the hall, the older man turned and pointed at Arnkel. "Odin curse you," he muttered. Then he looked up at the High Table and sighed, "And Odin curse Floki Magnusson, leaving us with this boy."

The doors slammed behind him and the bar was thrown across. In the tumult that followed, Gil stepped back from the table, and summoning Percy, turned toward his inner room. Aidan's fingers clamped on his wrist, so strong and unforgiving that Gil thought alarmingly of Floki. "The earl does not leave his table before his guests."

"What earl?" Gil groaned hopelessly.

"Sit down."

"Let me ...."

"*Now.*" Aidan jerked his arm down with such force, he lost his balance and half fell back onto his seat. Percy stared, clutching his wooden cup. Aidan gently beckoned him back to his stool. "Call for music," he said to Gil.

———

The music was long finished when Gil left the hall. The chieftains had departed, replete and cheerful, to their ships; all but Red Kol who sat yet with Magnus by the ale cask, exchanging stories of their youth. Shony had taken Janetta to her house. Percy was asleep, goat-less, in the earl's bedchamber, with Bjorn snoring contentedly outside the door.

The big man jerked awake as Gil passed him. "It's okay," Gil smiled. "I'm not going far and Hakon has guards everywhere." Bjorn rumbled back into sleep, and Gil picked a quiet path between his warriors, sprawled on sleeping benches, or furs by the hearth.

The night was winter cold, star filled. His eyes went to the black outline of his resting ship. Time to be away from here, for every reason: winter, freedom, shame. He looked up at the pole star, riding high now and thought with frustration of Floki, under the same stars but stubbornly following his own.

He stepped softly past the Nunnery, where Rachel and Danni whispered in the darkness, like sisters. The narrow windows of the church, beyond, glimmered with candlelight. He heard Aidan's gentle voice raised in the Vigils chant, and hesitated, but then shrugged and pushed against the wicker door.

It swung too readily a frail barrier in such a dark time. Aidan, kneeling before the small altar of his oratory, never moved. *Turn,* Gil cried silently, in a second wave of frustration. *You hear me. And I could be anyone. Anyone, with any weapon ....* But the chant continued, unwavering, and Gil knelt then, also, on the earthen floor, and waited, torn between fury and love.

Almost at once, exhaustion overcame him. He reached out a hand to steady himself, but his eyes were closing, his mind filling with edge of sleep dreams. Jerking awake, he gave up and rose to leave.

"Be patient," Aidan spoke without turning.

"I thought you didn't know I was here," Gil lied.

"Of course I know you are here. The Lord is also here. I speak with him first."

Gil knelt again, his frustration fading as the chant resumed, soothing and familiar, phrases of Latin breaking through, now, to meaning. When Aidan turned to him, at last, the lines of his weathered face, the shabby, patched sleeves of his habit, and his ever gentle smile were also so familiar that Gil suddenly found himself weeping. Brushing a hand across his eyes, he blurted, "It's late."

"And tired men seek the things of childhood," Aidan said, as once, a lifetime ago, he said of Floki.

"I'm not a man."

"And, if not a man, what?" Aidan smiled again.

"A stupid boy a stupider man left in charge of Hrolf's Isle."

"Ah," Aidan said.

"I'm sick of trying to please old men!" Gil cried. "Red Kol. Gunnar. *Magnus.* They *never* believed I could do it."

"You are angry that they do not trust your judgement." Aidan rose to his feet. "But, with the one who did, you are angrier still. Why?"

"Because he was wrong."

Aidan nodded thoughtfully, then moved with light,

youthful steps across the little building. The Noble Cat rose, too, out of the shadows, and followed. Laying his psalter down on the bench, the Ab sat beside it and beckoned Gil to join him. "About the ways of men, Floki Magnusson is very rarely wrong. He has a wise heart."

"He was wrong about Hakon," Gil said at once. "'An earl for the longhouse?' Right. So, he sits there and says nothing all night. And leaves it all to me!"

Aidan stroked the cat. "He is not yet ready to come out of the shade." He smiled at Gil's confusion. "He lives all his days in the shadow of his cousin. Without it, the light is too bright." He paused, twirling the cat's tail through his fingers. "Hakon will act, once you leave."

"What difference will that make? Hakon isn't in *my* shadow."

"Ah, but you carry Floki's shadow with you. He chose you." Aidan looked up at the altar, where the wax candles burnt low. "You make three enemies this night. And you can afford none. You must put this right."

"*Three?*"

"Gunnar. Sigurd …."

"And Magnus," Gil groaned.

"Magnus is not your enemy." Aidan shook his head at Gil's immediate protest. "Treat him with the respect he deserves. If Floki can kneel to him, so can you. Swallow your pride."

"He doesn't deserve any respect," Gil shot back. "He's a drunk who loves his ale horn more than his wife. Who's he to tell me about women … or anything."

Aidan laughed softly. "A man who has run his ship aground may not be the best helmsman. But he will know where the rocks are." Then, no longer laughing, he said, "He is not a fool. He is a strong man, growing old. He has raised a son he does not understand. A son who outshines him in every way. And unlike Hakon Ragnvaldsson, he does not care for the shade."

"So?"

"Lead him into the sun."

"What?"

"Is there nothing you have yet to learn from Magnus Redbeard?"

Gil sat in silence for a long while, looking up at the dark roof beams where the crow, Feannag, slept, dreaming, no doubt, crow dreams. "If it isn't Magnus, then who?"

"Arnkel."

"Arnkel? Arnkel got everything he wanted because of me!"

"Yes. And he will despise you for it because he defeated you. He will despise you also if you defeat him, but he will fear you. Which is safer. You must make him honor this marriage."

"He's not going to listen to me after tonight."

"He will listen to the earl."

"*Hakon*?"

"Hakon is not earl. His silence has spoken for him. You are earl and he will listen because the earl holds power." Gil raised a sarcastic eyebrow. Aidan pursued, "He works in your shipyard. He tills your land. He eats your grain."

"It's not mine. Nothing's mine. It's Floki's and I'm holding it for him until he comes back."

"And Floki holds it for an earl in Norway. Who himself holds it, though he may not be aware, for the King of the Universe, to whom he will relinquish it without a doubt and hold no more than he can touch with the crown of his head and the soles of his feet. And that, also, not forever. But for now, Gil, it is yours. You are earl and you must make peace on Hrolf's Isle before you sail. With Gunnar. With Sigurd. With Arnkel. And with Bergljot, who, though she deserves better, has chosen him."

Gil shook his head hopelessly. "I don't know how."

Aidan smiled. "When a man takes you for a fool, Gil, then play the fool."

Aidan's bell was ringing the first hour, with dawn barely brightening the sky, when Gil rose and left the longhouse. He glimpsed Shony hurrying to morning prayers, and two kitchen maids feeding hens. All else was quiet, but for the thud of an axe in the shipyard. *Does Eyolf ever sleep?* he wondered, making his way to the strand.

The chieftains' ships were shrouded yet, their crews silent

beneath their black tents. But smoke rose from the shipyard fire
and figures moved about in the dim light; Eyolf himself peering
into the bubbling cauldron of pine sap. Nearer the quiet sea,
Arnkel Fish-Tail crouched by the new-laid keel of a fishing skiff.
Seeing Gil, he stood and waited with a guarded smile.

"You work early," Gil smiled in return.

"What choice?" Arnkel hunched a shoulder toward the
grey-bearded master shipbuilder.

"Not a lot," Gil agreed with another smile. He sat down on
a stack of smoothed timber.

Arnkel watched uneasily, then, looking down at his hands,
he muttered, "What I say last night … too much ale."

Gil shrugged. Then he looked straight at Arnkel with wide,
honest eyes and said, "Pretty near the truth, anyhow."

Arnkel stared. "What say you?"

"Look," Gil ran an embarrassed hand through his hair
and pushed sand around with a foot. "I know I'm young. But
it's more than that. You're not that much older and …." he let
his voice trail off. "Some men just *know* about this stuff." He
paused. "Men like you." Surprise, and then wary pride, crossed
Arnkel's face. "I don't know how you do it," Gil said, stumbling
over the words. Then he paused and looked down at his foot
pushing more sand around. "Janetta is like that fortress at Mont
Tombe."

Arnkel laughed aloud, "And there you have help from the
earl … Floki," he added awkwardly.

"Which I definitely don't want with Janetta." Gil gave the
sand an emphatic shove.

Arnkel laughed again; then stretched lazily and settled
himself on the timber beside Gil. "It is not difficult," he said
with an easy grin. "You have only to tell them what they want
to hear."

"But what *do* they want to hear?"

Arnkel leaned back against the stacked timber, smiling
to himself. "Some," he said, "That they are beautiful. Some
that you bring them beads and brooches to show off to their
friends. *All of them* that never have you loved another like you
love them!" He paused, his smile fading. "That was true, with

Bergljot, in the beginning. She is …." he fell quiet. "But then!" he cried, "The girl in Norway! You see her … the hair, like white silk! And the eyes …." he shrugged, "What man can resist?"

"So, what did you tell Bergljot?" Gil said.

"She was different," Arnkel answered soberly. "Whatever I try, that night, it is Mont Tombe. The only thing she wishes to hear is 'I am Bergljot's man.' So be it! I take her up to Odin's Stone. And I show her how, if you look through it in just the right way, you see the sea and the stars together, which is so beautiful. And I take her hand through the stone and I say it. And she pledges to me, and then … oh, right there …." He smiled dreamily. "But I do not tell you about that."

"No," Gil said quietly, "You don't need to." He turned to face Arnkel. "But now, you tell me what *I* want to hear." Arnkel's smiled faded.

"And what is that?" he said uneasily.

"That today you will beg forgiveness of Bergljot and her father and brother. And tomorrow you will handfast before witnesses at Odin's Stone."

Arnkel sat very still. And then, with a steely edge to his voice, he said, "And if I do not?"

Gil pointed to the shrouded outlines of a hull at the edge of the shipyard.

"*Summer Dawn*?" Arnkel said, puzzled.

"Eyolf's knarr. She's sailing to Norway for timber, day after tomorrow. And you," Gil stood, "will be on her. If you're lucky, you'll catch a glimpse of *Silver Dragon* setting out for Francia." He gave Arnkel a friendly smile. "I may be a boy and I may be stupid. But she's my ship, and I am earl."

Gil walked with a jaunty stride back up the strand. Ari and Karl passed him, squabbling on their way to the unfinished pony pen. Ciarnan, wincing at the light, groaned a greeting as he and Ismail led the two new horses out to grass. Cheerful after his ale-free night, Ismail saluted Gil with a high-five.

Wood smoke and the scent of baking bread drifted down

from the hall. Gil quickened his step and then abruptly stopped. Magnus Redbeard stood in the open doorway, eyes squinting blearily, hair and beard tangled with sleep. Steeling himself, Gil resumed his pace. "A good morning, Earl's Father," he said as their shoulders brushed in passing.

"And a good night, before," Magnus laughed softly. "Though Gunnar Osvifsson perhaps does not agree."

Gil said nothing. Ignoring the greetings of those he passed, he strode through the hall, entered his bedchamber, and closed the door. Percy yet slept in a tangle of furs. Quietly, so as not to disturb him, Gil sat on his own bed and stared at the opposite wall.

Above the desk, the double-bladed Irish battle-axe hung where Floki had left it. He studied it for a long, silent while; then stood, crossed the room in two strides, and lifted it down from the wall. Shifting its heavy length over his shoulder, he left the room and walked without speaking through the startled men and women of his household, out into the wintry morning.

He found Magnus at the edge of the strand, staring seawards as if in search of a ship. He did not hear Gil approach until there were but ten strides between them. Turning, he acknowledged him lazily, then, an instant later, saw the weapon in his hands.

Gil watched the flicker of fear light in his eyes, and holding his ground in silence, let it grow. "Magnus Redbeard," he said, at last. Magnus nodded, his hand drifting uneasily to his sword hilt. Gil stood yet, unmoving, and then suddenly smiled. "Teach me how to use this thing," he said.

CHAPTER ELEVEN

Two days later, when Gil put out to sea, the Irish battle-axe went with him, wrapped in pitch-soaked sailcloth and stowed beneath the steersman's bench. The straw-filled leather mannequin on which he had practiced, slumped like a drunken warrior beside it.

Propped on a stake in the sand, it had endured a full day as his adversary. For half the morning, its tough leather resisted his clumsy efforts. But then he found the balance of the long haft and under Magnus' unforgiving eye, mastered the powerful two-armed swing, and, at last, the deadly twist of the wrists that turned the twin blades.

By midday, the leather was scarred and torn. At dusk, the mannequin lost an arm. And by nightfall, with Magnus pursuing his instruction by firelight, it was slashed through to its battered wooden core.

Arms burning, his whole body aching, Gil had accepted the grunt of approval that brought the lesson to an end, and with the axe over one shoulder and the mannequin over the other, returned triumphant to the hall. But he had dreamt that night of the slaughter at Cille Aidan, and Floki's treacherous guards; straw men, soaked in blood.

They sailed at dawn, with the wind in the North and the sea before them calm in the lee. The nervous ponies clattered up the gangplanks, followed by the islands' young men, love-knots from its young women on their wrists. Bold in her married woman's headdress, Bergljot Gunnarsdottir clung to Arnkel's arm, until, breaking free, he ran up the gangplank to his cheering friends.

The boards were drawn up, the ships floated, their prows turned seaward. Then, with the sails fluttering eagerly and his oarsmen on their benches, Gil jumped down into the water and strode up the strand to bid each of his gathered household farewell.

Aidan gave his quiet blessing, Shony a proud smile. Magnus granted him a gruff nod before tramping off to his work. Hakon Sea-Friend, eyes alight with cheerful envy, enfolded him in a brother's embrace. Men left behind to tend beasts and fields bowed respectfully as Gil passed. Old women pressed amulets into his hands. Small girls giggled and ran away. Boys, with dreams of Viking adventures, plucked at his lordly cloak and offered bloodthirsty advice.

Then, as Gil scrambled back aboard his ship, a flurry of hoof beats turned all eyes inland. Hair and skirts flying, boots pounding her pony's flanks, Asgerd galloped down onto the strand and, scattering the household, rode straight into the sea. Straining up to Ragnar on *Silver Dragon's* deck, she twisted a knot of braid around his brawny forearm, spun her wild pony, and galloped away, even as he held his trophy aloft.

Laughing, Gil watched her retreat up the hill track. Then he turned and surveyed his ship. The rowing benches were full, oars ready. Ciarnan and young Ari stood by the sheets. At the pony pen, Danni and Rachel, with sword belts once more around their waists, calmed the snorting beasts. Crouched beside the steersman's bench, Janetta comforted Percy, red-eyed from parting with his pets. Across the stretch of smooth water between the two ships, Ismail stood ready at his helm.

Gil raised his arm and swept it seaward, then nodded to Erling beside him. "Helmsman, take her out."

The sheets tightened, the sails filled, and with barely a dip of the oars, *Silver Dragon* and *Star-Seeker* slipped away from the land. The poet, Eoin, touched his harp strings and a haunting melody of parting drifted across the widening gap of sea. Aboard ship, Niall took up his own harp and the notes mingled, tying them yet to home with a love-knot of song.

But then Eoin's grey dog lifted its shaggy muzzle and began to howl, a long, keening note, drowning the twinned melodies in mournfulness. "Be quiet," Erling muttered under his breath. The younger men laughed. But as the sound followed them out into the tide, even the boldest fell silent.

But then, free of the lee, they caught the full force of the North wind. The ships heeled as they turned across it and the air was filled with the humming of shrouds, the creaking of masts, and the snapping of the bright golden pennant above. Aidan's bell rang three times from the shore. Ari and Karl cheered, boyish voices thin in the tumult, and Gil saluted Ismail across a stretch of open sea. Janetta sat boldly beside him, Lionheart whinnied his usual complaints, and Gil felt, at last, at peace.

They passed between the Spear Isle and Gauk's Isle, and turned eastward to the open sea, and then south, sailing again with the wind at their backs. The day was bright, a blue sky above, a light chop on the sea below. Threading their way between islands and skerries, they rode on before the strengthening northerly, until at sunset they were in sight of the Pentland coast.

White horses marked the swift tides of the crossing, and with the long hull bucking in turbulent waters, Gil took the helm. A ship's length behind, Ismail's *Star-Seeker* followed, steady in his wake. Blessed by a rising moon, they made landfall as the last light faded from the sky.

It was as desolate a shore as Gil could imagine, and without Hrafn Bare-Chin's spilled wine maps, he would never have found the little bay between its guardian sea stacks, nor navigated a course to its strand. No keel drags, new or old, marked the pristine sand. Sea birds wandered the shore as if they had never seen a man. Still, Gil sent guards out, as soon as they beached, to take positions on high ground.

Then, giving orders for driftwood to be gathered and the ponies led out to graze, he descended the gangplank with the broad-axe and the leather mannequin, drove a stake into the sand, and resumed his practice, cheerfully ignoring the laughter of his crew.

In the morning, the sky was clear and the wind yet steady from the North, and so it held as they journeyed on; a good omen Erling concluded, to balance the howling of the dog. For three days, they saw no sign of life. No watch fires on the land, no sails on the sea; neither knarrs to tempt Gil's young crew, nor warships of his enemy. But then, as the third night approached, he heard a sound of home. "A church bell?" he said, startled, to Erling.

Ahead lay a misty point of land, a long, low ness, reaching into the sea. The sound came again. Ciarnan rose from a board game and joined Gil and Erling at the helm. He pointed to a barely discernible tall round tower. "Colm's Port," he said, "A great *muinntir*. I knew one of its brethren, on Hy."

"They ring us a welcome."

Gil turned quickly. Arnkel Fish-Tail had quietly joined them, his sharp eyes sweeping the undefended shore. "And they are known for their hospitality. I think they wish to share their wealth." He laughed boldly. Ari and Karl looked up from their own games and ran to peer eagerly over the rail. Gil smiled, but swung the oar and set an unthreatening course to the shore.

They camped that night on a sliver of land, a small island, deserted but for sheep. Once again, Gil battled with his leather adversary by the light of the fires. "Janetta," Arnkel called when Gil returned to the ship, "he betrays you. See! Each night he takes another away with him. Look, there, his new love!"

Gil grinned and held up the battered straw figure. "Ah, the hair, like white silk!" he cried, pulling out bits of straw. "What man can resist?" Smiling cheerfully at Arnkel, he mounted the gangplank and stowed the axe and the straw man, beneath the steersman's bench.

The next morning, he again set a course that skirted the *muinntir*. Passing far out to sea, they crossed a broad firth that ran deep inland, with hills rising on either side. Erling tapped his arm and pointed to the great divide. "Glen Alban." Gil nodded. "This is where we fled," Erling said, "leaving you in Caledon. Here, in the mist, we lost Hakon Sea-Friend's ship."

Gil surveyed the calm waters, so innocent now, and let his eyes drift to the distant hills, the highest whitened with early snow. There, deep in the fastness, lay Camelot. There, amidst the ruins of Arthur's kingdom, Jocelyn Guidbairn held court. And there, too, stood Merlin's fearsome tower, where Gil had been his prisoner. Shutting that memory from his mind, he imagined instead the great walled Forest of Pentecost. And beside it, wild and overgrown, the Mews Garden where he and Janetta met. He called her to his side and pointed, "Home."

She laughed, leaning against him on the steering board. "Home is here," she said.

It was then he saw the sail: a white smudge coming toward them from the south, its pale outline catching the light as the ship tacked across the wind. "Ciarnan!" he pointed to the mast.

The Irishman jumped up from the bench he shared with Niall. As Gil headed up into the wind, he scrambled up the swaying mast and slung one leg over the yard. Clinging to the masthead, the golden pennant whipping just above his head, he shielded his eyes and peered into the glare.

"Warship?" Gil shouted up.

Ciarnan shook his head. "Knarr."

"Alone?" Arnkel called eagerly.

Ciarnan stared a long while. "I see no other." With a careful glance at Arnkel Fish-Tail, Gil called the Irishman down.

"How does she ride?" Arnkel asked, as Ciarnan's feet touched the deck.

"Low in the water." Ciarnan looked quickly to Gil. "Well laden."

"Ah," Arnkel shook his head, "That is dangerous. This wind," he looked around the calm sea, "it might well rise. And then? Laden ships founder. We must relieve him of his burdens." He grinned at his shipmates, and looking down at the two awed young boys, Ari and Karl, said, "It is our duty to keep merchants safe."

Gil nodded casually toward the sheltered firth, "I think he will make those quieter waters before this gathering storm overcomes him." He squinted up at the brilliant sky and gave the two boys a small smile. Disappointed, they turned back to Arnkel.

"*Silver Dragon!*" Svein Sveinsson called as Ismail brought

Star-Seeker up astern. "What holds you?" He looked up at their luffing sail.

Gil waved and pointed to the knarr which had altered its course so their paths would not cross. "Just showing him we're not a threat. Why ruin his morning?" Ismail laughed and Gil turned the oar, catching the wind again.

Arnkel's face darkened. Watching the knarr escape, he said, "You do not sail this ship alone, my friend. And some here would have this prize."

Gil studied the knarr, wallowing in the light chop as it angled toward the firth and Glen Alban. Well laden, indeed, with treasures for Camelot. He said, "There will be other seas and other prizes. These are dangerous waters and not just for him."

Erling nodded solemn agreement. "The sooner we pass through them, the better for all," he said. Arnkel gave an angry shrug. Gil looked calmly past him and signaled Ismail.

"Sail on."

All down the coast of Alba, Gil set a cautious course. If he saw a sail, he turned aside. When a smudge of smoke or the glow of a watch fire appeared ashore, he went far out to sea. At dusk, he chose his harboring with care, as far from any sign of habitation as he could find.

His crew grumbled, but seamen always grumbled, and, blessed by the faithful north wind, most seemed happy enough to enjoy the easy sailing and the campsites on the edge of the great forests; the hunting and the feasts of game around their driftwood fires.

Each night, Gil battled the straw man, to the amusement of all. Arnkel abandoned his mockery and instead gave his two young followers lessons in swordsmanship. But others took up the jest. "They say he beats that good wife," Svein Sveinsson mourned.

"Send him to the women!" Erling declared. "Hildigunn and Helga! They will deal with him!"

"Asa!" said Ragnar.

"*Grimhildr,*" Svein Snaggle-Tooth growled, to raucous cheers.

Gil smiled, barely hearing them, his mind and body focused on the long haft, the heavy blade. Left to right, right to left: remembering the moves Magnus had shown him in his one grueling day of instruction. Hands held side by side, or hands crossed. Though his wrists cried out for relief, he mastered it one-handed and learned to toss the haft from one hand to the next, and to swing it over his head as if chopping wood.

Their teasing and their chores finished, several of his crew would come to watch. When he managed at last to pass the broad-axe behind his back, and to throw it skyward and catch it again, they broke into spontaneous cheers. Sweating and triumphant, he ended his practice, and with his warriors carrying axe and mannequin behind him, returned to the camp.

The fires burned low, casting the dragon shadows of the beached ships over the sea. Above, the sky was more white than black, with stars. All around their small camp lay such darkness that an eerie feeling arose in Gil's heart that all places he had ever known had vanished entirely, and they were the only men left in the world.

As he stepped within the circle of light, singing greeted him and the sweet notes of Niall's ancient, mysterious harp filled the air. Danni, Rachel, and Janetta, sitting in a ring around him, sang the verses of a song of the shielings, the men and boys joining in the refrain.

Gil sank wearily down on a driftwood log, his eyes on Janetta's soot-smudged face. Wind-burned and tousled, she seemed more beautiful to him than ever. And hunting from her black mare's back and roasting game over her well-laid fires, more at home on these wild beaches than in any hall.

The melody of her song, haunting and familiar, awoke in him a fanciful dream of running away with her into the wild lands beyond. Of leaving cares and causes behind, to live like Derla lived: children of the shielings, wandering the hills. He raised wistful eyes, again, to the sky. The pole star yet rode high. And Frigga's spindle yet called him South.

The next morning, they crossed another great firth, well-trafficked with merchant ships. It was impossible to avoid every one, and once again his restless crew watched laden knarrs slip out of reach.

Gil knew he played a delicate game. Too little satisfaction would arouse resentment. But too much, too soon, was worse. They were all young and already missing home. Sea-kists full of plunder and heads full of battle tales, and they would turn their eyes north. And he had yet a long, long way to sail.

They camped that night on a windswept strand in Northumbria. The mood was somber, everyone weary of wind and sea. Niall's harp was silent. No one sang. The fire flared fitfully, burning the bannocks. Rachel threw one at Ragnar for complaining. The younger men played board games and quarreled. Svein Sveinsson and Erling argued over splicing a rope. Lionheart bit Hrafn for no reason at all.

Gil finished his practice early and then sat with Danni and Percy, washing Percy's collection of sea shells. Begun on their first night out, it now crowded his sea kist and threatened to move into Gil's "You'll sink my ship." Gil smiled.

Percy carefully handed Danni another shell. "They're for my goats," he said. "So they'll know where we've been." Rachel joined them, kneeling in the sand.

"Listen to modesty over there," she said.

Seated between Ari and Karl and surrounded by a dozen young men, Arnkel Fish-Tail was telling of the great battle he fought in the marshes of Caledon, when he sailed with Floki Magnusson through Glen Alban. Ari's eyes shone in the firelight. "How many did you kill, Arnkel?" Arnkel made a show of counting on his fingers and then giving up.

"Were you wounded?" Karl cried. Arnkel rolled up the sleeve of his tunic and showed a fading scar. Svein Snaggle-Tooth scratched his head. Erling looked patiently out to sea. Danni covered her face, giggling behind her hand.

"He forgets we were there, too!" she whispered.

Gil smiled. "Not exactly how I remember it," he conceded. "But it makes a good story."

Rachel tilted her head solemnly toward Arnkel's young followers. "They *weren't* there," she said. "And they think it's true."

Overnight, the wind and weather turned. Gil woke to rain and sleet spatting against the tent cloth. Clouds scudded across a wan grey sky. The ponies huddled, nose to tail, waiting eagerly for their pen. *The ship! The ship!* Lionheart whickered, as Gil led him down from his grazing.

See? I knew you'd like it in the end.

Leaving the strand under oar, he took his course from landmarks and memory, raised sail, and set off into the keening wind. They tacked far out to sea, before turning on another long broad reach toward the shore.

The ship sailed well; the oar steady, the sheets needing little attention. Board games were rested on sea kists, Ciarnan rising only at long intervals from his to re-set the tacking spar. Gil sat easily at the tiller, watching the dragon prow surge through the choppy sea. A glance over his shoulder showed Ismail's *Star-Seeker* cutting through their wash, three ships' lengths behind.

The wind strengthened and, and even tacking against it, they made better speed than in the calmer days before. Gil's mind ran forward, down the barely visible coast: *Einar's Bay. Hrafn's Ayre. Dofras. Then the narrow sea that lay between the pilgrim port and Francia* ....

By midday, the cloud was breaking, revealing bright blue patches, between squalls of snow. Sun splashed the yellow beaches. A stretch of fresh-ploughed field appeared ashore and vanished into mist. Another window in the cloud cover showed green pasture lands, before a squall closed in, hiding all in a veil of white. Behind it sounded the distant lowing of cattle. Lionheart neighed, sensing his own kind somewhere near. Then Gil heard again the sweet sound of home: a church bell chiming above the rumble of a distant surf.

He stood up, peering into the snow. Rachel ran to the rail and Danni, soothing her excited mare, mounted the side of the pony pen. The clouds parted and she turned to Gil and cried, "Look! Lindisfarne!"

He was closer in than he realized, closer than he ever intended. Clustered on their low island, the turf roofed buildings of Aidan's *muinntir* shone with fresh fallen snow. A thin white blanket covered the surrounding fields and glistened on the tall bell tower. Abandoning their games, his young crew gathered at the rail.

His eyes on the shore, Gil sensed, rather than saw, the movement behind him. He was half turning when the blow struck. Brushing the side of his head, it slammed into his shoulder, breaking his grip on the tiller and hurling him to the deck. Even as he was falling, his mind sought reason, imagining the halyard had somehow parted, dropping the heavy yard. *Only, it would never reach him ....*

In a mist of confusion, he sprawled below the steering bench, hearing shouts and cries and boots thudding on deck boards, all from a far distance. When, struggling one-armed, he turned and looked up, a sword blade glistened in front of his face, and Arnkel Fish-Tail was at the helm.

"Stay still," Arnkel smiled pleasantly. "No one is hurt. I do not steal the ship. I only borrow it."

Gil's eyes were on the sword blade, the hand that held the hilt, and the pale young face above it. *"Ari?"* he whispered. Wincing as feeling came back into his numbed arm, he braced himself to sit. Instantly, the sword jabbed closer to his face.

"Do not move!" Ari's voice cracked on the last word. Fear shone in his eyes, and the fingers on the sword hilt were white, but when Gil shook his head, the point jabbed up against this throat.

"Okay, okay. I believe you." Pulling back cautiously, he let his clearing vision pass down the deck. Karl was standing behind Ari, worriedly clutching the oar with which Arnkel had felled Gil. Beyond, three men stood shoulder to shoulder, their backs to him, raising a barrier of drawn swords against the rest of his crew.

One turned, looking nervously back to Arnkel. *Brand. Brand who had worked beside him all summer on Ulf Kolsson's farm. Tofi from the shipyard. And Gisli, who trained with the blacksmith.* All very young. All, he had thought, his friends.

Over their heads, he saw Erling watching every move. Their eyes met and Erling's hand closed on his sword hilt. Gil shook his head. He half turned, blinking and feigning dizziness. Ari flinched. The sword wavered. Beneath the steersman's bench, Gil glimpsed the gleam of steel. Half hidden by the straw mannequin, the haft of the Irish battle-axe lay just out of reach. Gil raised his head.

"Be careful, my friend," Arnkel's voice was calm, "we come about now and pay a little visit." He jerked his head toward the *muinntir.* "Then," he smiled, "She is yours all the way to Francia."

"Okay," Gil said quietly. "But you need to set the spar, or …."

"I sail on this ship before you ever see her!" Arnkel snapped angrily.

"And the sheets," Gil persisted, "The sail's luffing," he complained. "And *what's that*?" he cried, staring alarmed at the mast.

Arnkel looked up too, and so did Ari. Gil rolled, caught the arm of the mannequin with one hand and the haft of the axe with the other, and was on his feet in an instant.

Whirling, he slammed the heavy straw man into Ari's stomach, throwing him back against Karl. Oar and sword clattered to the deck as Gil spun the other way, and swung the axe blade in a flashing arc, a foot from Arnkel's face. With an outraged curse, Arnkel dropped the tiller, and, reaching for his sword, backed toward the rail.

Un-helmed, the ship lost way, and slewed sideways, her prow swinging down the wind. Gil swung the axe in a two-handed deck clearing circle and jumped to the steersman's bench. Bracing a foot against the tiller, he thrust it hard over the steering board, heading up into the wind. With his foot still holding the steering oar steady, he faced Arnkel, the battle-axe raised, "Drop the sword."

Arnkel shrugged and shook his head. "You do not do it," he said. "You are not Floki Magnusson, my friend." He leaned forward to take the axe and smiled. "Before you cut yourself."

Gil nodded thoughtfully. Then with his foot still on the tiller, he tossed the axe skywards, caught it just below the head, and slammed the long haft across Arnkel's knees. With a howl of pain, Arnkel scrabbled for the backstay and missed, and flailing wildly, fell backward into the sea.

Before he surfaced, Gil had a hand on the tiller. His ship secure, he turned, axe ready. Erling raised a cheerful fist; his other arm firmly around Gisli's throat. Brand and Tofi, disarmed and battered, were held secure by Ragnar, his big hands knotted in their unkempt hair.

A shout sounded off their steering board, as *Star-Seeker's* white swan figurehead rode into view. "Hey! What you do?" Ismail waved from the helm. Then, seeing Arnkel floundering, called, "Is okay. We save." Svein Sveinsson leapt to the rail with a coil of rope.

"Leave him," Gil ordered.

"Leave him?" Ismail's astonishment sounded even over the rush of the sea. But, turning his own oar to lose the wind, he headed up and obeyed.

Gil looked down at Ari and Karl huddled below the steersman's bench. He nodded to Ari, and pointed to the rail. "You next."

The boys clung together, trembling and sobbing. "It was a jest," Karl cried. Gil raised the battle-axe. Ari climbed to his feet, and, weeping like a child, stumbled across the deck and mounted the rail. Voices of protest arose among the crew.

Gil ignored them. He waited until the boy's young legs tensed for the jump. Then, aware that every man aboard was watching, he said evenly, "There are no jests at the helm of a ship, Ari. None." The boy nodded desperately. Gil waited again, then beckoned him down. A great sigh of relief swept the deck. Then the watchers turned uneasily to the sea.

Arnkel's shouts were thinner now. From the corner of his eye, Gil saw his head slip under. When he broke surface, his face was white with cold, his eyes dark with terror. His frozen

mouth moved silently and then croaked out one word: "Forgive
…."

Gil shook his head. "I am not Floki Magnusson," he said.
"He is a forgiving man." He looked up the deck. "Ciarnan!
Svein! Set sail." He turned the oar, the sheets tightened, the ship
gained way.

Above the whistle of the wind in the shrouds, he heard
Rachel's clear young voice. "He is dying, Gil."

"I do not care."

"Be sure," she said, "Before you take a life."

Still, it was not her plea that changed his mind, but Bergljot's
white headdress blowing in the wind as he sailed *Silver Dragon*
from Hrolf's Isle.

They put in at Einar's Bay, the rockbound cove beyond
Lindisfarne claimed by Floki's grandfather. Gil found the narrow channel with ease and rode in under full sail. Proudly,
Ismail did the same, and safe on the sheltered shore, they
exchanged a boyish high-five. Though there was little of the boy
left in Gil that night.

Numbly, he ordered fires lit and warming broth prepared.
But, stripped of his drenched clothing and wrapped in cloaks,
Arnkel lay unmoving beneath heaps of furs. Past eating, past
speaking, past even shivering, he stared mindlessly into the fire.

Released by Ragnar and Erling, and bereft of weapons, his
three followers sat apart, guarded only by their shame. When
Gil passed them while leading Lionheart and Grani out to grass,
Gisli called, "He tells us it is a jest! We win some silver and we
all laugh. Even you!"

"And you believed him?" Gil walked on without awaiting an
answer. When he returned, Danni and Janetta were struggling
to help Arnkel drink broth. His head lolled, eyes vacant. Gil
turned away and saw Rachel watching.

"He may die anyhow," she said. There was no reproach in
her voice, only sorrow.

Gil gave a bitter shrug. "Odin's will?"

"Your will," she said and walked away.

"What else could I do?" he shouted after her. She turned, still walking backward down the strand. The mist was rolling in, making her appear far and ghostly. "I had to. I had no choice." She said nothing. "I am earl now, Rachel. And the earl is the only law there is. *You* told me."

She smiled sadly. "And you told me you'd find a better way."

By nightfall, Arnkel had recovered enough to sit up by the fire. The girls brought him more broth and fresh bannocks and he ate, avoiding Gil's eyes; and, stronger still, mounted the gangplank and took himself off to the bed they had prepared for him aboard.

"He lives," Erling ruled cheerfully, and the mood of the camp lightened. Board games were set up and Niall played his harp and there was even a gentle song. Gil checked on the ponies and walked back toward the fires and the black tents, ready for bed himself.

But Erling stopped him at the edge of the camp. His jovial face was solemn and he beckoned Gil to sit beside him on a fallen tree. Rubbing his thick beard with the back of his hand, he said, "You are earl, and all decisions are yours. But I must say this one thing." He lowered his head respectfully.

"Say it." Gil braced himself.

"You make, this day, an error."

"I make a lot," Gil answered wearily.

"No. Only one." Erling smiled, his sunburnt forehead wrinkling.

"I shouldn't have thrown him in the sea."

Erling smiled again and shook his head. "You should have let him drown."

When Gil lay down, that night, beneath the awning, Erling and Svein sat yet with their board and playing pieces. "We enjoy our game," Erling said mildly, "and would finish it."

Gil nodded and smiled, knowing well enough they were guarding him against his own treacherous crew, but too exhausted to care. In wary silence, Ari and Karl dragged their furs into a corner of the deck and curled up like two beaten puppies, as near to Gil as they dared. When all was quiet, Janetta came from the girls' tent and wordlessly lay down in the darkness beside him. Gratefully wrapping his arms around her, he buried his face in the deeper darkness of her hair and slept.

In the morning, Erling and Svein were snoring peacefully beside their board. It did not matter. Arnkel, and any threat he might have posed, was gone; vanished into the forest beyond, taking with him Gisli, Brand, and Tofi, and half the silver in their treasure kist.

CHAPTER TWELVE

"It's so empty," Gil whispered, watching the bleak shore recede. It was midday. He had stayed on in the cove, mounting a search, more to allow time for a change of heart, than out of any hope of success. But no one was found, and no one returned, not even Tofi, who was younger even than Gil and who had wept, parting from his mother on the strand.

Now, with half a day lost, they sailed into the teeth of a gale. The sea before them was grey, streaked with white. Storm clouds lay over the forest and moorlands behind. The further out they tacked, the vaster and lonelier the shoreline appeared.

"Where will they go?" he said, aloud, to Erling, at his side. He felt a pain in his chest, like grief, at leaving them behind, so far from home. Even though it was their own free choice.

Erling shrugged. "There are men there."

"Men who will welcome four Vikings?"

Erling rubbed his sun-burnt nose and then said cheerfully, "They have silver. Perhaps they buy good favor?"

"Or they are murdered for it."

"Ah! You think too much like a Northman. No. I think some kind farmer takes them in. And then Arnkel seduces his daughter. And his wife! *Then* they are murdered." He smiled. "Cheer yourself. They find a road. They follow it to Lindisfarne. And there they beg mercy of the Ab, for they are shipwrecked, or so they claim. He finds them passage on some visiting merchant's knarr. And Arnkel is home before you, with some tale full of lies to explain himself."

"I hope so," Gil said quietly. "For Bergljot's sake."

Erling snorted. "For Bergljot's sake, I hope not. Better he

were under the sea, and she a widow."

"Alone with a child?"

"Not for long," Erling smiled again. "A fine woman. Some other will marry her." He paused, tugging at his beard. "Many men in our islands raise another man's child."

Gil looked out over the dragon prow, questing seaward, and then glanced quickly behind to see all was well with Ismail. "But the others," he said sadly. "They're just boys really. And I promised their fathers ...."

"Their fathers should have raised better sons." Erling slapped Gil's shoulder. "Their fault, not yours. You do well, young earl. But for that one mistake." With a grim smile, he wandered off in search of a game.

It was a short day, and all too soon, they were again seeking a sheltered strand. Too late for hunting, they shared a morose meal of dried fish and Bannocks, Gil measuring their diminishing supplies in his head, as they did.

His careful plans were in disarray. The silver in his treasury was now barely enough to replenish supplies at Hrafn's Ayre. There was nothing left over to reward his young crew and their need of reward was evident. Too wary, now, to complain, they slogged listlessly through chores on shore and shipboard, their Viking adventure reduced to a tedium of empty stomachs and damp feet.

The days fell into a weary pattern, with the alien shore ever unfolding off their steering board. When, rarely, they passed signs of habitation—farmland and smoke from strangers' hearths—they grew lonely for their own. At nightfall, young faces turned wistfully north.

Windswept camp sites blended, one into another, the monotony broken only by a successful hunt inland, and the luxury of meat. But soon the squabbling and resentments began, again. Games were forsaken. Stories dwindled for lack of listeners. Niall sang of old heroes of Ireland for lack of heroics of their own.

One night, the ponies wandered, delaying them further, while recriminations flew between the girls over tethers improperly tied, and Gil thought grimly of wolves. In the relief of their sudden re-appearance, he vented his fury on Lionheart, even though he knew it would have been a mare in the lead: *Next time I'll leave you! Let the wolves eat you!"*

Lionheart munched the remnants of some farmer's haystack. *There are no wolves on Hrolf's Isle.*

But we're not ON Hrolf's Isle, genius!"

Only Percy, who liked things always the same, seemed content; his friends around him all day long, and his precious cup and his newest shell hugged close under his fur, each night.

For Gil, there was yet another concern, greater than the loss of their silver. His crew was four men down: there were four fewer on the oars, when launching against the wind, four fewer to man the sheets and the tacking spar. Four fewer to reef the great sail in a sudden squall, or haul on the ropes when coming ashore.

And, though he kept the thought quietly to himself, four fewer in any battle, chosen or unchosen, they might fight. That one of the missing four was, but for Ragnar, the best swordsman aboard, mattered even more. Boys and farmers could manage in a brawl. But against schooled opponents, he needed warriors. And Arnkel Fish-Tail, dishonest and self-aggrandizing though he was, was undoubtedly a warrior.

Still, he could not avoid a fight forever; nor did he any longer wish to. Where earlier he had steered clear of passing ships, now he searched the horizon eagerly for sails. One timely knarr, and half his problems were solved. A swift capture, a show of swords, and they could sail on to the impromptu markets of Hrafn's Ayre with the swagger of Vikings, and silver to spare.

But now, the sea remained empty, taunting him with its peacefulness, and the first ships they saw were merchant vessels at Hrafn's Ayre, itself lying in the shallows behind the curving sand bar, protected by their very numbers. And so, like a fox humbled by hens, he beached his warships amongst them and set about seeking food for his crew.

A sack of cabbages and another of turnips was all he dared afford, but added to fresh-caught fish, netted by Ragnar and Ismail in the tidal pools, they made, at least, a change. Cheered by it, his young Northmen wandered innocently amid the merchants' campfires, admiring the exotic goods bound upriver for the markets of Deer Bay.

A fur trader, rightly judging them penniless, scolded them away from his beautiful pelts, and another only laughed and shook his head when Leidolf and Hamund, farmers' sons from Gauk's Isle, held out two small coins toward a roll of silk. Gil yearned to thrust silver into their purses as Floki Magnusson had done for him, but instead, watched silently as they returned to their tents empty-handed, twisting their fading love-knots around their wrists.

In the morning, they left at dawn, slipping out on the ebb tide, while the merchants sat around their fires, waiting for the flood that would carry them inland. The wind was light, the sheltered waters calm. A last star remained in the sky. Here and there, ashore, a man watched, wary eyes on the golden pennant.

"Glad to see us go," Gil said, with a smile, to Rachel who had come to stand beside him at the helm. As he steered seaward around shoals and sandbanks, she looked out over the dragon's tail at the grey river winding through salt meadows, toward Deer Bay.

"Homesick?" he nodded toward the distant town.

She shrugged. "Why does standing on the same ground make it feel closer, when it isn't distance at all, but time that lies between?"

He thought quietly. "It's like the love-knots," he said at last. "They tie a man and a woman together when the sea separates them. Time is just a bigger sea. And the land is the love-knot in between."

She raised an eyebrow. "That's rather poetic. I think you're turning into Floki."

His eyes on the grey horizon, he laughed grimly. "Just now, I'd like nothing better."

She smiled. "Be careful what you wish for," she said.

When, halfway through the day, they spotted the knarr, riding low in the water on course for Deer Bay, he remembered her words. But still he moved without hesitation. Signaling Ismail, he changed course and together they closed on the merchant ship. He hoped only that he could take it without bloodshed. That he would take it, was no longer in question.

It had appeared suddenly, breaking from a fogbank, a good-sized trader with a large expanse of sail, looming larger still than it was in the eerie light. Seeing them, its master jibed downwind, turning back to the safety of the mist. But, heavily laden and broad-beamed, his trader was no match for longships racing under full sail.

They were a scant two lengths behind when the knarr slipped through the wall of low cloud as through a curtain, vanishing like a ghost. Ismail hailed Gil and Gil thrust an arm forward. Side by side, they, too, slipped into the grey oblivion.

Silence fell all around, the sea itself smoothed as if pressed flat by the weight of nothingness. What sounds came, the soft splash of their own bow waves and that of their prey, and the ominous rumble of unseen surf, somewhere off his steering board, served as Gil's only guides.

"I trust he knows his sea," Erling muttered uneasily over Gil's shoulder. Aware he was letting another man set his course, Gil struggled with a memory from years ago, of the mist-shrouded waters as they sailed from Hy. And the fearsome fang of rock that even Floki Magnusson got wrong.

"Merchant," he said, as much to himself as to Erling. "Back and forth all the time."

The sail slackened as the wind dropped further, and then suddenly, she was there before him, becalmed and readying her oars. Gil swung the tiller, lest he run her down, and with loosened sheets, they glided smoothly up beside her steering board. Beyond the knarr, *Star-Seeker* closed in, a white-winged phantom.

Signaling to Ciarnan to drop the sail, he called to Ragnar and Svein for the grappling irons. Then the mist suddenly parted and what had been grey shadows aboard the knarr became men.

He saw at once that the ship was much larger than either of the two he had raided with Floki. And her crew, larger too, by far. A big, solid, workhorse of a boat, she was two-thirds the length of his own, with oar ports for a dozen men, each side. Several were already manned, as if she prepared yet to escape, while the rest of her crew, big, battle-scarred men with well-worn sword belts cinched around muscular waists; lined the rails.

A gust of wind shifted the loosened sail and Gil caught his breath. In the open hold amidships, crouched a further dozen men, crammed shoulder to shoulder amid the cargo of tight-lashed casks. For an awful moment he imagined he had attacked a warship by mistake.

But then he heard a shout from his own deck, bizarrely, in Irish. "Men of Tara?" The young poet, Niall, was on his feet, straining over the rail toward the huddled figures in the hold. One man half rose, throwing back a multi-colored cloak, worn over the shoulder in the Irish way, and shouted back, "Kinsman! Set us free!"

Erling nudged Gil's shoulder, pointing down at the iron cuff on the man's leg, the length of blackened chain linking him to his neighbor. "Slave trader." The Irishman caught up the chain and shook it furiously, and Gil understood the ship, then, and her hard-bitten, oversized crew. Silks and furs had no need of chains, nor warriors to quell rebellion; slaves were a dangerous cargo.

His counterpart at the knarr's helm, a wind-burned Northman with yellow hair in long plaits and a forked, ruddy beard, leaned casually against his tiller and raised a hand lacking two fingers, in salute. "Out a'viking, boys?" he called. Laughter engulfed the line of warriors at his rail.

Gil nodded. "Good guess," he said and won a laugh of his own. Out of the corners of his eyes he saw Svein and Ragnar waiting with their irons.

One of the warriors, a broad, bald man with a beard tucked into his belt, caught the quick shift of Gil's gaze, but seeing the grapples, he only snorted. "Picked the wrong ship, lads. Go off and find yourselves a nice little silk trader with a fat old Dane at the helm."

"Go home to your mothers!" another shouted, then. "If your mothers will have you." The laughter and the insults to their mothers that followed gave Gil a chance to meet Svein Sveinsson's eyes, across the deck of the knarr. Raising his head, he looked hard at her lofty yard. Svein nodded.

"Be quiet," the fork-bearded helmsman shook his head disapprovingly. "I am sure their mothers are fine women, all, and married indeed to their fathers." He smiled, as if he had all the time in the world to converse, and looked up at Gil's masthead where the golden pennant fluttered in the mist. "You know, lad," he said cheerfully, "I see that, and I run. But you are not the man I fear you are." His eyes roved Gil's deck, as if seeking someone, and returned to Gil at the helm. "And indeed," he added, "I hear that man is in Norway, causing trouble." His brown forehead wrinkled with puzzlement. Then suddenly his eyes bored into Gil's. "So, what you do with Floki Magnusson's Dragon?"

Gil blinked innocently. "I've stolen her."

"*You?*" The helmsman's answer was almost lost in the laughter of his crew. Shields were lowered and fierce postures abandoned.

"And he *is* in Norway," Gil added. "Hiding from me."

The men at the oars leaned back on their benches, howling with glee. The warriors at the rail pretended terror; two dropping their swords and holding up empty hands in surrender.

The helmsman, tiring eventually of the jest, smiled. "Fine, lad; now on your way. I would catch the tide ...." He turned back to his steering oar; then whirled, too late, at the sound of grapples skittering across his deck. "Oh, Thor's hammer strike you!" he groaned wearily, as his crew dashed to cut loose the tightening lines. But then Svein Sveinsson's iron flew, high up into the mist and over their yard.

Clattering into the mast, it scraped down, gouging the wood and snagged, entangled in the rakke. Svein hauled on his line and the knarr lurched onto her loadboard. As her crew scrambled for footing, the rakke splintered and the yard crashed down, enveloping half the deck in sail. Grappling irons rained from both sides, the three hulls thudded together, and Gil grabbed the battle-axe and jumped.

Its flashing arc cleared space enough for Ragnar and Ciarnan to follow. Behind them, his whole young crew jostled to join the fight. Ismail's Shetlanders were already scrambling over *Star-Seeker's* rail.

Aboard the knarr, Gil left his two best swordsmen to engage the captain and his bald mate, and the untried youngsters to deal with their crew, staggering out from beneath the fallen yard. Swinging the axe to open a path, he raced to the hold and hauled back the heavy sail.

"Kinsman!" A red-headed, smiling young man emerged from beneath and welcomed him with a stream of Irish. Holding the slave chain up in both hands, he stretched it across a thwart. Gil spun the battle-axe and brought the flat of the heavy head down with a ringing crash. The outstretched links bent and splayed. Two more blows, and they parted, jingling into the hold, while the loose end of the chain rattled through the slave cuffs, setting man after man free. Laughing grimly, the Irishmen set upon their captors in a flurry of bare feet and fists.

Gil looked up to the deck of his ship. Janetta, Danni, and Rachel were struggling together to calm the ponies. He pointed to the freed Irishmen. "Arm them!"

Forsaking their rearing, whinnying charges, they ran to the weapons kist and hauled out blades and axes of every size, flinging them down to the Irishmen. "Kinsman!" Gil's new friend cried gleefully and with a sword in one hand and an axe in the other, he plunged into the fray.

It was over too soon for the Irish; the pent up shame and fury of their captivity only half spent. But, wrong-footed and outnumbered, the crew of the knarr knew when to quit. Lined up against the rail, they laid down their weapons and held up their hands.

The fork-bearded helmsman dropped his own sword belt to the deck and lifted empty palms. His mockery had vanished, but not his easy nature. "I fear your efforts wasted," he said regretfully. "I am not a wealthy man."

"Less wealthy this night than this morn," Erling called. The captain nodded gravely, his long plaits flicking in the wind.

"I give you half the slaves," he said. "Any more are trouble." He shook his head concernedly.

"We are good with trouble," Ragnar smiled.

"All the slaves," said Gil. "And your silver."

"But I have none!" The trader raised his eyes to the heavens.

"That will be true this night," Erling agreed. Gil lifted the axe and studied its shining blades.

"Broadaxe!" cried his Irish friend, and trying out halting Norse, "We play some more?"

The captain shrugged and nodded to his mate. "The large kist," he murmured.

"Both kists," Gil said.

"There is but one ...."

"Which is both large and small?" Ragnar smiled again.

Scowling, the bald man retrieved two kists and with a glance at his captain, laid them at Gil's feet. Guarded by the battle-axe, Ciarnan knelt and opened both.

The larger was piled high with stolen treasure: strings of pearls, beads and crystal, silver platters and goblets, a jewel encrusted psalter. The shallow interior of the smaller contained a few pieces of hack-silver and a set of scales in a wooden case. "The tools of my trade," the captain said, "little more."

"The tools of *your* trade lie on the deck before you," Ragnar growled, nudging the captain's sword belt with his foot.

"What's underneath?" Gil said innocently.

The tip of Ciarnan's sword, prying at the wood beneath the scales, lifted it just enough to reveal the glitter of gold.

"Ah," the captain shook his head. "Would you believe I had forgotten that?"

"No." Gil grinned and got a cheerful grin in return.

They loaded the kists aboard *Silver Dragon*. Whooping and cheering, the Irishmen loaded themselves. Retrieving their grapples, *Star-Seeker* and *Silver Dragon* cast off, drifting away from the knarr on the gentle sea.

The captain looked up at Gil thoughtfully, "I do not know how you come by her, lad, nor do I believe your story, but whoever you are, you serve that fine ship well."

Gil gave a cautious nod. "Thank you," he said at last. He looked down at the trader's crew, disentangling their fallen yard. "Can you repair her?"

"Am I a seaman?"

They shared a respectful smile and then Gil took the helm and ordered his crew to raise sail.

The Irish slaves lifted the spirits of the Northmen like a clearing sky at the end of a dreich grey day. They were young. They were light-hearted. They were giddy with their unexpected good fortune. And they were warriors.

The first night, gathered around a blazing fire, they told their story, in Irish, translated by Ciarnan, and in their own ragged Norse. The red-headed spokesman declared himself Fergus, son of Gartnan, a noble king who, like Ciarnan's father, owed loyalty to the High-King at Tara. He held out his cloak before them. "This indeed, the Tara weave, known to your poet, as he, and Tara's harp, are known to me." He stared reverently at the fabled instrument resting humbly on Niall's knees. "To think that I would ever see it, more, and here on this far shore," he cried, before continuing his tale.

"And it was on behalf of the High-King that I, and all these, followers, too, of Gartnan, did battle against men of the North, raiding our shore." He seemed blissfully untroubled that his new friends were also men of the North, though Gil thought of Hakon and the cloak he himself wore, stolen from those shores.

"But they were many," Fergus continued, "And we, few, and some among us die that day, and some flee, and the rest you see before you, rounded up like cattle and driven aboard their ships, bound for the slave markets of Dublin. And then, but for you, the slave markets of Deer Bay and lives of labor for another's bread."

He shook back a tangled mane of curling ruddy hair, and, smiling within a bushy beard, grasped Gil's arm in a warrior's grip. "Broadaxe! My friend!"

As they sailed down the coast, other friendships rapidly formed. Divided evenly between *Star-Seeker* and *Silver Dragon*, the Irishmen meshed easily with their crews, finding common language in the common cause of the ships and the sea.

Each landfall, they threw their welcome weight against the ropes, scavenged the strand for firewood, joined Gil and Janetta in the hunting, or rode out with Rachel and Danni, seeking grazing for the ponies. Missing their brothers and sisters at home, they played games with Percy and ran along evening strands, gathering shells for him, like children.

Respectful of Gil, playfully flirtatious with the girls, strong-backed and uncomplaining, they made lighter every task on shore or at sea. At night, they all shared stories of their respective homes, and as Niall played, sang together; old songs of Ireland, and new-wrought songs of their own adventures composed in a day, by the Irish *file's* quick-witted son.

Stepping back with Gil from the heat of the fire, one night, Erling nodded with satisfaction. "It is well. The dog howls for Arnkel."

Startled that the omen at their sailing still played on Erling's mind, Gil smiled uncertainly. "Why do you say?"

"Arnkel leaves and takes those three striplings with him. And then *these* come to us. Twelve warriors! Odin smiles on us. The dog howls for Arnkel Fish-Tail."

On the fourth night, with the air already warmer, and the light more southerly, they beached at the edge of a great forest from which Janetta and Ismail returned with two fine deer. Gil brought out a cask of ale, and they feasted properly, celebrating their last landfall before Dofras, and the crossing to Francia.

Well-fed and with cheeks reddened from the fire and from drink, Fergus wrapped Gil's shoulders in a brawny arm and cried, "Broadaxe, my friend! Come with us to Ireland. Come to my father's hall. You will be welcomed like kings! And nowhere is the hunting finer, the feasting more splendid. And, for those who are free, the women more beautiful!" To the cheers that followed, he added hastily, "And more chaste!"

With laughter, then, and promises to test that claim, the Northmen cast hopeful glances at their earl. Gil smiled and shook his head. "I cannot," he said simply. "I sail to Francia."

"Ah, a pity." Fergus rocked back on their shared driftwood seat, his arm yet around Gil's shoulders. Then he loosened his grip and sat straighter. His eyes darkened with a new uncertainty. "But you will set us ashore in Dofras that we may seek another ship?"

Gil looked down at his hands, studying the rope burns in the flickering light and thinking of his disconsolate, diminished crew on the strand at Einar's Bay. He opened his mouth to speak and then closed it again. "I sail to Francia," he said, at last. He looked up urgently and met the Irishman's eyes. "I have friends there. Kin. There's a battle I must fight. I need them to join me. We're too few ...."

"A battle in Francia?" Fergus said cautiously.

"No. In Caledon. I sail to Francia, and then back to Caledon. By Glen Alban," he said. "Look, I'll take you there and then the way lies clear through the glens to the Sudreys. And Ireland."

"And then you set us free?" Fergus said.

Gil pulled back, horrified. "You're free now!" he cried.

Fergus smiled. "Yes. We are free." He laughed lightly and lifted a booted foot. "There are no chains. Only the sea."

He turned away and called to Niall in Irish for a favored song of Tara, and listened to it, a little sadly. But his cheerful nature revived at once and he returned his arm to Gil's shoulders. "Who is this enemy you go to fight?" But before Gil could answer, he cried, "No matter! An enemy of Gil Broadaxe is an enemy of mine. We join you in this battle! Ireland will not see us, until your cause is won!"

By the morning, the Irish warriors were all full of the battle to come, teasing the young Northmen that the glory would all be theirs. Erling smiled contentedly within his beard. "Odin's will," he said.

Gil said nothing. But when, in sight of the white cliffs of Dofras, he swung his oar and headed out to sea, he felt something in himself turn, too, setting a new, uncertain course.

Chapter Thirteen

"She is long away." Ismail shaded his eyes, peering into the white morning sky. Danni had flown first; Rachel, after. Gil looked up to where Rachel's Hawk circled yet, awaiting the Wild Goose's return. Then he glanced uneasily inland, over the forest and the bright tops of the distant tournament pavilions. Still seeing no sign of her, he turned his gaze to the sea beyond the bluff that hid the strand and their camp.

The tide was out; the bay a mere expanse of yellow sand cut only by narrow rivulets of sea water. Mont Tombe floated on the horizon over a shimmer of mirage. The November air was as warm as spring, the wind in the south.

They had come to the Frankish fortress a day earlier, at Saxt. Gil beached his ships as Floki had, where the inflowing river cut through the tidal flats, providing a certain escape route at the lowest ebb.

He ordered the masts lowered and the awnings raised. Then, while fires were kindled, he saddled Lionheart and rode through the falling tide to the edge of the tournament ground. Dismounting, he looped the reins over his arm and with the pony ambling behind, wandered barely noticed among the half-built booths of the merchants who followed the knights.

Struggling with the babble of languages, he eavesdropped on stall holders and armorers, blacksmiths and pilgrims, as in Frankish and Norse, Saxon, and Latin, the merits of contestants and their mounts were debated. Then he mounted his pony again and with soaring spirits cantered home over the fresh-washed sand. Because among the names of knights and heroes whispered in awe by youthful esquires and with dreamy smiles by the boisterous women with their high-kilted skirts, was the one name he had come hoping to hear: Lance'lot, the champion of exiled Camelot.

"Perhaps your father is not yet here," Ismail said, still watching the sky, "And so she does not find him."

Gil shook his head. "He's here. They're placing bets on him already. He has to be here. And the Vespers is Saint Martin's Eve. That's just five days away."

Ismail smiled. "You sure?"

"No." Without Aidan and his psalter, Gil's calendar was governed only by shortening days and rising stars. He grinned lamely. "But Rachel keeps track for me. They'll be here." He watched the hawk circle.

With his eyes still on the far horizon, Ismail said, "Do you think, ever, that Danni flies away north and does not return?"

"Back to Floki?"

Ismail shrugged uneasily. Gil shook his head. "No. Danni keeps promises. When we were kids, if she promised you a stick of ...." he paused, forehead furrowed, trying to remember. The taste, minty and sweet was in his mouth. "You know, that stuff you ate, but didn't eat?"

Ismail grinned. "No?"

"Anyhow, she kept all her promises. And this one, to Aidan, most of all."

"And then?" Ismail said.

Above them, the hawk darted suddenly from its circle, streaking out over the forest toward a distant dot that had appeared in the sky. Relieved not to answer, Gil smiled. "There she is."

He watched as her shape grew larger, while the hawk's diminished. The two birds passed in the air, the hawk homing to the point from which the wild goose had flown. Suddenly stooping, she plunged down toward the treetops. "She's found them!" he cried, turning to Ismail. But then a shout from behind took all his attention.

"Broadaxe!"

Gil spun around. Fergus strode over the crest of the bluff, a quiver of arrows over his shoulder, a bow held up in his hand. "Look, my friend, what your silver brings to me!" With his free hand, he flung back his cloak, revealing a new scabbard and sword. "And this!" So fine a weapon!" He caressed the hilt. "I am armed like a king. But how can I repay you?" he cried, dismayed.

Gil laughed, looking up again to the call of the wild goose. "By using it!" he said. He unbuckled his own sword belt and looping the ends held it up. "It's not my silver, Fergus. It belongs to us all. And my warriors must be armed."

His eyes were on the approaching bird. The sun glinted on her wings. As always, she looked joyful, as if the sky were her natural home and she returned to earth with regret. He raised the circle of leather to her. Then, out of the corner of his eye, he saw a flash of movement, as Ismail hurtled by him. Fergus shouted and sprawled in the beach grass, with Ismail pinning him down. The bow, and the arrow he had set to its string, skidded into the sand.

"Leave me!" he shouted, staring up at the goose. "I would have it!" He struggled up, red-faced, with Ismail still restraining him. Then the bird swept through her circle, and landed, a windswept and beautiful girl, at Gil's side.

"Welcome back," he said, and shrugging toward Fergus added, "Sorry. But you have an audience."

Fergus staggered to his feet, holding on to Ismail for support. "A Change-Thing?" he whispered.

Danni smiled encouragingly. Fergus edged closer, reached out a shaky hand and touched her. Jerking his fingers back, he cried, "It is real! It is you!" he shook his head wonderingly. "I have heard the old women speak of such things." Cautiously he touched Danni again, letting his fingers rest briefly on her arm. "Always, I laugh! But now, I laugh no more." Turning to Gil, he said. "And you know she does this? It does not trouble you?"

"Actually," Gil said. "I asked her to do it." Fergus stared. Gil said to Danni, "Are they there?"

"There's a pavilion," she looked back toward the forest. "Far

back in an oak grove. So well hidden that I flew over it twice
before I saw it."

"What color?" Gil asked.

"Grey. Or brown. Like Aidan's robes. Undyed cloth. I thought
they were pilgrims. But then I saw the chargers, tethered in a
line. And armor heaped beside the fire."

"It's them," Gil said. "Only exiles make camp in secret."
He saw the hawk rise up above the canopy of the forest and
streak back toward them, and he held up the sword belt again.
The hawk dove low and he glimpsed a bright flutter of cloth
gripped in her talons. Dropping it at his feet, she swept through
her circle and into her human form. Behind him, Fergus gave a
strangled cry.

Slipping to his knees, Gil took up the cloth and spread it out
in the grass. On a snowy white pennant designed to adorn a
lance the heraldic emblem of a great fir tree shown in brilliant
green.

"It is Green Tree of Caledon!" Ismail cried. "It is your father.
Lance'lot."

"They're about a mile from here," Rachel pointed back the
way she and Danni had flown. "There's a clearing, deep in
the forest. First, there's an avenue of beech trees. Then a track
leading off it. You'll see hoof prints."

"I know the place," Gil said quietly. He rolled the pennant
and gave it back to Rachel. "We'll find it." He nodded to Ismail
who was already drawing a circle in the sand with the tip of his
sword.

Fergus watched uneasily. "What does he do?"

"Ah." Gil smiled. He rested a hand on the Irish warrior's
shoulder. "My friend," he said, "I think you should take the
girls back to the ships," he smiled again, "so they won't be
frightened."

Fergus looked from Ismail to Gil and then back to Ismail.
"You mean so that *I* will not be frightened."

Gil shrugged easily. "Change-Things are scary. Some of
them scarier than others," he added.

"I am not frightened."

"Okay."

"I am a warrior of Tara. I fear no ghosts, no Change-Things, none of the faery world."

"Good!" Gil nodded again to Ismail who stepped within his circle, softly murmuring the blessing. Gil closed his eyes. He might be a change-thing himself, but the transformation always un-nerved him. When Fergus finished shouting in horror, he knew it was safe to look.

The Stag stood, yet in its circle, shaking its great rack of antlers and pawing the ground. Fergus was on his knees, hands half shielding his face. Danni and Rachel bent over him at either side, struggling not to laugh.

"You okay?" said Gil.

Fergus got stiffly to his feet and lowered his hands. White-faced and determined, he said, "I am not frightened."

"Great!" Gil gave him a big smile. "That's really great." Then, as the stag leapt free of the circle and trotted back and forth, he himself took its place.

Fergus held out a hand. "Wait." He looked at the stag and back to Gil. "*You?* You *also?*"

"Sorry about that." Gil gave him another smile. "Ready?" Fergus covered his eyes again and groaned, which Gil took to be agreement. Closing his own eyes, he murmured,

"Bless to me my sister,

Bless to me my brother ..."

At least, he thought, as the world sprang up, huge, noisy, and vibrant, around him, *his* Other wasn't scary. Though the whimpering sound Fergus made when Cat rubbed against his boot suggested otherwise. Deep within his feline soul, Cat felt a sort of kitten-pity for the Irish warrior, but when a second rub won only another moan, he gave up, crouched low, and sprang up onto the stag's shaggy back.

The stag jumped, its rough coat twitching frantically, as Cat set his claws in firm. *Sorry.* Padding gently, he strove to reach past the predator fear in Ismail's animal mind, to the human mind within. *Go for it.*

With a last shudder, the stag gathered himself and bounded away through the marshland to the forest beyond. Cat hunkered down, purring and padding. The rocking motion, the warmth of the shaggy mane of neck fur, the effortless strides beneath him, were soothing and familiar. *Like in Rome. Riding in the cowl of Floki's pilgrim's cloak, claws in the Northman's hair ....* He padded harder and was nearly asleep when Ismail's Stag stopped in the beech wood avenue, sniffing the air.

Cat raised his head, flaring his nostrils and half opening his mouth. *Wood smoke.* Then: *Men. Horses. Dog.* His hackles rose and his ears flicked forward, catching the jingle of harness, the distant clang of metal upon metal, a child's squealing laugh. Rising and stretching, he leapt to the ground and approached alone on stealthily paws.

The sounds grew louder. Horses whinnied. Men shouted. A hammer rang a steady bell note on an anvil. The yeasty tang of ale enriched the scents, and then, the aroma of roasting meat. Cat's nose twitched happily. He loped, tail high, toward the distant flicker of firelight through the trees.

A beaten track, rank with horse sweat and manure, crossed his path. He cleared it in a bound and darted into a thick bank of laurel. Then, lowering himself to his belly, he crept forward and crouched, tail swishing, at its edge.

Before him, in a forest clearing surrounded by enormous, brown-leafed oaks, lay the encampment of the knights of Caledon. A drab, grey pavilion stood in the shadows beneath one mighty tree, its peaked roof brushing the lower branches. Above its awning-draped entrance hung three shields, their bright colors defying the poverty of the tent cloth.

In the center, the Red Cockerel announced the Earl de Troye. At its left hung the Black Dragon of the Saracen knight, Palamedes, and, on the right, the Green Tree of Caledon. Cat's tail swished again, in excitement.

Across the clearing, a whole string of knights' chargers sheltered, like sheep in a thicket, beneath the boughs of another forest giant. Nearby, a blacksmith worked at a rough forge and a youth led two more horses back and forth, their sweaty coats steaming in the dusky air.

A fire burned in the center of the clearing, and there, where a gap in the forest canopy allowed a glimpse of the sky, sunlight sifted down onto the head of a woman roasting meat on a greenwood spit. A small white dog sat beside her, watching hungrily.

Around the open hearth, other women pounded grain, while men polished armor and mended tack. Two young girls plucked wood-fowl. Another milked a patient cow. Smaller children, armed with wooden swords, scrambled over a cart stacked high with provisions and made fortresses from jousting saddles and shields.

The garments of all, once fine, were patched and worn, the plaid cloaks of Caledon faded by southern suns. But the women laughed and sang while they worked and their children played happily, innocent of the lands they had lost.

Cat's nose twitched back and forth between the fresh milk frothing into the girl's wooden pail, and the meat sizzling succulently on its spit. Settling on the meat, he watched the woman at the fire. She was tall and slim, with plaits of yellow hair wrapped around her head. Leaning forward, she plucked a scrap of meat from the roast and held it up. The dog sat up on its haunches, whimpering, until she dropped the meat before it. *Never,* Cat flattened his ears. *Not for all the game in the forest.* He turned his attention to the milk.

A child's shout came from the trees and the woman straightened, wiping her hands down her rough apron. Gil's heart surged. *Ingirid! Janetta's stepmother.* She turned toward the fair-haired young boy who ran into the clearing, holding a bow in one hand and a fresh-killed rabbit in the other. He dashed past the fire and ran toward the pavilion. Ingirid reached out to stop him, but he eluded her, and shouting, "Papa! Papa!" he slipped between the tent flaps with his prize.

Forgetting the milk, Cat stared at the place where he had vanished. A low rumble of voices came from within the pavilion, interrupted once by an angry shout. Ears forward, Cat listened and sniffed the air. Then, with a quick check on the dog, he broke from his shelter, bounded to the provisions cart and darted into the darkness beneath it.

Beyond, a row of jousting saddles provided a cat tunnel and a stack of shields, a cat wall. But then there was only open ground before him. He looked back over his shoulder. The women worked and the children played, oblivious of his small furry presence. The absurd dog sat up, yet begging. With a tail swish of disdain, Cat trotted in full view to the foot of the pavilion and wormed his way beneath the out-stretched cloth.

Within, the air was murky with dust and rank with the scents of men and the horses they had ridden. And of dog. Tail bushing, Cat gauged the distance to a cross beam of the tent frame and leaped to it, landing silently on delicate paws. Below him, the gathering seated on rough benches took no notice; their attention fixed on the rustic High Table at the pavilion's rear.

Three men sat there, and two more, slender and young, stood facing them. A heap of tan-spotted hounds snored beneath the table, paws twitching in a dream-hunt. Warily, Cat raised his eyes to the men. In the center, his burly frame uneasy on his primitive High Seat, sat Janetta's father, Martin, the Earl de Troye. His powerful arm rested around her fair-haired half-brother, as he listened to his petitioners with weary patience. The child clung to his father's neck, his rabbit hanging now forgotten from his hand, staring in awe at his companions.

On the earl's left, his black hair and beard curling wild as a bramble thicket, sat the great Saracen knight, Palamedes. His long velvet tunic was frayed at the hem, its fur trim ragged and torn. His head was bowed, his dark eyes solemnly downcast; but the hilt of the sword at his side gleamed yet, polished with care.

Cat's eyes settled, then, blinking gently, on the man at the earl's right, and his paws padded at the sound of his voice. Lean and worn, his greying brown hair hanging untrimmed below his shoulders, his tanned face lined, Lance'lot, once Laurent Lake of Greene Mountain Falls, quietly addressed the petitioners, "No one doubts your courage."

"But no one will act on it either," the taller of the youths cried. "Will they, Sir Lance'lot?" He raised frustrated hands in the air and half turned away, revealing his face. *Elias!* Cat's ears flicked happily. *Elias of the Forest!*

"We will act." Martin de Troye's eyes flashed.

"Sir Martin," the second youth, smaller and darker, said softly. "When?"

Palamedes, who had remained sitting in thoughtful silence, slowly raised his head. Fixing his dark gaze upon the young man, he said, "You know this, my friend."

"What?" Elias cried. "When the sun rises in the west? When the moon falls into the sea?" He paused, cocking his head sardonically, "When Arthur returns?"

A troubled muttering passed through the men on the benches. Martin de Troye silenced them with a wave of his hand. Turning back to Elias, he said, "Yes."

Elias threw his hands in the air once more. "Then we will wait in this forest until our heads are as grey as yours."

"Ah, better a grey head than none at all, my friend." Palamedes' white smile lit his dark face. "But, list, your fears have little cause, your hopes, much. Arthur's return grows near. There are rumors ...."

"There are always rumors," Elias said wearily. "Arthur is in Frisia! Arthur is in Saxony! Arthur is in Rome! Even in Caledon, I hear the rumors. And none of them are true."

Martin de Troye leaned forward over his table. His boot brushed a sleeping hound, which woke and sniffed the air. Cat froze on his beam, every muscle tensed to flee. But the beast laid its head down on its paws again and snored.

"I know what it is like," the earl began, "to be young and restless ...."

"And I have heard *this* before, too!" Elias spun again, as if he would leave. Cat's ears flattened in sympathy. *Stay. Fight.* Elias turned slowly back.

With great dignity, he said, "I am not a boy to be humored with kind words. I am a man who has ridden in the tournaments and won fine ransoms. Paying my own way, I have ventured to Caledon. Darras, here," he laid a hand on his companion's shoulder, "young as he is, rode with me.

"We have travelled within the forest to the walls of Camelot itself. And under the very nose of the Golden Knight, won men to our cause. Morians and Gareth stay on there, risking their lives to win more. And I return," He said bitterly, "and find only old women, telling each other tales."

Martin de Troye jumped to his feet, hand on sword hilt.

"Outside." He jerked his bearded chin toward the entrance. "We will discuss this as knights."

Lance'lot reached out, and without looking up closed his hand on the earl's wrist and pulled him sharply down. "We are short enough of men," he said, with the trace of a smile. "Let's not lose any more."

He looked up at the young knights. With another smile, he said, "Courage is not enough, Elias. You do not lack that. But you lack an army. Nor have you ships to carry one across the sea."

"There are many here!" Elias cried. "And more come, every day. Five joined us at Dofras on our return."

"But not enough," Lance'lot's voice was gently unrelenting. "We have fought," he said, "and we have failed, Elias."

"Then stay here!" the youth flung back. "We will go and leave you!"

"But who will follow you?" Lance'lot pursued. "How many?" When Elias made no answer, he said solemnly, "If we go now, and fail again, our cause is truly lost. They will never rise a third time. Not even for Arthur." He leaned back in his chair, eyes half closed. Then, straightening, he said, "We must wait. He is our only hope."

Elias stood, silent, before the three great knights. Then he said simply, "Then we have no hope at all." Laying his hand again on his friend's shoulder, he turned away, this time not in anger, but in sorrow.

The younger boy, Darras, blinked back tears. Brushing a hand across his face, in pretext of smoothing back his hair, he looked blankly out over the gathering in the pavilion. And then, suddenly, his eyes opened wide and a smile of pure delight crossed his face. "Look!" he cried, tugging at Elias' sleeve. But when the older youth raised his eyes, there was nothing to be seen beneath the dusty tent cloth but a bare wooden beam.

Cat hit the ground running, wormed his way under the tent cloth, and dashed out into the sunlight, a tail's length from where Ingirid's white lapdog had chosen to sleep. Lying on its back, its small feet in the air, it woke with a start, flipped over and exploded in a flurry of high-pitched yapping.

Inside the pavilion, the hounds roused, baying in response.

Cat puffed up to twice the lapdog's size and swung a claw across its nose. Squealing, it retreated to its mistress, just as the hounds burst from the tent with Darras on their heels. "Gil?" he shouted. "Gil Lake of Tir nan Og! Show yourself!"

But Cat was a streak of orange fur, vanishing into the laurel and the forest beyond.

"It's hopeless," Gil said. "We might as well have stayed on Hrolf's Isle." He threw the last of his leg of roast pheasant in the fire and gloomily listened to it sizzle.

"No," Ismail said. "We stay on Hrolf's Isle, we do not meet the Irishmen. We do not meet the Irishmen, we do not have this good pheasant."

"Or the pigeons," Danni smiled at Gil.

"Great. We can spend the winter hunting."

Erling helped himself to more pheasant. "As good a use of spear and bow as any. And we have enough of those. The armorer shut up his booth and set out for home, on the business we gave him." He grinned, his beard bristling. "Go to your bed, young earl. In the morning, it is no longer hopeless."

"Fine," Gil said. "Wake me when Arthur gets here." Erling looked blank. "Arthur the king. The one we have to wait for." Gil looked out over the crackling flames to the fire-lit strand where the Irishmen were schooling his young warriors in swordplay. He turned back to Erling, "And don't treat me like a boy."

"I do not mean …."

"Just don't."

Erling sighed, looked around at the others, and then sat back with a weary shrug.

"Sorry," Gil muttered. "But I'm just so sick of being lectured to by old men. Elias standing there in front of the three of them … I might have *been* on Hrolf's Isle, with Gauk and Red Kol. And Magnus."

"But then it is not hopeless," Ismail smiled. "Gauk accepts you as earl. Red Kol lets Ragnar sail. And you raise a crew of old men's sons for *Silver Dragon*."

Gil shook his head. "This is different."

"Why?" Danni said quietly. "Because one of them is your father?"

"No." Gil looked away." But I would have thought," he added, "That *he* wouldn't have been so cautious."

Erling nodded soberly, picking meat off a bone. "Caution is, at times, the best shield."

"Then we are well shielded." Gil got up angrily and stalked away from the fire. Then seeing Janetta's gentle gaze upon him, he returned and stood staring into the flames and pushing sand into a little hillock with his foot.

Ismail said, "You see your father. Suddenly you are little boy. Listen to you. How you talk. And how you walk, even." He jumped up and, laughing, stamped off, as Gil had done, came back, and scuffed sand around like a petulant child. Gil balled his hand into a fist and spun to face him. "Oh, that very grown up, too," Ismail said softly.

Their eyes met and Gil ducked his head and again said, "Sorry."

"Is okay." Ismail's light hand was on his shoulder and suddenly he laughed aloud. "Hey! You look so funny, running from the forest. Like a fox with tail like this!" He held up his hands, a foot apart.

Gil smiled. "Well, you saw what was after me. And, hey, you looked pretty funny, too." He held his hands up to his head to make antlers and pawed the ground snorting through his nose."

"Well," Ismail said, "they run."

Gil smiled again and sat down and accepted an ale horn from Erling. But the dark mood lingered like the November dusk closing around his ships on their empty strand. Until this moment, he had not realized how much of all he had achieved since parting with Floki in Norway had been for one purpose alone: to ride beside his father on the road to Camelot.

Janetta came and sat behind him, and leaning against her knees, he was half asleep with ale and the warmth of the fire, when he heard the shout from the darkness over the sea.

"A ship?" he whispered, sitting up and peering into the

night. Fergus, Ragnar, and Erling were already on their feet. The sky was heavy with cloud, the sea, black. Only the white crests of breaking waves shone through the darkness as the flood tide engulfed the last of the sand bars.

"If there is a ship at all," Erling said, "she will be aground."

The shout came again, and over the sound of the sea, a faint splashing. Lionheart whinnied suddenly from the bluff where the ponies were tethered.

Gil jumped to his feet. "It's a rider. Someone's tried to cross the flats and got caught!" *Like I did*, he thought, grimly remembering Floki dragging him and Janetta from the sea. The shout came a third time.

Gil ran toward the surf, but boots pounded behind him and Erling's hand caught his shoulder. "He may be no friend of ours."

"But he's drowning!" Gil shoved his helmsman aside and plunged into the surf. "Bring ropes!" he called back to Ismail.

The panicked whinny of a horse brought a chorus of equine replies from the bluff. Gil strode through the water toward the sound. Ismail, a coil of rope over his shoulder, followed. On either side, Fergus and Ragnar joined in with drawn swords.

"If he is *not* a friend," Fergus grinned.

"Or it is a trick," Ragnar muttered.

"No trick." Struggling to keep his footing, Gil searched the fast flowing tide, seeing nothing. Then suddenly a horse's head reared up from the water like a rising dragon. White foam churned before its hooves as, snorting and wild-eyed, it struggled up onto firm ground, its drenched rider clinging desperately to its neck. Half-swimming, Gil reached the pair and together with Ismail led the trembling beast to the safety of the strand.

Firelight revealed its young rider. "Darras!" Gil cried.

The youth grinned happily at the row of drawn swords facing him and looked down at Gil. "I am right!" he cried joyfully. "It is you!"

He slid down from the horse and wrapped Gil in a dripping embrace. Stepping back, he smiled again. "I see you and I say to Elias, 'All is saved! We have men! We have ships!' But Elias says,

'You see a cat.' I say, 'No cat comes in among the hounds. It is a Change-Thing. It is Gil.' And I tell him you will be here, with the Viking. He says, 'A cat is a cat.'"

Darras shrugged cheerfully. "So, I come, myself. And I see your fires across the bay and ride for them. But the tide is flowing so fast! So, I nearly drown. The horse swims and I swim. And just in time we reach the shore." He held out the hem of his wet tunic and laughed.

"Get him dry clothes," Gil said quickly, to Ismail, and taking up the fur-lined cloak he had left by the fire, wrapped it around the youth's shoulders.

"Ah, it is no matter," Darras said. "A little sea water. A small price to pay for such good fortune." But, once assured his horse was cared for, he allowed himself to be led to the fire and dressed in dry clothing. Seated there and sipping the warmed ale Janetta had brought him, he smiled happily.

"How did you find us?" Gil said.

"Briant tells me. He remembers where the Viking rests his keel when Garlon and Allein cross with you from Dofras."

"Briant ...?" Gil said uncertainly.

"Sir Brandel's son. Your friend!"

"My friend?" Gil winced. "We betrayed him for a ransom."

"Ah, that is tournament." Darras shrugged. He rides now with Allein and Garlon. Briant's ransom freed Allein's father. Now all are friends. And all will join us. I knew you would return one day to lead us. Elias doubts, Gareth doubts, even Morians doubts. But I never doubt, though the seasons pass."

He looked around at the great ships on the strand, the campfires, and the shadowy figures of the Northmen and the Irish, gathered around storytellers and gaming boards or listening dreamily to the music of Niall's ancient harp. "Now, surely, they believe!" he said. "Such men and such ships to carry them. And the Viking, so famous a warrior!" he looked around again, and then turned curiously to Gil. "Where is he?"

"Being famous in Norway," Gil said.

"But you have his ship!"

"I have his ship," Gil agreed, still slightly stunned, himself.

"No matter then," Darras smiled boldly. "We are many and

we have you. When do we sail?"

Silence fell around their fire. Danni watched Gil steadily. Ismail met his eyes and raised an eyebrow. Rachel rose and filled ale horns, avoiding his gaze. Gil said, at last, "When my father sails with us."

"Your father!" Darras' smile faded. "But your father will not!" He shook his head in disbelief. Then he hunched over his bent knees staring into the flames. "Then Elias is right," he said sadly. "It is hopeless. Even with you." He dropped his head onto his folded arms, hiding his face.

Gil leaned forward helplessly. "Darras, if they won't rise for the three best knights in Camelot, because Guidbairn defeated them, they won't rise for me."

"Then that is simple." Janetta spoke so suddenly from the shadows that even Darras looked up. "You must defeat them, too," she said. "And prove yourself Guidbairn's equal."

"Defeat my *father*? And *your* father? And Palamedes? But they ...."

"On the tournament field," she said. "Where war is only play. And all knights prove their worth. Then," she said, "the Men of Caledon will follow you. And your father will follow you, too."

"Broadaxe!" Fergus cried. "She is wise!"

Gil shook his head uncertainly. But then Ragnar, who had sat throughout in silence, said also, "She is wise. All men respect the man who defeats them."

"Yes!" Fergus cried. He grasped the haft of the battle-axe that Gil had leaned against the ale cask after his practice. "This! This they respect." He stood up and swung it in a cheerfully drunken circle.

Smiling, Ismail stepped forward, begged modestly to try the weapon, and when Fergus relinquished it, handed it firmly to Gil.

Gil studied its fierce double blade in the firelight and smiled too. "Great!" he said. "I take them all on. Martin de Troye. Palamedes," he paused, "Lance'lot. Anyone want to place bets?"

"I am with Broadaxe!" Fergus declared at once. "Broadaxe! Broadaxe!" And the Irish all took up the chant.

"I, too, am with Broadaxe," Darras cried.

And then Erling stroked his beard and gravely announced, "I, also, am with Gil Broadaxe."

But Gil was no longer listening. The long haft firm in his hand, he stood on another far strand, seeing fear awaken in the eyes of Magnus Redbeard. Slowly, he turned back to Darras. "Can you get us horses?" he said.

Chapter Fourteen

"Lower your lance, Fergus!" Gil called. "You want to hit the middle of his shield." Clad in chausses, chain hauberk, and steel helm, Fergus sat astride the tallest of their fine new chargers, facing Ismail across a stretch of tide-washed sand. Ismail's pony, Chocolate, that looked big on Hrolf's Isle, looked small here. And Lionheart—Gil grimaced wryly as Percy trotted him down from the bluff—looked smaller still. "Ismail!" Gil shouted, "Cover your face!"

"Is hot!" Ismail protested. The late autumn sun shone with surprising warmth from a perfect sky.

"It'll be hotter on the tournament grounds tomorrow and we can't be seen, right?"

Reluctantly, Ismail drew the chain *ventaille* across his mouth and chin and throat, hooking it to his helm.

"Wonderful. Knights of mystery. I'm scared of you both already." Behind Gil, the girls looked up from the length of white sailcloth on which they were working and laughed.

In the days since Darras had come, the broad curving ayre on which the ships rested had been transformed into a school for knights, with Gil and Ismail teaching as they had been taught long ago at Einar's Holm. Lance targets—hoops of bent withies—hung suspended from posts in the sand. Two sailcloth sacks, stuffed with bracken and mounted on a driftwood horse, stood in as an opposing knight. A line of tethered chargers snorted and reared while Karl and Ari cautiously offered them water and hay.

When Darras rode off, two days before, to borrow mounts for the tournament, Gil had hoped for three. But at sunset, a whole string of splendid beasts came splashing through the tide. At their head rode a slender blond knight who shouted a joyous greeting, "Gil Lake! My father sends you seven horses, so well does he think of you!"

"Briant ...." Gil shook his head in admiration as the boy cantered the animals cheerfully into his betrayer's camp.

"And my father, three more!" The dark youth taking up the rear of the string, with Darras, smiled shyly. "For your skill won the ransom that bought his freedom."

Gil shook his head again. "More like my trickery, Allein," he answered quietly.

"But that is tournament," they laughed. "And soon we ride together again!"

The two young knights crouched, now, on the sand beside the girls, Briant admiring their work, and Allein admiring Janetta, with such shy innocence that even Gil could not disapprove. Gil turned to the waiting horsemen and shouted, "To the field!" And then, looking further along the strand, "Percy! Get out of the way!"

Mounted on Lionheart and determinedly advancing on their crude sailcloth knight, Percy looked up in surprise. "Oh!"

"Out of the *way*," Gil waved an arm and Percy quickly trotted Lionheart to safety as Gil signaled that the joust begin.

Shields raised, lances lowered, Fergus and Ismail charged, their mounts shod hooves kicking up clods of wet sand as they thundered towards each other along the strand. The crews of both ships gathered behind Gil to watch.

On the first pass, Fergus' horse stumbled and swerved and both lances missed their targets. On the second, they disarmed each other and held their restless chargers until Ari and Karl retrieved their fallen lances. "Is my fault!" Ismail apologized.

"Is both your faults, butterfingers," Gil returned. "Again. And don't be so polite."

Ismail nodded, lined Chocolate up, and charged again, his slender body suddenly steely and determined. Ducking past Fergus' wavering lance, he slammed the point of his own into Fergus' shield with a crack that echoed down the strand. Fergus lost his reins and then both stirrups, tumbled like a ragdoll over his horse's rump, somersaulted mid-air, and landed, sword in hand, on his feet. Spinning Chocolate around, Ismail stared in amazement.

Shouts and cheers arose in Irish and Norse. Erling and Ragnar thumped shields with their fists. Svein Sveinsson shrugged. "He is an Irishman. There are no greater horsemen."

Erling stroked his beard quietly. "Once," he said, "At Einar's Holm, I see Floki Magnusson ride a circle around his father's house, standing on the back of his horse. Do you know another man, of any land, who does that?"

Gil smiled, with a quick glance over his shoulder. "No. But I know a girl who could." Janetta ducked her head shyly and busied herself smoothing the square of sailcloth stretched between Rachel and Danni on the sand.

Ten passes later, when Fergus and Ismail had each unhorsed the other twice and both animals and men were soaked in sweat, Gil called a halt. Karl and Ari led Chocolate and the borrowed charger off to be rubbed down and watered. Gil turned to Ragnar Kolsson. "Our turn."

As Ragnar untied a tall black horse from the waiting string, Gil called to Percy to bring him Lionheart. Standing with thumbs hooked in sword belt, he waited as Percy picked a meandering course across the strand, making stabs at imaginary knights along the way. "Like, *now*?" Gil shouted.

Two invisible opponents later, Percy pulled Lionheart up before him and slid reluctantly from the saddle. "I want my own horse."

Gil smiled, tightening the girth. "You can ride Lionheart again. I just need him a little while."

"I want my own horse for the tournament."

Gil turned to face him with another, gentler, smile. "Tournaments aren't for kids."

"I'm not a *little* kid, Gil," Percy said. "I'm fourteen. Aidan told me when it was my birthday."

Gil nodded. "Okay. But not everybody rides in tournaments. Niall doesn't, because he's my poet. And you're my cupbearer …."

"I rode in the Mews Garden. I jousted with you. And then I *was* a little kid." He stood there, solemn and grown up.

Gil let go of the saddle and studied him seriously. "Tournaments are dangerous," he said then. "What if you got killed? Who would look after your goats?"

Percy rubbed his nose, thinking. "Aidan, probably," he said. He met Gil's eyes, his own unblinking.

Gil leaned back against Lionheart and then nodded again. "Darras," he said, looking up, "Ride back to the Men of the Forest, tomorrow, and get me the oldest, wisest horse you can find. An old charger that a father trusts with his youngest son."

Darras looked doubtfully at Percy. "You are certain?"

Gil saw Danni watching him too and said clearly, "I can't treat him like a child forever. Everyone grows up." He mounted Lionheart and rode out to meet Ragnar Kolsson. The moment they turned to face the big, black charger, Gil forgot all about Percy in the effort of keeping his pony from running for the hills.

He's too big! He's too big!

He's half the size of Doombearer and ….

He's Doombearer! He's Doombearer!"

He's NOT Doombearer. But if you run away, we WILL fight Doombearer.

I want ….

The ship. Fine. Have it. Gil swung down, pointed to the gangplank, and stalked off to the string of chargers. Lionheart's warm, soft muzzle bumped into his back. Gil turned, eye to eye with the pony. *Yes?* Lionheart blinked winsome eyelashes. With a sigh, Gil swung back into the saddle and cantered back to his place.

Cautiously reining the pony around, he again faced Ragnar and the black charger. Lionheart stood, trembling obediently in place, leaving Gil to cast wary eyes over his opponent. Ragnar lifted his lance from the leather fewter and slapped it under his arm. Swathed in chain mail, his genial features hidden by helm and ventaille, he settled rock steady into his saddle and gathered up the reins.

Gil saw at once that Red Kol's son was that rare kind of man who could learn by seeing a thing done once. *Like Floki*, he thought. *Only bigger and heavier. And if he hits my shield with that lance, he'll knock me to Norway to join him.* He tightened his own reins, raised his old Pouncing Cat shield, and at Ismail's shout, charged, knowing there was only one thing to do.

Two strides from Ragnar's galloping charger, he flung himself flat on Lionheart's neck. The lance flailed uselessly overhead and Ragnar lurched half out of his saddle with a shout of surprise. Whirling the charger, he lowered his ventaille and protested, "Is that allowed?"

"No," Gil said cheerfully, behind his own scarf of chain mail. "But it works."

It worked three more times, as Gil tried out increasingly inventive variations of Floki's unchivalrous tricks. On the fourth, Ragnar pulled the big horse around and galloped furiously after his opponent and his squealing mount. Reaching out with one long arm, he caught Gil's long hair from beneath his helm, hauled him out of the saddle, and dropped him on his butt on the ground. "Is *that* allowed?" he growled.

Bruised and winded, Gil got up, painfully, pulled off his sweaty helm, and grinned. "Only for Northmen."

"I understand now." Ragnar smiled and drank from a horn of frothy ale. "It is battle, without blood."

Gil nodded. "Mostly. But sometimes," he added quietly, "There's blood as well."

"But only in error."

"Not only." Gil looked out from the shade of the awning, where they ate and drank in the shelter of *Silver Dragon's* beached hull. Having finished their own meal, the girls were working again on their square of sail cloth. Only Gil had noticed that from time to time Danni, or Rachel, disappeared beyond the bluff behind the ships, returning later, windswept and tousled, to their shared endeavor. He said to Ragnar, "The tournament ground is really big. Out of sight of the heralds, the rules get forgotten."

"Then, they must be forgotten often," Ragnar grinned. "I ride the field yesterday, while they practice upon it. It stretches as far as from Red Kol's hall to the shielings. And there are trees and burns, thickets and hollows. There is no way that the heralds ever see it all. I do not see it all, myself, even as I ride it."

Gil tilted his chin toward the girls. "They see it all. And they will show us." He rose, finishing the last of his ale. "Come." Waving an arm, he beckoned Ismail, Darras, Briant and Fergus who had returned to jousting practice on the strand.

When they were gathered in a circle around the three girls, Danni and Rachel sat back on their heels, stretching the sides of the sailcloth out, while Janetta held the top firm. "A map!" Ragnar cried. "It is the tournament ground! Look, there, the viewing stands, there the broad field, and beyond the first of the burns …." He knelt in the sand, his finger lightly tracing the features marked in charcoal on the faded wool.

"It is beautiful!" Fergus knelt, also, and then looked up awed at Danni and Rachel. "Is this what you see? When you …?" He made wing shapes with his hands.

"More or less," Danni said.

"That wood *is* on the other side of the burn," said Rachel. They gave each other a sour look and both folded their arms.

Janetta said hurriedly, "Yes. It is what they *agree* they see when they finish the arguments."

"Never mind," Gil said, "It's close enough. That's the willow copse where the Golden Knight caught me. And there's the edge of the forest. And there's the beech wood ride."

"And there," Darras cried, "Is our camp. See, they even draw the Green Tree of Caledon!"

Gil smiled, his fingers brushing his father's heraldic device. His eyes strayed to the lightly sketched trees of the willow copse. *Beware the sheltered copses, the hidden ditches … beyond the sight of the many. There, vengeance is wrought. There, men are killed.*

And there he would use his father's own warning against

him, not in vengeance, but for his own essential treachery. He looked up solemnly. "Whatever happens," he said. "No one must be hurt."

That night, they spread the map out by the fire, and; gathered together around it, held their council of war.

Ragnar spoke first. Rising to his feet, he bowed formally to Gil and said, "When, the day past, I ride to the tournament grounds and I watch as these knights practice their skills, I see that even in this battle without blood, they are as any warriors. All have strengths; all, weaknesses. And those who know their own and learn those of their opponents, are those who win.

"Big men overwhelm with height and length of arm. But they are also heavier and need a bigger horse. No big horse turns as quickly as a small horse. I, and Fergus, too, are bigger and stronger, our horses bigger also. But you and Ismail are swift and agile. Your ponies, more agile, too. And you are skilled and use our strength and size against us."

"And when that fails," Gil said, "we cheat."

"But not in sight of the heralds," Darras cried. "They would expel us from the tournament, should they see."

"Then," Ragnar grinned, "They will not see." He looked down at the map. "Our battles must be fought here." He ran his hand along the outer reaches of the charcoaled tournament grounds. "Here, trees and hillocks will shield us from view. We must meet our quarry here."

Gil nodded agreement.

"But how?" Darras studied the map doubtfully. "The three best knights of Camelot will be in the thick of the melee, seeking the best ransoms."

Fergus smiled. "Then we must tempt them with something better."

"What is better than purses of silver and gold?"

"For some men, nothing," Ragnar said. "But some men prize glory, more. Others have a weakness for vengeance. Others for greater adventure. We must find the weaknesses of these great knights. And then we use them to defeat them."

Darras shook his head mournfully. "Then it cannot be, for they have none. They are indeed the finest knights of all who ride the tournaments, and though they seek silver, it is not for gain, but to feed their exiled followers. The end of that exile is their only goal. And when Elias calls them old women, he is wrong, for only concern for others stays their hand. All three are brave and true, and I have seen no weakness in them ever."

Gil said, "I saw weakness in Martin de Troye."

"The earl?" Darras cried. "But he is the fiercest of warriors."

Gil glanced uncomfortably at Janetta. "He gets angry," he said. "He would have killed Elias over an insult, if my father hadn't stopped him."

"Ah," Fergus cried, "anger is a weakness indeed. No man fights as well when angry, nor thinks as well, either."

"No." Gil smiled grimly, remembering his one extraordinary victory over his own earl, at Candida Casa. "I saw even Floki Magnusson defeated by it, once."

Ragnar raised an eyebrow. "Then what defeats Floki Magnusson, will surely defeat this earl as well. But what of the mighty Saracen? What weakness is his?"

Darras said hopefully, "He is a big man and rides a big horse … perhaps we are swifter?"

Gil shook his head. "He is the biggest warrior I've ever seen and Doombearer is the biggest horse. But they both move like lightning and turn as fast." He paused. "But he is not a Northman." He looked up at Fergus. "Can honor be a weakness?" he said.

Fergus thought carefully and then nodded. "If he holds it dearer than victory, yes." He thought some more and said, "And your own good father? His fame and valor are known to all." He smiled hesitantly. "But perhaps a son sees what is hidden from the world?"

Gil sat in silence, staring into the dying fire, suddenly a small boy convinced of his father's invincibility. "He did everything right," he said at last.

"No man …." Ragnar began.

"But he did! On the river, in the mountains, running or

climbing or skiing. He always won." But then a memory leapt into his mind of the one time his father had lost.

Puzzled, and then worried, Gil had waited at the race finish as runner after runner crossed the line, his father not among them. And then at last he had appeared, trotting slowly beside a struggling stranger, as if he himself could run no faster, guiding the man safely home. "Yes," Gil said. "He has a weakness." He looked sadly into the flames. "He is kind."

Fergus grinned and raised a triumphant fist. "The tempestuous man, we will anger. The honorable man, we will show dishonor. And the kind man ...."

"We will betray," said Gil.

The Irish warriors left the camp at dawn, splashing across the tide flats while the church bells of Mont Tombe rang Lauds. Before the stall holders set out their wares, before the scent of roasting chestnuts filled the air, and long before the contestants paraded the tournament field, they would be in their places at the forest's edge.

The Northmen followed, armed and laden with coils of rope and bundled fishing nets. And, rolled tight and tucked securely within Erling's shirt, the golden pennant from *Silver Dragon's* mast. Gil watched them set out on the inland route through the marshes to the beech wood ride and then turned back to Janetta.

"I do not need this," she said, holding up the hem of the chain hauberk that he had draped carefully over her slender frame. It was his own outgrown mail and, with the linen undercoat, hung almost to her knees, but it would be covered by the pilgrim's robes he had bought the day before. "I am only to be captured, and only by Ragnar."

"It's still a tournament ground. Things get rough."

"A nun does not wear chain mail."

He lowered the habit over her head. "This nun does." Grinning, he adjusted her veil. Then suddenly remembering his vision of her through the seeing stone, dressed in the habit of the Grey Sisters of Caledon, he leaned forward and kissed her.

"And nuns do not kiss."

"Oh, this nun does."

"Leave my holy lady, you Viking scoundrel!" Ciarnan barged in between. Clad in his own pilgrim's garb, he made a convincing companion to Janetta's nun.

"Hey, *I'm* allowed. It's Ragnar you have to fight. Only don't do it too well. He has to win."

"Do not concern yourself," Ciarnan winced, watching the Northman practicing kidnapping Gil's straw man. "He is not likely to lose. Have you told him he is not to kill me?"

Gil shrugged cheerfully. "It has to look real, doesn't it? Speaking of which," he stared past Ragnar, at the horseman in the distance. "Percy!" he shouted, "That's fine. That's enough. You don't have to do it again!"

"Oh!" Janetta cried, as the small rider tumbled from the back of his charger onto the packed sand. "That is five times! He will be only bruises!"

The horse, tall and lean with a back swayed by age, stopped in its tracks and turned its fine old head to its rider, sprawled motionless at its feet. "Look!" Janetta caught Gil's sleeve. "This time, surely he is hurt."

"Enough!" Gil repeated wearily.

"I'm dead!" Percy's high voice assured him. But he got obediently to his feet and led his new charger proudly away.

"Hey, he is good," Ismail smiled, joining Gil. "They will believe he is real knight."

"That's what I'm afraid of," Gil said soberly.

Ismail smiled again. "Is okay. I am there always. He does not leave my sight."

———

At Terce they set out on the track through the marshes, riding two abreast, with Ciarnan on foot leading Janetta's mare. When the tournament grounds were in sight, Gil reined Lionheart around to face his followers. They jostled to a halt, blocking the path of a farmer's cart. The man raised a fist. "Pilgrim beggars! Tournament scum!" With Frankish curses, he drove his oxen past, toward the bright pavilions beyond a fringe of trees.

Gil bowed an apology and was ignored. With a smile, he looked back at his motley gathering. Costumed and disguised, with battered armor and shabby clothing, they blended readily with the penniless knights and shoeless penitents crowding the countryside.

No pennants hung from their lances. No noble devices marked their shields. Gil's Pouncing Cat remained aboard his ship. Its replacement hung heavy and unadorned around his neck, giving no hint of his identity. A rough cloth over his saddle hid the Irish battle-axe in its sheath.

The helms surmounting Fergus and Ragnar's red heads bore signs of sword blows and blacksmith's repairs. Ismail and Percy wore ragged linen hauberks beneath their mail, tufts of padding poking through tears in the chain.

Briant and Darras, with cloaks draped over their own shields to hide the painted fir-cone that marked them as followers of Lance'lot, kept their faces down until the farmer was out of sight. Then they grinned up at Gil. "Tournament scum!" Laughing, they pointed at Ciarnan, "Beggar pilgrim!"

Clutching the habit that hid his sword belt, Ciarnan held out an empty palm. Janetta giggled behind her veil. "My lady!" Ciarnan cried, "laughter does not become your noble penitence!" He tugged reproachfully at her pony's lead rein. "I must hurry you from this unseemly company!"

Seated sideways on a saddle that was little more than a flat wicker basket strapped to the mare's back, she rode like an old peasant woman, her nun's habit trailing over the beast's tail. But when a burst of shouting from the tournament field sent the pony shying off the track, she only swayed gracefully, her balance secure.

Gil surveyed them with a smile and then, hunching a shoulder toward the tailgate of the lumbering oxcart, said, "Well, you convinced him. I only hope the herald doesn't throw us off the field."

"He will not." Darras smiled back. "I have seen knights with neither helm nor mail, riding old plough horses into the melee."

"And some," Briant said, "Ride well, for all their poverty.

Though," he added, "few engage them, for all know they will bring no ransom if captured."

Gil nodded. "I'm counting on that to keep us out of trouble."

"*We* will keep you out of trouble," Briant said with his kind smile. Remember, ride with red, for the Knights of Caledon ride always with blue."

Darras saluted Gil, "Goodbye, my friend. We meet as enemies upon the field. Though friends again, in the forest." Shaking back their cloaks to reveal the heraldry of their shields, the two young knights cantered away to the lists. Beyond the pavilions, the herald's horn sounded sharp in the autumn air. Gil turned back to his waiting company. "You all know your orders?" They nodded eagerly. "Fergus?"

"I seek the Red Cockerel," Fergus said. "Martin de Troye. The man of anger."

"Be careful. Angry or not, he is deadly."

"He must catch me to be deadly." Fergus drew his *ventaille* over his luxuriant beard. Gil turned to Ragnar.

"The Black Dragon. Sir Palamedes," the Northman smiled. "The man of honor."

"Not too honorable to wield a sword," Gil reminded him.

Ragnar laughed cheerfully and patted the black charger's neck. "This is a fine horse, and your lady a fine rider. We are in the forest before he unsheathes the blade."

Gil looked to Janetta and her escort. "And you Ciarnan?"

Ciarnan shrugged, looking blank. "I speak only Irish," he said, in suddenly stumbling Norse.

"Ah, right. Forgot that. Say it in Irish."

Ciarnan bowed his head modestly and answered in his native tongue. "I am but a humble pilgrim seeking Holy Rome."

Gil grinned, "Any more humility and I'll think you're Floki." Still smiling, he turned to Percy, sitting proudly on his charger beside Ismail and Chocolate. "Remember what I said?"

Percy nodded solemnly, "I ride behind the red pennant and then I ride for the golden pennant. I stay with Ismail whatever happens."

"And?"

"And I don't say your name."

"Even if I'm right in front of you."

"Even if you're right in front of me."

Gil pulled the boy's helm down and fastened the *ventaille* across his face. "What's my name?" Percy silently shook his head. "Cool."

The horn sounded again and cheers arose from the viewing stands for the knights riding onto the field. Lionheart's ears flicked wildly. Gil gathered up his reins. *It's okay.* He tightened his grip. *We did this before.*

WE DID THIS BEFORE! Panic shivered over the pony's skin. Skittering sideways, he worked up a buck.

Gil's knees clamped against the saddle leather. *You were great! C'mon. You're a real charger, now.*

A real charger. Mid-buck, Lionheart reconsidered. *A REAL charger.* Flattening his back and raising his head, he looked around. Then, with a shake of his mane and smug nip at Chocolate's haunch, he trotted proudly to the lists.

No one noticed them arrive; the attention of all fixed on the tournament field. Stall holders had abandoned their wares to mount the earthen banks behind the palisades. Farmers, wagon drivers and passing pilgrims crowded forward for a better view. Gil threaded a way through girls with flower baskets and small boys jousting on broomstick chargers, to a flower-decked gap in the palisade.

Reining Lionheart in, he gathered his small party around him, looking out onto the field where the contestants cantered in a wide circle before the viewing stands. Their horses trapped in brilliant colors, matching pennants on their fewtered lances, each bowed to the lord and lady of the tournament and then galloped out to the waiting herald. Raucous cheers announced the arrival of famous knights. Laughter, those less honored. Above, in the viewing stands, noblemen sipped wine and ladies in velvet and furs summoned esquires to bear ribbons to their favorites.

"Listen!" Janetta cried. "They call my father's name."

To shouts of "Troye! Troye!" the exiled earl cantered onto the field, his shield held up to the stand.

"The Red Cockerel," Fergus said softly, "My angry man."

"Go," Gil said. "Keep him in sight."

Fergus trotted out beyond the palisade, kicked his horse into a gallop, and stopping for neither favors nor honors, thundered across the field and disappeared into the milling scrum of mounted men behind the red pennant.

"And the man of honor," Ragnar nudged his big charger up against Lionheart's flank. "Is it not so?" Black hair and beard streaming in the wind, and the Black Dragon, his mythical Questing Beast, on his shield, the Saracen Knight took to the field.

"Palamedes! Palamedes!" the crowd chanted. Flowers rained down and young girls waved their ribbon favors, as he cantered past the stands. But, though bowing with great courtesy, he accepted none and turned his enormous coal black charger to the lines of blue.

"Be certain he sees you, when you make your move."

"*All* will see me," Ragnar laughed. He rode out at a canter, his long-legged charger taking him across the field with ease, and waved flamboyantly to the viewing stands. His height and red beard marked him out even when he joined the long line of horsemen behind the red pennant.

"Two down," Gil said, carefully watching the field.

"And one to go is me?" Ismail smiled.

Gil touched his bridle arm and pointed. "There."

A group of young knights cantered together before the lord and his lady. Briant's pale blond hair flowing from beneath his helm brought cheering and flowers from the girls on the palisade. Beside him, Darras and Allein displayed the fir-cone devices on their shields. Elias, tall and solemn, rode behind.

"Ah!" Ismail cried. "The Men of the Forest!"

"Face them on the first charge. When they engage you, no one else will try. Then ride for our pennant and the willow copse. Keep Percy in front. If anyone sees, they'll think you're after a ransom."

"I am!" Ismail grinned cheerfully. And with his hand firmly on the bridle of Percy's charger, led the boy out onto the field. When they had taken their place across from the Men of the Forest, Gil turned his gaze back to the parade of knights before the viewing stand. They were fewer, now, and the herald was sounding an impatient horn. Gil's eyes flicked from one bright shield to the next, searching with increasing desperation for the Green Tree of Caledon.

And then, suddenly, it was there. Lance'lot had slipped unnoticed onto the field, appearing among the circling contestants for the briefest moment, before galloping his white charger to his place. But the cheers following him were the loudest of the day and the chanting of his name rose like a swell on the sea. Gil stared after him, caught between joy at seeing his father and shame at what he was about to do.

"It is you!" Janetta whispered urgently. "Look! The herald signals you!"

Tearing his eyes from Lance'lot, Gil saw the herald furiously waving him onto the field; the last knight remaining; all others holding their restless mounts in two long, wavering lines. Turning swiftly to Ciarnan, he said, "This is it. Follow me out so you're right in the middle when he's ready to blow the charge. And here's hoping he doesn't speak Irish."

Ciarnan shrugged. "If he speaks Irish, I speak only Latin." He smiled and drew up the cowl of his robe, as Gil rode out onto the field.

"Oh, look upon him!" a girl's voice cried. "He is so small!"

"And so sweet!" cried another, "with his mane so long and his tail sweeping the dust!" A cascade of blossoms fell from the palisade, piling on Lionheart's head like snow. Twitching his ears, he whinnied in alarm.

"Hold back!" the first girl cried. "You frighten him!"

Flowers! Gil slapped his reins against the pony's neck. *Now you're afraid of flowers.*

They tickle. Lionheart shook his head and planted his forefeet firm. The herald shouted and one of his men rode across the field, a whip firmly in his hand.

Move, Gil pleaded. *Or that will REALLY tickle.*

But the girls on the palisade protested, shouting, "Shame! Shame!" until the man backed his horse away in confusion. Then, raising each hoof high, Lionheart picked a wary path through the blossoms.

"Behold!" the second girl cried, leaning over the palisade, "He dances! Oh, he is so dear, I would ride him myself."

"If there is a ride to be had," a cheerful, loose-haired woman called, "I would prefer his master." She leaned far out, blowing a kiss from berry red lips, and winning roars of laughter from the crowd.

Get us out of here! Gil pleaded, and with a desperate kick, sent Lionheart prancing and shying across the field. He was halfway to the herald when he realized the laughter was no longer for them.

The attention of the two lines of knights and the stout, grey-haired herald, himself, was fixed now on a point behind him. Easing Lionheart into a trot, Gil turned and looked cautiously back.

A hundred paces from the palisade, a barefoot monk walked calmly across the tournament ground, at his side a pack horse bearing a small, veiled nun. Pilgrim staff in hand, oblivious of the twin lines of straining warhorses, he stared straight ahead, as if his eyes already beheld the Seven Hills of Rome.

Laughter, shouts of amazement, even the furious notes of the horn, swept past the holy pair until at last the herald cantered from his place to confront them. Passing Gil and Lionheart unacknowledged, he trotted across the beaten ground shouting, "You fool! It is the charge. There are a hundred horses! A hundred great knights barely can hold them! Get off the field!"

The holy brother stopped and looked around, as if seeing all the great gathering for the first time. Then, with a small shrug, he continued walking until the herald dismounted, stamped directly into his path, and stood, blocking his way. "Do you not hear me?" he bellowed.

"I speak only Irish," Ciarnan said in Irish. "We make pilgrimage to Rome," he added helpfully.

The herald threw his hands in the air; then, looking around briefly for a solution, took hold of the horse's bridle with one hand and the cowl of Ciarnan's habit with the other. But suddenly a new sound broke through the laughter and jeers: the beat of galloping hooves. The herald whirled as the tall, red-haired horseman bore down on him and the unwitting monk.

The nun raised her veiled head, shrinking back in obvious terror as the horseman's great arm swept around her, lifting her from her mount and up before him on his without breaking stride.

"My lady!" Ciarnan cried in Irish. And, wrenching the wicker saddle from the horse's back, he mounted and raced fruitlessly after his lost nun.

"Villain!" roared Sir Palamedes, kicking his black charger, Doombearer, into a gallop. A dozen knights broke ranks to follow; Martin de Troye and Lance'lot at the front. But then the high notes of the charge rang across the tournament ground and eager challengers closed on each of the champions. Gil had a last glimpse of Ragnar with Janetta secure before him and the Man of Honor in hot pursuit, before the cloud of dust obscured all.

When it had cleared enough to reveal shadowy forms, the two lines had unraveled into the brawling chaos of the melee. Lances thumped against shields. Horses whinnied in excitement. Men shouted and cursed and rallied their friends, while loose chargers galloped in panic, and unhorsed knights fought sword battles on foot.

Gil spun Lionheart, searching the field. Ragnar and Janetta, and Palamedes, too, had vanished. In the distance Ismail chased Percy toward the willow copse, with Darras and Briant on their heels. And a hundred paces away, Lance'lot of Caledon pursued the brutal, practical business of tournament, defeating two challengers, one after the other.

He watched only briefly as, unhorsed and with shattered shields and splintered lances, they were led away by his followers for ransom. Then he turned his white charger back to the fray. A third challenger faced him: a skinny young knight on a remarkably small and furry horse. Looking down from the height of his own mount, Lance'lot studied his opponent.

Face masked by his *ventaille*, helm pulled low, Gil dipped his lance and bowed. Lance'lot loosened his own face guard and with a small, respectful smile, shook his head. But Gil's gaze was on the great white charger.

It's you. The monkish plough horse.

The animal bent his neck and pawed gently at the ground.

Gil heard him in his heart: *We ran together through the forest. The sky was filled with light.*

The Northern Lights ... the great pillars leading them through Caledon, fleeing the Golden Knight ... *You saved me.*

The horse blew softly through its nose. *My friend.*

Gil looked back to his father. Lance'lot again shook his head, and then deliberately turned his charger aside. But the white horse pulled hard against the reins, one beautiful dark eye fixed on Gil.

Let's play, Gil lowered his lance and kicked his surprised pony into the charge, leaving Lance'lot no choice but to engage.

Like a great white wave breaking over a ship, the monkish plough horse thundered toward Lionheart. But his ears were yet forward, his head held high, and at the last moment, he shied suddenly, whipping his master's lance from its target. The thud of Gil's own against Lance'lot's shield stunned him as much as his opponent.

I beat him! I beat him! Lionheart chanted, whirling for another clash before Gil even tightened his reins. Struggling with his unruly mount, Lance'lot turned to face them. The monkish plough horse again broke into its charge, but three strides away, kicked up its heels, skittish as a colt. Half unseated, Lance'lot yet kept his lance aligned, until a final shimmy from his mount undid his aim. Again, the point swung wide, just glancing the edge of Gil's shield. Gil ducked beneath it and once more his own lance thudded home. Lionheart spun in a whinnying circle, mane and tail flying. A cheer sounded from the viewing stands as Gil turned again to face his father.

Lance'lot's big hand held the white charger firmly in check. With a thoughtful nod to his opponent, he drew his *ventaille* over his face and then raised his lance again. Pulling sharply on his reins, Gil interrupted Lionheart's victory prance. *He's serious now. Stop fooling around.* But suddenly another cheer arose from the stands, and then laughter. And then, cutting furiously through the din of the melee, the sharp notes of the herald's horn. Gil looked at his father, unsure what they had done wrong. But Lance'lot had turned to face the viewing stands and the two riders who had claimed the attention of all.

Burly form hunkered down behind his Red Cockerel shield, Martin de Troye charged the red-bearded knight galloping toward him with whoops of Irish glee. "Fergus!" Gil cried. Lance held high in one hand, his shield arm punching the air, and his horse guided only by his knees, the Irishman closed on the exiled earl. Then, two strides from his opponent, he threw himself backward, arching over the cantle of his saddle, his helm skimming the horse's rump as the earl's lance flailed empty air. "Quick learner!" Gil grinned behind his *ventaille*.

And his admiration only grew as, pass after pass, Fergus tried out every dishonorable trick Floki had played on Palamedes and Gil, in his turn, had played on Ragnar. The herald's horn blew in protest and the herald's men rode to intervene, raising disappointed jeers from the stands. Whirling his horse one more time, Fergus charged the outraged Earl de Troye, and at full gallop, kicked his feet from his stirrups and jumped up on his saddle, as if to stand.

Shouts and groans greeted the audacious move and Gil watched, fearing disaster. But Fergus kept one hand firm on the high pommel of the jousting saddle. Then, with a quick flick of the other, tossed his tunic up over his head and dropped his britches to his ankles. Bare buttocks flashing in the sunlight, he swept past his opponent to howls of uncontained rage. With hilarity convulsing the stands and the herald's men closing in, Fergus had only time to pull up his britches and drop his butt back into the saddle before the Earl de Troye flung his lance to the ground, drew his sword and thundered after him, murder in his eyes.

Trusting the tall black charger and Fergus' own horsemanship to keep him safe, Gil returned to his interrupted joust. With the eyes of all yet following the fleeing pair, he quietly reined Lionheart around and cantered away from the stands. When Lance'lot also turned to seek his opponent, the skinny knight on the furry little charger was a hundred yards distant, waiting on a small rise at the edge of the fray.

In a gait midway between a charge and a romp, the white charger galloped toward them. Lionheart, ears flat, mane bristling, pawed the ground. *Don't get carried away*, Gil nudged him into line with his knees. *He's still twice your size.*

He's afraid of me. Lionheart broke into his vigorous short-legged gallop, and indeed the white charger shied away, as they met, though, from the set of his ears and the toss of his head, more in fun than in fear. Lance'lot, managing his absurdly playful mount with skill and good humor, did at last get past Gil's guard. But the lance merely tapped Gil's shield, barely moving it on his arm.

He's playing, too. Gil looked quickly back. Lance'lot swung his horse around in a long lazy arc. Then, tightening his lance under his arm, he hunched low over the white charger's neck and sent him pounding toward Lionheart, straight as an arrow shot from a bow. *And he's not playing now.*

Gil raced to meet the charge, but this time, when the two animals were paces apart, he hauled back on the reins, spun Lionheart about in his tight-footed pony turn, and galloped the other way.

A glance over his shoulder showed the monkish plough horse taking up the chase. Slower on the turn, but faster in the gallop, he rapidly closed on Lionheart's tail. Jumping a ditch and circling a tree, Gil again spun the pony and lowered his lance in another charge. The big white horse had only skidded to a surprised halt when Gil's lance struck his master's shield.

"Well played!" Lance'lot called, but Gil was again galloping away.

Dodging each other around thickets and scrub, leaping gullies and spinning to cross lances, they left the noise and the dust of the melee behind. The herald's horn faded. They were alone; testing each other in a running battle across the undulating land. Joyful and exhilarated in the shared excitement of the chase, Gil felt closer to his father than ever in his life.

And then, suddenly, the game was over. Ahead, fluttering over the distant beech wood, he glimpsed his golden pennant. And, in the willow copse before him, hidden beyond the sight of the many, the trap that he had laid.

With a cold emptiness in his stomach, Gil watched the two riders emerge from the shelter of the trees. The first, small and chunky, urged his tall, sway-backed old charger into a gallop, fleeing the wiry, slim knight on the brown horse, behind. Crossing in front of Gil and Lance'lot, they brought their own chase to a sudden halt.

In the open meadowland before them, the first rider turned to make his stand. The brown horse closed; lances thumped shields in a convincing clash. The two separated, turned, clashed again. Gil held his breath as, on the third pass, the slim knight's charge over-powered his opponent, sending him tumbling from his saddle, and landing on the beaten ground with a solid thud. Gil winced; seeing it rehearsed on the strand was not the same as seeing it here.

He looked quickly to his father, holding his white charger back, as he himself held Lionheart. Lance'lot leaned forward in his saddle, his eyes on the fallen knight. Percy played his part perfectly as Ismail turned his horse and trotted closer to his defeated opponent. Leaning down, he prodded Percy with the butt of his lance, and then, with a shrug of disinterest, turned the animal and cantered casually away.

Lance'lot stiffened in the saddle, and then, beckoning Gil, galloped to the aid of the man on the ground. In his concern, he did not notice that Gil had not followed. Nor, as he dismounted and bent over Percy, did he notice Gil's warriors emerging silently from the willow copse, with nets and ropes and swords.

The white charger, standing faithfully waiting, whinnied in alarm. Lance'lot whirled, reaching for his sword, and then froze. A circle of armed men surrounded him in silence, as into their midst trotted the small furry charger. Face carefully shielded, Gil swung down from Lionheart's back and faced his father.

Hopelessly outnumbered, Lance'lot looked briefly at the wide sky above, and then with a lightening hand, drew his sword. Gil jerked the broad axe from its sheath on his saddle and with one ferocious swing, sent the sword spinning from his father's hand.

The nets descended, pinning Lance'lot's arms to his side. Svein Sveinsson dashed forward, binding his wrists. And then, trussed and helpless, the great knight of Caledon was hoisted back up on his horse, and with the horse hemmed in by three of their own, led at a trot to the beech wood.

"Can I sit up now?" a plaintive voice begged from the ground. Gil looked down at the small round face, under its sturdy helm. "Only, I need to ... you know." Gil made a sound halfway between laughter and tears, and nodded.

"You were great," he said to Percy's carefully turned back, as the boy relieved himself against a clump of wildflowers. And then he boosted him up onto the sway-backed charger and strode back to his pony, the Irish battle-axe over his shoulder, and the ache of betrayal in his heart.

CHAPTER FIFTEEN

Bright with autumn light, the beech wood closed above Gil's head as he led his father into captivity. A drift of fallen leaves rustled beneath their horses' feet, but no wind blew and no birds sang. Behind, Ismail followed, with Percy again safely at his side. Ahead, a line of horsemen waited, dark shadows in the golden glow.

In the center, the Saracen knight, Palamedes, sat, disarmed and bound on his great charger, enduring his fate with the wounded dignity of a wild beast tamed. Beside him, Martin de Troye glowered in outrage at his captors, his fury only heightened by Fergus' cheerful grin. Gil's Norse and Irish followers circled them on foot, watching with silent curiosity.

Gil's eyes swept past them all, seeking Janetta, and came to rest upon her white veil, yet concealing her features as she sat behind Ciarnan on her black mare. Riding astride, now, her posture boldly defiant, she faced her father whose gaze passed over her, unaware.

Both imprisoned knights looked up at Gil's approach with their defeated champion. Palamedes' shoulders slumped sorrowfully. The Earl de Troye stiffened in fury. At Gil's side, Lance'lot greeted them with a wry smile. Then, turning to Gil, he said, "Our pavilion lies within the forest, sir. We will make good the ransom, there." Nodding toward his fellow prisoners, he added, "There is no need of bonds. We are honorable men."

Careful not to speak, Gil signaled Ragnar and Svein to untie all three, and when they had finished, led the way through the laurel thickets to the forest camp. His small army followed, with Erling last; the golden pennant of his earl retrieved from the treetops and tucked within his shirt.

Cheers greeted their entry into the forest clearing. The young girls jumped up from their querns, spindles fell still, and the smith at the anvil laid down his hammer. But then, like shadows, Gil's men stepped from the laurel, quietly surrounding the camp.

The shouts and laughter died. Children, running to grasp the bridles of triumphant chargers, stopped in their tracks. Eyes wide with apprehension, they watched as the three great champions of Caledon were escorted, humbled, to their own hearth.

"Papa!" a high pitched child's voice cut the sudden silence. Red-cheeked yet from sleep, Janetta's half-brother burst from the pavilion, running to his father. Then, seeing him amidst the ragged strangers, he stopped and turned back uncertainly to his mother, standing yet in the entrance of the pavilion. Noble and quiet, she acknowledged her husband's return with a small bow, accepting defeat as evenly as she would victory.

Then, emboldened perhaps by the inaction of his elders, the boy strode forward. Passing his defeated father, he stopped before Gil, tugged at Lionheart's reins for attention, and said, "Are you the Golden Knight?"

Lance'lot laughed softly, looking down at the child. "He is not, for we yet live. Defeated though we are." He raised his gaze above the boy's head and addressed a white haired old man with a withered arm hanging limp at his side, "Good Sir Lardons," he said, "bring the treasury. There is a ransom to be paid, fairly won."

Gil quickly shook his head. "There's no need," he said to the old man. Reining Lionheart around, he faced the three captured knights. "The only ransom we want is you."

"We are *hostages*?" Martin de Troye turned smoldering eyes on Gil.

"No." Unhooking his *ventaille* and raising his helm from his head, Gil said, "You are warriors." He brushed back his sweaty hair and faced his father. "Warriors who will lead us to win back Camelot."

Behind the prisoners, Ismail and Percy also removed their

helms; Percy staring in fascination at Lance'lot. Janetta swept back her veil and met her father's gaze with a determined smile.

"Daughter!" he cried, parent's joy mingling with anger and humiliation. With a shout of delight, his small son ran to his sister.

"My noble friends!" Sir Palamedes dark face lit with pleasure and he extended his mighty arms wide as if to embrace them all. And, as Ingirid hurried to welcome her stepdaughter, Martin de Troye turned his outrage on Gil.

"You!" he roared. "You risk my daughter in foolish horseplay on a tournament field. My daughter whom you claim to love!"

"He risks no one!" Janetta shouted back at her father. "*I* own what risk there is—and there is none—look!" She drew back her enveloping habit to reveal her hidden chain mail. "He dresses me in armor for my safety."

"Your safety lies beneath my roof!" Martin de Troye waved a fist.

"Which he would win back for you," Janetta raised a fist of her own.

The attention of all turned to the battle between father and daughter. But Gil kept his gaze on his own father's face, acutely aware that Lance'lot, sitting the while on his white charger, had said nothing at all. Their eyes met. Gil shrugged. "I'm sorry ...."

"No reason. It is tournament." Lance'lot gave his son a small smile. "All is fair." Turning then to Troye and Palamedes, he said, "Summon the Council."

While the huntsmen were called back from the forest, and the young knights from the tournament ground, Ingirid served ale to her husband and his victorious opponents. Under its cheering influence, his anger eased, and when his daughter reminded him that he, too, had snatched her from the lists, but a year earlier, he even smiled. "On this same field!" she declared.

"Yes," he mused dreamily. "And you standing up on your horse's back at the Tournament of the Ladies."

"Which I won," she said.

He smiled again. "Daughter, you should have been born a son, for you have a warrior's heart."

"I have a woman's heart," she returned. "But you have all

the son you need in my brother." And, while the watching child beamed happily, she held out her hand to Gil. "And I bring you another."

Troye cast Gil a grim look. "As you say yourself, Daughter, I have sons enough. But," he added with grudging respect, "he also, has a warrior's heart."

"Then we are well suited," she shot back, "for like is well to marry like, as all know."

"Broadaxe," Fergus interrupted suddenly. He stepped closer and nodded toward the forest. Gil, also, had heard the jingle of a harness, and Lionheart's snort of equine challenge. Reaching for his sword, he faced the dark wall of laurel. But then loud laughter and shouts announced the innocence of the approaching horsemen.

The first burst into the clearing: a young knight proudly holding up his prize money from the tournament. Others followed, their cheerful banter falling awkwardly quiet at the sight of their champions surrounded by armed strangers. Drawing their horses to a restless halt, they sat in uncertain silence until Lance'lot said, with a smile, "We are defeated, but there is no cause for alarm. It is but a family matter to be settled amicably."

He stood up from his seat by the fire and, stepping close to Gil, laid a hand on his shoulder. "This man is my son. He claims ransom from us, but it is a ransom I think you will happily pay."

The young men slowly dismounted, wary eyes upon Gil and his companions. Then one pointed suddenly at Fergus. "Look! It is he who played the fine trick. And his face is as comely as his bare arse!"

"It is so!" Two of Fergus' Irish kinsman agreed, laughing. And to the Forest Knights they cried, "He is our champion, Fergus Bare-Arse of Tara!"

"Ah, noble Bare-Arse," a third bowed dramatically.

Fergus smiled and sipped from his ale horn. "Each man may say that once," he nodded pleasantly. "The man who says it twice, dies."

In the instant hush that followed, Lance'lot laughed quietly. "See to your horses and come within the pavilion. Sir

Mondrames is here now," he gestured toward the forest, "The Council is complete."

Gil looked up. At the edge of the dark laurel, a man had appeared, wrapped in the long plaid garment of Caledon, his bow slung over his shoulder. Tall and lean as the grey dog at his side, he walked in silence to the pavilion.

The blacksmith, who had returned to his work, laid down his tools and followed, and the white haired Sir Lardons, lifting his limp arm across his body, rose to join him. Sending her small son to Janetta, Ingirid passed through the curtained entrance with her husband.

Lance'lot turned to Gil. "The Council awaits, sir. Go and claim your ransom." He smiled distantly, as to a stranger. His victory heavy upon his shoulders, Gil led the way into the tent.

Men moved respectfully aside, as a grim-faced Martin de Troye beckoned him to the High Table. The seat of honor at his right stood empty. Gil hesitated, willing his father to take his rightful place and knowing, as well, that he would not.

"Seat yourself, young earl," Palamedes urged him. "It is your duty," he added with a gentle smile.

Reluctantly, Gil accepted the offered place and faced the noisy gathering filling the pavilion. Benches overflowed and late comers stood all around the cloth walls. Darras and Briant smiled proudly amid the Men of the Forest. Elias caught his eye and nodded a silent salute. Gil's own men crowded the entrance, standing shoulder to shoulder, blotting out the daylight.

"Broadaxe!" Fergus raised his fist and the Norse and Irish cheered and chanted until Gil hastily shook his head.

"Allow them their triumph," said a soft voice at his side. "They are right to be proud."

Gil looked quickly to his right. Lance'lot, who had taken his place beside him, smiled with a sudden flash of warmth. But he turned away then, to address the lean huntsman, Mondrames, leaving Gil uncertain of what he had seen.

Something soft brushed against his foot. Startled, he looked down. A spotted hound raised its head and fixed soulful eyes upon him. Gil glanced up to the beam on which Cat had crouched and phantom hackles rose. But the hound only nuzzled his leg, then put its chin on its paws and went to sleep.

"Earl Martin," Lance'lot addressed his superior, "since it is one of my own blood who we gather to address, I ask that I may speak?"

"Speak." Troye gave a curt wave of his hand. "But speak loudly, lest his rabble drown your words."

"His rabble are now well behaved," Lance'lot said with a small smile. "And I ask our own rabble to be so, as well." He looked hard at Darras and Briant who were yet chanting, 'Broadaxe' under their breath. Then he swept the rough hall with a thoughtful gaze.

"I see from your faces," he said, "That you know already why we are here. And," he added with a wry smile, "you are as divided as ever on the terms of this 'ransom.'" Looking out over the benches, Gil saw the same division: young warriors in bubbling high spirits; their elders, watchful and grim.

"But we are united!" Fergus shouted, his arms around Darras and Briant. "Brothers, all!"

"I'd sooner be kin to a donkey," Martin de Troye growled.

"Ah, an honorable beast, the donkey," Palamedes smiled within his dark beard, winning a furious glance from the earl. Gil looked up at the Saracen knight, seated beyond Janetta's father, sensing an unexpected ally.

"When the High Table itself cannot make peace," Lance'lot said quietly, "there is little hope for the hall."

The ancient Sir Lardons got painfully to his feet. "The terms are dishonorable," he said with solemn gravity. "He defeats us with trickery."

"And when we smuggled warriors through the gates of Camelot, dressed as serving maids?" Lance'lot smiled.

The old man shrugged. Then straightening his back, he said, "I did not ride at Arthur's side to surrender to buffoons." He nodded angrily at Fergus. "Give them our silver and let us keep our honor."

Sir Mondrames, the huntsman, got slowly to his feet. Facing Sir Lardons he said, "Honor makes a poor porridge come winter. Give them our silver and our children starve." A weary sigh passed through the pavilion and Gil felt again the weight of victory.

"But I say to you," Palamedes rose, resolutely cheerful, "is it not an honor bequeathed to us, that this young earl who defeats us, yet desires our leadership?" The knights surrounding Fergus shouted agreement. A few of the older men nodded, too. But Lardons only shook his white head.

Lance'lot sat back and closed his eyes. When he opened them again, his gaze was faraway. Looking out over the hall and then back to his fellows at the table, he smiled sadly. "My friends," he said, "there is no honor without justice, and no justice in the world with Jocelyn Guidbairn on Arthur's throne." He turned then to Martin de Troye. "Accept these terms and seek justice? Or winter in poverty with Lady Honor?"

"I say accept the terms!" Palamedes declared at once. Gil's followers cheered.

"Silence!" Troye glowered. He looked to Sir Lardons. Again, the old man shook his head. "I see many boys. Few men. I say no."

The blacksmith rose suddenly. "Warriors, like metals, are tested in fire." He raised a soot-smudged hand toward Gil. "The scar on his face tells he has seen battle. I say yes, accept the terms." He sat down and folded his arms.

The huntsman turned then to Gil. "How many ships sail with you?" he said.

"Two," Gil answered.

"How many benches?"

"Sixteen, on each."

"And how many men aboard?"

"Sixty came with me from the North," Gil said. "With the Irish, we have seventy-two."

"And each Irishman worth two in battle, if not three!" Fergus cried. "And so, we are near a hundred."

Mondrames stroked his grey-streaked beard. "And we are a hundred more. You will be well laden, young earl." He raised a bristly eyebrow and smiled.

"There are ships at Mont Tombe," said Gil.

Troye shook his head brusquely. "Yes. And the earl of that

fortress will smile and offer wine, and, yes, his ships. But then, 'it is not the time.' Or, 'there are repairs needed.' Or a crew to be raised. And so, the months pass since you ask."

Gil shrugged. "I don't intend to ask."

"Hee-yah! Broadaxe!" Fergus shouted.

Martin de Troye cried for silence again, but the old huntsman quietly laughed. "I say yes," he said.

"And I say no," growled Martin de Troye.

At the end of the table, Ingirid slowly rose. Her beautiful face solemn, she smiled gently at Gil. "My heart goes with you," she said, "But my head, with my husband. His courage and skill are no less, but his wisdom is rightly more. The Men of Caledon who would not follow Martin de Troye, will not follow you." She shook her head sadly. "I, also, say no."

A groan swept over the young men on the benches. The old nodded sagely. All eyes turned to Lance'lot, the last of the council to give judgement. He looked gravely at Gil for a long silent time, but when he spoke, it was Ingirid he addressed.

"They will rise," he said, "and they will follow him. Not because he is brave, although he is, nor because he is clever, though he has shown himself that. But because he wins the hearts of men." He gestured towards Gil's determined followers.

"Young men," Martin de Troye snapped, "who know no better."

Lance'lot sat back. "The world belongs to young men, my friend." He smiled. "As once it belonged to you and I." Still, there was a weariness in his voice when he next spoke. "I say accept the terms."

The benches erupted in cheering. Martin de Troye shrugged his big shoulders. Standing, he addressed Gil, "The last vote is cast. Three say no. Four, yes. We accept your terms."

Gil carefully got to his feet. As carefully, he drew his sword from its scabbard, and, as Floki had taught him, laid it across his hands as he knelt at the feet of Martin de Troye, offering fealty to their new chieftain.

Fergus punched a fist in the air and shouted, "Broadaxe!" and the Irish and Norse broke into their chant. But then Lance'lot stood, and with his hand on his sword hilt faced them with such authority that they fell silent without protest.

"Go," he said. "Build up the fires. Whatever tomorrow holds, this night, we feast." When the cheering again died down, he said quietly, "I ask only one thing first: that I have a small time alone here with my son."

Emptied of its occupants, the pavilion seemed small and shabby. Daylight shone through rents in the cloth. A mouse scuttled over the beaten grass floor. Gil's phantom Cat whiskers twitched as he waited for his father to speak.

Shouts and laughter drifted in from outside, but, within, the silence stretched uncomfortably. Torn between pride and uncertainty, Gil glanced uneasily down the High Table, where Lance'lot yet sat studying his calloused horseman's hands. He looked up, suddenly, and Gil jumped. "You rode well," he said. "A fine chase."

"Thank you."

Lance'lot nodded thoughtfully. Then he looked up again and his eyes met Gil's. "You will steal the ships." Gil said nothing. Lance'lot looked down again, and then up, with a helpless shake of his head. "What can I expect?" he said wearily, "leaving you with that damned Viking?"

"Take that back." Gil laid his hand, without thinking, on his sword hilt.

"What?"

"You will not insult my earl. Take it back."

"Your earl?" Lance'lot raised his eyebrows and shook his head. In a quiet voice, he said, "I've lost you."

"No," Gil answered evenly. "But you will. Take it back."

They sat in silence. After a long while, Lance'lot said, "When you were little, I thought when you grew up, you would look like your mother. But you're grown, now, and you look like me." He paused, "Like I looked, once …." He shook his head again. "So long ago… I take it back," he said then clearly. "What is it your men call you? Broadaxe? Gil Broadaxe," he said with a small smile. "I will not insult your earl."

Gil nodded. Then, slipping his hand from the sword hilt, he said, "The lord of Mont Tombe imprisoned our people to lure us to his shores and betray us to the Golden Knight. If we had beached on his strand, we would have died there. He owes us his life. But we will settle for ships."

"Spoken like a true Northmen," Lance'lot smiled. He looked up at the peaked cloth roof, then turned back. "And where is that Northman, your earl? At the camp, awaiting word of your success? Or riding the tournament field, disguised as the pope?"

"He's in Norway," Gil said, "keeping a vow." He smiled back at his father. "Sometimes, even a Northman has honor."

Lance'lot sat back and studied Gil with narrowed eyes. "But then, how are you here?"

"He gave me his ship."

"He *gave* you ... and you, alone ...?"

"Hardly. Sixty men sailed with me from Hrolf's Isle. And then the Irish joined us," he added quickly.

Lance'lot watched him and then said, "Why?"

Gil shrugged. "They were slaves. They escaped from a ship off the Saxon coast. And we took them aboard."

"And they came to Francia?"

Gil nodded.

"Would they not choose to return to Ireland?" Lance'lot said.

"They will," Gil answered hurriedly. "Only, it wasn't possible ...." He stopped speaking and looked carefully down at his hands. Then he said evenly, "Okay. It *was* possible. But I needed them. Four of my own men deserted. The Irish are great warriors."

"Yes. Even when enslaved."

"They're not slaves."

"Then what are they? If fighting for you is your choice, not theirs?"

"You don't understand."

Lance'lot sat back and closed his eyes. "Oh, I do," he murmured. "This world ... this world corrupts the best of men."

"It's not like that," Gil protested.

His father opened his eyes and shook his head. "Gil, there

is only one thing in all of this I cannot understand and cannot forgive. You used the *child* to trick me. You put that child on a tournament ground. He could have been killed."

"He knew that."

"How can he understand what that means?" Lance'lot said angrily.

"How can any of us?" Gil said. He shrugged again, but his mind was far away and the face he saw before him was not his father's but that of the Golden Knight, confronting him on that same tournament field.

You will compromise. You will cheat and betray. You will become like all men.

He dropped his head into his rope-scarred hands and wept.

CHAPTER SIXTEEN

Gil halted his party in a stand of dark pines, a hundred feet from the causeway. The track ahead glimmered in the growing light. Above, the black bulk of Mont Tombe loomed against the fading stars. He signaled silently to Fergus and Ragnar and they slipped ahead, vanishing at once amidst the trees.

Seagulls wheeled and cried overhead. A forest bird chirped. Gil waited in silence with Lance'lot and Martin de Troye. The men behind them shuffled nervously, his own crew uneasy on this foreign shore, the forest knights wary of ships and the sea.

The earl leaned close. "It is dawn," he whispered harshly. "The guards will see us."

"No longer!" Fergus laughed softly, re-emerging from the shadows. His white shirt sleeves were dark stained. Ragnar stepped to Gil's other side, quiet as a ghost. Gil turned his face from the reek of fresh blood.

"How many?"

"Three. Two sleeping. One drinking ale. All sleep now." He shrugged easily.

Conscious of his father at his shoulder, Gil said quietly, "Good." A cock crowed from the heights of the fortress. He hurried his men forward, scrambling up onto the causeway and down the other side to the strand, fresh-washed by the falling tide.

A plume of smoke rose above the thatch of the roof: kitchen fires re-kindled that the earl of Mont Tombe might break his fast. Gil watched warily as it blotted out the dimming stars. His eyes swept the stone steps leading from the kitchen door.

A sleepy dairy maid on her way to the byre could undo them as swiftly as any guard.

Seeing no movement, he crouched low, running across the sand to the beached ships, his small army on his heels. Troye was right: it was later and lighter than he would have liked. But the tide was his master, not his servant, and their window of opportunity was small. Already, the surf was pounding on the bar. By sunrise, the wide bay would be dry land.

Ahead lay the nearest ship; a broad ungainly knarr that Svein Sveinsson had dismissed with disdain when they scouted the shore the night before. Gil ducked beneath her bow, with Ragnar beside him.

"Ah! There?" Ragnar gestured toward a lean warship pulled high up on the sloping beach.

Gil shook his head. "She's summered on the strand, strakes as dry as bone. Launch her and we'd be swimming while we rowed." He pointed down the strand where two vessels lay side by side, the strengthening light catching their painted figureheads.

Ragnar laughed. "A fine eye for ships, Gil Broadaxe. We sail like kings' sons."

"Well, earls' sons, anyhow," Gil waited in the knarr's shadow as his force gathered around him. "They sail from Dublin. Cousins of the earl of Mona. We owe *him* a favor, too," he said.

"You know them?" Fergus stepped, surprised, to Gil's side.

"No. But the kitchen maids couldn't stop talking about them. Even while they fed scraps to a cat."

"And the cat," Svein Sveinsson added, "listened very carefully."

Ragnar gave Gil a shrewd look. "Cats can be very wise. I knew one once that won a man a bride."

Gil smiled and turned to the sea. There was light enough now to see the white froth of the bar. The stretch of sand between the water and the sterns of the beached ships widened as he watched. The wind, rising with the dawn, was thankfully at their backs. The surf, alone, would be enough to fight. "Time to move," he murmured to Svein. He raised his hand above his head, swung it down, and ran.

Behind him, his followers broke smoothly into two groups, Svein leading half to the first ship, Gil and the rest taking the second. He had chosen the two crews with care: enough strong backs for the launch and the oars; enough experienced sailors to raise masts and man sheets. And enough swordsmen to meet any resistance. That role he left to his father, Palamedes, and Martin de Troye; though, with luck, stealth and dawn mist would save them the need of steel.

"Good seamen!" Svein Snaggle-Tooth grinned appreciatively at the tree-trunk rollers and the coils of rope tidily stacked beneath the bow.

"Better seamen would leave guards." Ragnar shrugged, shouldering a log, and Gil remembered how, even on his kinsman's shore at Mona, Floki had left half his crew aboard.

"They will next time!" he said cheerfully and ran up the waiting gangplank to take the helm.

The hull juddered beneath him as the ropes tightened, and then, with a lurch, broke free of the sand. Svein Sveinsson saluted him from the steering board of the second ship, as she, too, began to move. The rumble of oak keels on rollers broke the dawn quiet, but the fortress above remained silent.

Balanced easily on the moving deck, Gil turned his eyes to the sea and, alarmed how quickly the tide was falling, leaned out over the rail. The wet strand between the stern and the water widened even as his crews strove to cross it. Each wave broke short of the wave before it. Seabirds darted for gasping fish among the men's straining feet.

Beyond the surf, white foam and dark whirlpools mottled the surface of the bay. Further out, their spray hazing the air, three lines of breakers marked the thunderous bar. Gil searched for his own ships sailing out from the ayre, but the horizon was lost in a grey veil of mist. Still, inland, the light grew as swiftly as the sea retreated. It was full dawn when the scream came from above.

He whirled. Floating serenely above the fog banks of the strand, Mont Tombe shone pink in the first rays of the sun. The scream came again; a girl's voice shrieking in terror. Grasping the taut rope over his shoulder, Ragnar looked up from below.

"They've found the guards. Haul!" he roared, throwing his weight into his line. "Haul!"

"Swordsmen!" Gil shouted. But the three knights of Camelot were already running up the strand to meet the dark figures scrambling down the chiseled stone steps. Steel flashed in the dawn as others gathered along the ramparts above. Caught in broad daylight between land and sea, Gil's men were hens beneath hawks.

The rope teams strained, knee deep in the water. The stern splashed into the surf and Gil felt the ship lift beneath him. A clash of steel rang from the shore and he spun to face it. Backs to the sea, his three swordsmen faced a line of angry warriors.

In the center and a stride ahead of his companions, Lance'lot battled two, disarming one as Gil watched. Palamedes mighty sword swing sent three running back up the beach, while Martin de Troye saw off another. But more men were pouring out of the awakened fortress, some already crossing the strand.

"Haul!" Ragnar shouted again, the sea swirling around his thighs. The ship surged off the last roller and plunged into deep water, the rope men stumbling and splashing to get out of her way. Gil grabbed the tiller, holding her straight with a yet loosened oar until the bow was clear of the land. A ship's length off his steering board, Svein's own captured vessel rumbled into the surf, her crew, like Gil's scrambling desperately over the rails.

Then they were afloat, with only their swordsmen left ashore. "Get aboard!" Gil shouted as dark water opened between ships and strand.

"We sail!" echoed Svein from his own deck.

Palamedes flashed them his broad white smile, and dispatching a last fleeing warrior with the sole of his boot, ran for the ships. Martin de Troye thrust back two others and followed. Only Lance'lot remained, locked in combat with a lean black bearded knight, intent on his swordplay and oblivious of the cries from the ships. Gil thought suddenly of the Irish warrior, Padraic Njalsson, fighting his lonely battle on the Roman strand.

"Get aboard!" he shouted, and when his father still did not turn, cried, "I'm not leaving you. *Get aboard!*"

Lance'lot looked up, startled; then lunged forward, disarmed his opponent with two quick sword swings, and raced for the sea. Struggling through the surf in his heavy mail, he was hauled roughly aboard by two Irishmen in the bow and dumped, coughing and gasping, on the deck.

But in a moment, he was laughing. Sitting up, he wiped salt water from his beard and shouted to Gil at the helm, "Sorry, captain! Forgot you were waiting."

Gil fought a smile. Eyes fixed on the receding shore, where a dozen men struggled to launch the nearest ship, he called back, "Row." His father staggered obediently to his feet, took the bench opposite Ragnar, and bent his back expertly to the oar.

Gil returned his attention to the deepening water swirling beneath the stern, and gauging it carefully, summoned Svein Snaggle-Tooth to fasten the oar. Then, as his oarsmen brought the bow around, he sent Ari to ride the dragon and call his course.

A rope secure around his waist, the boy perched high on the curving prow, shouting back, "Load-board, steering-board," as Gil helmed a tortuous route between sandbars and shoals.

A quick glance over his shoulder showed Svein Sveinsson safely parting their wash. Beyond, on the already distant strand, the shouts of their opponents grew faint.

"Are they following?" his father called.

Gil smiled again. "They can try."

But, already, patches of yellow sand were appearing between their stern and the shore. Once, his oar stirred swirls of mud from the seabed and the tiller shuddered in his hands, awaking the grim memory of Kernow. But his oar held, and the hull slipped clear. Turning, he waved a warning to Svein, and the Shetlander swung his own ship aside, seeking a deeper channel.

The roar of the bar grew louder, and the boy on the figurehead half vanished in blown haze. But he stayed gamely at his post, gesturing with a free hand as the crashing waves drowned his voice: load-board, then steering-board, then load-board; and sinuous as dragons, themselves, the longships wound through the lines of surf.

And then they were free, past the white ramparts of breakers, out in the open sea. Gil turned to look back as Svein also cleared the bar. Beyond, Mont Tombe basked in morning sun, marooned above a broad expanse of golden sand, as if they had taken the sea away with them when they sailed.

Ragnar and a team of young knights raised the mast. The sail tumbled free. Karl and Fergus tightened the sheets and the prow of their stolen ship lifted like a sea-bird taking flight. Behind, Svein's ship, too, had spread her wings and as the two vessels gathered speed, the exhausted rowers slumped on their benches; then rose to stow their oars.

Alone at the helm, Gil felt the ship come alive beneath his hand, answering to the slightest turn of the oar.

"A fine ship," Lance'lot perched at the end of the steersman's bench.

Gil nodded, moving the tiller slightly to catch more wind. The sail strained, taut. The rushing bow wave sparkled in the rising sun.

"They will miss her," Lance'lot smiled.

Again, Gil nodded, thinking of the man who had helmed her last watching now helplessly from the shore. "She handles well," he said.

The mist thinned. Above, the sky was blue, though patchy fog still shrouded the sea. He glimpsed the ayre off his steering board and called, "Ciarnan!" gesturing to the mast. Lithe and fearless, the young Irishman mounted its swaying height and, straddling the yard, searched the horizon.

"You're a good seaman," Gil's father said.

Gil shrugged and smiled. "I'm a Northman."

Ciarnan shouted a warning down from the mast, and Gil headed up, and as the sail fell slack, rose to his feet, straining to see in the white glare. Grey shapes, vague and shimmering in the eerie light appeared and disappeared like ghosts. "There!" Lance'lot pointed over Gil's shoulder. But the mist thickened, for a moment closing again overhead, and there was nothing.

Sounds drifted across the water: a breaking bow wave, a gull's cry, and then, the sudden whinny of a horse. *Lionheart!* Gil heard the pony's confusion ... scenting him, searching for him …. Then a gust of wind rippled across the sea, the fog bank parted like shredded silk, and they were there: Star-Seeker off his load-board, and right before him, *Silver Dragon*, the sunlight glinting on her figurehead, and at her masthead, the golden pennant of his earl.

The decks of the two stolen ships erupted in cheering, and, after a wary hesitation, answering cheers of recognition came to them across the water. "Fine ships!" Erling Maiden-Face shouted to Gil, and from *Star-Seeker's* helm, Ismail added, "You say thank you?"

Gil swung his oar, called to the boys to tighten the sheets, and, buoyed on a swell of laughter, sent his four swans flying, out to the lawless sea.

———

But the journey, begun thus in a brightening dawn, ended in darkening shadow as each day's sailing drew them farther into winter and the north. Gales blew, unrelenting. Sails reefed, they struggled up the Frankish coast, beating against unforgiving winds, beaching wearily each night, scant distance from the harbor of the night before. The days shortened. Rain supplanted sun, and sleet replaced rain. They crossed to Dofras in snow.

There, at last, they could purchase provisions with the silver of their combined treasuries. But an army was expensive to feed. And the three knights' chargers, whose patient bulk crowded the hill ponies in their pens, needed more than winter grazing on wild shores. Beneath the storm-lashed chalk cliffs of the pilgrim port, Gil sent Fergus and his Irishmen off with a purse of hack silver to bargain with the merchants for fodder.

Martin de Troye's eyes followed the Irish down the strand. "You *trust* him?"

"Of course," Gil returned angrily. He saw his father also watching and grew angrier still. But, despite his anger, when he heard Irish voices among the seamen gathered around their fires, he fought doubt, himself.

But then the big red-haired warrior suddenly appeared, grinning broadly, his men following with sacks of straw and oats. "They argue the price," he said cheerfully, "but in the end, we agree." He tapped the hilt of his sword as he placed the purse with the remaining silver in Gil's hands.

Gil returned to the ships and held the purse up, in silence, before Troye and Lance'lot. The earl shrugged gruffly and walked away. Lance'lot smiled. "Did you tell them they were free?" he said.

Gil stared and then shook his head angrily. "Free? I let them *go*. I gave them silver and let them go."

"You showed your trust," his father agreed. "Your trust does not make them free men. Did you free them?"

"They *stayed with me*," Gil shot back. "There are ships all down this strand. They could have gone anywhere." He raised his hands in the air, and unable to meet his father's eyes, strode off to stare at the stormy sea.

They sailed on, the weather no kinder, the days shorter still. Beaching on lonely shores, they lived off the land: deer and wood fowl from the forests, and from the farms, mutton, meal, and cheese; some paid for, some not.

Nights were dreary; hungry men had no ear for song or story. Seasickness ruled the days; the ragged chop and roll of winter swells taking a toll of all but the hardiest of the Northmen. The forest knights lay on the decks, cursing the sea.

When a luckless merchant crossed their path, Gil took him, less for the need of his silver than for the cheering of his own weary crews. Then, with their fortunes replenished, he set his course for Hrafn's Ayre, trusting its booths of treasures and trinkets to cheer them further.

As at Dofras, Gil had the figureheads of the stolen ships— the dragon and long-maned horse that bore their names in runic script—taken down, lest among the ships crowded on the long sand-spit were friends or kin of their rightful captains. One sixteen-bencher was much like another: without their distinguishing ornaments, only the man who built them would know the Dublin ships, *Sea-Terror* and *Odin's Mare*.

But when they reached the entrance of the sea-road to Deer Bay, his caution seemed strangely unnecessary. There were no masts rising above it, no ships awaiting the tide. And when they rounded the point of the spit and entered the bay behind, the landward strand stretched white and empty, but for one small, upturned hull, a fisherman's skiff inverted against the weather.

Around it were strewn casks, ropes, and three dark heaps of sodden sailcloth. A deep keel drag through the remnants of the rapidly vacated camp marked the departure of a much larger ship. A thin column of smoke yet rose from a dwindling fire. The scent of burning driftwood only half disguised another, rank and sickening. Ragnar stepped onto the steering board and drew his shirt up over his nose. "What happens here?"

Gil shrugged, studying the shore. "Someone left in a hurry," he said.

Fergus joined them. He wrinkled his nose and pointed toward the heaps of rumpled cloth, picked at, as they watched, by a circle of gulls. "Too much of a hurry to bury their dead." With a jolt, Gil saw the heaps were shrouded corpses.

The stench of death aroused a grim memory of his first voyage with Floki Magnusson and the slaughtered village on the Pentland coast. He swung his oar hard and headed up into the wind. Behind him, the three following ships did the same, gliding with slack sails alongside.

"A raid?" Fergus said. Looking up and down the barren strand, Gil shook his head. It made no sense. There was little sign of a battle. And where were the merchants who flocked here? What raider had overwhelmed them all, leaving so little behind?"

"There's no one here," he said at last. "Whoever did this is gone." But then a sudden movement by the upturned hull sent Fergus and Ragnar running to the arms kist for their bows. With arrows set to string, they mounted the rail and stood watching as, stumbling and barefoot, a man emerged from the shelter of the skiff and staggered to the edge of the sea.

Beard and hair unkempt, tunic stained and half undone, he stood swaying, shielding his eyes as he peered out across the water. Then, in a rasping voice, he called, "Help us, I beg you. We are stranded. Help us!"

"Oarsmen!" Gil cried. "Take us in!" But even as he called the order his own mind was arguing: *But they have a boat.*

"Stand off!" He jumped at Svein's shout. "Stand off the shore!"

"They're stranded!" Gil called back. "They need help."

"They are not stranded! They are ill. They have the sickness. Stand off!"

"It is so!" another Shetlander shouted, standing up at his oar on Ismail's *Star-Seeker.* "The sickness comes to our island. Many die."

"The earl's own good lady dies," Svein Sveinsson fixed sorrowful eyes on Gil's face. "Take us to sea."

Gil thought of Hakon's kind-hearted mother, Gunnhild. So full of life; so quickly gone. "Help us," the man on the shore pleaded weakly.

"We can't just leave them," Gil said.

"We must," Svein returned. "Set foot on that shore and we leave you, too."

Gil stared. The big Shetlander faced him calmly and without rancor; but also, with iron resolve.

"He is right."

Gil turned, startled, to the soft, female voice. Rachel stood before him, looking sadly at the shore. "What is it?" he asked uncertainly. "Malaria? Like Eirik …?"

She shook her head. "That wouldn't matter. Malaria isn't contagious. *This* …" she looked again at the desperate man, "… is. That's why they were abandoned, Gil."

"So, I abandon them, too?"

She met his eyes, her own shining with tears. "It's not like home, Gil. Even if it's just measles or flu … these boys from their far islands …" she looked quickly around at his young crew, "… they have no immunity. We have no medicine. If you land there, a third … even half … may never see home." Quickly wiping her face, she turned and walked back down the deck to stand with Janetta and Danni.

Gil nodded slowly. He raised his head, gazing around at his ships with their slackened sails; their crews and captains watching him intently. Men shrugged. No one spoke. No one would meet his eyes. He turned at last to his father, willing him to say something, to find an answer. To tell him what to do. But Lance'lot waited silently, with all the rest. Squaring his shoulders, Gil turned back to the strand. Even before he spoke, he saw hope drain from the face of the man on the shore.

"Give them some water, some meal," Erling said gently, from the helm of Odin's Mare. "It's all we can do."

They brought *Silver Dragon* within a dozen feet of the shore, with oarsmen ready to draw back at once, and with Fergus and Ragnar standing at the rail, arrows trained on the sick man below. At the sound of voices, his two companions dragged themselves from beneath the upturned hull, and stood clinging to it for support, as a cask each of water and meal were unloaded into the sea and guided with boat hooks to land.

Then, as the oars dipped and splashed and the ship slipped away, one of the two shouted out, "Do not leave us! In the name of the good Christ, do not leave us alone!"

"Christian," Fergus murmured.

"Or they think we are," Ragnar shrugged.

Gil brought his ship around, and in the strengthening wind, called the boys to tighten the sheets. The cries of the men left behind were drowned by the rush of the bow wave, but the stench of death stayed with them, far out into the open sea, and they sailed on, late into the dusk, before they again put ashore.

Each night after found them on a wild strand, huddled around campfires or under rain sodden tents. Happily now, they relied on fish and game, and even dry bannocks and water, rather than risk what they met at Hrafn's Ayre. All desire for the bustle of booths and markets was gone. The silver in their purses would wait a better day.

In that way, fighting the ever recalcitrant sea, they made their way north to Einar's Bay. Relieved to bring all his ships safely through its daunting rock gates, Gil brought out ale, and even with the wind whipping its own melody from the strings, Niall played his ancient harp and they sang songs of love and home.

That morning, they set out yet again into the too familiar gale. "Does the sun never shine on this land?" Martin de Troye glared at the cloud-bound shore and shouted the words over the howl of the wind.

"Only on Caledon," Gil grinned, wiping spray from his face.

"And upon Tara," Fergus smiled within his sleet-caked beard.

"The sun always shines on home," Hamund's young voice was wistful in the gale.

"Even on Gauk's Isle!" his friend, Leidolf cried, laughing.

But Hamund only smiled sadly and sat twisting the love-knot on his wrist. And then, worn through by salt and sweat, it broke apart and in an instant flew from his arm. "My Valgerd!" He cried the girl's name as if she herself had been swept from him. But then the frayed ribbon caught, astonishingly, in the rigging, wrapping itself around a wind-shaken shroud. "I save you!" he cried happily; and leaping up on the rail, stretched high for it, fluttering just out of his reach. Gripping the shroud, he pulled himself up, his feet teetering on the rail.

"No!" Gil shouted from the helm, and he waved frantically for someone to stop him. Ragnar and Ciarnan leaped up together, reaching out even as the boy lost his footing, and then his hand hold, and, grasping his love-knot, plunged into the sea.

He was gone in an instant. The great ship swept past, the bow wave rolling over the empty patch of sea where Gil had fixed his eyes. With all his strength, he swung the oar, turning the prow into the wind. "Loose the sail!" Karl and Ari obeyed, staring back at the sea with huge, terrified eyes. But there was nothing but foam-frothed water in their wake.

Gil turned his ship and called for oars and each of his captains did the same. Sails lowered, oars dipping cautiously, they searched the empty sea, crisscrossing their own washes, rowing back and forth, calling, listening, calling again.

Once a fish broke the surface and an insane cheer greeted it, and then faded to wry laughter and then silence, and they searched on. Then, Gil heard a sound over the rush of the wind and shouted, "Raise oars!" and they all drifted, listening, until no one could deny it was only a gull, high overhead. The gale was rising, the day passing; they had no harboring in sight. Not a man complained.

And all the while, Gil yet saw the whole thing before his eyes: the love-knot, Hamund on the rail, the way he plunged straight down into the sea. "He went down so fast," he said wearily.

Ragnar dipped his oar and shrugged. "He does not swim."

Gil shook his head in frustration. So many of the island boys did not. "Maybe he hit his head ...."

"You see it all."

"... or I hit him with the oar? Did I ...?" But the steering oar, so well crafted by Eyolf Grimsson, transmitted the slightest vibration, and he had felt none. "He didn't even struggle!" he cried, anguished.

"He sees no point."

Gil bowed his head over the tiller. No. Overwhelmed by hopelessness or determined not to release the treasure he had saved, Hamund sank as if he were carved in stone. Gil saw him, even now, falling ever deeper into the silent darkness below, his love-token clutched yet in his hand, and knew he would see him like that, the rest of his own days. He raised his head and called the hardest order of his life: "Raise sail."

The yards rose up the masts, the sails fluttered down and were sheeted in, and the four ships resumed their interrupted journey. Janetta came quietly to Gil's side, and stood leaning against him in the way he loved saying nothing and understanding everything.

Her warm body close, his ship true to her course, he fixed his eyes on the north and rehearsed in his mind the journey he would make to Gauk's Isle, with a purse of silver—the correct amount ruled by his council—to compensate a father for his loss. Though all the silver in the world could not be enough.

And then the wind shifted, blowing her hair with its sweet scent over his face, lifting the golden pennant at the masthead. Backing west and then southwest, it settled, strong and steady, over his shoulder and the ship quickened, cutting through the waves. Above, the clouds lifted and took on a bright glow and then suddenly broke, sending shafts of sunlight over sea and land.

"Look!" Janetta cried.

Fields appeared, neatly mowed or freshly ploughed for winter. Cattle sprinkled the hillside and in the distance, over the thatched roofs of a cluster of buildings, a bell tower rose. The sweet chiming of its bell reached his ears. "Lindisfarne," he said quietly, knowing now exactly where he was: back in the very same waters where Arnkel Fish-Tail staged his mutiny and got thrown in the sea for his trouble. Arnkel Fish-Tail, who he did not leave to drown. And now the sea, having been denied Arnkel Fish-Tail, had taken Hamund in his stead.

He looked bitterly out over the ruthless waters, splashing so playfully in the winter sun, and for a brief moment, hated them, and hated everything about them, even his beautiful ship. But then the sun, sinking lower in a green, translucent sky, turned the wave tops pink and gold. A single star and a crescent moon trembled above the masthead, lifting the darkness from his soul. Ahead, a gentle bay beckoned and, arms around his love, he steered a grateful course to its strand.

And then, onward from that moment, their journey seemed charmed. The wind came behind them, steady and true. Game filled the black cauldrons in the star-filled nights. Even as they entered Glen Alban, no ship crossed their path on the tranquil sea, but for one small skiff, its sail flitting in the dusk; some fisherman returning to his rest.

In the frosty morning, the tide obeyed their wishes and the sparkling blue river carried them inland. The forest gave up its trees and the longships rode their sea of logs into the Great Loch of Alba. And there, in the shadow of a dark fortress, they dropped anchor in a sheltered bay and for the first time since the flight from Mont Tombe, Gil slept the night through.

CHAPTER SEVENTEEN

Lionheart woke him, a small whicker of greeting in the pre-dawn darkness. *Go to sleep. It's night, still.* But the whicker came again, untroubled, but insistent. Gil groaned and pulled his sleeping fur over his head.

With the ships at anchor in deep water, a safe distance from an uncertain shore, there'd been no grazing that night, no gallop along the tide-washed strand. *Soon*, Gil thought of the steep climb beside the Falls of the Fugitive, *Soon you'll have all the exercise you want.*

But then Janetta's black mare, Hrafn, gave a frightened neigh and instantly Gil was fully awake. Throwing back the fur bedroll, he sat up. The sky above was star-filled. Frost sparkled on the tips of the fur and on the silver trim of his scabbard lying at his side. The soft glow of starlight defined the length of the ship: the black awnings draped over the lowered mast, the frost-maned ponies in their enclosure, the blunted prow, bereft of her figurehead in these dangerous waters.

But for the shuffling beasts, all was silent; his men sleeping peacefully beneath the awnings, or out on the open deck, the girls in their tent.

Yet, something was wrong. His eyes searched the deck again, finding nothing. *Nothing. And no one. No one at the prow. Where was his guard?* His hand shot out, fingers closing on his sword belt, drawing it closer. *Too light.* With a jolt, he realized the scabbard was empty.

"Do not seek your sword." Gil's hand froze on the scabbard. Soft, barely audible, the voice came from behind and above; from the steersman's bench below which he always slept. "It is not there."

He whirled. Silhouetted against the stars a man sat calmly at the helm, where his guard, Fergus, would sit. Only it was not Fergus: no folds of Irish plaid draped the figure, but a Northman's cloak, the hood drawn close, the face in darkness.

Gil's mind flew to Arnkel's mutiny, and then, more frightening still, to the lost, sea-wrapped boy from Gauk's Isle. "Hamund …" he whispered shakily.

"Have I been so long away you forget my name?"

Relief flooded Gil's heart, followed instantly by outrage. *"Floki?"*

"Hush, Warrior, men yet sleep."

"Where are my guards?" Gil cried.

A hand drew the hood aside. Starlight shone on the familiar pale hair and eyes, the cheerful smile. "Be at peace, Warrior, and do not shout. Do I harm friends of my friends? I only ask them, courteously, and indeed in Irish, to be silent. But they will not, so they have been made so." Floki smiled again innocently. "Though how you find so many Irishmen, I do not know; to have one at each end of your ship and yet more asleep on deck."

He waved a hand toward the snoring warriors wrapped in their distinctive plaids. Gil was on his feet, staring all around. *"Where are they?"*

Floki sighed and stood as well. Placing a hand on Gil's shoulder he turned him toward the shore. "Safe under that great tree," he pointed to the dim outlines of an enormous branching oak, "And within the *vallum* of the small chapel beyond, so none may harm them and they may listen as my friend there sings his office."

"Your friend? You have a friend *here?*"

"I have friends everywhere. Who would not enjoy me?" He smiled, and wrapping Gil in an affectionate arm, gave him a rough shake.

"I can't imagine," Gil muttered. Smarting from the humiliation of his ship's guard overpowered and his sword lifted from his side, he stepped out of the embrace. "How did you get them there?" he said suddenly. "And how did *you* get here?"

Wide awake now, he stared at the quiet waters of the

sheltered bay, his four dragons tugging gently at their anchor lines. "Where's your ship?"

Floki enfolded him again within a friendly arm and pointed down. Barely visible in the shadows, a small skiff with lowered mast lay tethered to *Silver Dragon's* stern.

"*That?*"

"Yes, Warrior. She is not mine. I borrow her in Norway. But she handles well."

"In Norway?" Gil's voice rose in astonishment and men stirred on the deck. "You sailed from Norway in *that?*"

"It is a long way to swim, Warrior. I get distracted. Too many fish. Look now," he said sorrowfully, "you have broken their sleep."

But the voice that had stirred the slim figure peering out from the flaps of the girls' tent was not Gil's, but his own. Ghostly in her linen underdress, Danni stood for an uncertain moment. Then, with a joyful cry, she leaped forward, running barefoot past the pony pen, disappearing beneath the awnings and reappearing, still running, nimble as a deer among the sleeping men, hair flying loose, arms outstretched.

"Ah," Floki cried, "*Here* is one who gives me welcome." And releasing Gil with a friendly shove, he jumped down from the steersman's bench and caught her as she flung herself into his arms.

Laughing and kissing and whispering, they embraced; she blithely oblivious of her state of undress, he cheerfully delighting in it, until Gil, wishing he could vanish, muttered, "Uh, Floki ..." he nudged a shoulder toward the shore, " ... the guards?"

"Ah, indeed." Floki turned also to the shore and released Danni regretfully. "But lass, you wear little and it is cold," he said, as if just noticing. She nodded happily, but he was not satisfied until he had wrapped her in his cloak, safe from the dawn wind and the eyes of awaking warriors, and escorted her to her tent.

He returned as silently as he left, appearing suddenly again out of the darkness. "Come," he said softly, "We bring comfort to those good men; they, too, will be cold, though not so welcoming of me. So, I would have your company. But first," he smiled, "I would return this." He held up Gil's sword in the starlight, then pressed the hilt into his hands. "I do not wish you to murder me in your sudden waking."

Gil took it in silence, stuffed it back into its scabbard and buckled the belt around his waist. Still without speaking, he climbed down into the little skiff which Floki had drawn alongside, and they slipped away from *Silver Dragon's* stern under oar, making no more sound than the splash of a leaping fish. Shielded by the longship's hull from the guards on her three companions, they set out for land. Only Lionheart's friendly whicker marked their departure.

"*He* greets me," Floki said pointedly.

Gil sat silent.

"I am away months, Warrior! What? You do not notice? In all this time you do not once miss me?"

"Oh, I miss you," Gil said softly. "I miss you on Hrolf's Isle when your chieftains treat me like a child. I miss you off Lindisfarne when Arnkel Thorleiksson tries to steal your ship."

"I tell you not to trust him." Floki looked over his shoulder at the shadowy shore.

"Right," Gil muttered. Then he said slowly, "And I miss you when Hamund falls in the sea and drowns in front of me and there's nothing, *nothing*, I can do."

Floki was silent, gently dipping the oars. "Hamund of Gauk's Isle?" Gil nodded. "I am sorry, Warrior." He paused. "A good lad. Kind." Then, after another silence, he said, "Do you think I never miss the men who taught me? Redbeard? Or Ragnvald? Or, indeed, even my *mother*, from whom I learn the use of a sword?"

Gil shrugged.

"Besides," Floki pursued, looking over Gil's head to the anchored longships, "I do not find Fish-Tail at the helm, but you. And you have raised a crew on Hrolf's Isle, and more in Francia. I give you two ships and you make them four. Why are you not proud?"

"Because Hamund drowned," Gil said quietly.

Floki fell silent, dipping his oars and pulling so smoothly that they still made no sound at all. "Shall I name you the men who die in my command?" When Gil said nothing, he sighed and looked up at the stars. "And where *is* Fish-Tail? Beneath the sea as he deserves?"

Gil shook his head. "I threw him in, but I had him hauled out."

"You will regret this one day."

"I regret it already," Gil said. "He ran off with half our silver and three of my men." He shrugged. "But you had *me* hauled out."

"You see!" Floki laughed delightedly. "I, too, regret this already! I raise an ungrateful whelp who gives me no welcome when I return. Now, get out and pull us in, we are in the shallows."

They drew the skiff up on a small muddy beach, stowed the oars, and picked their way along the overgrown shore. Ahead, Gil saw the high branches of the great oak, its dead leaves shivering against the greying sky. There was still no sign of Fergus, or of Fionn, who had kept guard at the bow.

"How did you find us?" Gil asked suddenly.

"I see you at sea." Floki turned and smiled. "A long way off. But I know my dragon, even with his head tucked under his wing."

"I saw your sail!" Gil cried. "In the firth! Such a small sail, I didn't pay any attention."

"Not wise, Warrior. Even a small sail has a ship beneath it. And even a small ship, at least one man aboard. What is his purpose that he is not home at his hearth?"

Gil nodded. The light was growing and they could see each other properly. He looked back at the beached skiff. "I can't believe you crossed the Northern Sea in that."

Floki shrugged. "I am but one man; why should I need a bigger ship? You do this, too, without difficulty."

Gil smiled wryly, not convinced.

"It is so, Warrior," Floki insisted. "Nothing I meet there is worse than the seas of the Holy Isle. *Land* is the problem, in a ship, not water. In the open sea the winds are steady. I tie the oar, and even sleep. And wake to the mountains of Caledon. And before them, four fine swans!"

"So I go ahead of you, into the river. The skiff draws little water. Only once must I drag her in the shallows. I am in the Great Loch well before you. And so, I pay a visit to this little chapel," he gestured to the dark stone building, dimly glimpsed now, beyond the oak, "and find there a father who knows me from the days I rest at the Field of the Church, after we meet with the dragon. You remember?"

"Oh, I remember," Gil glanced uneasily at the waters of the Great Loch, dim yet in the shadow of their surrounding hills.

"He is of their brethren and now serves the people of this strath. And *he* welcomes me without question," Floki added. Gil said nothing and with a shrug, Floki continued, "And so, with him, I watch you come into the bay and cast your anchor here, as I know you will, for you sail to the Falls of the Fugitive. Though that you must not do."

"Why?" Gil protested. "It's the road to Camelot."

"That is why."

Floki looked out across the water to the dark fortress on its promontory above the bay. A wisp of wood smoke rose above its thatched roofs and Gil thought of Mont Tombe. "They also watch you arrive," Floki said. "I see men on the walls. But since you show no interest in them, they show none in you, knowing you will soon be gone."

"But *where*?" Gil said, "if not the Falls of the Fugitive?"

"I will tell you. But later." He paused at a low stone wall. "Listen."

Gil heard the familiar Latin chant, a lone voice singing the psalms of Prime. He remembered Aidan, the night he had gone to him in despair of his failures as earl. And yet, he was here, within reach of Camelot; an army at his command.

Floki took off his sword belt and, laying the weapon down, stepped over the wall. "You, also, Warrior. We come to holy ground."

Gil did the same, uneasily, though, because he had become aware of another sound, a scuffling and grunting, as of some fierce and angry beast. Involuntarily, he glanced again at the loch.

But the sound was nearer, on land, coming from beneath the

oak tree by the chapel. "Floki ..." he whispered, "There's ...."

"I hear it, Warrior. Yes. Wild swine roam these forests. Great boars, with mighty tusks! There must be some near." Gil thought regretfully of his sword, lying outside the *vallum*, but Floki had quickened his pace, as if eager to do battle with these beasts, bare-handed. "Ah! They are here!"

Taking up a fallen branch, Gil ran to join him. But, reaching the tree, he saw no wild boar, but two men, bound with sturdy rope to either side of the enormous trunk, gags in their mouths and fury in their eyes.

"Fergus!" he cried. "Fionn!"

Wriggling around as much as their bonds allowed, they stared at Gil in astonishment. Then, gesturing awkwardly with half-pinioned limbs, they snorted and grunted in renewed outrage until Floki, with a kindly smile, stepped close and removed each of their gags.

"Slaughter him, Broadaxe!" Fergus roared. "He steals your ship!"

Floki shook his head, smiled again, and pointed to *Silver Dragon* floating serenely in the dawn. "Safe at anchor, her crew enjoying their rest," he said in Irish. "As you would also," he added sorrowfully, "would you only be silent."

"Silent when you take Fionn's sword and mine?"

"But you *would* wave them *about*," Floki said.

"He holds a blade to my throat and binds me!" Fionn, young and dark, turned boyish eyes to Gil, "I fail you, Broadaxe, but he is so swift."

"I fail you, too," Fergus growled. "But loose these bonds and give me a blade and I make amends."

"You see?" Floki sounded genuinely hurt, "he will be all for waving it about again." He turned to the Irishman and nodded. "You will, will you not?"

"I will gut you and flay you and leave not enough of you to feed one crow."

Floki sighed. "I am sorry, Warrior, but they are not reasonable. Where do you *find* these Irishmen?"

"Do you know him?" Fionn asked, suddenly awed.

"Very well," Gil said. "He is my earl."

Fergus' angry face paled, and turning to Gil he ducked his head in the only gesture of submission he could manage. "Then I must serve him," he said in a low voice. "As I serve you." He looked up, fixed his fierce blue eyes on Floki's and said, "Forgive me. I have offended greatly. But I knew neither your name nor your rank."

"My name is Floki Magnusson," Floki said with a small smile. "But your earl flatters me. I am but his helmsman. Albeit, a good one," he added. Then assessing Fergus carefully, he said, "And you who wear the Tara cloth, what name and rank are yours?"

With what dignity his position permitted, the Irishman said, "I am Fergus, son of Gartnan, a warrior of Tara until my bondage."

Floki paused and raised an eyebrow toward Gil, but when Gil only shrugged, he turned back to Fergus. "I know the name of Gartnan. A great chieftain, renowned through all Ireland."

"I know your name as well," Fergus said uneasily.

Floki laughed. "But more in condemnation than renown! Do not be concerned," he said, "My battles in Ireland are done. Warrior!" he turned to Gil and gestured to the small knife Gil wore always at his belt, "Cut them free."

They set out again in the skiff; Floki, the dutiful helmsman, manning the oars. But aboard the anchored longships, many were now awake and observing their approach, first in puzzlement and then with shouts of recognition and delight.

Floki nodded and smiled. "Ah, Warrior, that must be an important man that so many acknowledge him. Perhaps you should enquire who they greet?"

"Perhaps I should," Gil agreed, watching as Floki stowed one oar and stood, guiding the skiff alongside *Silver Dragon's* hull, with the other. "On the other hand, perhaps I should just do this." He jumped up and dove hard at the Northman's legs, tipping him off his feet and over the rail. With an astonished shout, Floki splashed full length in the sea.

Fergus and Fionn cried out in alarm. The welcoming cheers from the longships faded in confusion. "Broadaxe! Do you lose your wits?" Ragnar called from above.

But Floki broke surface laughing so hard he could barely swim. "Warrior!" He gripped the skiff's hull and reached up a plaintive hand. "Help me," he gasped, still laughing, "Before I drown."

Gil smiled, unmoving. "Ask me nicely."

"What say you?"

"Try 'May I board your ship?'"

"Warrior ...." Floki's pale eyes flashed for an angry instant, but then he was laughing again. Covering his dripping face with his free hand, he murmured, "Ah yes. Ah yes. I understand." He looked up, and suppressing another bout of laughter, said meekly, "Gil Lake of Tir nan Og, *may* I board your ship?"

"*Yes*, Earl Floki." Gil reached out and caught his hand. "Welcome home."

Floki scrambled aboard the skiff, drenched through and laughing still. "Ah, this is justice," he declared to the watchers crowding *Silver Dragon's* rail. "This is justice. I raise up blood of my blood." Then catching sight of Lance'lot among them, he cried, "And there is the man who sires the audacious cub! Be proud, my friend! He learns well the lessons I teach!"

Raising anchor, Erling, Svein Sveinsson, and Ismail had their oarsmen draw their ships in close beside *Silver Dragon*, roping the hulls together as they would for battle. But this was for a happier cause, a morning feast in honor of their returning earl. Or, at least, as good a feast as could be made of dried fish and cold meat.

But scarcely was food served and wine poured and formal greetings made to all, then Floki drew Gil to one side and turning him to face the fortress across the bay said quietly, "Warrior, what see you there?"

Gil studied the dark outline, still murky in the overcast dawn. Smoke yet drifted over the roof tops, but all else was so still that he could hear the wing beats of the white birds flying up from the thatch. "Nothing," he said.

"Not true. You see what you have seen before. On Yula's Isle," said Floki.

"The doves," Gil whispered.

Seeing the direction of their gaze, others quickly joined them at the rail, Troye and Lance'lot sipping their wine, and Ismail with his arm discreetly around Rachel's waist. Lance'lot watched the birds setting out across the grey loch, buffeted by strengthening winds. "Messengers?" he asked quietly.

Floki shrugged. "Men keep them for meat as well, for they always return, no matter how far they fly."

"Unless," Rachel suggested, "they fall prey to a hawk?"

Floki laughed. "Indeed. But which? They are many. Still, since they spread their wings, we must spread ours."

"You fear treachery?" Troye glared at the silent fortress.

"No," Floki smiled, his eyes sparkling, "but I always expect it." He turned to Gil, "Now, Warrior, while there is yet time."

The three helmsmen returned to their ships, clambering from deck to deck, their half-eaten breakfasts clutched yet in their hands. Ropes were loosed, the hulls separated, masts raised. Before the last white bird had vanished into the cloud-heavy sky, their sails were tumbling free.

"What's my course?" Gil said uncertainly. Floki sat beside him on the steersman's bench, with Percy hugging him joyously, under the folds of his fur-lined cloak.

"Straight to the far shore, as if indeed you would beach. Only do not. There is no beach."

"Wasn't planning on it," Gil said, eyeing the distant rocky hillside plunging steeply into the loch. He glanced back. Floki's little skiff, tethered to the dragon's tail, bounced contentedly in their wake. Behind, the three longships heeled before the rising wind as they cleared the shelter of the bay.

White caps splashed the choppy grey water. Karl and Ari tightened the sheets. *Silver Dragon's* prow lifted, her sail billowing taut. "She rides well for you," Floki said.

"She rides well for anyone," Gil said. "She's a beautiful ship."

Floki smiled, ruffling Percy's hair. "Eyolf's master work," he said. "Something about the wood that summer ...." He paused and said carefully, "How was my father when you left him?"

Gil kept his eyes on the forbidding shore to which he sailed and said, "Well."

"Did you part in friendship?"

Gil hesitated. Then he nudged the Irish battle-axe at his feet. "He taught me how to use that," he said.

Floki glanced at the weapon and nodded. "Then he serves you well," he said. He looked down at Percy and laughed gently. "And what of you, Cupbearer? How are your goats and your new ram? Are *they* friends?"

Percy poked his head out from under the cloak. "Gil made me leave them behind. In a pen. *Outside.*" He glared accusingly at Gil.

"Then we will leave *him* in a pen, once we are home."

"Thank you," Gil said. "I look forward to that. Will you tell me where I'm going before I hit the rocks?"

"There are no rocks until you are an oars length from the shore," Floki said mildly. Then turning suddenly, he said, "And what troubles you, my friends?"

Gil took his eyes from his course and saw Ari and Karl had briefly left their posts. They ducked their heads, whispered and exchanged punches. Then Ari pushed Karl forward. "Earl Floki?" the boy burst out. "Is it true you fought a dragon on the loch?"

"No."

"Arnkel said you did," said Karl.

"I did not fight it. We discussed if I would be its dinner and agreed I would not."

"Arnkel said he rescued you," said Karl.

Floki's eyes narrowed, but he smiled when he said, "That is not true. My lady rescued me. Perhaps Arnkel lies to spare me shame?" He shrugged lightly. "Though it is no shame to me to be graced by such a lady."

Ari edged out from behind Karl. "Can I see your scars?"

"No. But if you wish to swim, I will help you. Then you may have scars of your own." He made to rise, smiling cheerfully, and with shouts of alarm they dashed back up the deck.

Percy slid further under the cloak, his eyes huge. "Is it real?"

"Yes," Floki laughed softly. "But it is only an animal, like a bear or a lynx. And it does not like the wind or the storms, so we will not see it today."

Percy nodded and smiled and got up to tell Danni so she would not be afraid.

"Hope you're right," said Gil.

"I am right. The good father who cares for me at the Field of the Church tells me this. And he tells me something else, as well." Gil looked up. "He tells me that there is another road to Camelot."

"Where?"

Floki pointed westward, along the approaching shore. "There is another pass. You do not see from here, so tightly does it wind up into the hills, and so hidden and narrow the bay where it opens onto the loch. They call it the Boar's Tail, for the way it twists and turns. But it leads up through those steep hills, just as does the way of the Falls of the Fugitive. And it enters the same high strath you crossed in the blizzard, only to the east and the north. And it will not be guarded, even if the Falls of the Fugitive is."

"Why should the Falls be? It wasn't when we came last."

"For that reason," said Floki with a smile. "Now I tell you what to do." He paused and sat straighter. "No. I do not. You tell me."

"Oh, *thanks*," Gil said. "So, what, I just keep sailing until I'm an oars length from the rocks? *Then what*, Earl Floki?"

"If you wish. But were it me, I would drop my sail before that. And also, my mast. Though the water is indeed so deep, you might pass beside the hillside with the masthead brushing the trees. And none would see you there."

"Ah," said Gil. He glanced quickly back at the fortress.

"No, they will not see. A sail, yes. These low hulls against the dark hill, no."

"How far along the shore to the Boar's Tail?"

"No distance for good oarsmen. And you have many." Floki looked back at the three following sails. "All those Irishmen with the broad shoulders and the short tempers." He watched a moment longer. "The Saracen helms Ragnvald's gift," he said. "I know the work of Shetlanders. But who gives you the others?"

Gil smiled, judging the distance to the shore. "A cousin of your cousin in Mona."

Floki tilted his head quizzically. "Indeed. I am surprised."

"So will he be when he finds out."

"Ah! Northman!" Floki cried, delighted.

Gil raised his head and signaled to Ari and Karl to loose the sail.

The track up the Boar's Tail Pass mounted as steeply as the burdened hill ponies could climb, while only the long legs of the two knights' chargers saved the heavy beasts from defeat. Pressed into service as pack animals, Doombearer and the Monkish Plough-horse bore their humbled state with dignity, though, laden as they were with arms and provisions, they had to gather themselves and leap to clear rocks and ledges. Still, they followed their masters without need of bridle or tether, as Palamedes and Lance'lot led the way through the pass.

Look at that, Gil nudged Lionheart who, with no other burden than Percy's small frame on his back, still picked his way with the reluctance of a wet-footed cat. *Why do I have to haul you everywhere?* Lionheart slid back on his haunches and flattened his ears. *One buck, and you are dinner. I do not lie.*

Gil heard giggling behind him, and saw Rachel, Janetta, and Danni hiding their laughter behind their hands as they struggled with their own charges. Behind them, Ismail led Chocolate, patiently coaxing the laden animal while Elias and Darras pushed from behind.

"My friend!" Darras called to Gil. "I smell the great forest! We are near!"

Gil smiled. They were a long way yet from Camelot—two, even three days march—but he understood the happiness of an exile nearing home. He raised his head, looking beyond the boys and the pony, to the long line of men winding their way up from the shore. In spite of the steady rain, they strode cheerfully, enjoying solid ground under their feet after so many days on shipboard.

But Gil missed already the long seas rolling beneath his keel, and the song of the wind in the shrouds. He looked quickly to Floki, walking between Erling and Martin de Troye, knowing he was the one man here certain to miss them, too. The three were deep in conversation, only raising their heads when obliged by some obstacle in the challenging path.

At times, the track snaked up the course of a tumbling burn. At others, it skirted the steep slopes of the hillsides enclosing the narrow defile. Three times they crossed the stream bed, sliding on moss covered rocks, the horses splashing and clattering through the water. When Gil looked back, mid-stream, at the narrow, sheltered bay where they had beached, the four great ships; shrouded already by their black awnings; appeared no larger than the skiff in which Floki had crossed the Northern Sea. And the skiff, itself, was but a scrap of driftwood.

Pleased with the height they had gained, he studied the camp. Tents had been pitched and smoke was rising from campfires. "Svein wastes no time," Ismail called, smiling. "He will have a longhouse when we come back."

If we come back. The words came unbidden to Gil's mind and he thrust them aside, though Lionheart's ears still twitched uneasily. *Not talking to you. And we* will *come back.* Most of them would, anyway.

He looked one more time to where the third of his forces left behind settled in for their long, disappointed wait. Deprived of the battle for which they had travelled so far, they played yet as vital a role: guarding the ships that were the lifeline to home.

Svein Sveinsson had accepted charge of the camp with a brief nod. Calm and practical, the Shetlander knew ships and the seas that lay to the North. And, if things did not go well, as Floki might say, he could lead the remnant home in *Star-Seeker's* wake.

To Svein Snaggle-Tooth, weather-beaten from so many summer journeys, Gil had entrusted Odin's Mare. And a fair-haired Irishmen called Bran, who had proved himself as skilled with ships as any Northman, would take *Sea-Hunter's* helm.

But it was to Ciarnan, who had sailed beside him to Rome and back, that Gil relinquished *Silver Dragon*, though he had turned for an instant to her true master, as he did. But if Floki questioned his judgement, nothing in his manner would say. Nor, if he had better choices of his own, did he speak them. Torn between pride and his own self-doubt, Gil glanced again at the three men walking behind.

Floki looked up suddenly, raised a hand in salute, and leaving his two companions, loped easily up the hill to join him. Tweaking Lionheart's ear as he passed, he turned Gil toward the eastern flank of the pass and directed his gaze to a jumble of stone at its summit. "Warrior, what see you there?"

"It's a fortress," Gil answered at once. "But it's empty. A ruin. I saw it from below." He gestured toward the track on the far side of the burn.

"A ruin, yes," Floki agreed. "But also high. I would see from there. And my lady," he glanced back at the girls and their ponies, "will see further still."

Little remained of the old hill fort but a few rotting timbers within a jumble of mossy stone. But its lofty setting still commanded a fine view of the Great Loch and its surrounding hills. While Danni laid out a circle of dead bracken on the grass, Gil and Floki climbed to the highest vantage point on the tumbled walls.

Turning from the loch, they looked out across the moorland of the high, broad strath to the dark forests of Caledon in which lay Camelot. The rain was turning to snow and Gil thought warily of the blizzard in which they had struggled so desperately. He peered through the falling flakes for a glimpse of the ruined chapel that had saved their lives. But it was yet too far.

Still, the snow, this day, fell lightly, riming the fallen stones and dusting the heather, but flying light and harmless before their feet. "You were right," Gil pointed to a thread of blue smoke rising from a hilltop to the west. "That's above the falls. He's set a guard."

"He would be a fool, if not," said Floki. He looked quickly to Danni, standing at the edge of her circle, and scrambled down to her side. "There is a guard, beyond. You will see the smoke of his camp. You must go nowhere near him. And over the forest, you must fly high. Above bow-shot. Above the talons of the peregrine."

Danni tilted her head and smiled. "I will fly where I must fly to see. Or there's no point in flying at all." She stepped closer and laid her fingers on his lips. "Did I protest when you kept your vow in Norway?" She shook her head gently. "For your own life, you have too little fear. But for mine, you have too much."

"Ah, but without your life, I have no life." He smiled winsomely and leant to kiss her.

She laughed and pushed him away. "Without me you have all the women in the Northlands."

But he was, then, suddenly solemn. "No. Without you, there is never another." And even when she was high above them in the snow-filled sky, the solemnity remained.

They waited, wrapped in their cloaks, sheltered by the half-fallen walls. With his gaze still on the sky, Floki said, "Hakon Sea-Friend is to be wed."

"What?" Gil sat up straight. "To Gudrun?"

"Of course to Gudrun. What else has this all been about?" Floki smiled wryly. "So now our household will be joined to that of Gudrun Helgisdottir. We are honored. They are honored more; though they, of course, believe it the other way around. But we will not fight over that. Nor over the lands, nor the beasts, nor the silver. That will be decided by men with grey heads in Norway. And men with grey heads in Shetland and Hrolf's Isle." He laughed softly. "It is my hope that all is settled before the bride and groom also have grey heads." He looked back up at the sky, still smiling.

Gil asked, "What happened to the stepmother?"

"She, also, will wed."

"I thought she *was* married," Gil said.

"Indeed, she was. But she is again a widow. Her husband met with a better swordsman. These things do happen." He gave a small regretful shrug. "But never mind," he added cheerfully. "She will soon have another."

"Who?" Gil asked.

"Were it her choice?" Floki laughed, "Some other young warrior with more lust in him then sense. But it will not be her choice. Ragnvald will choose." He paused. "She and her child are given sanctuary in Shetland. Lands and honors, and indeed a husband, appropriate to her state. Ragnvald and Hakon will oversee this."

Gil sat in uneasy silence. Then he said cautiously, "Do you trust her?"

"Of course not. But were a man to slay every foe in whom he has no trust, he would live in a lonely world. This is how peace is made, Warrior. That is never without risk."

Floki stood and searched the sky from horizon to horizon. Then he took his seat again, beside Gil. "I am pleased for my cousin," he said. "This is a good match. He is all dark caution; she, impatient fire. So, a goad for one, a bridle for the other, and together they plough a straight furrow." He laughed. "And with her lands in Norway and his in Shetland, they make a love-knot of the sea! I am pleased for my cousin," he said again. "Sea-Friend is a fine man. The best of all our family. I am pleased he makes so fine a marriage."

"But you won't dance at his wedding," Gil said suddenly.

Floki looked again at the sky. "No."

He fell silent then and for a while there was no sound but the wind sighing around the old fortress walls. "The ghosts of men watch with us," he said then.

Gil shivered and looked over his shoulder.

Floki smiled. "Do not fear. You will not see them." But Gil felt compelled to look once more.

"Do *you* see them?" he said uneasily.

Floki smiled again. "And if I were to, would it matter? What are they, but what we will become? What are we, but what they were once?" He laughed and knocked the snow from Gil's hair with a friendly slap. "Erling Maiden-Face sings your praises," he said.

"Does he?" Gil said, startled.

"He does. I learn how you master the Irish battle-axe. And how you help Fish-Tail to swim. I learn of your cleverness in Francia." He paused. "I am proud."

"Thank you," Gil said, startled again.

"I learn, too," Floki said then, "How you win the slaves."

"They're not slaves."

Floki sat quietly, watching the snow settle. After a long while, he said, "They are free, then, these Irishmen?"

"Do you see chains?"

"I see young men far from their homes and kin, setting out for a battle that cannot be their own."

"You sound like my father."

"I am flattered."

"Don't be. He calls you a damned Viking."

Floki leaned against the snowy stone wall, laughing softly. "That I go out a'viking I cannot deny. And I may well be damned, though that he cannot know." He stood then and surveyed the grey sky for a long while. Then resuming his seat on the tumbled stones he said, "I think you become too much blood of my blood, Gil Broadaxe. I send you back to your father's care."

"You send me nowhere," Gil said angrily, but Floki only laughed again before falling quiet. Gil sat in silence watching the snow slowly turn the landscape white.

"I hold no slaves," said Floki.

"They're *not* ...."

"Oh, silence, Warrior, and listen," Floki said patiently. "I hold no slaves because I have not the need. But, did I require them to defend my people or feed my household, then I would. And so, there is no virtue in my not holding them. Nor do I say you do wrong." He paused thoughtfully, and then said, "To take a man's freedom for a season may be fair. Just payment, even, for their rescue. But when a man dies a slave, you have taken his freedom forever. We go now into battle. Some will die."

Gil shrugged angrily. "So, what do I do?"

Floki smiled. "You are earl."

Only the sound of wing beats over their heads kept Gil from punching him.

"She comes, Warrior!" Floki jumped to his feet, holding up

the circle of his sword belt as she swept; a grey-white ghost; out of the grey and white sky. He caught her, bird become girl, before her feet touched the snowy ground. Laughing and breathless with the joy of her flight, she leaned against him, the snowflakes that had dusted her feathers yet scattered on her hair.

But at once her face grew solemn. Stepping from his arms, she brushed snow from her sleeves and stood in silence.

"What do you see?" he asked uneasily, "That your face is full of sorrow?"

"They have burned the Convent of the Grey Sisters," she said. "They have taken Guinevere."

CHAPTER EIGHTEEN

"Oh, a grievous wrong," the knight, Palamedes cried sorrowfully.

"The devil is in him, and the devil take him!" Martin de Troye stalked back and forth, brandishing fists. But it was neither Palamedes' mourning, nor Troye's fury, that gripped Gil's heart, but the look of grief on his father's face, for a loss he had no right to grieve. Caught between pity and anger, Gil was glad when furious shouts among his men called him away.

It was the third argument he had been called on to settle since they made camp, and it was not yet nightfall. He had found a fine campsite, in woodland bordering a small river, high in the hills. Game was plentiful, the river leaping with fish. Wood for fires and shelters was ready at hand.

They had broken their march in full daylight, with time to send out huntsmen and fishers. Time to build shelters against the snow. To light fires and prepare a feast. Whatever the morning brought, his men would sleep, this night, warm, dry, and with full bellies.

Still, nothing pleased anyone. Arguments flared like sparks in ripe grain. Gil barely settled one, when another demanded his attention. Warriors sent to hunt resented those assigned the "fool's work" of building shelters. The shelter builders sulked, their hunting skills demeaned. Camp sites were claimed and re-claimed. Mock sword battles broke out with lengths of brushwood. Leif and Briant's tired efforts at a lean-to ended in a half-hearted fistfight.

Turning from cajoling the two boys back into friendship, Gil was confronted by three angry girls and a clutch of belligerent ponies. "Grani always gets the best grazing. Always." Rachel shoved the dapple grey out of Frosti's way.

"Like when?" Danni, earl's lady, pouted with girlish outrage.

"Oh, grow up, both of you," Gil muttered. Then Lionheart bit Hrafn and all three girls turned on Gil. Taking Lionheart's lead from Janetta, Gil hauled his offending pony off to a lonely patch of grazing far from the camp. *You know,* he sighed, *just at the moment, I'm on your side.*

He stood watching the pony munch grass and enjoying the peace of solitude as dusk drifted down, concealing the smoke of their newly lit fires. The only sound that reached him was the urgent clashing of steel on steel as the older and wiser of his men used the time to practice their skills. He leaned against the animal's warm flank, compassion for his fractious followers settling like the dusk. They were tired and hungry. And afraid.

Ahead lay the great adventure his island boys had dreamed of as they set sail from Hrolf's Isle. But now they were close and had seen a friend die. The forest knights who had dreaded the ships, had looked wistfully back to them as they climbed away from the strand. Like Lionheart. He gave the pony's rump an affectionate slap and returned to the noise and clamor of the camp.

The huntsmen joined him, appearing one by one out of the dark, drawn like moths to the flames. Furred and feathered bounty hung about their necks and they brandished their bows in triumph.

Then Fergus stepped out of the shadows; a fine roebuck slung over his shoulders, his broad grin lighting the gloom. Fergus, son of Gartnan, the best of his huntsmen, the cheeriest company, the swordsman he turned to first. Gil greeted him happily, hiding the conflict in his heart. But as his eyes swept over the men and boys gathered around his campfires, he wondered, sadly, which of them would fall for lack of that captive sword? Still, they had come willingly, and this man, however willing, had not.

Wearied by indecision, Gil stepped within the circle of firelight. There was little respite there. Rachel and Danni, back from tethering ponies, argued about the arrangement of plucked fowl on a cooking spit. Erling was in the midst of a dispute with Ari and Karl. Troye was yet raging. Palamedes, yet mourning. Even the greenwood fires crackled restlessly.

Only Percy, happily kneading a huge mound of barley dough, was content. And Earl Floki Magnusson, stretched out in front of the fire, studying his Latin psalter, peaceful as a monk in his cell. Rising briefly, he held the book out to Rachel to query some point, and then, stretching languorously, returned to his place by the fire. He glanced up as Gil stepped resentfully over him. "All is well, Warrior?"

Gil opened his mouth to state exactly how un-well all was, but was confronted at once by Karl, holding up a bloody moorhen in outrage. "Erling says I am to pluck this! It is woman's work! I am a warrior."

"Okay, okay," Gil said as Ari arrived waving a wood pigeon. "Look," he said, "Ismail's gutting fish. And he's …."

"If only women pluck fowl," a quiet voice spoke suddenly behind him, "Then only women eat them."

The boys turned pale, clutched their resented birds and nodded, "Yes, Earl Floki."

As feathers flew beneath boyish fingers, Floki beckoned Gil. "Warrior. Come sit."

Gil took a place on the log on which Floki leaned. "Yes?"

"Tired men become like small children. They wish not to be reasoned with, but to be told what to do." Floki looked back at his book, tracing a line of the Latin with a finger.

"That's all?" Gil started to rise.

"A moment. I finish this. Sit. Rest. It is good for you."

"Floki, there's work …."

"There is always work." Floki closed the book and slid it carefully into its leather satchel. "And how are *your* lessons?" he asked mildly.

"*What?*"

"Have you learned what Aidan teaches you? Or can you still not add up the number of your fingers?"

Gil laid his hands flat on his knees and stared up at the overhanging trees. "Do you think," he said slowly, "That I just possibly might have enough to do right now?"

Floki shrugged. "I make peace in Norway. I arrange my cousin's marriage. I sail the Northern Sea. And still I have time for lessons. Here...." he leaned over and swept pine needles and melting snow from a patch of earth. "Here, write your numbers here—or shall I write them for you?"

Gil stared harder at the trees. Then he looked around suddenly, aware of low laughter from the shadows behind. His father sat in the shelter of a great pine, quietly skinning a rabbit. "What's so funny?" Gil said sharply.

Lance'lot laughed louder. "He has no more luck than I had! Even with that sword at his side." He turned to Floki, "It is a lost cause, my friend!"

"Ah, then," Floki said at once, "all is well. For I grow fond of those." He reached up and slapped Gil's head. "Enough. We are serious now. Come," he beckoned Lance'lot closer. "And you as well, my noble friends," he called to Palamedes and Troye. "Now we talk."

He stood, and beckoned Danni, too, and when they had all taken places on the log beside Gil, he picked up a limp, ruffled moorhen from the heap of game by the fire and sat cross-legged on the ground, facing them. And, though he thus looked up to them all as he plucked the bird, he was somehow still totally in command.

"I hear many things," he said softly. "Many worries and many angers, also, as you talk. For you are very loud, and I have little choice but to hear, though at the same time I seek to study." He smiled. "But I am clever, and hence able to do both." Lance'lot laughed softly. Troye cast Floki a sour look. Palamedes nodded, puzzled. Floki continued, "This, then, is what is important...."

"What is important," Troye shouted, "is they have violated church sanctuary and taken our queen!"

"No. What is important is that you think they have."

"You think they have not?" Troye's brows lifted and he shook his head impatiently.

Floki smiled and shrugged. "Perhaps the sisters leave willingly to seek other shelter?"

"The Mews Garden!" Palamedes cried joyfully. "Did not the good Change-Thing see smoke from its chimneys?" He beamed at Danni and she nodded. Troye gave her an uneasy glance but turned back to Floki.

"Having burned their own convent in leaving?"

Floki smiled again. "Perhaps hunters stay in it, once abandoned. They drink ale and are careless with fire?"

"A likely story," Troye growled.

"Which story is more likely?" Floki said. "You hear one; Palamedes another. Each hears what his heart tells him. Sir Palamedes, ever hopeful. You, sir," he faced Martin de Troye, "ever angry. And in anger, or in hope, you would act before you think. But still, you *know* only this: There is smoke from the chimneys of the Mews. The roof of the convent smolders on the ground. And there were footprints in the snow."

"For some are left behind, surely, to *die* in the snow! Is not *that* important?" Troye roared. "If we were men and not scholar boys lectured by you, we would be mounted and riding this night to their rescue!"

Floki smiled at Danni. "Had the byre yet its roof?"

She nodded. "And the guest house, too."

"Then they will not die in the snow, having better shelter than we have ourselves. But you, my friend," he turned back to Troye, "will die indeed, should you seek to cross high ground this night. I beg you, be patient." He paused and then said quietly, "All speak of what was seen. But none speak of what was *not* seen. Why is that?"

"How can we?" Lance'lot began.

But Gil said, "She saw no one."

"Ah, one among us thinks!"

Troye turned red, but Lance'lot smiled and looked proud. Gil said, "There was no one in the fields." He paused, meeting Danni's eyes. She nodded. "Where were they?"

"Where indeed?" Floki finished plucking the hen, rose, and placed it on a heap by the cooking spit, and returned with another.

Troye shook his head impatiently. "It is winter. They are at home at their hearth-sides! There is no work to be done in their fields."

Floki pulled wing feathers from the bird. "I am a farmer,

my friend. Summer or winter, there is always work in the fields. Why do they lay down their tools?"

"To free their hands for swords," Gil said. He met Floki's eyes. "He knows we're coming."

Palamedes sighed. Troye raised a fist. But Lance'lot said, "He has always known we would come."

Floki smiled. "But neither the day nor the hour. The fires of the convent yet smolder. What does that tell you?"

"He is a heathen!" Troye shouted. Floki waved him away, his eyes on Gil.

"It's recent. Like, yesterday. He knows exactly." Gil sat in silence, staring at his hands. "You were right about the doves," he said then. "He's been warned."

But Floki shook his head lightly, surprising him. "The doves were but a signal. He does not plan this in a day. But he has indeed been warned."

"We are betrayed," Palamedes' dark face contorted in sorrow.

But Lance'lot said, "But by whom? We sail as fast as the wind takes us. Who could reach him faster?"

Martin de Troye spoke with grim assurance, "One with no need to set sail at all. Four of our men left Francia for Caledon. Two, only, returned."

A stunned silence fell, broken at last by a sorrowful sigh. "It is hard for young men," Palamedes said, his dark eyes full of compassion. "Hard for so many years to keep faith."

"You think ...." Gil's voice croaked with astonishment, "You really think ...."

"The boy, Gareth, would not be responsible," Lance'lot said. "He would do as Morians ruled."

"Morians!" Gil turned in outrage to his father. "Morians would never, *never* betray us."

Palamedes smiled gently. "And the young indeed trust. At times, too much."

Gil jumped to his feet. "I won't hear this." His father reached out to him, but he angrily pushed his arm away.

"Warrior. Sit." Floki continued to pluck feathers from the hen without raising his eyes. "It does not matter."

Gil stared at his bowed, blond head. "It doesn't matter that they call my friend a traitor? Morians, and Gareth, too, who had the courage to stay and fight when *they* all kept themselves safe across the sea? They accuse *them* of betraying us?"

"It does not matter who betrayed us." Floki removed small tufts of fluff from the plucked bird. He looked up. "Though, no doubt we will, in time learn. Perhaps even at the convent when we reach it."

"You would *go* there?" Martin de Troye's brows rose in astonishment. "It is a trap!" he declared. The others joined in with more argument, but Floki rose again, and giving the plucked moorhen to Rachel, sat once more, arranging his fur-lined cloak carefully around him.

"The ermine," he said, stroking the dark-flecked white pelts, "Is sly. It springs the trap unharmed, steals the bait, and goes on its way." He looked up at Gil and smiled, and Gil smiled slowly back.

"But good sir," a cheerful voice addressed Floki over Gil's shoulder, "The many ermine in that cloak were not clever."

Gil spun around. Fergus was standing at the edge of the forest, grinning broadly.

"Ah," Floki returned at once, "but they chose their fate willingly, so honored were they to adorn me!" He swirled a flap of the beautiful garment around himself with another smile.

"Stop playing like a girl!" Martin de Troye roared. "We are in trouble!"

But Fergus' laughter drowned out further protest. Then, still gleeful, he said, "Forgive me, for I am but a servant, but I hear you talk, for, as Earl Floki says, you are not quiet."

"Ah, here is another who comes willingly," Floki said. "Servant though he is. Come," he beckoned Fergus to join them. The Irishman came with dignity into their circle, and bowing to each, seated himself at a respectful distance on the trampled forest floor.

"Sir Palamedes speaks truth," Floki said then. "It is hard for a man of any age to keep an exile's faith. How tempting the hearth-fires he remembers. How tempting the fields he ploughed. The cattle-beasts he knew, each by name. What matters in the end who is his earl if those things, again, are his?"

"You speak as one who surrenders," Troye said querulously.

"All men surrender, my friend. Either to death, or to life. It is only the second who matter here. Dead men carry no arms." He paused and leaned forward, "But who among those who worked these fields did so willingly? Who among them now bear arms by choice? Who among them will not rise and claim their own if given the chance?"

"All!" Fergus punched the air with a joyful fist. "All will rise!" Palamedes smiled his white smile. Floki turned once more to Gil.

"It is, again, King's Table," he said. "He moves a piece. Yes! We are betrayed. He knows that we are here. But we see his move. So, we know he knows. He is ready for us. But we are now, again, ready for him."

"More than ready!" Fergus cried. "A day hence, we meet, at last, the enemy of Broadaxe!"

"You, too, are young," Lance'lot said with a gentle smile. Gil regarded Fergus steadily and then shook his head.

"It does not matter," he said softly. Then, rising, he addressed the Irishman, "Fergus, son of Gartnan, there is a ship, below on the strand, your kinsman, Bran, at the helm. By dusk tomorrow, you and all your men will be aboard, and by dawn, sailing Glen Alban, for Ireland."

Fergus got slowly to his feet, his face in the firelight white with shock. Crossing the ground between them, he came and stood before Gil. Then, as slowly, he sank to his knees. "Get up!" Gil laughed awkwardly. "It's just what I owe you."

But the Irishman only shook his head. Then, with a voice heavy with emotion, he said, "Forgive me, Broadaxe ... I know I fail you and it grieves me bitterly, but I swear on the Blessed Mother's holy name that I will not fail you again! I beg you, do not send me away!"

Gil stared in astonishment, an astonishment he saw mirrored in the eyes of the three knights of Caledon. Then he heard laughter behind him and turned to see Floki raising a hand of welcome to the Irishman, his eyes yet sparkling with mirth.

"You knew."

Gil had handed Lionheart and Percy over to Janetta and gone back to join Floki and Ragnar Kolsson, walking at the rear of the long column of men. Floki smiled and said nothing, only pointing out a landmark to Ragnar as if Gil had not spoken. It was again dusk. Gil's aching legs told him how far they had walked, crossing the high moorland and descending now into the forest. But he matched the Northman stride for stride, where once he would have trotted to keep up.

"The Irish," Floki said then, "are a wonderful people. The finest of poets, the finest of musicians, the finest of horsemen. The finest warriors." He paused, ducking under a low hanging pine bough, and smiled. "But their sense of honor is as absurd as Palamedes'. And they cannot resist a fight."

Gil nodded grimly. "You could have told me," he said. "This hasn't been easy."

Floki turned to face him. They were eye to eye now, virtually the same height. "If we know a friend will not accept a gift," he said. "What value our giving it?" He stopped walking then and laid a hand on Gil's arm. "Listen."

Over the sound of the wind in the tree tops, and the river in the ravine below, Gil heard a distant roar of falling water. "There is a cataract beyond," Floki said.

"I know it!" Gil cried. "It's the Linn of the Rainbow Bridge. Where Palomides heard his Questing Beast!" The scene from that winter's day leapt vividly into his mind ... the rush of wind from nowhere, the sound that seemed to freeze even time, and the great knight leaping the stream on his black warhorse and galloping from their sight. "It's where he left us."

Floki smiled and looked skywards. "The wind roars in these great trees."

"But this was different. We heard it too." Gil paused, because another scene filled his mind now and another horseman: the horse white, the knight, Lance'lot. "It's where my father fought Guidbairn and made him raise the Bridge with Merlin's Stone."

The stone, even now resting in his own pocket. "It's where I crossed to Tir nan Og."

Floki nodded then, gravely, though he said only, "I, too, pass this linn, but I see neither bridge nor beast. Still," he smiled again and shrugged, "There is a fine pool and the ground around it level and well sheltered. Were it me, I would break our march beside it and make camp. And only at dawn seek out this convent forsaken by its nuns. But of course ..."

"I know," Gil said wearily. "I am earl."

It was a very different camp from that of the night before; without fires and without shelter but the overhanging boughs of the trees. Darkness was falling when they reached the linn, made darker by the forest all around and the heavy cloud cover above. The wind had turned southerly halfway through the day, thankfully melting the snow, and with it, the signs of their passage through the whitened land.

Still, though the track was beaten black mud, the turf beneath the ancient pines was dry and springy with moss. The cataract itself glowed eerily white against the black rock cliff and cast a haze of spray over the dark pool at its foot. The rowan tree trembled, yet, over the stream, its branches delicate as black lace.

But when Ari and Karl pleaded to be told how it had saved Palamedes from the Golden Knight, the Saracen would not speak of it, nor of the bridge that rose from the black pool to carry his adversary into another world.

Indeed, no man spoke much that night and even Niall's harp was still. They ate their meagre meal of cold bannocks and scraps of dried fish, and slept, huddled beneath the dark trees, wrapped in their cloaks against the night.

Gil lay awake, with Janetta in his arms. She had crept there in silence as she often did, but would be gone when he woke, and none would know she had been there. So silently did she come and go that sometimes he wondered if he had dreamed her. But now, feeling her healthy young body in his arms, he knew no dream would ever match her presence.

Above, the clouds had broken and stars shone brightly, entangled in the pine boughs overhead. *Like diamonds in her hair.* He thought then, that when all was done and there was peace in Camelot and on Hrolf's Isle, he would go raiding and bring her diamonds. Though where he would find them, he had no idea. *Floki would know.* Half asleep, he determined to ask him in the morning.

The roar of the Linn was hypnotic, weaving itself into a half-dream of his great ship sailing the Roman Sea in the warm southern night, the bow wave sparkling with green phosphorescent light. And then suddenly the light was all colors and the bridge was rising from the pool ....

He woke. No bridge, no ship; only the girl in his arms who cared more for stars over her head than for diamonds, anyhow. He drifted off and then suddenly was intensely awake. *The bridge.* For the first time since that far summer day at the Lookout Rocks, they were all together; himself, Danni, Percy, and Rachel and Ismail, and his father, too. Merlin's Stone was in his pocket and the door lay open to their world. He lay stunned by the simple possibility: they could go home.

But at once faces and voices crowded into his mind: Karl and Ari, awed and trusting. Ragnar and Erling awaiting his orders. Briant and Elias and Darras, gallant and brave. Fergus and his warriors. Aidan, watching on the strand as he sailed. Loyal Hakon Sea-Friend. Palamedes. Lionheart! Floki Magnusson who had given him an earldom. Janetta.

She stirred in her sleep and a lock of her hair brushed his cheek, catching in his rough, young beard. Tightening his arms around her, he understood at last his father's unbreakable pledge to this world. He, too, was bound to it by an entanglement of duties and friendships, debts and honor and love. There was no return. No going back. No home but this. The anger he had carried so long thinned and vanished like the mist above the Linn. He woke and it was dawn. But the girl in his arms was gone.

The day was clear, cold and still. Frost stiffened the moss underfoot and the rocks of the Linn were white with rime.

Before the winter sun touched the high treetops, they were again on the road to Camelot.

Gil sent the young Irishmen, Cormac and Fionn, on ahead, running swiftly through the forest to ensure the way was clear. Then he set out, walking beside his father, at the front of his long column of men.

At the fork in the track, they waited until the scouts came loping back, having found no sign of men, nor horses, on either path; indeed, no sign of life at all. "The forest itself sleeps," Fionn said.

"Even when we climb a tall crag, as stands there," Cormac pointed to a jagged rock face rising through the trees, "and see down to open fields, there is no man."

Martin de Troye joined them and stamped his feet on the frozen ground. "Who would be out, who had no need? Even the birds seek their nests."

Floki smiled, looking up at a patch of blue sky caught in the swaying pine boughs. "When the lynx hunts, then, also, the forest is still. But if they are here, they are not close. We go on."

Gil turned to the left, following the less used track that led to the Convent of The Grey Sisters. Blocked by fallen trees, and narrowed by encroaching saplings, it was now, in places, so faint that once he veered astray on a deer path before finding the right course.

They passed the meadow where he had met Guinevere carrying firewood and where on a long past summer day, Janetta had been captured by the Golden Knight's raiders and taken, a prisoner, to the Mews Tower. The old, lichen-encrusted apple tree was half broken by a gale and the raspberry canes were a nettle-tangled thicket. No wood-gathering queen greeted them this time, and, feeling again the lonely desolation of lost Camelot, he led his men on.

Walking cautiously, half expecting to hear the bell of Prime, and yet knowing he would not, he came at last in sight of the convent walls. The tall wooden gates stood half open, as if the occupants had fled in haste. Frost glistened untouched on the cobbles of the courtyard within. The fire had taken the roof timbers of the nunnery, as well as the thatch, leaving only smoke-stained stone. But the guesthouse stood, just as Gil remembered it, and beyond the ruins of the convent, the byre was also untouched.

Sending Ari and Karl up onto the walls to stand guard, while the rest of his followers took shelter amid the trees, Gil drew his sword and walked between his father and Floki Magnusson, through the empty doorway of the roofless, fire-blackened shell.

The interior was a jumble of fallen timbers and charred thatch, sodden from yesterday's snow. Still, when he kicked a mound of straw aside, a tendril of smoke yet rose. A sickening memory rose with it, of the slaughtered, burnt out village on the Pentland coast. Gil fought against panic as Lance'lot and Floki quietly searched the ruin.

But there was nothing to fear: no charred, diminished bodies huddled in the ash. And, indeed, there was nothing to find throughout the wreckage of cells, refectory, and chapel. No sacred vessels glinted, incorruptible by fire. No treasured psalters lay charred as in the sea-cave on Hrolf's Isle. Even the rough pottery bowls of the refectory were simply gone.

"This is a very courteous fire," Floki said mildly. "All escape. And with all their goods." Gil turned to him uncertainly, and Lance'lot raised an eyebrow. But then a shout from the boys on the convent wall sent all three running to the door.

The warning cry had brought a dozen of their warriors in from their concealment in the forest. Now, with drawn swords and raised bows, they encircled two grey-habited figures cowering in the cobbled courtyard. Faces hidden by their white veils, the pair clung to each other like terrified children.

"Lower your blades!" Palamedes shouted, coming around the corner of the guesthouse. "Can you not see they are harmless?"

Sheepishly, the warriors lowered swords and turned bows aside. But Gil heard Floki laugh beside him. "A scrap of grey cloth can hide many things," he said quietly. "But an innocent heart sees only innocence." He walked purposefully to the two nuns and said with surprising gruffness, "Explain yourselves."

"Good sir," the first spoke in a high, quavering voice, "We

are Sister Felicity and Sister Cecilia," she took the hand of the
second nun, "humble daughters of the Convent."

"I see no convent, only a ruin," Floki persisted. "Why are
you here?"

"Good sir," Sister Cecelia spoke in a voice even higher and
more terrified, "A terrible fire burns the roof of our convent,
leaving us without shelter in the snow! But our good Christian
king gives us his hunting lodge in the Mews Garden below,
where we may stay until he rebuilds our home."

"A good Christian king, indeed," Floki said. "But such
are the fruits of pilgrimage." He smiled sunnily and the two
sisters nodded their veiled heads so vigorously that Gil caught
a shadow of a young face behind. "So why are you not with
them?" Floki said then.

"But, sir!" Sister Felicity spoke, "Could we leave our gentle
kine calling to be milked?"

"Ah," Floki gave them another sunny smile. "Of course you
could not. I will tell your Good Mother how well you tend the
dairy."

"You go to her?" the second nun squeaked.

"Of course. Now you have told me where to find her." He
smiled again. "But come. We will sing a psalm of thanksgiving
for your deliverance from the fire." He slipped his psalter from
the satchel he always carried, knelt, and crossed himself with
elaborate humility.

Warily, they also knelt. Opening the book, Floki turned it
carefully, handed it to the sister called Felicity, and began the
Latin psalm from memory in his beautiful clear voice. Their
own were less beautiful and less clear, and their Latin, even
to Gil's ears, oddly muddled. When they had finished, Floki
again crossed himself, took the book back, turned it once more,
and replaced it in the satchel. Then he stood and smiled again.
"I thank you." And stepping forward he slipped his powerful
hand beneath the nun's veil and stroked her hidden cheek.

"My friend!" Palamedes cried, indignant. "You go too far."

Floki laughed. "Some might say, not far enough." Turning,
he signaled the boys down from the wall. "Come, we leave these
holy dairy maids in peace."

Once outside the convent wall, Palamedes turned again to Floki in dismay. "I must protest, my friend. That was unkind. The poor child shook with fear."

Then Fergus laughed heartily. Half amused and half reproachful, he said, "No doubt the first time a man ever touches *that* cheek!"

"And likely the last," Floki smiled. "For soon the good sister will wear a beard."

"What?" Gil said. Confused silence fell on the men gathered around them. "What are you saying?"

Instead of answering, Floki looked around until his eyes fell on Rachel, standing with the ponies in the shadow of the trees. "Pretty Hawk?" he said. "When our friend burns Cille Aidan and leaves it roofless, who was last to flee?"

"Aidan," she answered at once.

"And who stayed behind and tended animals?"

"Aidan."

"He did not leave you, a young woman, alone there?" Floki asked uncertainly.

"Of course not," Rachel shook her head. "You know that."

"Yes. And so do we all." He jerked his head toward the convent. "If any need stay behind, it would be their Good Mother. She leaves no nuns. Not even her most witless nuns who have neither Latin nor psalmody and cannot read enough to tell the book is upside down. She leaves no nuns and indeed, no nuns are here. Nor any girls at all."

"What? They are *boys*?" Troye raised an astounded eyebrow. "Are you sure?"

Floki smiled, his eyes sparkling. "Good sir, if you wish further proof, I bid you hunt for it yourself."

Troye shook his head, his own eyes blazing with outrage. "But why? Why set them there in this blasphemous act?"

"To give us the message just given," Lance'lot said then. "And carry to their master our response." He paused, studying the convent wall. "It is, indeed, a trap."

"What now?" Gil said quietly.

Floki also studied the grey stone wall. "You have two courses," he said then. "In the less safe course, we keep our word to the holy nuns and follow the track to the Mews, just as they will report. Within sight of the wall, we turn eastward, and while he rides to draw closed the snare, we circle the Forest of Pentecost and find refuge. Sir," he turned to Lance'lot, "in that high, hidden valley where you made your home. And thus, we spring the trap."

"And if they are lying in ambush *along* the track awaiting us?" Troy demanded.

Floki smiled. "Then we make a fine lining for his cloak. It *is* the less safe course."

"And the safer course?" Gil asked uneasily.

Floki was quiet. He looked again at the blank convent wall and when he spoke, Gil saw the regret in his eyes. "They are young and likely acting under threat. But without them, he does not know we are here." He faced Gil. "Kill them."

CHAPTER NINETEEN

Aware of all the eyes on him, Gil stared at the convent wall. The wind dropped and the forest fell silent, as if it, also, waited on his word. But he kept his own silence until he could force enough conviction into his voice to mask the turmoil in his heart.

"When we hunt the deer," he said, then, his eyes passing over the solemn faces, "Do we go out onto the open hill, where they can scatter in four directions?" He saw Fergus shake his head. "No!" he continued, "We trap them in a ravine or a valley, with only one way out." He looked straight at the Irishman who nodded vigorously.

Palamedes' face broke into its broad smile. "So, too, when we hunt bow and stable! The beaters drive the hart between the lines of waiting bowmen, that stable in which it meets its fate."

"The Mews Garden walls are the bowmen's trap," Gil said then. "And, like the huntsmen, he won't make his move until we're all within, with only one gate and no other escape." He turned to Lance'lot who nodded thoughtfully. Martin de Troye allowed him an uncertain shrug. But the one man whose judgement Gil truly wanted, gave him only a courteous smile, impossible to read.

Gil looked back at the convent wall. "We'll keep our word to the holy nuns," he said wryly. "And by the time they reach him with news of our plans, we'll be on the far side of the Forest of Pentecost. Before he's closed the gates and searched the Mews Garden, we'll be crossing the river. And by the time he sees his trap is sprung," Gil said with a cautious intake of breath, "we'll be in my father's home."

He saw men nodding and smiling in agreement. It was a good argument, and if he was right, he would have spared two young lives. Though, if he was wrong, others, his own, would die. They all knew; still, no one spoke. He was earl.

They set out at a steady walk, held close together on the flanks by the confines of the track. Gil and Lance'lot took the lead, and at the rear, Troye and Palamedes urged stragglers on. Ragnar, Fergus and Floki roamed freely, with bows raised and arrows set to the string. But even with those three as guards, Gil never took his hand from his sword hilt until, within sight of the Mews Garden walls, they turned to the east and left all tracks behind.

There, he followed his father through the ancient trees Lance'lot knew so well to the edge of the walled Forest of Pentecost. Already they were far from the North Gate used by the huntsmen, and the wall was overgrown, and in places frost and fallen trees had broken it down.

For once, the sense of abandonment gave Gil comfort. No one rode here, neither knight nor stone mason. When they passed the walled up East Gate and he knew the whole breadth of the hunting forest lay between them and Guidbairn's forces, he allowed a brief halt. It was midday and they ate a hurried meal, and then went on, skirting the miles of wall as the winter sun made its short journey along the southern hills.

A small, decorative tower marked the wall's turning point, and they left it then to follow its own way westward and went out into the trackless land beyond. There, Lance'lot again led until they reached the river, and the waterfall flowing down from the Hidden Valley was in sight.

The river was high with snowmelt and by the time they had thrown a guide rope over it and shepherded all across, dusk was falling. Wet and cold, Gil's men looked to him hopefully. "Not far." He smiled, pointing to the hill track rising before them. "And we'll warm up climbing."

As they mounted higher, forsaking the forest for heather moorland, he was aware of a new light brightening the sky, strengthening even as the daylight faded. A hand tapped his shoulder lightly. He turned and saw Floki's white smile. "Odin's Maidens dance."

Gil craned his neck, following the shifting veils of the Northern Lights above, and whispered, "They hang their shields on the stars."

It seemed a happy omen, and he grinned and quickened his pace. He was well ahead even of his father, when he scrambled over the last rocky outcrop onto level ground. Before him, the small, hidden glen was magical with frost; the aurora lighting the snow-covered heights around it.

Snow yet lay on the bent grasses and the roof of Lance'lot's abandoned hay barn. The vast holly tree that screened the entrance of the cave-house was trimmed with stars. Gil turned and watched, quietly triumphant, as his small army crested the rise in twos and threes. Tired, but smiling, they trudged happily toward him. He waved a hand in greeting and then ran on with a child's eagerness to his father's house.

His hand already gripped a branch of the holly, when he caught the faint scent, borne by some capricious shift in the wind: wood smoke. He jerked back by saving instinct and the blade that flashed through the dusk missed his face by inches and buried itself in the wood of Lance'lot's tree.

He heard shouts behind him and the scuffle of running feet, but his sword was already in his hand. Raising it high, he lunged at the shadowy figure struggling to free the buried blade. But then a pulse of flickering aurora lit his opponent's strained young face, and Gil froze. "Morians!"

With a joyful cry, the man let go of his sword. "Gil! My friend! You come ...." Then something swished over Gil's shoulder, as if the wind had taken solid form. A small sharp thud cut Morian's sentence short. He gasped, then swayed and stumbled, and with bloody hands gripping the arrow buried in his chest, he slipped slowly to his knees. Shaking his head, he looked up at Gil with a bewildered smile. Then his eyes widened for a moment. He whispered urgently, "The *muinntir!* The *muinntir!*" and then fell forward onto the turf, the shaft of the arrow snapping beneath his weight.

Gil reeled back. Open-mouthed with shock, he spun around, turning on his own men, "Who did this?"

Ragnar Kolsson stood quietly apart, his bow string yet

trembling from the arrow's flight. With a brief bow, he said, "You are safe?"

"Safe?" Gil whispered. "Safe ... you stupid idiot!" His voice rose in fury. "It was Morians! My *friend*! You killed ...."

The flat of a hand cracked across his head, sending him crashing into the tangle of holly boughs. Ears ringing, he struggled to regain his footing, but the next blow caught his chin, knocking him to the ground. Then the hand closed on the front of his tunic, hauling him back to his feet.

"He saves your life!" Floki's voice in a whisper held more anger than any other man's shout.

Lance'lot spoke suddenly from the dusk. "The man attacks you with a sword."

"It was a mistake!" Gil cried.

Floki twisted the cloth of the tunic and pulled him close. "How was *he* to know that?" Then he jerked Gil around and released him, staggering, in front of Ragnar. "You stand," Floki whispered. "You apologize. You accept the loyal service of a warrior. *Now!*"

Shaking with grief, humiliation, and fury, Gil faced Ragnar, who stood, yet, in noble silence. "Ragnar Kolsson," Gil said numbly, "Forgive me. You did well defending me. Thank you." Ragnar bowed again, formally, and stepped back.

Gil bowed also. Then he swung fiercely around and punched Floki so hard that the Northman staggered, stumbled, and sprawled in the trampled mud. Shouts of amazement from the gathered warriors were followed by a hasty shuffling of retreating feet. But Floki calmly sat up, wiped blood from his mouth, stood, and nodded solemnly. Then he laid a gentle hand on Gil's shoulder. "Come now," he said. "We say prayers. And in the morning, we bury your friend."

The morning was cold and still. The clash of their spades against stones echoed across the high valley. There had been fresh snow in the night, and before they could even mark out the grave, it had all to be cleared.

Sweat trickled down Gil's back from the effort, damping his shirt and chilling him further. He paused spade in hand, looking up to the guards watching from the ridges. Floki paused, too, and leaned on the rough handle of his spade. "Your father keeps a good house. A tool for every need." He smiled bleakly, his cut lip bleeding again. Gil said nothing. They both bore the marks of yesterday's encounter. Neither had spoken of it.

"There is no justice in battle," Floki said. "There is no sense in battle. There is no reason for men to do battle, for all they win ends here ." He gestured lightly at the half dug grave between them. "But they will do it, all the same."

Again, Gil said nothing. He was weary with grief, weary with hunger and weary of argument. They had debated bitterly into the night, gathered around the fire in Lance'lot's cave-house. Outside, more fires burned and tired men; all but the five standing guard, slept among the tethered beasts. Under the wood and turf roof, sagging, now, between the rock walls, Lance'lot, Troye, and Palamedes faced Floki, Gil, and Erling Maiden-Face across the fire, while the girls moved, in silence, between them, preparing food. From the shadows at the rear of the cave, where Morians lay silent and cloak wrapped, Percy watched with wide sad eyes and a solemnity beyond his years.

"He didn't betray us!" Gil cried angrily. "He recognized me. He was so happy ...."

"In the dark, you see this?" Troye rose and stalked from the fireside. Palamedes studied Lance'lot's rusting tools and said nothing.

"He called me his friend."

"And would he not, *were* he not?" Troye returned from the shadows.

Erling Maiden-Face nodded gloomily. "The Wise Ones tell us, 'Beware of befriending an enemy's friend.'"

Gil whirled on him. Floki laid a hand on his arm. Shaking with frustration, Gil cried, "*He let go of the sword!*"

"Gil," His father's voice was somber. "Sometimes we see what we want to see and hear what we want to hear."

Gil had jumped up then and run from the cave. As once long before, it was Floki who followed and found him quietly weeping beneath the ever shifting aurora. He stood beside Gil for a long time, watching the curtains of light. Then he said, "A man at his feasting table wears a fine tunic, a silver collar, arm bands of gold. When he goes out to the fields, he lays those fine things aside and takes up rough tools."

Reluctantly, Gil glanced toward him. After another long silence, Floki continued, "So, too, when he goes to battle, he lays aside that fine thing, his heart, and judges only with his head." He smiled sadly. "With my head, now, I tell you what matters: If you are right, we are safe here. If you are wrong, Guidbairn knows this place and awaits Morians' word to close the trap. The only man certain of the truth lies shrouded, now, in your father's house. So, we must find it ourselves. Send Ragnar and the Irishman out at dawn on your swiftest mounts. Let them ride the countryside, seek out the men of Caledon, and learn from them our friend's plans."

Gil stared up at the restless sky. "No." He met the flash of anger in Floki's eyes with a smile. "I'll send my Stag."

Floki shook his head, briefly puzzled. Then he laughed softly. "Ah. The Saracen."

———

Dusk was again falling when they lowered Morians into the ground, and Ismail had been gone since daybreak. As Floki read from his psalter, Gil stood between Elias and Darras, scanning the dimming valley for a glimpse of his returning Stag. Then, as clods of frozen earth thudded into the grave, he stared straight ahead, aware that half the men surrounding him thought his dead friend a traitor.

When they were done, a stone with Morians' name scratched into it was set on the dark mound, and Janetta, Danni, and Rachel brought circlets of ribbons for it, for want of flowers, or berries, or a single bright thing in all the winter valley.

Shivering and stamping their feet, the men drifted away to their fires. Gil waited, alone, as the stars came out, not wanting to leave and let Morians slip forever into the past.

"Warrior?" Floki had appeared suddenly out of the night.

"Come. Your people need you. They are tired and afraid."

"You think I'm not?"

"I know you are. But you are earl." Floki spoke so gently that Gil couldn't be angry.

"Morians wanted to be buried in holy ground," he said. "And I've done this." He shrugged sadly at the mound of turned earth, already sparkling with hoar frost.

"Where a good man rests is always holy ground," Floki smiled.

"But he *asked*!" Gil cried, anguished. "It was the last thing he said. 'The *muinntir*. The *muinntir*.'"

Floki was silent for a long while. He laid a hand then lightly on Gil's shoulder. "When all is done and there is peace, we take him down to the *muinntir*. Until then, he rests well here, under so many stars." He gestured at the sky, more white than black with the Milky Way a river in spate over the hills. Then he turned Gil quickly toward the lip of the high valley. "Look there!"

The night mist lay thick over the marshy land below and the Stag came up out of it, like a sea creature rising from the deep. Breath smoking the starry air, antlers sparkling with frost, it mounted the hill, so wild and fierce that Gil doubted it was Ismail at all.

But then, scenting them, it shook its shining rack and broke into a weary trot. Strides away, it reared up, pawing the ground. Turning itself in its circle like a settling cat, it bowed its shaggy antlered head, bent forelegs and then haunches, and then sank down into the frosted heather.

Before Gil's eyes, the beast dwindled and faded until nothing remained of the mighty creature but a slender, exhausted boy, kneeling on the frozen ground. Ismail raised his dark head and gave a tired grin. "Is *long* way!"

Gil and Floki helped him to his feet, walking on either side as he stumbled toward the distant glow of the fires. "I am *everywhere*," he said, and then his voice grew solemn. "And everywhere is same! In fields, in farmyards, always there are women, there are children, but never men."

"None?" Gil said.

Ismail shook his head. "Women dig. Women tend animals. Women follow the plough."

"Grimhildr ploughs," Gil said.

"Ulf and Bjorn plough also," Floki said quietly. "She is not alone. What do you tell me, Saracen?"

Ismail studied the Northman in the faint light. Cautiously he said, "Once, the Believers do terrible thing. A village angers them. They take the men. They take the boys. Kill all. Only women and small girl children left."

"Who tends the fields?" Floki said.

Ismail shrugged. "There is hunger."

They had reached the great holly tree. Through its branches came light, wood smoke, the scent of baking bread. Floki said, "A land without men is a land without food. I think he is not such a fool. Nor," he turned to Gil, "do I think Morians sought holy ground. Come." His sudden smile lit the darkness. "Food and then sleep, for before day breaks, Warrior, we ride."

"Cats hunt at dawn." Floki's light laughter drifted back through the forest darkness.

Gil leaned forward on Doombearer's back, peering grimly through the trees. "So they tell me." Above the swaying pines, a sliver of rising moon had joined the stars, lighting the Northman's bright hair and the pale haunches of the Monkish Ploughhorse on which he rode. "What am I hunting?" Gil asked.

Floki laughed again, half turning on the white horse's back. "The Men of Caledon. Mind you do not catch too many."

Gil shook his head uncertainly, resting one hand on Doombearer's shining mane. Riding Sir Palamedes charger after Lionheart felt like walking on stilts; the ground impossibly far down and his head brushing branches.

"The beast suits you." Floki grinned back at him. "They do not call you Gil Sliepnir now!"

Gil winced, remembering Lionheart's miserable whinny of dismay as he rode out of the Hidden Valley, leaving him behind.

I'll come back. I just need something with longer legs ... to keep up ... right?

"We rode this way once," Floki said suddenly. "And this fine animal carried us both at a gallop. No longer. You grow. Look there, there is light in the sky."

Gil turned and saw a faint line of brightness in the east. "This Cat had better start hunting," he said.

"It shall. We are close. See there, through that gap, is our friend's fine keep. And beside it, that tower where I found you."

Gil stared at the black shapes bulking against the stars; Guidbairn's great square hall overshadowing the ruins of Arthur's. And Merlin's Tower, as forbidding yet as on the night they fled it on the back of the Monkish Ploughhorse.

Floki slowed the white charger and reined it to the edge of the track, allowing Doombearer room to come up beside him. "He knows we are here," he said then. "He knows how many ships and hence how many men. He knows we cannot defeat him with this force alone. We need the Men of Caledon.

"But he, too, needs the Men of Caledon, to work his fields, fish his rivers, serve his household. A kingdom empty of men is no kingdom. And so, he imprisons them until we are defeated. Where now, Warrior, can he hold a hundred men?"

"The *muinntir*," Gil whispered. "Morians knew. They're in the *muinntir*."

Floki nodded. "Secure from all but passing cats."

In the shadow of Camelot's outer wall, they dismounted. Floki backed the two obedient chargers into a stand of young firs and tethered them loosely. Gil drew a circle with his sword tip in the pale dusting of snow. The light in the east had strengthened; the stars above fading. The *muinntir* was a dim charcoal silhouette beyond the wall.

"You must be swift," Floki said, as Gil stepped into his circle. "You must not be seen. And you must return with this knowledge: where are the guards and how many? Are the doors barred from within? Are the prisoners chained? Who carries the keys?"

Gil nodded. He sheathed his sword and closed his eyes. *Bless to me my sister ....*

"And Warrior?"

Bless to me my brother ....

"I am alone here, one man hiding two horses as big as clouds."

Bless to me, O Changeless One ....

"Be back before sunrise if you wish to see me again in this world."

My Change-Thing, My Other.

"And do not sleep!"

Cat arrived, twitching cold fur and shaking snow from his paws. Then he sat down, washed between his toes and yawned. Cats did hunt at dawn. But cats also slept at dawn.

"And if you do not see me again in this world," Floki grasped his scruff, "Avoid me in the next!" With a deft hand, he tossed Cat onto the coping of the wall. Cat landed on four agile paws, sat down to wash his ruffled coat, and trotted away along the capstones.

When he reached the nearest of the tall, arched windows of the *muinntir*, he leaped across to the sill. Shards of broken glass still littered the stonework, but he landed perfectly among them, small paws unscathed. Aware of the light behind him, he crouched low and, shielded by the twisted lead of the window frame, looked down into the long nave of the church.

On either side of the central aisle lay rows of cloak shrouded forms, as if an entire chapter of monks had been struck dead in the midst of their prayers. But Cat's ears told him all yet lived, breathing softly in their sleep, or muttering and shivering on their beds of stone.

The roofless building gave scant shelter. The dawn wind blew through it and snow whitened the sleepers' cloaks. Cat puffed his fur in sympathy and looked hopefully toward the fire smoldering before the ruined altar. But it was too far and too wanly burning to warm either himself or the sleepers on the floor. Even the men standing around it slapped their arms and stamped their feet, their breath puffing frostily on the air.

Cat's eyes opened wider. *The guards.* Remembering his purpose he dutifully counted: *Four paws, plus tail, plus one ear.* Another man, big and bulky, relieved himself insolently against the altar. The hot human piss smell wrinkled Cat's nose. Something metal jangled as the man adjusted his clothing. *Plus another ear,* Cat counted. Swiveling his head, he spotted three men with ready bows balancing on high window ledges, and another four at the great door at the foot of the nave. *That made another whole cat.* He swished his tail, pleased with his mathematics.

Seven plus seven; fourteen men to guard a hundred. A creak and scraping at the door brought Cat's head around in an instant. A sliver of grey light appeared and a slight figure entered, set down a basket before the men, and retreated. The sound came again at the door, the bar outside sliding shut. *But no bar within.*

The basket was carried up the nave and Cat stretched his neck out, sniffing happily. *Food.* The scent rose above the heavy stench of unwashed bodies, sour ale, and more sour urine. And then suddenly there was a scent Cat knew—a boy scent, familiar despite the passing of time. A friend scent—*Gareth.*

Cat rose, stepped over the lead frame and, picking his way through the splintered glass, crept to the inner edge of the sill and leaped down to the stone floor. At Cat level, the smells were as thick as sea fog, but he picked from them the one he sought and followed it, trotting purposefully between the huddled prisoners, belly low, tail straight, a pale shadow scarce bigger than the rats that scurried from his path.

He found the boy near the front of the nave, where the broken remnants of the wooden choir stalls had been piled for firewood. He had made a small shelter of two and curled beneath them. Cat wormed in beside him and reached out a tentative paw.

Gareth jerked awake, searching the darkness with wide, frightened eyes. "Get off me!" He swept terrified hands down his cloak.

"Hush," a man whispered out of the night. "You bring the guards."

"There are rats!" Gareth cried.

"The guards are worse," the man mumbled, and slept.

Flattening his ears at the rat-insult, Cat put out as soft and un-rat-like a paw as he could manage and patted Gareth's face. The boy shrank back and then stared hard and whispered, "A cat?" he sat up joyfully and Cat jumped at the rattle of chains through leg irons. "*The Cat*! Gil ... is it you?"

Cat turned in a circle and purred. Gareth reached out for him but he slipped free. "Please. I am alone so long." Reluctantly, Cat stepped closer and allowed his back to be stroked. The boy wrapped a rough cold arm around him. "So warm!" he whispered.

Deep within Cat, a feline compassion arose, a kitten-comforting kindness that brushed human protest aside. Settling down, he puffed out his fur, making of himself a warm, soft pillow. Arm around him yet, Gareth slept, and beside him, Cat slept, too.

He woke in grey daylight, stirred by the scent of food, the sounds of waking men, and the clanking of metal on metal. Sitting up, he washed his face and paws and looked around. The fire burned higher; a black cauldron hung over it, and the guards were ladling something interesting into bowls. Released from their chains, a line of men waited hungrily. Cat sniffed the air and considered joining them.

A guard approached, drawing the loosened chain noisily through the irons of the nearest man. "Up!" he said gruffly, nudging Gareth with his foot. Cat hissed. The guard looked down, peering into the murk. "What is here?" he growled.

"Leave him!" Gareth, suddenly wakened, gathered Cat into the crook of his arm.

"It is but a stray cat," the man beside him said. "What harm does it do? Let it stay and give the boy comfort."

"Let it stay and chase your rats!" another called. There was laughter and faces turned toward Cat and Gareth in the dim light.

The burly guard who had defiled the altar strode closer. Holding up a ring of heavy keys, he shook it threateningly at Gareth. Then he leaned down until his foul breath was in Cat's nostrils; his murky eyes peering into Cat's as if seeking the boy beyond.

Cat's paws quivered. *He was running through the forest; the terriers on his heels; ahead, the false safety of the snare ... and then he was Gil, dangling helplessly, the hunters surrounding him and that face, the face of the bullying guard of Merlin's Tower ....*

The man straightened abruptly and turned to the first guard. "Kill it," he said.

"No!" Gareth wrapped Cat tight in his arms. Cat felt the guard's boot thud into the boy's ribs, and, yowling in fury, pulled free. "Run!" Gareth cried, gasping for breath. "Run!"

"Run! Run! Run!" The prisoners on either side chanted. Cat ran, darting between the rows of men who scrambled aside to let him pass and then crowded together to block the pursuing guards. With feet thudding after him and shouts of alarm sounding outside the *muinntir* as well, he abandoned hope of his windowsill and sought refuge low down, beneath benches and choir stalls and under the fallen rood screen, until in the dark shadows footing the walls, he found escape.

A hole pierced the stonework; black and dank and littered with rat droppings, but fresh air wafted through it, scented with snow. Worming in, with wary whiskers brushing stone, he wriggled the length of its narrow tunnel and tumbled out over the carved stone lion that marked its lip. Crouching down beside the lion, he explored his circumstances with eyes, ears, and nose.

The shouting had died down both within the *muinntir* and without. Peaceful light fell on the old church and its protective wall. As Cat watched, the tops of the tall firs beyond turned gold. *Sunrise!*

Driven by a rare sense of urgency, Cat trotted to the foot of the wall and made the top in three scrambling bounds. All was quiet beyond. The two big horses dozed, side by side, in their thicket. Floki stood yet, just as Cat had left him, calmly waiting. Seeing Cat, he made the smallest nod of greeting, but did not move. Neither when Cat jumped happily to the ground, nor when the snare whipped out of the sky, capturing him in its circle.

He didn't warn me! was Gil's first, furious human thought. He leaped up, angrily shaking his snared foot. Calm yet, Floki turned his head slowly from side to side, and then Gil saw the bowmen; six in all; standing in the shelter of the trees, each with his set arrow aimed at the Northman's heart. As he watched, the nearest two turned, and adjusted their aim to his own.

A rustling and snapping of branches brought the two horses' heads up. Gil turned without thinking to the sound, and heard his two bowmen tighten their strings. But his eyes were fixed on the three figures emerging from the forest.

Two were warriors, armed and ready like the six surrounding Gil and Floki. But the third, walking between them seemed to wear his sword, with its gold-embossed hilt, only as noble decoration.

Dressed in a golden cloak of ermine-trimmed velvet, and a tunic embroidered in silver, his burnished leather boots disdaining the rough ground, Jocelyn Guidbairn, the Golden Knight, smiled the distant, gracious smile of a king.

Setting his eyes on Gil's face, he shook his head sadly. "Ah, sorrowful indeed," he said, and then turned his gaze pointedly on Floki, "to be betrayed by a friend."

A friend. A friend! A sea-wave of doubt flooded Gil's mind. A friend. Not Morians who they buried together, but Floki. Floki appearing in the skiff, claiming to sail from Norway. Floki who knew all their plans and directed all their moves. Floki who had not warned Cat of the snare ….

But then Gil caught the triumph in Guidbairn's eyes in response to the outrage in his own and remembered his treachery in Merlin's Tower. *You appear unfortunate in friends.* Doubt warring with shame, Gil turned helplessly to Floki.

Floki met his stunned gaze with a wry smile. Then he spoke one sentence in the softest of voices. For a confused moment, the words made no sense. Then, startled, Gil realized he was speaking in Irish: "Do you trust me?"

Gil opened his mouth but could not find words.

"Do you understand me?" Again, in Irish. Guidbairn glared from one to the other, a stranger to the tongue.

Gil breathed in deeply, nodded, and gave the Irish

affirmative, "It is so." Then he turned to Guidbairn and looking straight into his brilliant eyes, said, "None of my friends have betrayed me. Not Earl Floki. And not Morians either."

"This is true. Morians did not betray you." Gil whirled to the voice. A man stood in the shadows at the edge of the forest. He stepped forward into the morning light, dressed in finer garb than ever on Hrolf's Isle. "I betrayed you," said Arnkel Fish-Tail.

CHAPTER TWENTY

Flinging back his fine cloak, and hooking his thumbs in his sword belt, Arnkel crossed the small clearing with a lordly swagger. Awkward in their own new finery, Gisli, Tofi, and Brand followed him into the light. When their eyes fell on Gil and Floki, their faces lit with momentary joy, extinguished at once by shame. They stood bunched together, staring at the snowy ground while Arnkel, smiling broadly, circled their prisoners.

"A fine catch," he pronounced. "I cast my net for one fish and catch two."

Gil heard Guidbairn laugh softly and struggled to contain his fury. But Floki laughed also, then.

"Be careful, Fish-Tail," he smiled at Arnkel, "Skiffs have foundered for too heavy a catch."

Arnkel stood very still, his own smile fading. "I wonder, now," he mused, "will men yet call me Fish-Tail when this catch is gutted and hung to dry?"

The three boys moved closer together, and Gisli, the youngest, let out a small, choked cry. Floki laughed, again.

"They will, Fish-Tail," he said cheerfully, "For you, like a fish, are slippery. And you, like a fish, are cold. And you, like a fish, swim with any tide. But tides turn, Arnkel Thorleiksson. So, if you are wise, you will beg forgiveness of your young earl, who is more kind-hearted than he should be and may yet spare your life. For if you do not, that life is forfeit to his sword. Or to my own."

Arnkel laughed incredulously. "Floki Magnusson, you do not change! And where do you exact this punishment? At the threshold of Valholl? For you are but one word from that place, my friend."

"Oh, come, come!" Guidbairn strode in between, holding up his hands. "It is unseemly that my guests should quarrel. For surely, you are all my guests now?" He bowed graciously to Gil and Floki. "And we will soon repair to my hall, where I may show you the courtesy you deserve.

"But first," he shook his head sadly, "there is a small unpleasantness." He looked up at the six warriors who had never once relaxed their stance. "My bowmen's arms grow weary. And to give them rest, I must have you bound." With a great show of distaste, he took from Arnkel Fish-Tail two coils of rope. "It is for your own safe-keeping, I assure you, for your reputations precede you, and these men are of a nervous nature. Here!" He smiled again. "This young boy will do the work and show you every care, since you yourselves have trained him." He dropped the coils of rope into Gisli's hands and thrust him forward.

The boy turned terrified eyes on Arnkel, but Arnkel only shrugged. With small, uncertain steps, Gisli crossed the clearing. Gil saw tears shining in his eyes as he stood before them, clutching the rope with trembling fingers.

"It's okay," Gil said. "You have to do it."

Gisli sobbed audibly and stepped closer. "Forgive me, Earl Floki," he whispered. "I do not know ...."

Floki smiled encouragingly. "Of course I forgive you." The boy looked up, wiping tears from his eyes with the back of a dirty hand.

"You do?"

"Does not the good father, Aidan, say we must forgive?" Gisli nodded uncertainly. "Now, do as you are told." Floki stepped carefully forward and made a slow, deliberate show of raising his arms, arranging his cloak over one shoulder, and then crossing his wrists behind his back. "You also," he said to Gil. "*Just* as I have done."

Gil nodded, and repeated each action until he, too, stood with crossed arms awaiting their bonds.

Gisli came first to Floki, gingerly slipping the rope around his wrists. "And does he not also say," Floki added, "that what is bound on earth will be bound in heaven? And what is loosed on earth will be loosed in heaven?"

Gil cast a puzzled glance sideways. He saw the boy pause, and then with a quick light of understanding in his eyes, bend his hands to the task. Fastening the last knot, Gisli left Floki and came to Gil, and only when he had finished binding him, did Gil himself understand. Letting his cloak fall from his shoulder, he explored his bonds beneath its shelter: loose enough that he could move both hands and fastened with a seaman's knot that would release with a single tug.

Guidbairn studied them both concernedly. "I trust the boy has caused you no discomfort?"

"No discomfort at all," said Floki with a cheerful smile.

"Ah," Guidbairn made a small, gracious bow, "that is well then. We may proceed." He turned as if to lead the way and then spun back. "But wait!" he cried, "I forget my manners! Your people have a custom, have they not, of laying down their weapons at the door of a host?"

Gil looked quickly to Floki.

"Indeed so," Floki agreed.

Guidbairn slapped his own forehead in irritation, and gestured to their bound arms, "And now I have made this impossible. Forgive me, I beg you. The cares of my kingdom ...."

Floki smiled his understanding. "The cares of a ruler are many. Indeed, weighed down by care, even this young earl has shown himself forgetful. Though, surely, not this day!" He moved closer to Gil as he spoke and jostled him affectionately. Gil felt the light touch of a hand beneath his cloak, slipping his father's knife from its sheath.

Guidbairn had turned again to face the three Hrolf's Isle boys, his face brightening. "Surely one of these will help you lad," he pointed a finger at Tofi's chest, "relieve them of their swords."

Floki moved back as Tofi approached. With a respectful duck of his head, the boy unbuckled Gil's sword belt, his fingers brushing innocently by the empty leather sheath at his waist. Sword and scabbard in his arms, Tofi retreated to Arnkel and laid them down. Then, with shaking hands, he faced Floki.

Floki smiled. "Very good. Now do for the helmsman what you do for the earl." Again, he jostled Gil cheerfully, and when he stepped forward to be disarmed, the knife was again in its sheath.

But for all its small comfort, Gil knew it was, like Gisli's clever sabotage, a pointless victory. Guidbairn's warriors yet surrounded them as they walked the short distance to the gates. Grinning broadly, Arnkel Fish-Tail carried their surrendered weapons at the rear. The wall beside them was lined with watch towers. And when the great gates of Camelot were dragged open, the cobbled roadway ahead was guarded throughout its length by Guidbairn's men.

Ever the cheerful host, Guidbairn himself strode between Gil and Floki, pointing out works and improvements underway. Numb with hopelessness, Gil barely heard. Once before, he had come within these gates, expecting to die. That he had survived was little comfort. The man who had rescued him walked bound beside him now. Fate was not outwitted, only postponed.

"The sun is well risen," Guidbairn smiled solicitously, "You will be hungry. We shall break our fast together!" He laid a lordly arm across each of their shoulders. "But first," he continued, "forgive me if I succumb to pride, but there is one structure on which my craftsmen have labored long, that I would show you." He stopped walking, and turned, turning them with him. "You will remember this old tower?"

Gil froze. It stood before him as it did yet in nightmares: roofless, its stone walls fire-blackened, its high windows; bereft of their eerie visions; the empty eyes of a skull.

"Merlin's Tower, I believe they called it in the old days?" Guidbairn prompted.

"I remember," Gil whispered.

"But, no longer! You see now, much is changed."

Still numb, Gil nodded. A wooden structure surrounded the building, a scaffolding, running just beneath the sills of the windows. Beneath it, brushwood and straw had been piled, overlaid with lengths of timber. Despite Guidbairn's praise of his workmen, the whole of it seemed hastily constructed of rough wood. The flight of steps rising to the scaffold still bore shreds of bark. It all might have been thrown up in a day.

But the Golden Knight continued to sing its praises. "From this broken shell, they have constructed a splendid new kiln. A mere spark set to the kindling, and flames arise, draw through those empty windows, and all of the tower becomes a chimney. And the heat! Hard to imagine ...." He paused, turning to Floki, "A most unusual design, would you not say?"

Floki studied it in silence. Gil shrugged uncertainly, seeing nothing that resembled the grain kilns of Hrolf's Isle. Untroubled, Guidbairn said, "Come, I will show you."

Leaving the others behind, he led Gil and Floki to the foot of the stairs. The steps were narrow and uneven, and, unbalanced by his bonds, Gil mounted them clumsily. When he stumbled, Guidbairn slipped a hand behind his bound arm. "Lest you fall," he smiled.

Gil shivered. *Why not just throw me off?* They had reached the level of the scaffolding. Arnkel, the guards, and the frightened boys were far below. *What was he waiting for?*

Guidbairn faced them on the narrow walkway. "You have seen the plentiful fuel that will fire my kiln. Now," again he smiled, "let me show you the sweet grain within."

The nearest window was but a few steps away. Gil stumbled again, his legs shaking with dread. Were the bones of his skeletal companion yet chained there? Were there more bodies, sights even worse?

"Look! Look!" Guidbairn cajoled eagerly. "What is there to fear?"

Staggering, Gil joined Floki at the low sill and, steeling himself, looked down and gasped. Two dozen white-veiled women sat huddled together on the stone floor, their grey habits spread around them like the wings of resting doves. "The Sisters!" he cried.

"You see," Guidbairn said, "nothing at all to fear."

Gil could not take his eyes from the captive nuns. They sat in a ring, centered on a single sister who, with head bowed over a psalter, softly chanted a Latin psalm. When the others sang the response, he thought again of doves.

A sudden sob broke through the chant and another of the sisters rose to her feet. Without ceasing her song, the leader held out her arms, and the nun ran into her embrace. Her veil slipped back and Gil saw a terrified young face, a girl with pale features and dark hair.

"Oh, these people," Guidbairn said reproachfully, "they send their children into such a life so young. A rare flower," he confided then, "do you not think? Just thirteen years …."

Thirteen. The age Janetta was when he met her, imprisoned in another tower.

The woman holding the girl raised her head as with the fingers of one hand she turned the page of her psalter. Gil stared at her gentle features, her strong, lean frame: the wood-gatherer of the convent meadow, the motherly comforter of the guest house! "Guinevere," he whispered.

"Ah, yes," said Guidbairn mildly. "A beauty, also, in her day."

Floki laughed. "The errant queen," he said with a knowing smile. Gil turned on him, outraged, and felt fingers bite into his wrist.

Guidbairn returned the smile. "Penitent, shall we say?"

Floki nodded innocently. "And this, then, is her penance?"

Guidbairn raised his hands in protest. "Surely not! Would I punish such as these?" He shook his head. "It is for their own protection I keep them locked away. Imagine if any of these ruffians, below, were to come within reach of that girl?" He paused, with an elaborate show of dismay. "They are all far safer within the tower, I assure you." Then, looking down at the sisters, he added, "But, of course, for some stray, unexpected spark …."

Seeing Gil shiver, he leaned forward solicitously, "Ah, my guest, I keep you too long in the cold. Come."

They walked in silence to the hall; Gil not knowing, nor caring, what lay within. He had seen down into the heart of the Golden Knight, and knew he could see nothing worse.

Outside the iron-studded doors, Arnkel made a show of laying down the sword belts Tofi had taken from them and stepped insolently over them as the doors swung open. Guards stood on either side, bristling with weapons. Guidbairn led the way between them. "At ease, my men, at ease," he said cheerfully. "We are among friends."

He turned to Arnkel, "I beg you, care for my guests while I make arrangements for our repast." For the first time, he left them, passing through a side door, and out of sight. The guards moved to a bench at the side of the entrance hall, where a great fire burned in an enormous hearth. Gisli, Tofi and Brand huddled in a lonely clump, as near the flames as they were allowed. But Arnkel yet lounged within ready reach of Gil and Floki, though preoccupied in flirtation with a passing kitchen maid.

Gil studied the maid; a well-fed, rosy-cheeked girl; wondering if she even knew of the tower and its occupants. Turning cautiously, he let his eyes drift over his surroundings. In height and breadth, the entranceway exceeded his whole longhouse on Hrolf's Isle. The inner doors, gilded and painted with hunting scenes, spoke of the grandeur of the Great Hall beyond.

On either side, smaller doors opened into corridors. The one Guidbairn had entered led, he guessed, to the kitchens, since the maid disappeared through it as well. The scents of cooking drifted out as the door swung shut behind her. Gil said in a low voice to Floki, "I will not eat his food."

"You will," Floki returned at once. "Had he wished us dead, we would be, so it will not be poisoned. King's Table, Warrior. The guest accepts hospitality."

Guidbairn reappeared, followed by men carrying planks and beams of wood and women bearing platters of food. The guards hastily vacated their places and a trestle table and benches were set up before the hearth.

Guidbairn beckoned Gil and Floki. "The Great Hall is cold, its fires not yet re-kindled. We will breakfast in simple comfort, here, close together, as befits old friends."

Floki grinned cheerfully. "Are we to set faces to the trough like happy swine? Or may I call the boy?"

Guidbairn laughed. "So comfortable am I in your presence, I had quite forgotten! You!" He pointed at Gisli, huddled with his friends at the door. "Untie them."

Gisli crossed the broad stone floor with downcast eyes, stepped behind Gil and Floki, and making a show of struggling with the knots, released them from their bonds. Offering them the bench nearest the fire, Guidbairn took his own place across from them and called for the women to serve.

Gil had seldom seen so much food, nor been so hungry, nor found it so hard to eat. With each mouthful he remembered the hunger of the men in the *muinntir*. With each sip of ale, he felt the fear of the imprisoned nuns. Filling his stomach seemed an act of treachery. But beside him, Floki ate and drank with apparent pleasure, praising one dish and another. "A fine table," he said, as they finished.

"Oh, modest enough," Guidbairn shook his head, "But this night ... this night we will do you justice." He sighed, then, and looked down, studying his hands. "But first there remains one other unpleasantness to be dealt with, as regretful to me as it is to raise such a matter with guests."

"Raise it," said Floki with a small smile. "What troubles a host, troubles a guest more. Who wishes to offend?"

"None, I am sure." Guidbairn made his kingly bow and then with another sigh added, "There are three treasures within your possession that rightfully belong to me. I would now have them back."

"What is rightfully yours must be returned," Floki agreed.

"Ah," Guidbairn turned slightly toward him, "I see you are a reasonable man."

"What are these treasures?" Gil broke in sharply. He felt Floki's boot nudge his own beneath the table but did not back down.

Guidbairn looked again at his hands. "Possessions," he mused. "Surely they are trivial things, and yet they can matter—a weakness, no doubt." He raised his head. "The first is but a small cup, a modest thing, but the Church holds it in such high regard that a shrine was prepared for it in my walled forest. Now the shrine stands empty. I have pledged before Peter in Holy Rome that I would make this right." His brilliant blue eyes bored into Gil's. "I must have this cup."

Before Gil could answer, Floki said, "We cannot oppose the

will of Holy Church. Nor thwart a penitent's vow."

Guidbairn stared for a long while at the young Northman, and said at last, "You are indeed a reasonable man. The cup shall be returned?"

"We cannot oppose the will of Holy Church," Floki said again, and before either Gil or Guidbairn could speak, he added, "And the second thing?"

"Ah, yes." Guidbairn still stared distractedly at Floki. "The second. A small thing, but an object of superstition among these people; safer for all if in my possession. I would have Merlin's Stone." He looked hard at Gil. "It would be wise to surrender it without argument. My guards have rough hands."

"I don't ...." Gil protested.

"Give it," Floki said. And when Gil mouthed *What?* he repeated, "Give it."

Reluctantly, Gil slipped the precious stone from his pocket and handed it to the Golden Knight. Guidbairn beamed his thanks, secreting the stone at once within the folds of his velvet tunic. "You are proving more affable companions than I might ever have hoped."

He sat back, tenting his fingers thoughtfully. "Now, but one matter remains, and, that resolved, all may be peace between us. You dine at my High Table as the honored guests you are, and in the morning, you, and all your companions and, indeed, your saintly queen, go free." He sighed and raised his head, "There is a young woman ...."

"No." Gil jumped to his feet, reaching instinctively for his surrendered sword. Floki also stood.

Guidbairn said calmly, "Before you consider leaving my presence, think carefully where you will go. The countryside is hostile, the weather poor, armed men surround you on every side. Surely some arrangement with my request is preferable?"

"Never!" Gil shouted.

Floki laid a restraining hand on his arm and said in a voice as calm as Guidbairn's, "With your permission I would speak alone with my earl?"

"Your earl?" Guidbairn looked from one to the other and then gave a shrug and a brief nod of agreement.

Gil walked stiffly beside Floki to the far side of the entrance hall, turned to face him, and said, "He can kill me if he wants. I am not giving him Janetta."

"Do you trust me?" Floki said in Irish.

"What difference does it make?" Gil shot back angrily. "I am *not* ...."

"*Do you trust me?*"

With a weary sigh, Gil gave the Irish affirmative.

Returning to the table, Floki took his place, pulled Gil down beside him and said, "We will speak of the woman."

"Ah, yes," Guidbairn smiled a long, slow smile, "My tarnished bride." Gil's whole body tensed with fury. Beneath the table, Floki's hand closed on his wrist. "Hardly any longer a creature of value," Guidbairn continued, "her honor compromised," he smiled knowingly at Floki, "It is said, by more than one—indeed, they say she was set apart on an island for your pleasure alone." Gil stiffened. Floki's fingers tightened their grip.

"Surely even I would not share her with a longhouse?" The two men laughed together, Gil held fast as an animal in a snare.

"But still," Guidbairn said regretfully, "I have offered her marriage. We are betrothed and Holy Church requires I wed her, if only to put her immediately aside." He paused and shrugged, "A convent perhaps. Regardless, she must be returned."

In the silence that followed, Gil was aware of the crackling of the fire, the shuffling of the guards' feet, and Arnkel Fish-Tail's low triumphant laugh. Floki said, "We will need a messenger."

Guidbairn leaned forward. "We are agreed?"

"Perhaps the boy with the ropes will be of service again?"

"Yes, yes." Guidbairn said impatiently, "if we are agreed?"

"It is a trick!" Arnkel shouted. "Their men will slaughter him!" Behind his back, Gisli watched calmly, a quick flash of understanding crossing his intelligent young face.

"I give him a pledge of safe passage," said Floki. "Have you a scribe?"

"Of course," Guidbairn returned loftily. "And a library of fine books for his pleasure. I will send for him."

Floki smiled. "Leave the scholar to his books. Send only for his vellum and ink, and I will scrawl the message myself. My poor Latin will prove it my own work."

Guidbairn stroked his beard warily. "And if I send this messenger, how will he find your people? Do not pretend to me they camp in ready view."

"Two fine horses brought us here," Floki said. "Mount him on either and it will return ...."

"The horses are ill-trained!" Gil kicked Floki's leg under the table. "He will need a guide."

Floki's eyes narrowed. "Ill-trained. Of course. And this guide?"

Gil faced Guidbairn. "The knight, Gareth, who you hold in the *muinntir*, knows the way."

"A traitor," said Guidbairn.

"But unarmed," Floki put in. He nodded toward Gisli, "This young warrior's sword will keep him loyal."

Again, Guidbairn sat stroking his beard, his eyes drifting from Floki to Gil and back. Then abruptly he summoned two of the guards and sent one in search of ink and vellum and the other to the *muinntir* for Gareth.

The big doors closed behind them and Guidbairn turned again to his guests. Abandoning his kingly demeanor, he leaned forward and whispered, "Let there be no treachery. You will pay for it with your lives."

Floki sat very still, his back straight, his handsome young face calm. "I respect your claim to what is rightfully yours. Now, I beg you, respect the honor of my word." He spoke with such quiet dignity that for a moment Gil, himself, was convinced.

Guidbairn's eyebrows rose slightly, but he inclined his head as if in apology.

"I know little of kings and great halls," Floki continued. "I am but a poor farmer from the Northlands. But we also have our courtesies. In our halls, a guest comes laden with gifts. Yet, I come to you empty-handed. I beg you, let me send for my harper, that he might play, and for want of a gift, I may dance for you instead?"

Guidbairn stared and then suddenly laughed out loud. "Who would have thought you of such a delicate nature?" He flung back his head, laughing again. "Send for him! Dance for me. Dance indeed."

Gil watched the Latin letters grow across the creamy vellum as, psalter open beside him, Floki inked out the borrowed words of his message: *Mihi crede.* Carefully laying down the quill, he turned the vellum to Guidbairn. "That is correct?" he asked innocently.

Guidbairn glanced with irritation at the writing, and then looked quickly aside, his gaze wandering around the entrance hall. "Yes, yes. Very good."

Gil fought a surprised smile; one poor scholar knowing another: *He can't read it.*

Floki also smiled, a slight quirking of his lips as he bent his head to his psalter again, and keeping his place with his left hand, took up the quill again with his right.

The two boys, Gareth and Gisli, sat stiffly waiting at the end of the table, Gareth stunned by his release, Gisli sniffing forlornly at the odors drifting up from the kitchens. Floki laid down his quill and returned it and the ink to the scribe's ancient wooden case. With a cloth from the case, he blotted the new words dry: *Volare sicut avis ad naves.* Guidbairn flicked his eyes over it and nodded, "Yes, yes."

Floki rolled the vellum, tied it with a cord from the box and wrapped it in a strip of cloth torn from the ragged sleeve of his shirt. Then he turned to Gisli and Gareth. "Ride, now, to the Green Tree of Caledon. Give this," he laid the vellum in Gareth's hands, "to the lady, Rachel, who will know well my stumbling grammar and uncertain hand."

He reached then, within his shirt and drew out a worn leather pouch. Untying the cord by which it hung around his neck, he opened the pouch and showed Gisli its contents. The boy's eyes widened at the glint of amber and gold. "Give this to my lady, Danni, as proof you come from me." Gisli nodded, awe-struck.

Facing them both, Floki said, "To the Knights of Caledon,

say this: Bid the lady Janetta ..." he paused and whispered wistfully, "my wildcat .... Bid my wildcat come now to her betrothed as once she came to Floki Magnusson."

Gil gasped at the words. Trust crumbling, he reached out a hand in protest. But his eyes fell then on Floki's bare forearm, exposed by the torn sleeve. A vivid white line ran its full length, the scar wrought by Janetta with Grimhildr's knife. An image flashed before him of Floki, blood-soaked aboard *Silver Dragon*, wrestling with his murderous wildcat. *As once she came ....*

He sat back, feeling a powerful calm descend. Floki again addressed the two boys, "Bid my cupbearer bring the Cup of the Chieftains, that we might drink the health of the king, and my harper bring his harp that I may dance before his table." He paused and then said clearly, "And bid Fergus son of Gartnan bring my cloak of many ermine, at once at the last note of the harp, lest in dancing, I take a chill." He folded his hands primly.

Guidbairn rolled his eyes. "Is that all?" he asked with exaggerated concern.

"That is all."

Guidbairn rose to dismiss the boys, but Gil said suddenly, "Wait." Startled, Guidbairn faced him. "I would ask a favor," said Gil. The Golden Knight made his gracious bow. "There is an old man in the camp," Gil continued, "a warrior of the old days, for whom I am named. He taught me so much. He'd be proud to see me, sitting beside a king. May he join us?"

"Of course, of course. I would be honored."

"Good," Gil smiled and to Gareth and Gisli said, "Bid Erling Maiden-Face bring my namesake to my side." He glanced at Floki and caught the slightest sparkle of laughter in his modestly downcast eyes.

Guidbairn escorted Gisli and Gareth back to the guards to be led out to the waiting horses and returned smiling benevolently. "If you will forgive me, the duties of my kingdom call. I have arranged for a room in which you may rest and refresh yourselves until the pleasures of my table, this night."

Bowing, he summoned two more of the guards and indicated the door opposite the kitchens. Numbed with tiredness, Gil followed, allowing himself a brief hope of a bed and even hot water in which to wash.

The door opened on a stone corridor that ran several feet before turning abruptly. Hurried ahead by the guards, he rounded the corner and lurched against the stone wall. Before his feet, steep stone steps descended into darkness. A cold wind blew up from below, carrying a sickening stench.

Suddenly, his arms were pinned behind him by rough hands, and stumbling wildly, he was forced downward and then thrust around another bend into a cavernous grey space. A boot slammed into the small of his back, kicking him down, and he sprawled on a wet stone floor. Floki landed beside him, rolled over and jumped to his feet. But behind them, a door thudded shut and with a jangle of metal keys, the bolts were thrown.

Stunned by his fall, Gil got slowly to his feet. Floki looked beyond his shoulder at something behind his back. "Warrior," he murmured, "face me." But Gil turned by instinct and, in the dim grey daylight drifting down from the one high window, he saw it.

It was nothing so blessedly pure as bones. The eyes were gone, and where maggots had worked at the flesh, the nose gaped, an empty hole. The skin of the face, stretched like tanned leather, revealed the shape of the skull beneath the young, shining hair. Shrunken lips exposed the wide grin of death. The odor of corruption rose amid a buzzing of flies.

Surprising himself with his own calm, Gil looked down at the corpse. "How long before that is us?"

Floki laughed, startling him. "The question all men ask and none can answer. But when that day comes, Warrior, it will not be here."

"Why not?" Gil said angrily. "He's tricked us into giving him everything he wants. Why should he ever let us out?"

"To further enjoy our humiliation. He is far too hungry for evil to allow us a simple death. This," he gestured to the chained corpse, "is just to remind us who is in control."

"He's an animal," said Gil.

"No. He is that far worse thing: a man. And being a man, he

is greedy. And being a man, he is proud. Too proud to admit he has no Latin. See, Warrior." He took his psalter from its leather satchel, and, sitting cross-legged beside the ravaged corpse, laid it open on his knees. "*Mihi* ... that is me. And here ... *crede* ... that is trust. Trust me. Rachel will laugh at my errors, but she will understand. And here ... *volare sicut avis* ... fly like a bird ..." he turned several pages, "*ad* ... *naves* ... to the ships. A Northman is only as safe as his ships. By sunset, our ships, forewarned, are afloat. When battle is done, there is escape."

Struggling to keep his eyes from their grim companion, Gil said, "How could you be sure ...?"

Floki smiled, "Why does a man keep a scribe?" He closed the psalter and slipped it into the satchel. "We summon to his table a cup of wine he dare not drink, a wildcat bride he dare not wed, and a cloak of ermine with teeth for his throat. And," he ruffled Gil's hair, "an old warrior who cannot even walk. King's Table, Gil Broadaxe! Well played!

"And now," he stretched his arms, "we sleep. The day is long and the night will be longer." He looked over his shoulder at the dead man. "And do not fear to trouble his rest. He is not here. He walks the green hills of Caledon, on a summer day." He stretched out on the dank floor and Gil did also, and slept.

CHAPTER TWENTY-ONE

She came out of the darkness as if out of his dream. Gil sat up, uncertain if he were dreaming still, since it was of her he had dreamt and in his dream, it was they who walked the green hills, not of Caledon, but of Hrolf's Isle, and it was indeed a rare and perfect summer day.

"Warrior."

He turned. Floki was on his feet, carefully screening the ravaged corpse from view. "Your lady is here."

"Janetta?" he whispered and then jumped up to run to her, but she shook her head and then Floki's outstretched arm was blocking his way.

She stood just beyond the doorway, where light from above drifted down the stairs, wearing clothing he had never seen before: a white linen dress embroidered in gold, and a cloak of deep green velvet. Her black hair was piled high on her head and jewels sparkled at her throat. She was exquisite and yet his heart fell. *He has given her clothes.*

She stepped a foot closer. "My husband desires your presence. He awaits you at his High Table."

"Your *husband*," Gil whispered, fury rising even though he knew it meant no more, nor less than "betrothed."

Again, she shook her head, tilting her chin slightly toward the stairs. Floki, still holding him back, pointed to the wall behind her where a faint shadow gave away the presence of a man, just out of sight.

Gil barely noticed. His eyes were fixed on Janetta's, reading in them the silent message as clear as in any language: *Do you trust me?*

Yes. Forever. With my life.

The shadow moved, and with a cheerful grin, Arnkel Fish-Tail stepped into the light. "Forgive my intrusion, but I am sent to guard her chastity. A daunting task with one so generous with her favors."

Floki's hand closed on Gil's shoulder, holding him firmly back, but Gil remained calmly looking into Janetta's eyes, Arnkel's words a distant meaningless blur.

"Perhaps indeed," Arnkel said, "she handfasts through Odin's Stone with one? The other? Both?" Gil still did not move and Arnkel shrugged sourly. "Come." He turned his back and strode up the stairs. But Floki bowed then to Janetta.

"My lady?"

"Yes," she said, smiling gently, "Please come." With Gil at her side and Floki shadowing them, they climbed the stairs, turned the corner into the corridor, lined now with flaming sconces, and followed Arnkel out into the entrance hall.

It, too, was lit by torches for all its length, casting flickering shadows over the cluster of people in the center of the vast stone floor. At first, Gil saw no one but the guards in their chain mail and helms, standing in a circle, unsheathed swords held ready. Among them, the boy, Gisli, turned his unhappy face away and stepped aside, leaving a gap in the ranks of armed men through which Gil saw Percy, small and wide-eyed, clutching his precious cup.

Gareth stood with a manly, protective arm about his shoulders and another around the *file's* son, Niall, who clung to his ancient harp as Percy did to his cup. But it was on none of the three that Gil's gaze rested, but on the beautiful young woman beside them: Danni, earl's lady, wearing the amber necklace and smiling a welcome to her love.

Gil turned quickly to Floki. Joy and concern warred on the Northman's face, but as he strode forward to embrace her, two hulking guards with raised swords blocked his way. He stopped, took a step back and gave them a look of withering scorn, which, raising his gaze, he cast on the remaining guards as well.

"What is the risk here?" he demanded. "I am without arms,

as is my earl," he waved an inclusive hand toward Gil. "And there? A child, a harper, a man already your prisoner, and a young woman as gentle as she is lovely."

No one answered, but the two nearest guards sheathed their swords and stepped sheepishly back, allowing him to pass. Before he did, he addressed the others with startling authority. "Put those blades away. You make yourselves look fools."

Gareth suppressed a giggle and the sheepish look spread from face to face. One by one, they sheathed their swords also and stood with empty hands. "Now, stand over there," Floki ordered. "You are frightening the child." Percy sniffed and gave a dramatic sob.

With a shuffling of feet, they obeyed, moving in a disorderly clump to the far wall. "I thank you," Floki said with a brisk smile. They ducked their heads and Gil knew right then that whoever sat in the High Seat in whatever hall, Floki Magnusson was earl.

An amazed shout of protest sounded behind them. Floki whirled. "You, also, Fish-Tail. Go." Gil held his breath, but a burst of laughter from the ranks of the guards sent Arnkel stamping, red-faced with fury, across the hall.

"I thank you also," Floki called after him cheerfully, and then with open arms strode to meet his lady.

The warriors in the hall fell silent as the two embraced and kissed, ignoring them all with lofty disdain. Then Floki stepped back and his face grew solemn. "I bade you fly."

"And we flew." She smiled and looked up at the rafters. Following her gaze, Gil saw the sparrow hawk staring down with her glittering yellow eyes. "No one said we might not fly back," Danni said.

Floki raised an eyebrow and shook his head. "The ships?"

"Afloat." With another smile she added, "When you fly from danger, then so do I."

He laughed then, in defeat. Glancing at the baffled guards, he said, "I fear I lie to them. Lovely you are, but gentle? Never." He kissed her again and lightly touched the amber necklace that once he had offered at Einar's Holm. "This also is lovely, but only a sliver of moon to your sun."

She reached beneath her hair for the clasp. "I must give it back."

"No," he protested. "I would have you wear it."

She shook her head. Loosening the golden chain, she clasped it between her palms. Then, taking its worn leather pouch from a pocket at her waist, she slipped it within and returned both to him. "One day. But this is not our day." Reluctantly, he accepted and tied the cord around his neck once more.

Danni looked up at the rafters. "Rachel says your grammar is terrible," she said cheerfully.

"I thank you." He gave her a wry smile. Then he held out his arm to Percy who ran happily to his side, the wooden cup bouncing on his chest. "Fish-Tail," Floki called then. Arnkel turned angrily. "I would have now the two blades you laid down at the door."

Arnkel laughed, shaking his head in astonishment. "Would you? You *truly* never change."

Floki raised his eyebrows. "Fish-Tail, I am not an idiot. How else may I dance the dance of Alba for your master? Here," he said, turning to Niall. "Give them to the harper. He is of the *filidh*, who neither bear nor learn the use of arms. But, oh, I beg you, place guards around him if you must." He gave an exasperated shrug.

One of the guards snickered. Arnkel turned redder and ordered Brand to bring the swords from outside the door. Shyly, the boy obeyed, returning with both sheathed blades. His eyes on Floki for reassurance, he offered them to Niall. Slinging his harp behind his shoulder, the *file's* son enfolded the swords and their scabbards clumsily in his arms.

"Very good," Floki smiled. "My lady?" he said to Janetta. And with her slight figure in the lead, they walked in a column to the magnificent entrance of Guidbairn's Great Hall, the guards shuffling obediently behind.

The elaborately painted panels stretched from wall to wall and rose to wooden pinnacles and scroll work above, so though the hall was screened from view, gaps in the carved wood let through air, light, and a murmur of voices.

As the doors were dragged open by two of the guards, Gil

saw a swift shadow sweep from the rafters and dart through a tear-shaped opening into the hall beyond. Floki looked up and smiled.

Gil stepped over the threshold and looked up, startled by a jolt of recognition. The long stone hall with its tapestries and flaming torches, and benches already filled with rowdy warriors and their women, was but a grander version of Gudrun's hall in Norway, or even Ragnvald's in Shetland. But the High Table, itself, raised on a dais and set before a huge hearth in which whole logs were burning, was more than simply familiar. He knew it; he had seen it before. The royal tapestries, the blackened lion head sconces, the twin doors in the paneled wall either side of the hearth and the regal golden pennant mounted above: all were seared in his memory, exactly as he saw them through the eerie window of Merlin's Tower.

Though now it was not Palamedes and the Men of the Forest, seated beneath the pennant, but Jocelyn Guidbairn himself. Bare headed, but for the golden circlet of royalty set on his blond hair, he rose to his feet as they entered and held out a welcoming arm.

On either side of his gilded High Seat, empty chairs awaited. Further down, knights and ladies had already taken their places. Gorgeous in the silks, velvets, and jewels won by their new allegiance, they leaned forward, eager eyes fixed on the returning bride. A muttering of gossipy tongues filled the air and sly laughter arose from the benches. Guidbairn silenced them all with a clap of his hands. "Stand and greet my lady and our honored guests."

Voices stilled, they hurriedly rose, leaving only one old man seated at an end of the High Table. So small and bent that Gil had not noticed him before, he was clad in a habit of the same undyed wool that Aidan wore. Grey beard drooping on his chest, he dozed wearily in his chair until, jolted suddenly awake by a neighbor, he struggled to his feet.

"Ah, the holy scribe," Floki murmured sadly. "A lonely sanctity in this house."

Gil pitied the old man, summoned from his quiet cell to sit, forlorn and forgotten amid the splendor, all for Guidbairn's vanity. His bent form trembling, he leaned stoically on his staff as the two ladies nearest the High Seat left their places to escort Janetta to the table. She walked between them with the calm assurance of a queen and as she took her seat at Guidbairn's side, a hush of respect fell over the hall.

Blue eyes burning with triumph, Guidbairn signaled Floki to take the seat of honor at his right. Floki shook his head.

"I beg you, sir, that is my earl's place." He bowed to Gil. "I am but the helmsman."

With a look of exasperated disbelief, Guidbairn said, "As you wish."

Gil turned to beckon Niall to join him and saw a shadow flash above their heads, dart unnoticed over the High Table, and perch high up, talons sunk in the royal pennant on the wall. He heard Floki laugh softly. "Wishing to correct my grammar, no doubt."

Fighting a smile, Gil mounted the dais with his poet at his side to take the place accorded his rank. Floki and Danni followed, with Percy between them, but the boy stopped directly in front of Guidbairn, and, tugging at Floki's cloak, whispered hoarsely, "Is he really a king?"

"Manners," Danni murmured.

But Floki smiled. "Would he wear a crown if he were not?"

Percy nodded solemnly. "Maybe."

The knights at the table laughed and one shouted, "An honest man!" But Jocelyn Guidbairn did not join the laughter.

"Take your places," he said. "We have delayed enough." And when Percy stepped closer, cradling his cup and peering at the crown, he flinched and turned away. "Music!" he called sharply to his own musicians, waiting below. "Music for our guests!"

Alarmed by the anger in his voice, they began a noisy melody on lute, drums, and pipes, and serving girls hurriedly appeared with jugs of wine and platters of meats. Gisli and Gareth found places on the benches, and Brand and Tofi rose quickly to join them, their allegiance to Arnkel forgotten. Arnkel himself sat among Guidbairn's warriors, his treachery insufficient to earn him a higher place.

Facing again a meal that in itself felt like treachery, Gil was dimly aware of Floki conversing cheerfully with the heavily armed warrior placed pointedly beside him. But the voice that held his ear was Janetta's, blending intimately with Guidbairn's lordly tones, slipping so readily into their shared Frankish tongue. He sipped his wine and stabbed at the venison before him.

"You do not eat," Guidbairn said solicitously. "Perhaps it lacks salt?"

In an instant, Gil was in Merlin's Tower, thirst-racked, struggling to swallow, sickness rising up his throat. He thrust the plate away and gulped more wine.

"My friend," Floki turned companionably to Guidbairn, "tread carefully." He smiled, a deadly glint lighting his eyes. Then he jumped suddenly to his feet. Every face in the hall swiveled toward him and at the foot of the benches, two bowmen rose and pointedly set arrows to strings.

Floki smiled at them and called, "I thank you for your hospitality!" drawing laughter from the knights at the High Table. Guidbairn again did not laugh. Still smiling, Floki pushed back his chair, and taking Percy with him, walked to the end of the long board, where the old monk sat dazedly nibbling at his food, and passing in front of him, led the boy to stand in front of Guidbairn again.

Taking the wooden cup from Percy, he filled it with wine and held it up. "Drink with me from the Cup of Arthur," he said, his voice, though soft, carrying out over the suddenly silent hall. Leaning over the table, Floki held it within Guidbairn's reach.

But with all eyes upon him, the Golden Knight rose from his chair and stepped hurriedly back. His face was white, and his hand, held up as if to ward off a threat, trembled.

"Drink!" Floki smiled. "Have you no thirst?" And when Guidbairn stepped further back, he said more loudly, "I offer you the Cup of the Forest of Pentecost! Camelot's greatest treasure!"

The knights and ladies laughed, pointing at the modest vessel. "He plays the fool!" one cried. But an older man growled at Guidbairn, "And makes the fool of you."

"Here," Floki said, "if you will not drink to Camelot's king, I yet shall." And holding up the wooden cup, he shouted, "To the king!" and drained it dry.

Then, lowering the cup, he turned to face the hall and with the same authority with which he cowed the guards, called out, "Let all men know the cup has been offered, and the cup has been refused!" He placed it once more in Percy's hands. A confused babble of voices started up. Guidbairn's knights turned to him in irritation.

"Give it to the holy father!" Guidbairn gestured to the old man, his voice shaking.

Floki shook his head sorrowfully. "What is rightfully yours must rightfully be returned only to you."

The muttering at the table grew louder, and when Guidbairn attempted to silence it, one man demanded, "What is the truth of this? What fear you in this clumsy child's toy?"

"Nothing!" Floki cried cheerfully. "He fears nothing. Is he not your king?" Then, sending Percy back to Danni, he leaped down to the floor and summoned Niall. To Guidbairn he called, "Though you will not drink with me, yet I dance for you!" And he unsheathed both swords.

Benches scraped back and armor creaked as a dozen warriors rose to their feet. Floki laughed, ignoring them, and held up both blades before Guidbairn. "Fine steel, would you not say?"

"Very fine," Guidbairn muttered, watching him uneasily. "Very fine."

"But surely yours is finer?" said a sweet girlish voice. Gil turned sharply. Janetta gazed innocently up at Guidbairn and laid a shy hand on the magnificently jeweled hilt of his sword.

He laughed indulgently. "It is also a fine blade," he said. His eyes were yet on Floki who waited with the two swords while Niall took his place on the end of a bench and rested his harp between his knees.

"May I see it?" Janetta asked.

"What? Yes, yes. Of course," Guidbairn muttered. Still distracted, he unsheathed the blade. She gasped.

"It is so *long*!" she cried, eyes widening. The ladies at the table giggled and one of the knights laughed out loud. Guidbairn smiled.

"Yes," he said. "It is long."

"May I hold it?" Janetta reached out her small sun-browned hands. With another smile, Guidbairn laid the weapon across them. Lifting the blade, she gingerly wrapped her small palm around the tip. "Ohhh," she murmured throatily, "it is so sharp!" The man beside Gil coughed suddenly, shuffling his feet. "I fear to pierce myself!" Janetta cried.

A voice down the table called out, "Ah, but he does that for you!" Guidbairn threw back his head and laughed. Then a chord from the High-King's harp drew the attention of all back to Floki. But when he stepped forward to begin the dance, Guidbairn's sword still lay on Janetta's lap.

Standing very still, Floki raised both blades high. Hands reached for sword hilts, and men leapt to their feet as he flung one, and then the other above his head, as he had done on Hrolf's Isle. And, as on Hrolf's Isle, the women in the hall cried out in relief as the hilts slapped faithfully into his hands.

Then, kneeling, he laid his own sword down, crossed it with Gil's, rose, and bowed to Guidbairn as he had to his father. But here he asked for no blindfold, and when Niall began again to play, he made no joyous shout but stepped in silence over the swords. Then, with his cold grey gaze fixed on Guidbairn's face, he began the slow, graceful steps of the dance.

The music, the intricate footwork, the lithe upright stance, were all as Gil remembered them, but the dance was subtly different, no longer a celebration, but a challenge. The moves were warrior's moves, the upraised hands, though empty, carried deadly threat, the dancer's gaze, a swordsman's gaze, unflinching on Guidbairn's face.

The hall fell utterly silent, but for the light scuff of the dancer's feet and the trembling notes of the ancient harp. Men and women watched, mesmerized. Even the bowmen at the foot of the hall let their weapons sag in their hands. Jocelyn Guidbairn sat still as stone but fear yet flickered in his eyes.

Niall's fingers quickened on the strings. Floki whirled, leaped, and spun. Yet even as the notes grew louder, a new sound came to Gil's ears, a soft murmuring, as if a wind was blowing all around the high stone walls. He looked up at the windows and saw only darkness. But as the harp music grew louder still and the dance faster, the murmuring of the wind rose, too. And now he heard new sounds; the voices of men, the clanking of armor, and even the clash of a horseshoe on stone, as if Guidbairn's Great Hall was as haunted as Merlin's Tower.

Still, bewitched yet by Floki's dance, none on the benches seemed aware. Gil shook his head, shaking away a dream that did not vanish. Then he looked up and, meeting Janetta's eyes, knew that she heard it too.

Floki spun, swept up one sword, spun again, and swept up the other. This time there was no filial submission. A blade in each hand, he faced Jocelyn Guidbairn as with a last sweep of the strings, Niall stilled his harp.

A look of alarm crossed Guidbairn's face, and he half rose. But his gaze was over Floki's head, on the painted wooden screen at the foot of the Great Hall. The knights and ladies, too, were on their feet, and the guards arrayed along the walls closed in, their eyes flicking from the distant doors to the High Table.

On the benches below, men and women turned to each other in confusion, all hearing now the impossible sounds beyond the screen; low voices, the jingle of mail, the creak of saddle leather and then the whinny of a horse; an army gathering, not outside the fortress, but within.

"Guards!" Guidbairn shouted, but the shout died on his lips.

Gil whirled. Guidbairn sat frozen, his head drawn back, his crown askew and his own sword held hard against his throat. Fingers enmeshed in his hair, Janetta wrenched his head back further, exposing the flesh to the blade. In a calm, clear voice, she cried to the ancient monk, "Good Father! Do not let me die unshriven, for I do murder now!"

Her sword arm tensed and with a gasp, she closed her eyes. The old man jumped to his feet, priestly duty strengthening his failing limbs. Guards swarmed in like wolves, one already raising his sword. But Gil was there first, his father's knife slashing the sword arm to the bone.

Then Floki was beside him, leaping up onto the table, a

deadly blade in each hand. But it was the hawk that warned Gil, sweeping with a wild cry from her roost on the pennant, clipping his head with her wings, drawing his attention out to the benches and the bowmen at their foot. He was moving even as the bowstrings hummed.

Flinging himself over Guidbairn, he wrapped his arms around Janetta's waist, and ignoring her cry of protest, dove with her to the floor. The jeweled sword clattered beside them as the arrows hissed over their heads and crashed into the hearth, showering the fleeing guests with fire.

Amid the curses of his knights, the cries of their ladies, and the clash of steel on steel, Guidbairn yet sat utterly still, staring in disbelief and then horror as the doors in the painted screen burst open, slammed wide by the force of three fewtered lances.

Their chargers reined shoulder to shoulder, Lance'lot, Palamedes, and Martin de Troye galloped into the hall and, with mighty Doombearer in the center, lowered their lances again and closed on the High Table, sparks flying beneath steel-shod hooves.

All around them, sword-wielding Northmen and Irish poured through the broken doors, and behind, the freed Men of Caledon, armed with wooden staves and their own broken prison chains. Half were mounted on unharnessed beasts loosed from Guidbairn's stables. The rest fought on foot with equal ferocity.

Bareback on a bridle-less pony, Fergus, son of Gartnan waved an expansive hand over their heads. "Earl Floki! Your cloak of many ermine!" he shouted joyously.

Guidbairn scrambled to his feet and with his guards crowding around him, fled in un-kingly haste toward the nearest door. Stumbling, he slipped to one knee and his golden royal circlet tumbled with a clang onto the stone floor. He paused, fumbling for it, and then abandoned it and surged upward, driven by terror as the clattering hooves halved and then quartered the distance to the dais.

"Take the child!" Floki shouted to Danni and with her arm around Percy, she dashed to the safety of the wall. The ladies at the table ran. The knights drew swords and backed away. Guidbairn and his guards reached the door.

Gil leaped up to follow and beside him Janetta clasped the fallen sword in two determined hands. But then Floki was there, flinging them both down to the floor and throwing his own body across theirs, as the chargers mounted the dais and, soaring above them, cleared the High Table and slammed into Guidbairn's defenders. Lances skewered those who yet stood. Pounding hooves trampled the fallen.

Then Erling Maiden-Face, bushy beard flying, dashed up to the dais on a wild-eyed horse and tossed the Irish battle-axe to Gil. "Your namesake, Broadaxe!"

Abandoning knights and hall, Guidbairn bolted through the door, slamming it shut behind him and throwing the bar. Gripping the broadaxe in both hands, Gil ran through the carnage to batter his way in. But again, Floki was there, hauling him back. "A rat in its nest has teeth. We deal with him later. There is work yet here."

Saluting the three mounted knights as they whirled their sweat-soaked horses, he jumped down to the floor of the hall. Gil turned with him and faced the battle now raging between Guidbairn's followers and his own.

The long room was a flickering, flame-lit chaos of fallen tables and broken crockery, loud with the clash of swords and the neighing of frightened horses. In the midst, his own men fought as the fine warriors they were but they were outdone by the sheer vengeful savagery of the Men of Caledon. Grimly wielding their rough weapons, they spared neither wounded nor disarmed, cutting down any who attempted to flee.

Sickened by the unbridled violence, Gil braced himself, gripped the broadaxe two-handed once more, and ran to the edge of the dais, kicking a fallen cloak from the path. But his boot caught in the grey bundle, thudding against something unexpectedly heavy. He kicked impatiently again and then looked down and saw the heap of ragged cloth was the body of a man, wrapped yet in his blood-soaked habit: Guidbairn's scribe, run down by the chargers' merciless, innocent hooves.

Too old and frail to flee, he had been left to be trampled

because no one had remembered him. Because *he* had not remembered him.

Anguished, Gil remembered him now, running to Janetta's aid, and saw him, suddenly, as Aidan. Not the powerful seaman-priest he knew, but Aidan grown old and frail, yet driven, still, by the same unquenchable faith.

Shame and grief fused in fury and Gil jumped down to the floor with the broadaxe in his hands, seeking the one man he saw, in that moment, as the true cause, not just of the old priest's death, but of Morian's and even Hamund's of which he was surely innocent: Bergljot's betrayer, *Silver Dragon's* deserter, Arnkel Fish-Tail.

Blind to reason, his vision narrowed to a single focus, he searched the hall and found him where he would expect to find him, deserting yet again. Abandoning the boys he had led into mutiny, he made his furtive way along the wall to the doors.

"Stop him!" Gil shouted stupidly to a hall full of battling men. But one man did hear. Erling Maiden-Face raised his head to the familiar voice, booted a struggling opponent out of the way, and bolted across the hall in pursuit.

Still, it was Gil, racing through the mayhem, who reached Arnkel first, slammed the battle-axe into the door post, and barred his escape. Whirling, Arnkel met Erling's ready sword with his own. Gil wrenched the axe from the wood as the two clashed blades.

"Maiden-Face!" Arnkel grinned. "I trim your beard, too!"

"Floki Magnusson names me Maiden-Face," Erling growled, "None other." He thrust hard past Arnkel's defense, slashing his tunic and drawing blood. But Arnkel fought fiercely, height and arm length in his favor. A quick lunge opened a gash of red down Erling's cheek.

Erling countered with a brutal kick, slamming his boot into Arnkel's knee. Gil heard the crack of breaking bone. Arnkel howled and staggered. Erling stepped back, eyeing his opponent carefully, and abruptly turned his back.

Gil stared, astonished. Erling smiled within his vast beard. "You kill," he said, with a shrug.

Regaining his balance, Arnkel lunged forward, sword raised

in both hands over Erling's head. Willingly, savagely, Gil swung the axe, all his anger behind it. Arnkel split open like the straw man, streaming blood and entrails as he collapsed to the floor. Choking with shock and fury, Gil raised the axe to strike again.

"Enough." An iron grip held back his arm. "Enough," Floki said gently. "We are done."

The rage receded, ebbing like a falling tide, leaving him weak and shaking and brutally aware of all around him. At his feet, the remains of Arnkel gasped and gurgled into silence. Turning, sickened, from it, he stared again at Erling Maiden-Face watching with calm satisfaction.

"Why?" Gil whispered, bewildered.

Erling smiled and shrugged again. "It is better you do it." His smile broadened. "I would marry his wife."

Gil covered his face with one hand, half laughing and half crying. When he raised his gaze again, his father was before him, mounted yet on the Monkish Ploughhorse. "You do well," Lance'lot said simply. "Battle is awful. We all know that."

Gil nodded. Slowly he turned around. Blood-sodden bodies lay amid trodden food and spilled wine. The survivors huddled behind a barricade of benches, guarded by Ragnar Kolsson from the unforgiving Men of Caledon. Surprised at their feasting, abandoned by their fleeing king, and overwhelmed by sheer numbers, however rudely armed, Guidbairn's warriors had been easy prey.

His own were now sprawled, exhausted, throughout the vast hall, the boys chattering in the excitement of victory, the older men quietly cleaning their swords. Beneath the light of a flaring sconce, Danni and Ismail tended their few wounded.

Gil turned quickly, seeking Janetta, and felt his heart lift when he saw her, safe on the back of her father's charger. Martin de Troye saluted him with cautious respect. But then Janetta slipped down from behind his saddle, and, still holding Jocelyn Guidbairn's sword, walked proudly toward Gil. Her eyes never leaving his, she stepped calmly around the butchered corpse of Arnkel Fish-Tail, taking no more notice than of a gralloched deer.

"Daughter!" Troye called.

"I am his," she said, without looking back.

Gil felt a pang of sorrow for the look of forgotten love on her father's face. But then she was in his arms, her trophy abandoned at his feet.

And I am yours, his heart cried. *But I am not of your world!*

He released her, shocked by a thought long forgotten, rising up to haunt him now. Dazed, he looked around the hall, quickly seeking those he was pledged to protect. Warriors' ladies, some newly widows, sobbed in each other's arms. Kitchen maids cowered forgotten, in corners, still clinging to their platters and jugs. Guidbairn's musicians huddled by a pillar, sheltering Niall, a fellow innocent in their midst. Relieved, Gil looked for Percy and found him holding a basin of water while his sister bathed wounds.

Rider-less ponies milled, neighing, as Gareth and Leidolf herded them toward the door. Through the cacophony of equine complaint, Gil heard a familiar inner cry. *I want the ship!*

"Lionheart!"

He was there, ears flat, mane bristling, eyes white-rimmed, nipping at his rider's leg. "Elias!" Gil saluted, "be careful!"

"Broadaxe!" Elias jumped down. "I borrow Sliepnir. But he is not happy!"

"Tell me when he is," Gil said. Yanking Lionheart's head down by his forelock, he looked him firmly in the eye and led him to where Niall hid by the pillar. *Make yourself useful.* Boosting the boy aboard and handing up his precious harp, he slapped Lionheart's rump and walked away.

Floki joined him, holding out his sword and scabbard. "Arm yourself, Warrior," he said with a smile, "for now we hunt rats."

Gil nodded and strapped the sword belt around his waist and lifted the battle-axe from the stone floor. He turned to the broken doors, but a shout and a peal of laughter spun him around.

Cheering Irish warriors had righted the fallen table on the dais and seated themselves down its length. In the center, Fergus lounged gleefully on Guidbairn's High Seat, his booted feet on the board and Guidbairn's royal circlet on his wild red head. Tipping the golden crown over one eye, he raised a dented goblet, "Behold! Fergus son of Gartnan! Once a slave, now King of Camelot!"

"He makes mockery," Martin de Troye growled angrily. "Camelot has no king but Arthur."

But Gil only smiled and shook his head as laughter exploded throughout the hall. The laughter spread, wry and half-choked; the laughter of men on the edge of weeping; the bolder and brasher, the closer the tears.

And then, above it all, Gil heard a faint cry, a bird cry, urgent and compelling, and looking up, saw Rachel's hawk sweep low through the broken doors and into the hall. Brushing the rearing ponies' heads, she flew, arrow fast and arrow straight, to Floki and slapped against his unprotected arm, her talons drawing blood. She mewed again, an uncanny, desperate cry, and in that moment, Gil smelled the smoke. His gaze met Floki's and even as the hawk again took flight, they were running for Merlin's Tower.

———

Gil burst from the gates of the fortress and it stood before him, the flames of Guidbairn's vengeance lighting the night sky. The grassy hill flickered with firelight. The rough scaffolding smoldered and smoke swirled into the empty windows. The door, locked and boarded over, was charring from the fire set at its foot. From within the stone walls, soft voices chanted, "*De profundis domine ...*"

"The bastard! The bastard!" Gil cried. He turned and saw his father watching in disbelief.

"Guinevere?" he whispered.

"And all the sisters," Floki answered. He reached for the battle-axe, but Gil was already running to the door.

Fergus, the crown still askew on his head, mounted the grassy slope beside him, struggling up the burning scaffolding toward a window. Palamedes rode Doombearer, wild-eyed but obedient, to the wall, and standing on his saddle strove to reach another. Gil swung the axe against the unforgiving timber barring the door.

It sprung back, bouncing off the wood as if it were steel. He swung again, his shoulders jarring with the force. On the third swing, he felt give, drew back, and struck again. Cleansed of Arnkel's blood by the splintering wood, the blade sank deep and the beam split. Instantly, Ragnar Kolsson and Erling were at his side, wrenching at the barrier with bare hands.

Tearing it free, they flung it down and Gil attacked the iron lock. Shards of metal flew, but the bolt held.

"Stand back!" his father's voice spun him around. Lance'lot and Martin de Troye, holding their dancing chargers shoulder to shoulder, lowered fewtered lances and charged, tearing through the door as if it were a curtain of silk.

Smoke billowed as they reined the terrified beasts around. Gil and Ragnar hauled splintered wood free. And then, out of the haze of choking air, still quietly chanting, the Grey Sisters emerged, walking calmly two by two, the youngest at the front, and at the rear, all their charges safe, the Good Mother and Guinevere. Surrounded by their cheering rescuers, they sang to the end of the psalm.

The youngest nun broke free of the column and ran to Guinevere. Safe in her arms, she looked up at Gil's father, astride the Monkish Ploughhorse. "Are you Lance'lot?" she murmured, awestruck.

"He is," said Guinevere. She too raised her gaze to his and a look passed between them, as sweet as an embrace. Gil felt the old anger for only a moment and then it was gone, replaced by a gentle peace. "And this knight," she turned suddenly to Gil, "Your son?"

"My son." Lance'lot's voice was thick with pride. The peace deepened and then a wild shout brought all peace to an end.

"They return!" Fergus cried, reaching for his sword.

Gil looked back the way they had come. Beyond the fire lit faces of his warriors and the Men of Caledon, he glimpsed a glint of steel as shadowy lines of figures emerged from the darkness, advancing on the burning tower. Orderly, disciplined, neither wearied by battle, nor humbled by defeat: "No," he murmured to Floki. "No one returns. These are new. It's like in Rome. He's kept half his force behind."

Floki laid a hand on Gil's shoulder and briefly rested his forehead on it. Then he looked up and laughed, "And as in Rome, we are again his fools!"

"What now?" Gil watched his men turning, wearily and warily, to meet the foe.

"Now, Warrior," Floki said quietly, "I think we die. As well we deserve."

"Right." Gil nodded, disconcertingly proud to be included.

"But first we fight," Floki grinned suddenly and unsheathed his sword. "And save all we can save. Good Sir," he turned to Lance'lot who stood beside them, holding the bridle of his horse, his eyes on the shadowy forms in the distance. "Quickly, while darkness hides you, take the sisters back through the gates to the forest. The smaller and weaker on your chargers. And take my harper on that miserable beast he rides. Keep them at your side."

Lionheart let out one long whinny of protest. Gil stroked his soft muzzle. *Go with him. I'll follow,*" he lied, as the pony was led away.

"And you, Sir," Floki addressed Martin de Troye, "Go, too, with the wounded and the boys."

He paused and whistled suddenly and in a moment Rachel's hawk appeared, darting out of the night and landing again on his wrist. He looked deep into her glittering eyes. "When night passes, you will lead them North, to the ships." He held her close and kissed her sleek head. "Farewell, Pretty One," he whispered and flung her to the sky.

He turned then to Danni, standing behind him with a protective arm around her brother's shoulders. "My lady," he said, "Tend my household." She nodded acceptance; the understanding between them complete. But Percy, sensing their sorrow, began to cry. "No tears," Floki leaned down to him. "You must go, too, and tend your goats." He straightened, and still looking into Danni's eyes, beckoned Ismail. "Good Saracen! I entrust them to your care." He raised a hand to her cheek, let it fall, and turned hurriedly away.

Numbly, Gil faced Janetta. "Go with your father. I'll join you at the ships."

"I do not leave you."

"You must."

Troye reached out his arms, "Daughter, I beg you."

"No."

Gil turned to lay gentle hands on her shoulders and found himself facing Jocelyn Guidbairn's sword. He heard low laughter behind him.

"Surrender, Warrior. She will use it. This I know."

Gil shook his head. "I don't want to lose you," he whispered, tears streaking his face.

"You never lose me. I am yours, always." She stepped to his side, the smallest and fiercest of his company.

Palamedes lifted two of the Grey Sisters onto Doombearer's back and with a look of parting sorrow sent the great charger to join the Monkish Ploughhorse. Then, turning to Floki, he said, "I also do not leave."

"Nor do I ask you," Floki smiled. "How can I? Were we not to ride Caledon once more?" And with Gil on one side and the Saracen knight on the other, he led their remaining force into battle.

Midway down the grassy slope he paused, signaling the eager Irish to hold back, that they might keep the higher ground. Gil looked down and saw Guidbairn's men halt as well. Bereft of their horses, half-blinded by the light of the fire behind, they began a wary charge.

Sword in one hand, throwing axe in the other, Floki stood utterly still as warriors closed on every side. Then, with a joyful shout, he flung both weapons up over his head, whirled, caught them, and still laughing, ran to meet them.

Then Gil was fighting too, his sword yet in its scabbard; the deadly Irish battle-axe held in both hands. Like a scythe, it cleared ground before him. Men fell, and men turned and fled. On either side they met Northmen and Irish, and behind them, a slim fairy-wisp of a girl, as deadly with her stolen steel as any man.

And, as the uneven battle turned inevitably against them, Gil thought exultantly, what better way to die, if he must die, than fighting like a Northman, with this girl at his side? He heard a distant last whinny from Lionheart and exulted again. They were in the forest, the escape achieved. His people, most of them, were safe.

But those who remained were now driven back, step by step, up the hill, and each step, Gil knew, brought them closer to the end. The heat of the growing fire scorched his back. Sweat soaked his tunic. His face was drenched, his eyes stinging. His strength fading, he cast the heavy battle-axe through the fire lit doorway behind him and drew his sword.

Fergus, staggering now from exhaustion, accompanied his sword swings with a string of Irish oaths. Erling Maiden-Face stumbled and nearly fell. Even Palamedes struggled to hold his place.

Only Floki seemed invincible, light-footed and light-hearted, laughing as he fended one charge after another. And yet, it was Floki who called surrender. "Enough." He lowered his sword and stood unprotected. "We are done."

Gil saw he was addressing not themselves so much as a tall man in the opposing line who had fought with the plain efficiency of a paid swordsman, a warrior by trade. With a nod of his head, he lowered his own sword too.

"Spare my people," Floki said quietly. "They fight only from duty. They have no quarrel with you."

The man nodded again, but looked over his shoulder, and out of the darkness Jocelyn Guidbairn appeared, mounted on his white charger, and dressed in his armor of gold. "Once again, you are a reasonable man," he said. "And so am I. So am I." His gaze shifted from Floki to Gil and Janetta and he waved dismissively at the exhausted warriors. "Let them go."

Erling stepped to Floki's side. "I do not leave you."

Floki laughed, "Tend the widows, Maiden-Face," and when Erling protested again, he only smiled fondly and turned him away. But Fergus held his ground, shaking his head vigorously. The stolen crown, bouncing on his red curls, brought cries of outrage from Guidbairn's followers and laughter from his own.

"I vow to serve Broadaxe," he proclaimed. "I cannot leave."

"Then serve me," Gil said. "Guard my people." He met the Irishman's eyes, and with a defeated sigh, Fergus nodded. Then, whirling around, he yanked the golden crown from his head, flung it at Guidbairn's feet, and led his men into the night.

Guidbairn jerked his head sideways, and in response, four of his warriors lifted a great wooden beam to their shoulders and brought it into the light of the flames. Two others joined them, and shifting the beam before them, they walked purposefully up the hill.

"Warrior," Floki nodded toward the darkness, "Now you."

"No."

His eyes on the approaching beam, Floki said, "It will not be a simple death."

"I die with my earl."

"And leave them with none?"

"Ciarnan is earl. I've named him my heir."

Startled, Floki said, "You learn too well." He smiled, proud and regretful at once; then turned to face the six. At a signal from the Golden Knight, they lunged forward.

Gil threw shielding arms around Janetta, but with the beam a yard away, Guidbairn shouted, "Halt!"

Leaning down from his horse, he addressed Janetta gravely. "My lady," he said, his voice surprisingly gentle, "he cannot save you. I can. Come to me. I will wed you and make you a queen. Surely better than the fire?"

"With him, I am already a queen," she said.

Guidbairn straightened, his eyes gone cold. "Then burn with him." He gave a quick flick of his hand and the six warriors charged. Floki and Palamedes took the force of the wooden beam with their shoulders but only stalled it a moment. Then it was again moving forward, thrusting them, resisting and stumbling, remorselessly toward the flames. The black doorway yawned and then they were through it, in the darkness and the smoke and the unbearable heat.

Gil was barely aware of the doors being closed, the bar thrown, the hammering of nails that hardly mattered now, since, choking for breath, he was struggling even to stand. Straining for air, he raised his face and was startled to see through the flickering veil of smoke, the dancing light of the aurora. "Odin's Maidens," he whispered, tightening his arms around Janetta,

"They hang their shields on the stars...."

He felt arms around himself as well; Floki's and Palamedes', linked around them, making their own shield. "Breathe deep," Floki said gently, "It is the smoke that kills. The flames will never reach you in this world. Breathe deep. Let all go."

Gil obeyed, coughing and fighting like a drowning man, feeling Janetta already growing limp in his arms. He thought of his ship and the sea and the island in the tide-race, far to the North.

A sound grew, above the crackling of the flames; a roaring that seemed both within and without, filling all the tower until the stone itself seemed to tremble around them. "List!" Palamedes cried. Surprised, Gil realized he heard it too. Palamedes turned his great bearded head up to the stars. But they had vanished and the sky had grown blue, and then sunlight broke through the windows of Time Past and Time Present and Time Yet to Come, and last, of Time Out of Time. *This is death* ....

But Palamedes shouted, "List! List! It comes at last!"

Floki, too, looked up, his grip around Gil's shoulders loosening. The sun was shining now through the stones of the walls themselves.

Gil stared at the blue sky; and then, all around, the green summer trees, the sparkling blue river, the hot, sunbaked surface of the Look-Out Rocks. The roaring rose in strength and pitch, a screech and a scream, and at last he saw it, streaking overhead.

"The Questing Beast!" Palamedes cried.

"It's an F-16," whispered Gil.

CHAPTER TWENTY-TWO

"Is this heaven?" Still locked in his arms, Janetta looked wonderingly around.

"Uh, not exactly," said Gil. His eyes swept over the sky, the river, the overhanging trees, the dark whirlpool of the Indian Kettle pool; all unchanged ….

Slipping from his embrace, Janetta stepped with the same wondering gaze to the edge of the rocks, where a gap in the wall of firs revealed the white clapboard of his mother's house. "Wait," Gil called.

He turned back to Palamedes who longingly watched the sky, ear cocked to the distant rumble yet sounding. At his side, Floki quickly assessed their surroundings, reading the landscape the way he read the sea.

"Warrior, it is summer. How is this? And that bird is no bird of Caledon." He pointed to a branch hanging over the Indian kettle pool.

"It's a blue jay," Gil stared at the branch, the same branch where he and Danni saw Percy's Stonepecker bird … *the stone! Merlin's stone!* He slapped his empty pocket.

"Where are we, Warrior?"

"Tir nan Og," Gil said with a slow intake of breath. *And how do I get them home?*

"List!" Palamedes grabbed his arm, jabbing a finger at the sky. "It returns!"

The rumbling drew nearer, rose again to a roar and then an air-shattering howl. Janetta covered her ears, staring terrified at the sky. Palamedes' face lit with his joyful white smile. "Behold! Behold!" he cried as it shrieked overhead and vanished once more.

Janetta cautiously lowered her hands. "Alas," Palamedes sighed his disappointment. Floki spun suddenly around, his alert gaze again on the river.

"Warrior ...."

But Palamedes wrapped an arm around Gil's shoulders, pointing again at the sky. "Had I only my bow to bring it down!" he cried mournfully, "It would be mine at last!"

"Could be," said a voice from below. "But if you ask me, getting the damn thing in the freezer's when the *real* trouble starts."

Gil whirled. The familiar kayak floated gently in the dark waters of the pool. Paddle resting across the little hull, the kayaker ducked his blond head, setting the eagle's feather dancing. "Ivan!" Gil cried.

"Hey, pal," Crazy Ivan nodded toward Floki who stood, hand on sword hilt, his lean frame tensed for battle. "Only joking."

Without taking his eyes from Ivan, Floki said, "You know this man?"

"It's Ivan!" Gil said. "My father's best friend!"

Floki released his hold on the sword. "Then I would have him my friend as well." He bounded lightly down the rocks and reached a hand to pull the kayak ashore.

"A friend of Lance'lot! Here!" Palamedes' sorrow at the loss of the beast vanished in this new delight. "How wondrous!"

"Wondrous the bastard has any friends at all," Ivan muttered, "Dropping this on my head." He glanced uneasily up toward the house as he handed his paddle to Floki.

"Is my mom at home?" Gil asked warily.

Ivan stepped out of the kayak. "Think so. But hang a minute, dude."

Floki turned the paddle carefully in his hands. "This is as he showed me in the cave in Caledon," he murmured. Then, pulling the kayak ashore and stowing the paddle, he said to Gil, "This is the small boat of your father!" But Gil was turning already to the path through the woods.

"Wait!" Ivan scrambled quickly up the rocks. "Let me check if the coast is clear."

"Clear?" Gil turned back. "Clear of what?"

"Cops. You're a wanted man." He grinned, but his eyes were solemn.

"Wanted? For what? Running away from Dr Fairchild's clinic?"

"I think they could live with that." Ivan paused, glanced quickly at Gil's companions, and then returned his gaze to Gil. "He's missing, Gil. No one's laid eyes on him for a month. Not since we hared out of there on my bike." He paused again, "They think, maybe ...."

"A *month*!" Gil cried.

"Bit less, maybe. Three weeks?"

Gil's mind flashed through time, seeing the boy he had been standing here with Ivan. Then crossing to the Wandering Pool. Searching the ruins of Cille Aidan, captured at roofless Einar's Holm; brought before Floki Magnusson, earl of Hrolf's Isle. Mastering the skiff in the tide-race, and then *Sea-Raven*. Helming *Silver Dragon* to Norway and Francia. And Rome. Rome!

The High-King's Harp and Cat snatched from the warm dark night and hurtled back to the clinic. Hearing, impossibly, the roar of the old Norton as he made his own escape. Then, battling tooth and claw with Fairchild ... and again, the Roman night.

He followed me! And I had the Stone and we took the Harp ....

"Of course he's missing," Gil said. "He couldn't get back." *Until now.*

"What dude?"

Gil shook his head.

... Rome. The battle in Peter's Church. Eirik's grave in the sand. Floki's vow and the long sail north. Yula's Isle and the ship-burning ... He touched his scarred face.... Home to Hrolf's Isle and then Norway once more. His summer earldom. And south again, with longships at his command ....

"Ivan, I've been away, like ...."

"Years. I see that," Ivan said solemnly. "I wouldn't have known you. For a start, you've grown about a foot." He grinned.

"But the odds against *another* Viking messing with my day on the river seemed a bit steep." He leaned closer, then, peering at the Yula's Isle scar. "Fall off your bike?"

"Something like that."

"I bet." Ivan dropped his gaze to the sword at Gil's waist and then raised it again to Gil's companions, studying their faces, their costumes, and their weapons, with growing amazement. "Well, Dude, at least you didn't bring the horse."

Gil grinned weakly. "He'd be easier to explain." He turned suddenly, hearing an unmistakable voice, calling Ivan's name. "Mom?" He peered up at the wood path.

"Ivan?" Her voice was high, uncertain. "Is Brian with you?"

"Talk of explaining," Ivan muttered. He stepped hurriedly to greet her.

"I heard voices ...." She stopped just within the shadow of the trees, looking smaller and thinner and somehow younger than Gil remembered her. He saw her raise her hand to shield her eyes. Her face growing pale with shock, she stumbled into the sunlight. "Laurent!" She stepped closer, reaching out shaking fingers. "Your face," she whispered, "What's happened ...?

"Mom," Gil shook his head, his eyes filling with tears. "It's me. It's not Dad. It's me." He swallowed hard, "I'm home."

"No." Her lips trembled. He struggled to read her face; her voice ... disappointment? Disbelief? Relief? "Oh, Gil!" she cried anguished. "You aren't even a child anymore!"

But then, just as suddenly, she was his mother again. Raising her eyes to his companions, taking in their unlikely presence and more unlikely appearance, she yet took charge. "Come. Quickly. Into the house before anyone sees." She stretched out her arms to shepherd them before her.

Ivan nudged Gil. "Better take that," he pointed down at their feet, "It's a dead giveaway." The Irish battle-axe lay just as it had fallen in the burning tower. Feet away, the jeweled hilt of Guidbairn's sword glittered in the sun. Gil took up the axe and gave Janetta the stolen sword. Side by side, they walked the well-worn path to his home.

Inside, the house smelled of wood smoke, baking, and a

thousand memories. "Are you hungry?" his mother said, as if he'd just come in from school.

"It's okay; we've just eaten." *At the High Table of Camelot.* His mind reeling, he turned to his companions.

Palamedes strode happily from one end of the living room to the other. "Here! The Hall of Lance'lot!" He held his arms wide. "From here he rode forth!"

Janetta stared with frank innocence at Gil's mother. "But you are so young! And Lance'lot ...." she stopped and turned uncertainly to Gil, and then back to his mother. "Forgive me ... I do not understand."

"Time," Gil muttered, searching his mother's face, "It's like I told you, only ...."

"It's alright," she said. Tears brightened her eyes. "I believe you now." She stared at him, imploring it not to be true and seeing in every aspect of his appearance, that it was. "You were a boy!" she cried fiercely. "I told them! You couldn't kill *anyone.*"

Gil shook his head. The battle-axe lay on the floor between them, a reproach to everything he had become. She covered her face with her hands.

Ivan moved to comfort her, but Floki was there before him, a respectful hand on her shoulder. "All men leave home as boys," he said, "and return as men. But he is a good and gentle man. You raise him well."

She lowered her hands and looked up at Floki as if really seeing him for the first time. "Who *are* you?" she asked.

"I am Floki Magnusson," he smiled, "your son's helmsman." He paused. "Earl's helmsman. It is a great honor."

"My son ...." she turned from him to Gil, without comprehension. Her eyes fell on the Irish battle-axe and she crouched suddenly, reaching for it.

"Don't," Gil said, too harshly. Then, as she jumped back, he shrugged and added lamely, "It's heavy."

Janetta wrapped her arm around Gil's, their fingers enmeshed. "Surely," she said, "It is right that an earl defends his people?"

Gil's mother stood facing them both, seeming to see them, also, afresh. "And you?" she whispered softly, her gaze, curious but not unkindly, fixed on their entwined hands.

"She is mine," said Gil.

"And you are hers." She smiled wisely and he nodded. Then she turned and whispered passionately to Ivan, "What are we going to do?"

Outside, something crunched on gravel. *A skiff drawn ashore.* Gil whirled to the window. Palamedes also turned, and his face lit with excitement. "A beast!" he cried, "with eyes like the sun!"

A heavy thud wrenched Gil into the 21st century. *Door. Car door. Not a skiff. A car.*

"And a man!" Palamedes gasped. "A man escapes its belly! Haste, before it swallows him again!" He started forward but Ivan swiftly blocked his way.

"Don't go hunting that one, pal," he grinned. "It bites."

Gil stared out the window. A big SUV was parked in front of the house, a man in uniform walking up the path. He thought for a moment of Guidbairn's guards and then said clearly, "Police."

His mother pulled him back into the shadows, her eyes wild. "Hide! Upstairs!"

"No time," said Ivan. Gil, too, heard the knock on the door, polite but firm. "Got to bluff it out."

"*Bluff*?" She shook her head hopelessly.

"Sure," he smiled. "If *you* didn't know him, he sure won't."

"But what about ...?" she waved a distracted hand at Palamedes, Floki, and Janetta.

"Just makes it easier," Ivan grinned. "He won't see the wood for the trees."

"He is right, Warrior," Floki said quietly. "Men seek only what they expect to find. They expect a boy. The see a man. It is like the Cup of the Chieftains. We hide in plain sight."

Ivan turned to face Floki. Looking him up and down carefully, he said, "You're one sharp dude."

"What is dude?"

Ivan grinned. "Let's say 'friend.'" He leaned closer, eye to eye with the Northman. "Do you trust me?"

With a slow smile for Gil, Floki said, "It is so."

Ivan looked blank.

"It's Irish," Gil said. "It means 'yes.'"

"*Irish?*"

"Don't ask," Gil sighed wearily.

"Right," Ivan said. The knock came again, louder. He nodded to Gil's mother. "Better let him in."

Gil watched from just inside the living room as his mother opened the door. Over her shoulder, he saw a lean, sun-tanned man with dark hair and a white smile, like the men of Rome. The man took off his hat, held it in his hands, and gave an apologetic shrug. "I'm sorry, Mrs. Lake. I know you'd call us if you heard anything, but I still have to check."

"Joe?" Ivan suddenly strode forward. "Joe Vignato?"

"Hey, *Ivan!*" the man relaxed, a bigger smile lighting his face. "Hey *man*! Haven't seen you since we hauled that idiot in trainers and sweatpants out of that blizzard! How's it going? Busy on the river?"

"Day off. Hey, Joe, want you to meet someone."

Gil shrank back, but Ivan was already ushering the man into the living room. Joe Vignato stopped, just inside the doorway, his dark brown eyes moving warily across their faces. "A little early for Halloween folks."

"Ah, they're always like this." Ivan stepped around him and stood beside Floki. "They're Gamers. Some big convention down in the city. Everybody comes in character."

"Oh, I *see*," Joe Vignato nodded, a little uncertainly. "Okay," he pointed at Floki, "Thor. Right?"

"No," Floki smiled. "Nor Odin. I am Floki Magnusson. Earl's helmsman."

Vignato looked puzzled. "You foreign?"

"*Joe*," Ivan put an arm around Floki's shoulders. "This is my *cousin*. My cousin from Norway. Remember? I told you about him …."

Joe Vignato scratched his head. "Sorry, Ivan." He shrugged good-naturedly, "Must have slipped my mind." Then he looked right at Gil. "That's a pretty convincing scar." He moved closer.

"He wins it in battle," Floki slipped gracefully in between them. "He is Broadaxe, my earl."

"Okay," Vignato grinned. "Getting it now." He pointed to Palamedes, "Let me guess. Prince Valiant!"

"Good Sir," the Saracen bowed, "You honor me too highly. I am but Palamedes, Knight of Arthur."

"Of *course.*" Joe Vignato slapped his own forehead, "On the tip of my tongue." He turned then to Janetta with a fatherly smile. "And you, young lady ... no, don't tell me. I should be good at this. My little daughter's an encyclopedia of Disney princesses. Aurora? No. Not Merida ... Elsa! Right? Wait 'til I tell Marie I met a real princess!"

"But I am not," Janetta said. "I am Janetta, daughter of Martin de Troye. An earl, but not a king ."

He smiled indulgently. "And is this your sword, Princess Janetta?" Adjusting the gun belt at his waist, Vignato crouched happily over the weapon on the floor. Floki, too, crouched briefly beside him as he examined the lavishly decorated hilt. "This really gold?" Vignato laughed teasingly.

"I do not know," Janetta looked modestly downward. "It is not mine. I have stolen it."

Vignato's eyes opened wide. "You what ...?"

"In the Game!" Ivan said. "Hey, Joe, don't get carried away."

Sheepishly, the police officer stood, straightened his back with a wince, and laid a hand on his hip. The sheepish look vanished in an instant. Hand yet on his empty holster, he whirled. Floki stood beside him, holding his gun.

Fear flashed in Vignato's eyes, but Ivan just laughed cheerfully and tapped Floki's arm. "Ah, pal," he shrugged toward the officer, "Joe kind of needs that."

"It's a weapon, Floki," Gil said quickly. "It's, like, his sword."

"This?" Floki turned the gun over, studying it incredulously. "How is this a weapon?"

Joe Vignato's mouth fell open. "He's never heard of a gun?"

"He was home schooled," Ivan reached for the pistol.

Gil's mother nodded vigorously, "By Quakers." Gil stared amazed. *She can lie!*

Joe Vignato narrowed his eyes. "In Norway?"

Ivan wrapped his cousinly arm around Floki's shoulders again. "Trust me on this one, dude."

"It is so!" Floki laughed, and still laughing, he handed Ivan the gun and drew his sword.

"Whoa!" Vignato backed away, turning to Ivan who held the pistol safely out of his reach. But Floki only smiled and, laying the weapon across his outstretched hands, offered it to him in exchange.

Vignato accepted it gingerly, weighing it in his own hands. Floki turned to Ivan and took back the gun. Studying it again, he said, "You kill men with this?"

"Aw, c'mon," Vignato shrugged. "We're pretty peaceful up here. People get the wrong idea." He grinned suddenly, clasping the hilt of Floki's sword. "What about you, Thor? How many do you kill with this?"

"I do not count," Floki said quietly. He extended the pistol to Joe Vignato and took back his sword in return.

"Right," Vignato looked briefly uneasy. "Well, that's a pretty good line." With his gun safely back in its holster, he allowed himself another smile. Then, scratching his head again, as if remembering his job, he said, "Hey, folks, you got any ID? Driver's license, bank card ...? I won't tell the Masters of the Universe."

"Joe," Ivan looked pained, "are they going to carry that stuff and ruin the image? C'mon."

"Okay, okay. Just thought I'd ask." He turned to Gil's mother, "Now don't you worry too much about your son. Kids, they do these things, even when they aren't ..." he waved a finger in a vague circle around his ear and then stopped himself. "And it wouldn't amaze me if the good doctor, himself, wasn't in some kind of a pinch. Lot of money in these clinics ...." He trailed off with an awkward shrug as Ivan escorted him to the door.

Palamedes watched with joyful fascination as the big SUV drove away. "He climbs again within its belly! So patient a Beast!"

Ivan turned to Gil. "Right. *That's* not going to work twice. We're out of here." He looked them over carefully. "But first, you're going to have to shed the threads. Take them upstairs and stay there. Your mom and I got to hit the Mall."

"This was your bedchamber?" Janetta sat shyly on the edge of his bed, gently stroking the cover. Gil nodded. The quilt, his old Jurassic Park favorite, and indeed all the room, was exactly as he had left it; his desk and his laptop, the bookcase with his collection of outgrown toys, and the big globe he got for his tenth birthday. All waiting unchanged for a boy who was never going to return.

"Such terrible beasts!" Janetta examined the threads of the quilt. "Who weaves this fearsome tapestry?"

"And who carves these mighty dragons?" Palamedes, ducking his head beneath the low ceiling, held up a large plastic T-Rex in one hand, a Stegosaurus in the other. Gil smiled and shook his head.

The room felt smaller than he remembered, but it was still larger than the earl's bedchamber on Hrolf's Isle. "Warrior?" Floki had examined all of it, his hands passing lightly over the wallpaper, the window with its shadowy fly screen, the bedframe, the table lamp, and the objects on the desk; as if absorbing and memorizing the entire construction of the house. Now he stood looking out the window, holding the globe in his hands. "How many days on that river to the sea?"

"The sea?"

Floki spun the globe. "All rivers flow to the sea, Warrior."

"Maybe ten?" Gil guessed lamely. Floki spun the globe again, studying it intently. Gil came closer. "It's a map," he said cautiously, "A map of the whole world." He hesitated, touching the smooth surface, "It's like this. Round."

Floki traced a line with his finger. "Of course it is round. What other shape do you wish, square?"

"I thought you thought ..." he shrugged, "it was maybe flat ... and if you went too far, you'd, like, sail off the edge or something?"

Floki stared at him. "And were it like that, would I indeed sail *anywhere*?" He slapped Gil's head, "Idiot."

"But where did you learn ...?"

"Aidan tells me this when I am a child. I watch my father sail away and when he is far out to sea, his sail grows lower and lower, until it vanishes and I run crying to Aidan that my father's ship sinks ... and he shows me how it goes around the curve of the *round* world, until I can see it no more." He paused. "But it is what every man who goes to sea learns with no need to be told. For he can see it himself, can he not?" Floki looked back at the river. "All rivers run to the sea. And the sea, Warrior, will take us home."

"Ah." Gil also looked out the window. He smiled sadly. "*This* sea, Floki ...."

The door latch clicked behind him and he whirled. "Sir Palamedes?" he cried. "Where are you going?"

Palamedes bowed courteously. "Without, to the forest. Need is upon me ...." He waved vaguely toward the concealment of trees.

"Ah, *right*," Gil said. "Right. You don't have to go out. We do that inside the house."

"Within?" Palamedes wrinkled his nose in disgust.

"Not even behind the byre?" Janetta asked, wide-eyed.

They gathered around him at the bathroom door, as, turning on faucets, running the shower, and flushing the toilet, Gil demonstrated the wonders within.

Palamedes nodded gravely at each. Janetta giggled. Floki crouched on the floor, laying his hands on a pipe. "The water flows. I feel it. From the river?"

"From the ground," Gil said. "There's a well. In the cellar."

"Where are the donkeys?" said Palamedes.

"*Donkeys?*"

"We see this, Warrior," Floki said. "In the fields by the Roman Sea. Donkeys turn a wheel. The water rises ... do you never *look*?"

"Oh. Right." Gil closed his eyes, frantically recalling long ago physics lessons. "There's a motor. Electric. It's ... like ... a mechanical ... a *man-made* donkey."

"Warrior?" Floki raised a sardonic eyebrow.

"Trust me," Gil said. "It works."

"How?"

A shout from below saved him.

"Gil?" Ivan, laden with shopping bags, craned his neck up the stairs. "Get yourselves into the 21st century." He tossed the bags up. "Twenty minutes. Dave's on the way with the pick-up. We're going to The Pond. Your mom's making sandwiches."

"No, Ivan's making sandwiches." Clutching an armful of clothes, Gil's mother passed Ivan on the stairs and disappeared into the guest bedroom with Janetta.

Gil emptied the bags on his bed, and having distributed tee-shirts, underwear, flannel over-shirts and denim jeans to Floki and Palamedes, quickly started pulling on his own.

"Warrior?" Floki was already dressed. "What is this thing? It stitches the cloth like needle and thread, and then," he ran the zip of his jeans down revealing his new Y-fronts, "parts it. And yet nothing is torn."

For a moment, Gil was equally baffled. Then he cried happily, "A zip! It's a zip" Oh, I've missed these!" he drew up his own with satisfaction.

"How wondrous the minds of men!" Palamedes happily zipped himself in. "And were there need ...."

"Right," Gil said quickly. "There's one thing. We sort of don't ...."

"Warrior," Floki gave him a sour look. "Do I uncover myself in front of the women at home? No. Nor shall I here."

"Why not?" Gil said, backing away, "They'd only laugh." He waved cheerfully and ducked out the door.

In the kitchen, Ivan stuffed their own garments into two roll-top waterproof sacks. "For when you get tired of the L.L.Bean look." Then he straightened and surveyed them carefully. "Not bad. Not bad." He grinned at Floki and nudged Gil. "He'll be fighting the women off. Except there aren't going to be any."

"Just as well," Gil muttered, not quite used to his denim clad earl, lounging against the kitchen counter like a rock star. He had taken the globe downstairs with him and was studying it now as he had studied the construction of the house.

Gil heard giggling outside the kitchen and found his mother and Janetta in the hallway; Janetta wearing skinny jeans, a pink tee shirt with a sparkly silver cat on the front, and a hairband with cat ears. "Look!" she cried, patting her jeans, "I am a boy!"

"Well, not exactly," Gil smiled. "But it's real nice."

Outside, tires crunched again on the gravel and an engine rumbled to a stop. Gil looked around alarmed. "No worries." Ivan came from the kitchen with a tray of messy sandwiches. "It'll be Dave. Hey, a Mall-Rat!" he grinned at Janetta and handed Gil the tray. "Eat those. I'll get the stuff into the pick-up."

Palamedes strode by, chicken sandwich in hand, and peered out the living room window. "The beast returns!" he exulted.

"Good name for it," Ivan said. "Only this one doesn't fly and you can't shoot it down either. But," he smiled cheerfully, "you can ride in its belly." Palamedes eyes lit. Ivan led him to the door. "Gil, get geography-man out of the kitchen. We've got to roll."

Floki sat at the kitchen table, hunched over the globe, his tanned fingers tracing the northern outline of the British Isles. "Take it with you." Gil grabbed his arm and pulled him up. "We're setting sail."

Dave climbed down from the cab of the pick-up and lowered the tailgate for Ivan to load the two dry-sacks. It was the same faded red Nissan that Gil remembered, with the dent in the hood from the time Dave hit the deer. The load bed was piled with freezer boxes, crates of beer, kayak and fishing gear; just as it always had been when Dave, Brian, Ivan, and Gil's father drove off for strictly no-kids weekends at the pond. Gil felt absurdly proud, at last being included.

"Hey, Dave," Ivan grinned as Gil and Floki joined Palamedes and Janetta, gathered around the pick-up, "Come meet my Norwegian cousin."

His eyes on Floki, Dave walked past Gil without recognition; then stopped and stepped back, staring. "Jesus. Ivan told me, but I didn't … hell, you've grown a foot!" He looked around at Janetta and Palamedes, and murmured, "It was all true … that day on the river …." Gil nodded. Dave put his hand to his forehead. "Sorry. Can't quite get my head around it."

Ivan held up the Irish battle-axe. "Maybe this will help."

Dave said, "Jesus," again. "That thing real?" He took it from Ivan.

Ivan, loading their sword belts and Janetta's trophy, said over his shoulder, "Looks real to me."

Dave weighed it in his hands. Turning to Floki he said, "Yours?"

"It is his," Floki nodded to Gil.

Dave studied Gil again, uneasily. "You use this thing?" Gil said nothing.

Ivan took the battle-axe again and loaded it beside the swords and added the globe. "Throw a tarp over that stuff," Dave called up to him. "Anyone asks, it's trout rods."

He climbed back into the cab and started the engine. Janetta jumped back at its throaty growl, and Palamedes' hand scuffed the hip of his jeans, reaching for his absent sword. Floki stepped closer and laid his fingers on the vibrating hood. Then he moved back and walked in a circle around the vehicle.

"This is a cart, Warrior," he said mildly. "As we see in Francia and Rome. But, with neither horse, nor oxen, and yet it moves. These beasts, as the donkeys, are also man-made?"

Gil nodded. "We call it horsepower," he said helpfully.

Ivan grabbed Floki's arm, guiding him firmly up into the cab between himself and Dave. "Auto-mechanics 101 is at the mountain place. Let's roll!"

In the back seat, Janetta giggled and clutched Gil's arm as the Nissan began to move. Gil's mother waved. Dave picked up speed. Palamedes shouted, "To the Field!" and Floki examined the dashboard, turning knobs and pressing buttons. Water splashed the windshield, followed by wiper blades.

"Hey!" Dave protested. Floki moved on to raising and lowering windows, winning a delighted shriek from Janetta. Then he hit a button and a male voice boomed into the cab.

"Avaunt!" cried Palamedes, whirling in his seat. Floki also spun around; then leaned over Ivan to peer out the window. Turning back to the dashboard, he stared at a speaker.

" … and riding at number seventeen in the charts …"

A female voice wailed amid a jangle of sound. "Alas!" Palamedes twisted in his seat again. "She cries in pain! Who harms her?"

"She's fine," Gil said. "She's singing."

"Singing?" Floki turned from the speaker to Gil.

"It's music."

"*That?*"

Dave reached over and switched the radio off. "Better?"

"Ghosts," Palamedes whispered. "Gone as swiftly as they come."

Floki studied the speaker. "Where are they?" he said.

Ivan rested his head back and closed his eyes.

"Warrior, we need a ship." It was their fourth night at the mountain place and, seated at the oilcloth covered table, Floki was again studying the globe.

"Lend you my kayak," Dave said, cheerfully opening a can.

Floki smiled. "Raise a mast on her and I say yes."

"Beer?" Dave offered.

Floki smiled again and shook his head. "I am thinking. Ale does not help."

"Helps me," said Dave.

"Helps me, too." Brian Gross was on his fifth. He raised his beer can in a toast. "Trying to get used to having a Viking for a son-in-law."

"You must wait until the marriage day. We are but betrothed."

Brian looked blearily at the young Northman and then at Gil, sitting on the floor by the woodstove with Janetta curled beside him. "You're not making this up? Danni ..." he smiled wistfully "... she's really grown up? Like you?"

"A little older," Gil said quietly.

"She is very beautiful," Janetta said. "And very kind. And her brother is a fine cupbearer. He sits always beside the earl." She nodded encouragingly, making her cat ears bounce, tickling Gil's chin. He was half asleep in the heat of the fire, but not ready to relinquish her to go to their separate rooms.

Floki said gently, "He is my fosterling. I am his father until he returns to you." He returned his attention to the globe.

A bird called out in the night. Gil sat up quickly, disturbing

Janetta, but it was only another blue jay, its sleep troubled by the distant growl of a motor coming up the track. Palamedes, dozing contentedly by the stove, jumped to his feet, as a headlight swept the cabin windows. "Behold, the shining eye!" he cried happily. "The man-made charger returns!"

Dave grinned, "With Ivan, the man-made Knight of Camelot."

The cabin was home to Ivan's sprawling collection of antique motorbikes, and on their first day, Palamedes and Floki had mastered riding pillion. By the end of the third day, they were motorbike jousting with saplings, in front of the cabin. In between, Ivan stripped down and re-constructed engines in front of them, then did the same with an old shotgun. He called it "learning by doing."

But Gil slipped away with Janetta, and rowed across the small lake that gave the mountain place its name. They walked in the woods on the other side and sat by the shore. Gil looked up at every bird cry. Jays, buzzards, once a bright cardinal that delighted Janetta. But no grey and black crow. No Feannag.

Three weeks past Saint John's Feast. Two months until Saint Matthew's ... but what difference did it make? The whirlpool of the Indian Kettle was beyond his reach. Not all cops were Joe Vignato.

The screen door banged and Ivan came in, grinning. "My charger is fed and watered, and now it's my turn."

Dave handed him a beer. "Good day on the river?"

"Didn't lose anybody."

Brian looked up from his beer can. "See that cat anywhere?"

"Saw an otter. Otters carry eggs."

"I see otters every day. It wasn't an otter."

"Cats don't swim."

"This one did. And it wasn't an egg. It was a rock."

Ivan dumped his helmet on the table beside the globe. "How's it going, cousin?"

"It goes well," Floki smiled. "I find my course."

Ivan pulled up a chair. "Show me."

"This," Floki said, his fingers tracing the North Atlantic, "Is the sea we cross. For here," he tapped the surface, "Is the place you say we are; here the river where stands Warrior's home, and here," he spun the globe, "stands our own."

Gil straightened up, trying not to disturb Janetta. "Floki," he said evenly, "The sea *we* crossed ...."

"I know, Warrior. The sea no man can sail. And yet we cross it, do we not?" He turned back to Ivan. Janetta yawned and stretched, sitting up, as Gil rose to join them.

"Here then," Floki said, "are our islands. Hrolf's Isle is not there, for the scribe who writes the map makes one island of all, but see, there is Pentland. And there," he ran his fingers upward, "Ragnvald's home islands, Hjaltland, and here, Norway, where we meet with Gudrun ...."

"Wait," Ivan stood and pushed his chair back, "Let's do this right."

He disappeared into his room and came back moments later holding something in his hand, something oblong, flat, shiny, familiar ... iPad! Gil's memory raced back. Ivan settled on his chair, pushed a button, stroked the screen, and held it up to Floki. "That better?" he said. His fingers yet on the globe, Floki turned to the screen, comparing images. He nodded slowly.

"It is better. There is Hrolf's Isle and the Spear Isle. Look, Warrior, the Horse Isle also. But," he shook his head, "he is also wrong, this scribe." He touched a space of empty blue. "The Holy Isle is not there."

Gil smiled, "Then he's left the best bit out."

Floki turned the iPad around, studied the back, turned it again, and gently stroked the screen, as Ivan had done. Delighted amazement lit his face, "It lives!" He turned to Ivan. "My cousin, what is this thing?"

"Ah." Ivan leaned back in his chair, eyes closed. "Right," he said at last. "It's a book. A kind of book. With," he paused, "a lot of pages."

Floki looked doubtful. Turning the slim oblong, he studied the edge. "I can neither see them, nor turn them."

"Like this." Ivan pushed a button and the map disappeared, pushed it again, and the map returned. With two fingers, he spread the map out until the North Atlantic was in view. "Show me your course."

Floki took the iPad again and in perfect imitation of Ivan, extended the map, narrowed it, moved it north and south; always checking back to the globe. "Trust me, cousin," Ivan said quietly. "It works."

He paused and Dave, who had joined them, added, "Just don't ask us how."

"I do ask you how," Floki smiled cheerfully, "But first, I use this clever thing." He brought the British Isles in close, "Look, Warrior," he held it up to Gil, "the coast of Alba ... and beyond, Francia, and there, look! The Great Pillars and the Roman Sea." Gil shook his head. "I am wrong?" Floki narrowed his eyes.

"No. You're right. But how?" Gil asked. "You've never seen a map."

"But I have seen the *seas!*" Floki flicked the blue Mediterranean. "All of them. The map," he touched his blond head, "is here."

Dave stopped midway through opening another beer. "Wait a moment. Wait a moment," he came closer, "you *memorize* it?"

Floki shrugged. "How else do I find my way? Besides," he said to Gil, "I do see a map. Aidan shows me in his books. Long before the Northmen come to our islands, a man sails from the Roman Sea and writes a map. It is often wrong, this map, but still, he is a fine seaman."

Ivan took the iPad, typed two words, and then handed it again to Floki. Gil saw an antique map of Europe, the Northmen's lands at the top, only a band of sea to the west. "Something like that?" Ivan said.

Floki looked, for a brief moment, unnerved. "How is Aidan's book here?"

"It's not," Ivan said. "Someone's seen it and made a picture of it."

"A scribe? It is copied?" Floki turned the iPad over and

explored its smooth seams for an opening.

"Uh, Cousin …."

"Learning by doing," Floki smiled.

Gil grabbed the iPad. "Uh, no. It's not in there, at all."

"Then where is it?"

Gil waved his hand weakly toward the ceiling. "Sort of in the sky?"

Floki gave him a sour look. "Held up by the angels?"

"It's Wi-Fi," Dave said. "It travels in the air."

"Radio waves," Brian burped helpfully.

"Look," Ivan took the iPad. "I'll ask it." He typed again, saying aloud, "How does Wi-Fi work?"

Floki watched him and then turned suddenly to Gil. "Warrior, why do I have you work with Eyolf, building *Sea-Raven*?"

Gil grinned, "So if I run her aground and wreck her, I can build her again?"

"Very good!" Floki gave him a brief nod of approval. Then he turned to Ivan, Brian and Dave.

"And here you have this wonderful thing you do not understand. And so, you ask this thing you do not understand, to tell you what you do not understand. What happens," he took back the iPad and held it in the air, "should you run *this* aground?"

Ivan sat down and took a long swig from his beer. "Where's Rick when I need him?" he said plaintively.

"Rick the telemarker?" Dave asked.

Ivan nodded.

"Good skier," said Dave.

"Good kayaker," "said Brian."

"Good skier, good kayaker, and good *physics teacher*!" said Ivan.

He looked up with a wan smile. "Here, cousin, let me find your map again for you."

"I have it," said Floki. He turned the iPad quickly and showed Ivan. "I do as you do. Learning by doing." He smiled and looked back at the screen. "But," he continued, "though the scribe is a fine seaman, and sees our shores, these," he trailed his fingers northward across the Atlantic, "he does not see. The

Churchmen's Isles lie here." He touched a scrap of land alone in the northern sea.

"The Faroes," Ivan said softly.

"I sail there," Floki said, "when I have fifteen winters. I find no churchmen, only Northmen and sheep. But I see the wild geese fly in from the west, and I know there is a land beyond. And this is so." He stroked the screen, bringing a larger island into view.

"Iceland," Dave said.

"Indeed. The Land of Ice and Fire. My father, Magnus Redbeard, has seen it. And so has my lady. For she flies there, from here, wing and wing with the wild geese."

Brian sat down dazed. Floki smiled and brushed a hand over the top of his head, like he might do to comfort Percy. Then he turned to Gil, "This," he touched the digital map, "is where she crossed to home. Here, we also cross. We need, only, a ship."

Gil shook his head. "Floki, we could have every ship in the Northlands, and we could sail all the way to the Northlands, but we still can't cross. I haven't got Merlin's Stone."

Floki raised his head slowly, "Warrior?"

"I gave it to Guidbairn."

"Ah." Floki laid the iPad carefully on the table and sat back. "Indeed so. And at my command. It does not occur to me that we might have need of it." He turned and looked wryly at Dave. "I think, friend, I have that ale."

"Is that the seeing stone?" Ivan asked. "The one the bird brought?"

Gil nodded. "One like it. The crossings are like doors. The stones are keys."

"But Danni ...." Brian protested.

"Her Change-Thing crossed. Her Other," Gil said, "Birds, animals ...."

"Cross at will," Floki said softly. "Only men cannot. I thank you," he accepted a beer can from Dave and opened it like an expert. "Warrior ... does, perhaps Feannag ...?"

"Why do you think I jump up at every bird cry?" Gil turned to Dave. "Could I maybe have one, too?"

They sat gloomily around the table, staring into their beer. "While you were studying wildlife," Ivan said to Brian "You didn't happen to see a big grey and black crow?"

"I wasn't studying wildlife," Brian grumbled. "And it wasn't wild. It came to me."

"Cats do carry things," Janetta said helpfully.

"Thank you."

"Kittens. And mice."

"But why swimming?" said Ivan.

"I don't know. Look. I'm down at the river, hauling my boat out, and I see this thing in the pool, by the Indian Kettle. And it's swimming toward me with something white in its mouth."

"Egg. Otter." Ivan grinned.

"Then it climbs out on the Lookout Rock, shakes itself off and puts the thing down and *looks* at me. You know the way cats look. And it isn't some fancy oriental thing that might swim. Just an ordinary stripy guy. Good looking cat, though."

Dave grimaced. "Kittens have scruffs and mice are, well, squishy. How does a cat carry a rock?"

"Who *knows*? Maybe that little hole in it helped. It was one of those white pebbles you get on a beach."

"Wait a minute," Gil sat up straight. Floki lowered his beer can.

"Anyhow, it drops it and jumps back in the water and when I look up from the rock, it's gone."

"Drowned," said Dave mournfully. "Swallowed by an otter." He shoved Brian and Brian pushed him away.

Ivan said carefully, "Brian? Is that rock still there?"

"No."

Gil looked at Floki and smiled weakly. Floki leaned back and closed his eyes. "Ah, Warrior," he said with a gentle laugh.

"It's in my pocket," said Brian.

They had two more beers to celebrate. Gil sat spinning the seeing stone gently on his finger. Brian said, "So it *was* a cat."
Ivan bowed an extravagant apology.

"A Noble Cat," Gil smiled, closing his hand around the
stone.

"What *is* that thing?" Brian mumbled sleepily.

"Our ticket home," Gil grinned at Floki. "Helmsman?"

"Yes. A ship."

Ivan nodded, "Got a feeling I should save this for the sober
light of day, but how exactly do you plan on getting a ship?"

"As always we do," said Floki.

"And how's that?" Dave joined in.

"We build one in our shipyard," Floki said. "If, of course,
there is time."

"And if there's not time?" Ivan said.

"We steal one," said Gil cheerfully.

Ivan grimaced. "I could see that coming a mile off. Only, I
didn't expect it from you." He turned back to Floki. "Cousin,"
he said painstakingly, "That is not legal here. It is against the
law. Understand?"

Floki nodded. "Were it not, it would not be stealing, would
it?"

"Can't argue with that," said Dave.

Gil finished his third beer and reached for a fourth. Floki
took it neatly out of his hand and put it on the table out of reach.

"One step ahead of me," Ivan grinned. Then he said
regretfully, "I can't allow this, Gil. What would I say to your
dad? What will I tell your *mom* for Heaven's sake?"

Gil sat still, instantly sober. Then he said slowly, "Tell her I
have to help my father protect my people. And this is the only
way."

"I got another way."

Gil turned quickly. Brian lurched up from where he dozed
beside the snoring Palamedes, yawned, stretched, and said, "I
know a boat you can have for nothing. Hell, the guy'll probably

throw in a box of cornflakes if you just take her away."

"Sounds like just the kind of thing you want to sail the North Atlantic in," Dave grinned.

"Oh, but she is." Brian scratched his side and shuffled over to the table. "Okay, she's small, but she wouldn't be the smallest to do it. And she'd be one of the best."

"What's this, Brian?" Ivan said, quietly curious.

"Rick's father-in-law's *Jack of the Beach.*"

"The old South Bay Cat? She's gone, Brian. The old man's long gone himself and so is his boat. Anyhow, he gave her to some kid, years ago."

"*Fifty* years ago. The *kid's* an old man now. Hey, it's a long story. Tell you in the morning." He yawned again and stumbled toward his room. "Better yet, let the guy tell you himself. It's quite a tale."

———

They saw the boat before they saw her owner; a beautiful little thing, riding gently beside the marina pontoon. Broad beamed and with a shallow draft, even with her fixed mast set far forward and her stern rudder, she made Gil think of the fishing skiffs in Eyolf Grimsson's yard. Both he and Floki knew her at once.

———

Ivan had found a video of another, built to the same design, and, after swearing not to ask how YouTube worked, Floki was allowed to study the little catboat flitting on bright water on the screen.

"Very good!" he smiled, and then added, "I will need oars, a spare sail, if possible; tools to fashion a mast, should need arise. Wait." He had gone to the room he shared with Dave and Palamedes and returned with a leather purse. "I have no scales," he said, "nor do I know the price, but take what I have." Opening the purse, he spilled a weight of hack silver across the table.

Dave and Brian stared open-mouthed. Ivan gently scooped the silver into the purse and handed it back to Floki. "I turn up at the bank with that, cousin, they'll call the cops. This one's on me. I need a longship someday; it's your round."

———

They had left at dawn, with the Nissan loaded up with foul weather gear, sleeping bags, camp food, water bottles, fishing rods, maps, charts, rope and tarps to serve as an awning. Gil's mother had driven up before daylight with the last of Ivan's carefully ordered supplies. She shook hands with Floki and Palamedes, kissed Janetta, and threw her arms briefly around Gil before stepping back with a determined smile.

"About Dad," Gil said suddenly. "I want you to know ...."

She quickly put a finger to his lips. "I understand. I don't need to hear."

"Gotta go, Laura," Ivan said apologetically.

She nodded and a gentle look passed between them, startling Gil. At the door of her car, she called back suddenly, "Tell him he gave me a wonderful son!"

On the long drive down to the Connecticut shore, Floki sat in the back seat of the Nissan's cab, studying Google Earth; only relinquishing the iPad when Palamedes' protests became too insistent. Dave had shown the Saracen knight a marvelous thing: a window into a world of knights and castles in which, with cries of "Avaunt!" and "To the Field!" he directed a miniature warrior into battle.

Ivan sat between them to keep the peace.

Though, when deprived of the screen, Palamedes was content staring out the window at the many marvelous beasts, some of enormous size, which joined them on the road. And, craning his neck, spotting dragons, far off, trailing their smoking breath across the sky.

Janetta sat between Gil and Dave in the front, subdued and sorrowful from the parting with his mother. "She is so kind and wise, like Ingirid, my stepmother." She wept quietly on Gil's shoulder, her cat ears trembling.

"Do you like my home?" Gil asked cautiously.

She raised her head and nodded. "The fine house by the river, I like very much ...." she said. "And all of your friends, also ...." she trailed off uncomfortably and looked out the window at an enormous shopping mall, and then another, afloat in a sea of concrete. "But Tir nan Og," she shook her head, "I thought it would be like Caledon," she said wistfully, "with still greater mountains and more beautiful forests ...."

Gil watched as a giant warehouse slid by, its fields of parked cars glittering like knights in armor. "It was," he said, "Once."

———

Gil heard a shout and turned from the boat. A man in jeans and a sweatshirt walked toward them along the pontoon. His hair was grey, but still thick, his face weathered. He swung one leg awkwardly with each stride, like a lame old warrior from Hrolf's Isle. "That must be him," Gil said.

The man held out his hand. "Name's Rob."

Ivan introduced them. He and Rick had set it all up the night before, where they were to meet and the time. Rob looked them up and down, his eyes settling on Floki. "Gotta say, you sure look the part. Where'd you say you were from?"

"Norway," Ivan said. "He's my cousin."

Rob nodded and said, "Well, well." Then he looked down at the catboat. "Bit of paint peeling there," he muttered to himself, his eyes on the black lettering at the bow. "So, what do you think of *Jack of the Beach*?"

"She is very beautiful," said Floki.

Rob nodded. Gil imagined any other response would have resulted in a sudden swim. "Oh, she is that." Rob's eyes, a saltwater grey-green, turned dreamy. "Imagine being fifteen years old and someone trusts you with that?"

Startled, Gil looked momentarily at Floki and slowly nodded.

Rob rubbed his stubbly chin. "Nobody ever trusted me with anything. Dad said I always wrecked everything ." He grunted something and continued, "I had a job at the marina. Didn't sail or anything. But I worked on this old guy's boat." He paused and snorted, *"Old guy* was a damned sight younger then than I am now, but that's how kids see things. Anyhow, sometimes he'd take me along. Then one day he took me out, and out there," he gestured to the misty waters of the sound. "He handed me the sheet and the tiller and just pretended to go to sleep."

Gil laughed delightedly, remembering the fishing skiff and the tide-race of Hrolf's Isle.

"I was shit-scared. But it was still the best day of my life. The wind, the sparkle of the water, the feel of her responding to my hand." His eyes were bright. "Anyhow, that's how it began. He made a sailor of me. He made a man of me. The right kind. I was well on the way to being the wrong kind ...."

"I was heartbroken when he said he was going to sell her. He wanted to do bigger things. Got himself a lovely ketch, but that's another story. Meanwhile, I was like a kid whose puppy's got run over. He found me on the dock, crying." Rob paused, shaking his head in amazement, "And he did it. He just gave her to me. All legal and proper." He shook his head again. "And I'll tell you, he wasn't known for throwing money around. And if I'm honest, at times he was an old curmudgeon who could irritate the hell out of me. But I loved him.

"And I loved her." He looked down at the catboat. "She and I, alone out there, fair or foul; sun, gales, once nearly lost in the fog. But, what the hell, she always brought me home.

"Anyhow, that was fine when I was young and like everybody who's young, couldn't imagine anything else. But I'm not young now. I've got arthritis all over the place. Some days, I can't even get down into her, much less take her out. Sometimes, when I'm a bit fed up of it all, I think maybe I'll sail out one day, lash the tiller and just sail on ... but it wouldn't be fair to the grandkids ....

"Anyhow, got a call a few weeks back, some people wanting to put her in a museum. Oh, yeah, I can just hear him: *'the harpies of the shore ....'"*

"'Shall pluck the eagle of the sea,'" said Gil.

Rob nodded, impressed. Floki, Dave, and Ivan stared in amazement. Gil shrugged. "We learned it at school. I liked it ."

"Glad you learned something at school," said Ivan.

"Then, other day, the museum people get on to me again. Talked it over with the family. They all say it's my call. So, I went up to the cemetery and stood there, like an idiot, and asked him, what do I do? Guess what? Old bastard didn't say a word."

"He is not there," Floki said mildly. He had slipped down onto the boat as they talked and was quietly moving from end to end, examining tiller, centerboard, rudder, and rigging with his light, sure hands. He looked up the slender mast, and then, with his eyes on the swaying masthead, added softly, as if to himself, "He sails the green seas; a fair wind over his shoulder." With a quick smile, he stepped up onto the rail, dove into the water, and disappeared from sight.

"What the hell?" Rob shouted.

"It's okay," Gil said, because even Dave looked startled. "He'll just be checking the hull."

Ripples spread out and dissipated. The murky water stilled. Silence fell.

"He all right? He's been down a long time."

"Good swimmer," Ivan said, with a glance at Gil.

After another minute of hobbling, agitated, along the pontoon, peering into the depths, Rob said, "Hey, I'm getting worried here. How long can the guy hold his breath?"

"Really long," Gil said.

"He's a pearl diver," Ivan said.

"He comes from a whole family of pearl divers!" Gil added. "You know, free diving ...."

"*Norwegian* pearl divers?" Rob screwed up his eyes, then opened them wide as something dark splashed beside the boat. "Hey, you see that?"

Gil and Ivan shook their heads and looked at the sky.

"There! There it is again ... hell, it's a goddamned seal! I've never seen one in here."

A smooth dark head suddenly appeared, vanished; a quick tail splash, then empty water. "I think it's gone under the boat!" Rob leaned out so far that Gil reached to stop him from falling in. "Hey, will your friend be alright? Do those things bite or anything?"

"They're friendly," Gil said through gritted teeth. *And I'm going to kill this one if it doesn't get its fishy ass up here fast.*

Floki broke surface, laughing, his long yellow hair in merman tendrils. "Not before time," Rob grumbled, reaching down a hand. Floki took it and scrambled easily up onto the pontoon. He laughed again. "Well built and well kept. A fine little skiff for any sea." Rob rubbed his stubble again and looked proud.

He threw himself into their preparations, as if his heart was sailing with them, leaving his lame old body behind. He gave them his own supply of camp food, and a set of inflatable rollers to save felling trees when they beached. He dug out the catboat's old sail, for a spare, found them two pairs of long oars, and even fitted the oarlocks himself.

Gil winced as the drill bit into the fine old wood, but Rob slyly grinned. "Museum folks gonna love this." That night he offered them a place to stay in his small house on the shore. But they slept, instead, out on the beach and rose with the morning star yet in the sky.

In the dim light, they gathered on the dock. A dog barked somewhere. Gulls mewed. Their gear was stowed and lashed down. Floki and Rob readied the sail and the oars and climbed back up onto the pontoon.

Rob ran his eyes over the four going to sea, his gaze settling on Janetta. "Now, little lady," he said, his voice softened with fatherly concern, "you sure you want to do this? Some big water out there." He hunched a shoulder toward the sound and the Atlantic beyond.

Janetta smiled, the dawn wind trembling her cat ears. She took Gil's arm. "I sail with him to the end of time," she said proudly.

"*Okay,*" Rob nodded approvingly at Gil. "Well, you've sure got one fan."

Ivan stepped forward, holding out the iPad. "There's about twelve hours charge. Won't last you all that long, but it'll give you a good start."

Floki laughed and shook his head. "I leave that, that you may study it, and when next we meet, you may tell me how it works. Now, I find my way as my fathers found theirs. Besides, I have this!" With a slow smile for Gil, he held up the Falling Star, and the needle of the small metal compass swung resolutely North.

Ivan grinned. "I'll miss you, cousin."

Floki smiled again and jumped down into the little catboat. "Come with us!"

Ivan's eyes drifted eastward to the misty sea. "Don't tempt me." He shook his head. "I have people to care for."

"As have we." Floki laid his hand on the tiller. Rob and Dave loosened the bow and stern lines and threw them down. Palamedes and Janetta took up oars, a few strokes taking them clear of the pontoon. Gil hoisted the gaff-rigged sail, catching the rising wind. The little craft gently heeled, her bow lifting quizzically, like a kitten sniffing the air. "Helmsman," he called, "take us home."

About the Author

A lison Scott, the daughter of two writers, Alexander Leslie Scott, master of the western detective novel, and artist turned short story writer, Lily Kay Scott, was born in Manhattan. Her brother, Justin Scott, is a master of thrillers, mysteries, and sea stories, including the Isaac Bell Adventures. A Junior Year Abroad from her American university took her to Scotland, where she met her future husband, Clement Skelton--an actor, playwright, film cameraman, Battle of Britain Spitfire pilot, and monster hunter. She had her first baby while living on the shores of Loch Ness.

From an apprenticeship in Gothic romances, she went on to publish her first hardcover novel, A World Full of Secrets, writing as Alison Scott, while her husband became C.L. Skelton, writing successful family sagas. After she was widowed, she continued writing while raising their two sons, Professor Alasdair Skelton, geologist researching in climate change, and actor and gardener Justin Skelton.

As Alison Scott Skelton, she has published several works of contemporary and historical fiction in the US and Britain; among them, *Different Families, A Murderous Innocence, Saving Grace, An Older Woman,* and *Family Story.*

The Warriors of Tir nan Og, the six-book series that opens with *The Underwater Bridge*, is her first work for a young adult audience.

Curious about other Crossroad Press books?
Stop by our site:
https://www.crossroadpress.com
We offer quality writing
in digital, audio, and print formats.